SECRET IDENTITIES

ISBN 9781695858091

Lion of Stone Publishing

to my mum, who always encouraged me to write,
to steve, who forced me to use first-person,
and to fate, who read it; before, during, and after.

Part One: Abyss

1.

"Abyss!"

Legion jumps from the fire escape and lands, near-noiselessly, next to me. He's dressed in his usual shades of green and tan— a bomber jacket with his name stitched carefully across the back, some loose joggers, and running shoes. The costume is finished with an odd black mask, made of plastic and cloth, settled over his face. It covers his forehead, trails down his nose, and then a second piece clicks into place over the bridge of his nose, hiding his mouth and his cheekbones. Only his slant brown eyes are visible; hard and unrelenting.

The night is young, but the sky is dark. Even still, I slide my sunglasses back on to my face before I turn to face him, ensuring that my eyes are hidden from view. I find that, now, covering my eyes in low-light does little to impede my vision. I'm grateful for it. It means I can keep them covered.

"Where to tonight?" Legion asks, steady and low as he always is when he's got the mask on. Even knowing him in both of his identities, I don't have to wonder why no one has worked it out without being told. There is a noticeable divide between them. When I see him like this, in his costume, his voice muffled by the mask, I can only think of him as Legion.

"Do you ever feel like we're playing dress up?" I ask flatly, instead of replying to his question. "We do these patrols. We help where we can."

"But?"

"But superheroes aren't common, anymore." They haven't been since the sixties— and that was only because they'd helped out in various war efforts over the decades previous, and, when they got home, had nothing better to do. Once nerves settled, and lives went on, caped-crusaders faded out of existence peacefully enough, and superhumans found other uses for their abilities. "And we're wearing costumes."

"Uniforms," he corrects, shrugging. "And superheroes are around. You know, Europe has all sorts of them running around. They've got special forces of them."

"Yeah," I reply, "that sounds totally true."

"It is," he protests lightly. "Remind me to show you when we get in. I was reading about it last night."

I sigh. I don't even know why I'm arguing the point, anyway. It's not like I'm going to stop doing this. Even if I do, sometimes, more often than not, feel like a kid playing dress-up, it's not as though I don't agree with his motivations. He wants to make the world better, and I can't blame him for that. I can even help him, like I have been for the past sixth months.

"All right," I finally say, pushing away from the brick wall and crossing my arms. "Where to tonight?"

"I think I asked you that."

A car horn blares through the quiet night, and a pair of headlights turn on to the road. Legion and I jump backwards, further into the shadow of the alley, and wait for the car to pass by without noticing us.

"We need a base of operations," I whisper to him once it's out of sight. "Somewhere that's not— you know, where we live. If you want to keep your identity secret, we can't keep crawling out of your fire escape."

"Now who's playing pretend?" he teases, heading out into the street with a mock salute, leaving me alone in the dark alley.

Watching him take a sharp left, I can't help but think that we need more than a *base* is a *leader.* Someone with the resources to help us do this properly, so that we don't have to wander aimlessly through the city streets at night, hoping to stumble upon something. If this is what he needs to be doing, then I'll help him, but I can't control him or guide him or make sure he's going to the right places. With just the two of us, we're mostly on our own, with no one to help us should we need it.

I make my way out of the alley and turn right.

I'm doubtful that I'll find anything, but I have a lot to think about.

2.

"Mom," Xander says, as he sits down next to me at the breakfast table. His hair is sticking up in all directions and his eyes are still bleary as he attempts to shake himself awake. As I'd expected, neither of us had found anything to do, and we'd arrived home at three a.m.. I woke up at seven good to go, but Xander needs more sleep than me. Years of studying has immunised me to exhaustion.

His mother, the amazing Ki Pae, tips her head in acknowledgement. She's standing at the stove of the galley-style kitchen we're facing, preparing a breakfast soup. It smells divine. I never realised how amazing Korean food is until I started living with the Pae's. "Yes, my darling son?"

"I'm going for lunch again today."

She turns away from the stove to face him, a hand on her hip. "That's three times this week," she points out, "I'm starting to think you're taking advantage."

She'd made a similar comment the first time Xander had gone to lunch, and I hadn't understood it any better then. Since then, he's been going out to lunch fairly regularly, with someone who he only refers to as 'Cee'. I haven't been able to find out anything else. I suppose I could just ask, but if Xander wants to keep it a secret, I'll let him. There are very few things that he keeps to himself.

It's a miracle he even has a secret identity at all.

"Never," he promises her, holding up three fingers. "I'll leave a duplicate in the shop, so I won't even be gone."

Ki hums suspiciously and takes her usual seat at the head of the small rectangular table. Xander sits at the other end, with me between them. In the eight months since I moved in, we've fitted ourselves into a simple, happy pattern. We eat breakfast together in the mornings, and at night, Ki sends us off only after we promise to be careful. I was sort of surprised, at first, that Ki knew what her son was getting up to at night, but it only took a few weeks of knowing them to understand just how close they are.

He couldn't keep a secret from her if he tried, and he never would.

"What about you, Abyss?" Ki asks me, startling me out of my thoughts. "What are you up to today?"

I shrug. "I'm going to the gym. Other than that, I'll be hanging around if you need me."

My gym isn't the nicest one in the world; I'd go so far as to say it's one of the worst. The paint on the walls is chipping and the equipment creaks dangerously. There are a few punching bags, though, and it's cheap enough that I can afford it on the pennies I make transcribing audio clips. I help out in the flower shop, too, sometimes, but I refuse to let Ki pay me for my efforts. She already gives me a place to live, rent free, and that's more than I could ever repay her for.

"I may have to," she says, but she's looking at her son. "What with Xander slacking off."

He throws his hands up in protest. "Cee has a lot to talk through, okay? I'm just looking out for him."

Ki hums again, but lets the subject drop. The flower shop opens at ten in the morning on Saturdays, and it's already a quarter after nine. We eat our breakfast in relative silence, and I curl back up on my sofa-bed in the living room while they shower and get ready. I'm struck, once again, by how similar they are. The only word I can think of to describe Xander is *wiry*— tall and thin, but tightly wound, all lean muscle. On the rare occasions I've seen him without a shirt, even I can admit that I'm impressed. Ki is similar, although in her age she's adopted a much softer appearance, leaning in to the roundness of her face. I think, from pictures, that Xander's face is more like his dad's, but the rest of him is all Ki.

While I wait for the bathroom to free up, I pull my laptop up on to my legs. It's one of about three possessions I had with me before I left, and although it's looking a little worse for wear now, I can't afford to replace it. Nor would I want to; it's got nearly ten years worth of study notes on it— everything from high school to the first year of my doctorate— and, unfortunately, my portable hard drive was not one of the other two things.

Sometimes, if I'm feeling especially torturous, I'll open up my old study notes and scroll through them. It's been a little over a year since I left school, and every so often it collides with my chest and makes it hard to breathe. Anxious with school, anxious without it. But I miss it, more and more every day.

Ki and Xander both make their way through the living room on their way downstairs to work. Their apartment is situated above the flower shop, which means that I can see the very top of the sign through the window. The sign is dark green, with the words 'PAE'S FLOWERS' painted across it in careful font. It may not be the most creative name, but they make up for it by providing beautiful bouquets that everyone in the city would willingly pay an arm and a leg for. I once overheard two customers talking about how the Caesar family would *always* come to Pae's Flowers for their arrangements. Xander's never mentioned it to me, so I'm inclined to think it's untrue, but it equally wouldn't surprise me. They are very, very good at what they do.

Ki pats me affectionately on the shoulder when she walks by and Xander shoots me a wide grin. Once the familiar sound of the shutter being raised passes, I drag myself up off the sofa-bed and to the bathroom to brush my teeth. I leave through the fire escape, because I'm not keen on trudging through the flower shop. Without a front door apart from the flower shop entrance, the fire escape and the wide window are the main points of entry for most visitors.

The Pae's have lots of visitors; it was something that took me months to get used to. Xander's friends from church are constantly dropping in and out; picking him up on Thursday nights for something they call Institute or taking him to dances on Saturdays. Ki's got a circle of friends as well, again mostly from church, who pop by at least once a month to chat and have lemonade. Then there's Xander's old school friends, Ki's neighbour buddies, their joint visitors from various other places that I can't keep up with. Dinner guests, lunch guests, sometimes even *breakfast* guests, although those slowed down once they realised I was sleeping in the living room.

The Pae's are overwhelmingly social creatures, and I don't think I'll ever get used to it.

The gym is fairly quiet when I get there, which isn't all that surprising. It's fairly quiet no matter what time of day I turn up. I pull on a pair of boxing gloves that don't feel exactly right on my hands— none of them feel right, gym-owned and broken in oddly— and make my way through a pre-set routine. It's good, and I work up a sweat, but it's not the same as working with someone.

Xander does martial arts, but has explicitly told me that boxing isn't something he's interested in.

I'll have to find another workout buddy at some point.

I move on to free weights, and then abs, and finish with a run. I leave the gym panting and tired. It's early June, and the sun is shining,

15

beating down against my skin. I like the summer. People don't look at my sunglasses so oddly in the summertime.

Walking home, I feel sweat sticking to almost every inch of my skin, rubbing uncomfortably against my clothing. Not for the first time, I wish I had the money for the C-Corp sportswear collection. Apparently, it's the most breathable and absorbent sportswear on the market. People talk about C-Corp products as if they're made of gold, but it's well-deserved. The Caesar Corporation— as is its proper name— is constantly striving towards developments across all areas of life, combining scientific method with every possible venture to ensure that the best of the best becomes available to the public.

That's what they say in their mission statement, anyway, and given how well-respected the company is, I'm inclined to believe it. The ads may get redundant, sometimes, and I may get sick of seeing the children's faces on every supermarket tabloid, but there was always good reason that I wanted to work for them.

It's not all about products, either. They've got full departments dedicated to pure research, with labs that I drooled over when I was lucky enough to take a tour in high school. I was twelve at the time, and even then I would've sold both my kidneys for a chance to play with their equipment.

I would've had the chance, later, if it weren't for... outside influences.

Xander is heading out to lunch when I get back, so I shower as quick as I can and join Ki downstairs to cover the shop floor for her when she needs to go to the backroom. I tie a green apron around my waist and stand behind the counter, trying to force myself to smile and look pleasant.

It's weird— surreal, even. I'd never have considered myself especially emotional. I always prioritised my studies above everything else, and my determination was considered my defining character trait. But I know that I used to laugh more. Smiles used to come easily, and I know that I used to scream in frustration or terror.

But for the past year, it's felt sanitised. I'm aware that I'm happy or content, sad or distraught. I'd even argue that I feel these emotions more intensely than ever before. They just come out wrong, or not enough, like my face and body stumble over the motions and movements that I've known since birth.

A baby cries out when it needs to communicate. I haven't felt tears prick my eyes in over a year.

It's not that I'm a robot, like Xander jokes sometimes, when my face is blank and I speak in a monotone. I just… struggle. It's like my emotions exist separately from my body, like my mind is detached from the physical world. It's not always a bad thing (it has it's perks, being able to shut off completely) but it makes it incredibly difficult to ignore the fact that I'm not a regular human.

I'm not superhuman, either, no matter what Xander and Ki say. I'm something else. I'm not entirely sure what, yet.

The bell above the door chimes, startling me. My deep train of thought is rattled, and I can almost physically feel my brain shooting back into place in my skull, like it had been somewhere else entirely. Knowing what I can do, I'm terrified that, maybe, it actually was.

I have my back to the door, so I take a half second to collect myself and force a smile to my face before I turn around. It's only Xander, returning from lunch, so I let the expression fall with a tiny exhale. He grins at me, bright and bold and beautiful as ever, and pulls himself up so he's sitting on the counter.

"How was lunch?" I ask, and I don't bother trying to infuse any particular emotion in to it. Xander has more than enough emotion for any given room, and he never seems offended by my monotone. "How was Cee?"

True to form, he knows that I'm teasing him regardless of how my voice sounds. He rolls his eyes. "Lunch was amazing. We went to that fancy café on twenty-third street, you know the one."

I do. I know that it's outrageously expensive, too, and suddenly Ki's comment about taking advantage makes a lot more sense. "Alexander," I say, and he scowls at my use of the name. "Are you a sugar baby?"

As I expected, he bursts into ruckus laughter, throwing his head back and clapping his hands against his thighs. "Oh my gosh," he says once he's calmed down a little. "*No.* It's not like that at all. Don't get me wrong, he's cute as the day is long, but no way. Not a chance. He's an old friend of mine."

"An old friend with money," I can't help but point out. "You could do worse."

"I could do better, too," he returns quickly. I have to wonder what Cee is like, to elicit such a response from Xander. He's the nicest person I know. I've never heard him say a bad word about anybody, and that includes his exes. Since there's not a chance in hell that Xander *is* taking advantage of the situation, I have to assume they just have that sort of friendship, where mockery plays an important role. It's hard to imagine Xander having that sort of friendship, but I suppose, in the grand scheme of things, I haven't actually known him all that long.

"He's coming by tomorrow," he says, shrugging his shoulders up to his ears. "After we get home from church. You can meet him then."

I'd be lying if I said I wasn't curious.

Still, instead of responding, I take off my apron, scrunch it into a ball, and throw it at him. "You should get off the counter," I tell him, putting on a stern voice. "What happened to leaving a duplicate here in your place? I've had to cover for you."

He grins, jumps off the counter, and puts on the apron. After a brief pause, a duplicate appears noiselessly next to him. The duplicate is identical, down to the clothes and the flyways in his hair. I reach out to tug him out of sight.

"You said you wanted a secret identity, Alexander," I tell the duplicate as we walk upstairs. He just shakes his head at me. "The shop is full of windows. If you want to keep it a secret, you can't go doing stuff like that."

"Don't worry," he says, taking off the apron and tossing it on the floor. It'll disappear in a few seconds, because for all that the duplicates are flesh and blood, the clothes they appear wearing don't seem to be real. "No one was around to see. Plus, you're always looking out for me." His brow furrows. "Us. Whatever."

"I can't protect you from being a dumbass," is all I say in return, before I sink on to the sofa bed. When I look up again a moment later, the duplicate is gone.

3.

I tag along with them to church the next day. I don't specifically believe in it, but it's nice to get out of the house sometimes. The only other place I go is the gym, and at least the church has people to talk to. Sometimes the missionaries look hopefully at me, but I can normally brush them off without too many hurt feelings.

As usual, we arrive five minutes late and the meetings still haven't started. Xander calls it 'Mormon Standard Time'. I call it 'dumb'.

When the first meeting ends, Ki rushes out to make it to her class before the people she's teaching. Before I can stand, a friend of Xander's and an acquaintance of mine settles in to the pew ahead of us to have a chat. It's Ava Layton, a wide eyed girl with ochre coloured skin and straight brown hair. She always looks like she belongs somewhere hot and dry, with a glamorous disposition even while she's picking paint out from under her fingernails.

She's one of Xander's best friends, and also his ex-girlfriend.

"Hello, hello," she greets, smiling softly at the two of us. As usual, her fingers are stained with paint and graphite. She may have decided to major in clothing design, but she's passionate about art in general. "I wanted to tell you that I've created a new mock-up for your mask."

I glance around, but thankfully Ava is keeping her voice low. No one is paying us any attention. Even still, I have to repress a sigh. There's got to be a better way to discuss this sort of thing. I don't have a secret to keep, but Xander's been pretty explicit in the fact that he wants to keep Legion and himself separate. Granted, I don't know how effective it will be when he's got me hanging around all the time, but it's been working out for him so far.

"I can bring it around today, if you like," Ava's saying.

"Not today," Xander shakes his head. "I've got a friend coming around."

Ava shrugs and stands back up, tipping her head in the direction of the classroom. Xander and I follow after her, chatting about much more innocuous things. They've been close since they were fourteen, dated for a year and a half when they turned sixteen, broke up amicably and became, if possible, closer than ever before.

I've never dated anyone seriously; starting high school as early as I did meant that my peers were all significantly older than me, and I was too busy to seek out anyone my own age. Once I started my bachelors, I went on a few dates here and there, but nothing came of any of them. I remember my best friend, Julia Lago, gushing about the eldest Caesar boy, but I'd never fully seen the appeal. Dating was just never a priority.

But Xander has dated at least semi-regularly, and somehow manages to stay friends with all of his exes. I don't think it's possible to hate Xander, in all honesty. He's got more friends than I know people, and keeps up with all of them. It would drive me crazy, to have that many people in my life, but not Xander. He smiles and chats and *loves*. I think it'll kill him one day.

The rest of church passes in a blur. As I sit idle in Sunday School, I wonder if Cee is another of Xander's exes, if maybe he's the only one to elicit bitterness in him. It doesn't seem likely; Xander never sounds angry when he talks about Cee, only teasingly frustrated and fond.

Before we leave, Ava grabs me by the arm. She doesn't bother lowering her voice, but I don't have a secret identity. "It would really boost my portfolio if I could design a costume for a superhero," she says, looking meaningfully at my sweater. It's the same one I wore last night.

"It's not like I've made a name for myself, yet," I point out, and she shrugs.

"I've seen a few videos crop up online. Legion, too," she's casual about it, which I appreciate. I do wonder, sometimes, if my lack of secret identity does help to protect Xander's. Hiding in plain sight, and all that. "You're more popular than you realise, you know."

I don't know what to say to that, so I just shrug. "You can design me something, if you like."

She fist pumps, hissing out the 's' in an over-exaggerated 'yes'. "Thank you, Abyss! I'll make it the best superhero costume ever!"

I don't doubt it. She helped Xander pick out his joggers, stitched his name on to the back of the jacket, built the mask that sits over his face. I'm sure whatever she makes for me will be amazing.

I offer her the smallest, most low-energy of smiles. "Xander's got a friend coming today," I say. "I should get going."

"Of course!" Ava grins, waves, and lets me go.

When we arrive back at the flower shop, there's a young man leaning against the door, playing on his phone. I can't get a good look at his face from the angle we approach at, but he has thick, dark curls that a Renaissance sculpture would envy. As the car rounds the corner and slows to a stop, he looks up and waves.

William Antonio Caesar the Third, the second eldest of the Caesar family and heir to the Caesar Corporation, is standing on our doorstep.

I open my mouth to ask what we should do, but Xander has already jumped out of the parked car and raced towards him. I'm left sitting in the backseat, reeling, as the eldest Caesar boy grins and claps a hand against Xander's shoulder good-naturedly.

Ki, presumably seeing my expression in the rear-view mirror, laughs. "Didn't he tell you?"

"*That's* Cee?" I say, letting some incredulity come through in my voice.

"He didn't tell you," she repeats, shaking her head fondly. "They were best friends as kids."

"They were?"

"Caesar was at our house every day it felt like," Ki smiles, waves at the boys through the passenger window. "They met at a playground when they were seven. Spent most days together after that. That family was always good to us, even after they moved to Greece. Those boys would've been… thirteen."

I watch through the window for a few more seconds as he and Xander laugh and pick at each other, play-fighting like school kids. Xander is still wearing his church clothes, with the sleeves of his white shirt rolled up, and the Caesar boy is dressed in a baseball tee and jeans. It's bizarre.

"Come on," Ki says, and I realise that she's already out of the car. I scramble out, closing the door with a slam behind me.

The boys look up. "Abs!" Xander shouts, which is completely unnecessary given the distance between us. I nod at him, unsure what to say. Ki heads into the shop and upstairs, locking the door behind her. I guess we'll head up through the fire escape.

"You must be Abyss," the Caesar boy says, coming over to me and extending a hand.

I shake it, trying to come up with something to say. I still can't wrap my head around the fact that Xander knows the Caesar family well enough to go to lunch with the eldest boy. Mostly, I can't believe that he never told me. It would've been the perfect thing for the game of two-truths-and-a-lie we played at some church activity he dragged me to a few weeks ago, and yet he never brought it up.

I wonder if his other friends already knew, and that's why it wouldn't've worked.

My mouth moves without me fully intending it to. "I used to want to work for the Caesar Corporation. The internship program is amazing."

He doesn't seem offended by my outburst; I assume he must be used to having people tell him things like this out of the blue. I'm just glad I didn't say something even more embarrassing. The only other thought in my head is: *I didn't know you had dimples.* He just says, "Charlie'll be glad to hear you say that. It was her pet project for a while."

Jocelyn Charlotte, the eldest of the four Caesar children. She passed up the opportunity to run the company and instead chose to study Journalism. In doing so, she all but handed the company to the young man in front of me. He's still smiling, and I take a half-second to really look at him.

I can see why Julia called him *gorgeous*; he's got a strong jaw and pretty almond coloured eyes. His face is covered in a smattering of freckles, and he's got broad shoulders that make him look taller than he is. In reality, he's not that much taller than me.

"Xander didn't tell me who was coming over," I say, turning to face him.

Xander just shrugs. "Caesar," he says, and points to me. "Abyss. Abyss, Caesar. Now that we all know each other, let's go upstairs. I want to take my tie off. It's too hot out here."

I shouldn't be, but I'm surprised when Caesar heads in the direction of the fire escape without prompting. Ki did say that he'd spent lots of time here, but it's still odd to me.

Julia collected magazines that had this guy on the cover.

I'm trying very hard not to be starstruck. I never thought I'd be the sort of person who would lose my cool around famous people, especially lately. With my emotions all detached and sanitised, I would've thought I'd be put at an advantage; instead, the opposite seems to be true. I'm incredibly aware of how surreal this is. Old idolisations are coming to the forefront of my mind, reminding me over and over that the person in front of me is *William Antonio Caesar the Third*, the heir to the company that I *dreamed* about working for.

When we get upstairs, I suddenly realise that I hadn't folded up the sofa bed. I don't usually; Ki doesn't seem to mind sitting on the bed when we're in the living room, and it's easier than refolding it every single day. But when we crawl inside through the window, I can't help but wish I'd folded it up today. Caesar's got more money than I could spend in a lifetime, and I'm sleeping on a sofa-bed in my best friends house, doing audio transcriptions so I have just enough money for clothes and a gym membership.

"It looks exactly the same," Caesar says, after he's straightened up and looked around. "It's funny how some things never change, isn't it?"

I look around the living room, taking in the old-school box TV that we hardly ever use, the low coffee table strewn with newspapers and magazines, the bookshelf stacked high with everything from Korean novels to the one textbook I'd had in my bag and can't bring myself to get rid of. The whole room is bathed in a yellow-tinted light from the tall lamp in the corner, and Xander has decorated any empty space with plants and flowers.

Caesar seems, oddly, right at home. The space suits him standing in the middle of the room in a wrinkled baseball t-shirt.

Ki, from the kitchen, calls out, "It's good to see you again, Caesar."

"You too, Mrs. Pae," he replies, raising his voice just slightly. "Anything I can help you with?"

"I'm only reheating some leftovers for lunch," she says, "do you want anything to eat?"

"Only if there's spare."

I sit cross-legged on the sofa bed, and after only a half-second, Xander has flopped stomach-first next to me. I flick his ear. "I thought you wanted to change?"

He offers an exaggerated sigh, dropping his face onto a pillow. "That seems like a lot of effort."

I shake my head and flick him again so he'll get moving. Whining all the way, he stands and disappears around the corner to his room. Maybe I didn't think this through; now, I'm alone with Caesar.

"So," I say, trying to inject some sort of inflection into my voice. I don't think I succeed; it takes too much effort these days. "You go by your surname?"

Caesar shrugs and leans against the bookshelf. He sounds teasing when he replies, "Is *Abyss* on your birth certificate? I don't think you're one to talk."

"It was between that and Chasm, so I think I picked the lesser of two evils."

"Chasm sounds pretty badass," he replies, grinning. It's not quite so brilliant as Xander's smiles, but it's nice; lopsided, dimpled. "Why wasn't *Void* a contender?"

It's an obvious enough question. I wish I had an obvious enough answer. Thankfully, Xander chooses this exact moment to burst out of his room, changed, and announce, "I'm hungry."

"I'm making you lunch right now!" Ki replies from the kitchen. "Come eat!"

We all make our way to the kitchen, settling down around the table as Ki hands out plates of reheated Indian food from last night. She and Xander take seats at opposite ends, and Caesar and I sit across from each other. We eat in silence for a few moments, until Ki ultimately breaks it.

"I'm sure I would've heard if you were moving back," she says to Caesar between mouthfuls of samosa. "Are you staying with your family?"

He shakes his head. "No, just me. I think Eliza is going to move back for school, but that won't be for another year or so. You know my dad's rules about the company— there's work for me to do here. I'm supposed to start working the mailroom every other weekend. And I'm studying, too. I have to finish business school. It made sense to do that here, where the business is based."

I don't know what he means by 'rules', but Ki nods like it's familiar. I wonder how close their families actually were.

Caesar answers my question for me when he says, "How are you, though? I haven't seen you since… Mr Pae's funeral. I wish we could've done more."

"Your mother already did too much," Ki replies, patting his arm and smiling at him. "It was hard, at first, but these past few years have been a lot better."

Xander nods. He only ever looks sad when his dad comes up in conversation. I never know how to comfort him; I didn't know Kwan Pae. I know that Xander looks like him, though, from the pictures on the bookshelf of them huddled side by side. They have the same brown eyes that squint when they smile, the same tiny nose that scrunches when they laugh. Xander smiles easily and freely, never hesitates to laugh, and sometimes Ki gets an expression on her face that's equal parts wistful and proud.

There's a brief, comfortable silence, before Ki asks, "Just business school, then? Nothing else you're doing?"

Caesar grins again. "Well, once I arrived back, I ran into this girl— literally, ran into her—"

"You didn't tell me you *literally* ran into her!" Xander cuts him off, his typical smile firmly back in place.

"That was quite literally the first thing I said to you."

"Uh, it *literally* was not!"

"I feel like we've said 'literally' too much," I add dryly, and Xander laughs. Caesar looks at me oddly, like he'd almost forgotten I was there. I tip my head at him and smile.

"And why is running into this girl so exciting?" Ki asks, and Caesar looks between her and Xander before huffing and rolling his eyes.

"Wait!" Xander says, and he's practically bouncing in his seat from excitement. "You haven't told Abyss yet, have you? Tell her how you told me."

There's several seconds of silence, before Caesar shakes his head. "I *can't*."

Both Ki and Xander look as confused as I feel.

"Can't what?" I ask. This whole conversation has taken a very bizarre turn in the last few moments.

Caesar leans back in his seat and looks at me for too long to be considered normal. Then he shakes his head, throws his hands dramatically in the air, and says, "I don't know! I just... can't."

"But you're doing it fine," Xander says, furrowing his eyebrows together.

"I know!"

"Calm down," Ki says, and Caesar takes a breath that can only be described as steadying.

"So," I say, and Caesar snaps his eyes to me. "You're superhuman."

"How do you know?" he says, eyes narrowed defensively.

"She's a genius," Xander says, "an actual, certified genius."

He's making fun of me, but I don't particularly mind. Instead of acknowledging it, I turn to Caesar and continue: "It was obvious enough from that conversation alone. But, also, your mom is a superhuman. It stands to reason that you and your siblings would be too. And given how excited Xander was for you to tell me in the same way you told him, it seems likely it's something... extravagant."

Caesar leans forward, resting his folded arms on the table and staring at me intently. Something in me shifts under his gaze, but my body stays stock still. There are some perks to having my emotions kept entirely separately from my physical body. It never moves if I don't want it to anymore.

"I'm a telepath."

4.

It's not what I was expecting.

Honestly, I'm not entirely sure *what* I was expecting, but somehow this revelation takes me by complete surprise. Telepath. William Antonio Caesar the Third is a telepath. Okay.

"Why couldn't you tell her the same way you told me?" Xander says in an exaggerated whine, smacking his hand against the table.

Caesar pulls the side of his lower lip between his teeth and shakes his head. "I dunno."

I sigh, push my middle fingers up the sides of my nose and under my sunglasses, rubbing at the corners of my eyes. I can't believe I'm considering it; I've only just met the guy. But he trusted me with this—making me one of a very select few, I'm sure. I'm not sure where, exactly, this conversation is going to take us, but it seems like a tit-for-tat kind of situation.

Before I can make up my mind, Caesar is continuing on in his story. I'm torn between relieved and disappointed.

"Anyway," he's saying, "I ran into this girl, and she was really freaked out. So, instinctually, I slipped inside her head to calm her down."

"That's something you can do?" I ask curiously. "Influence people's emotions?"

Caesar shrugs and moves his hand in a so-so motion. "Not exactly. But once I'm in someone's head, I can usually figure out the root cause of their emotions and offer comfort, or something. She was… all over the place. I could barely keep up with what was upsetting her. Didn't help that she was thinking in mostly French. But one thing that I did notice was all the numbers floating around her vision. And," he cuts me off with a teasing smile when I open my mouth to ask what he means by that, "yes, I *do* see out of their eyes. It's one of my favourite things to do. I can literally see things from other people's perspectives."

"Huh," I say. It's a surprisingly intriguing ability. I've never thought of what telepaths could do, beyond reading people's thoughts. But it seems like Caesar, at least, has a plethora of various connected abilities. I make a mental note to ask him about them later. After I explain why I think he can't read my mind.

"What do you mean *numbers*?" Ki asks, and that's a fair question.

"Like, numbers," he says, screwing his eyebrows together. "It's hard to explain if you can't seem them, but they're like… percentages, I guess? Odds. She just called them 'the numbers'. The thing was, I couldn't get rid of them, not even temporarily, and if they'd been some sort of… hallucination or imagined thing, I would've. It wouldn't have stuck, it would've returned right after I left, but I would've been able to get rid of them."

"You know from experience?" I ask, pursing my lips.

He nods. "Yeah. My younger brother, Carlos," he says, as though I wouldn't know the name of the younger son of the Caesar family, "went through a spell of terrible sleep paralysis. He kept seeing things in his room in the middle of the night. I stayed awake in his bed for, like, three weeks, helping to get rid of them so he could sleep."

"When did you sleep?" Ki demands, and Xander laughs fondly at her mothering. I crack a smile myself.

"During the day," Caesar assures her. "The point is, I know I can get rid of things that aren't real. These numbers… they were."

"So she was superhuman," I say, and I don't bother adding any emotions or movement into this statement, my voice my usual monotone. "What's so special about that?"

Caesar gives me an expression that's sort of a glare, but too curious to carry any real heat. It must be odd for him— I'm sure, usually, people are easy for him to (literally) read, and I'm something of an enigma to him. "She didn't know they were real," he says, and I have to admit it surprises me. "She thought they were just… a weird way she processed things. When I explained to her that I couldn't get rid of them, I asked her what she used them to, uh, process."

He pauses significantly here, which makes me want to roll my eyes. It's all drama.

Xander ruins the moment for him by saying, "she used them to win at cards!"

Ki and I turn to look at each other, and I offer a confused huff of a laugh. "What?"

Caesar smiles fondly at Xander, shaking his head. "The numbers were probability. We tested it together by rolling dice. In theory, the numbers should've always given her a one out of six chance, no matter what number she was thinking of, but these numbers… they factored in everything. I don't know exactly how it worked, but she'd think *hmm, what the odds that it'll land on five?* and the numbers would answer, and she'd always be right. It's like, they were aware of the wind, how many times I'd shake the die, whether it would catch on a groove… She was never wrong."

"And the same held true when playing cards, I take it?" Ki asks, leaning forward on her elbows.

"Yeah," Caesar nods. "She always knew when to hold or fold, or what cards I had when we played go-fish. It was kind of crazy. I think, after she'd realised what she could do, she wanted to show off, because she dragged me to this grimy casino and won every single game at least once."

"So, she's basically psychic," I say, unimpressed, "and she uses it to gamble?"

"Wouldn't you?" Caesar challenges.

I can honestly say that I wouldn't. At least, not as exclusively as this mystery girl seems to be. I would've used it for science. Which sounds a lot more noble than it actually is— I would've double checked the safety measures on the experiments I was performing. Or… I might've just used someone else. It's hard to say. I was, frankly, obsessed.

"So, she took you to these casinos," I say, brushing over it. "What does that have to do with you being back?"

"Well," he says, and he rubs at the back of his neck. "I never really thought about the fact that superhumans didn't always know how to recognise their ability. Or how to deal with it even if they did. And when I helped her, I just felt like I should be doing more to help other superhumans, too. I mean, my mom is superhuman, like you said, but I've never been open about my ability. I thought it might be good to… reveal it."

Xander grins at him. "He told me when we were eleven," he explains to me. "I was the first person outside of his family to know."

"And, until recently," he says, smiling quite genuinely at me, "he was the only one to know. After years of not being in proper contact with him, he still hadn't told anyone. There's not a single speculation online about me being telepathic, even when people are talking about how my siblings and I are *probably* superhuman. I knew I could trust him."

Xander, somehow, manages to beam even brighter at that. "Course you can."

"So when I was heading back here for school and work, I decided to meet up with him to ask what he thought about coming clean with it," Caesar smiles, "I think I've made my decision. Telling you was something of a… practice run."

"Why me?" I ask, because it seems like a reasonable enough question even if it is, at least somewhat, emotionally charged. "I mean, you could've told someone you actually know."

Caesar leans back in his chair and smiles at me. "Telling someone I actually know isn't as scary. But Xander trusts you, so I was pretty sure that even if, after telling you, I changed my mind… I could trust you to stay quiet."

The thought makes me warm, somewhere deep inside. I offer him a gentle smile in return. "But you haven't changed your mind?" I clarify. "You're going to tell everyone?"

"Soon. Probably next week. Can I trust you to keep it quiet until then?"

I nod.

It doesn't take more than a few moments of silence for Xander to start not-so-subtly staring at me. When I don't immediately move to speak, a duplicate starts pattering around the kitchen, cleaning up. It's his way of letting me know that Caesar does, in fact, know that Xander is superhuman. As if I wouldn't have figured that one out already. He may not have developed his ability until after Caesar moved away, but I'm certain that the minute Caesar revealed why he'd wanted to meet up with Xander, he was excitedly talking about how he was superhuman, too.

But I'm not Xander.

It's only when Ki fixes me with a look that reminds me of my mom that I start to feel guilty. Caesar may be a complete stranger, but he has trusted me with a secret that he's trusted very few people with before. And I haven't told him anything.

Not that he seems to be expecting anything; he's sitting across from me, looking between the two Xander's with an intrigued expression. Even if he *knew*, I doubt that he's seen it in action as much as I have, even just in the past week.

"Let's move into the living room," Ki suggests, and I think it's her way of helping me to relax.

"I'll grab drinks," Xander says, and a second duplicate appears to dig through the cabinets for sparkling juice and glasses.

"This house is too small for three of you," I say, gesturing with my chin towards the galley-style kitchen, where the two duplicates are fighting over the space.

Xander shrugs. But when the first duplicate is done clearing our dishes, he dissipates it with a dramatic, but unnecessary, wave of his hand. I don't know why he bothers— I've seen his duplicates flicker out of existence without any movement on his part. When I tried to ask him about it, he just shrugged and said it's fun.

He and I have different ideas of fun.

Regardless, we all stand and make our way to the living room. Xander and I take seats on the sofa bed, while Ki sits cross legged on the coffee table and Caesar takes the armchair. We're all quiet for a few seconds. Xander elbows me and gives me an incredulous look.

I heave a dramatic sigh, which takes more planning that I'd like it to, really, and effectively draw everyones attention.

"I have a hypothesis as to why you can't read my mind."

"Oh?" Caesar says, smirking at me. "What's that?"

I can't tell if he's being condescending or angling for humour, but either way I'm annoyed by it. I'm an actual, certified genius, and when

I say I have a hypothesis, I'm already pretty certain it's fact. I make a point to scowl at him before I continue. "It's a complicated story."

He gestures for me to go ahead. I take off my glasses.

I see the very instant that it clicks in his head that I'm something inhuman. For the past year, my eyes have been... different. I thought they were solid black, at first, pitch dark. But upon closer inspection, I could see the swirling, nebulous colours— green and blue and pink— and flecks of light that look like stars. When people first look at them, they don't see any of that.

When people first look at them, they see the Void.

"Okay," Caesar says slowly, staring at me. I slide my glasses back on and he shakes himself. The Void has that effect on people. "So... you're superhuman, too."

"Not exactly," I say, and it's my turn to smirk. "I'm a universe."

5.

The story I tell Caesar goes like this:

The last thing I see before the experiment begins is my lab assistant. I say 'my', but the lab belongs to the university, and she's volunteering for extra credit. But I felt important having one, even if it was only for a few hours. The last thing I see is her, double and triple checking some readings and then giving me a formal looking nod. I give her a thumbs up back, realising only a second later that it makes me look even younger than my age.

There are downsides to finishing high school early and whizzing through university and being a year into a doctorate at eighteen years old. Not many, but a few. Like being stared at as though you're five when you're trying to run an experiment that will prove or disprove the existence of alternate universes.

Personally, I'm hoping for proving. I keep thinking of JuJu— Julia Lago, that is, my best friend. She'd wanted to be here, but her class schedule wouldn't allow it, and I know better than anyone that she can't afford to miss any more of her media studies classes if she can avoid it. Besides, it's not like I won't be around later to tell her about the results, and she'll be there when I present my findings and do a proper showcase of the device, and that's the real, important stuff.

But she is the whole reason for the experiment, anyway, so I can understand why she wanted to be here. After all, I wouldn't've choose to study astrophysics with such intensity if it hadn't been for her showing off her ability to me when we were kids. She couldn't resist gripping my arm and showing me all the different universes she could see.

People call her an 'illusionist', but I know better. Those places and people she shows me are real, and I'm going to prove it. She inspired all of this.

With very little fanfare, I flip the heavy switch to turn on the machine I've been working on for the last year.

I'm a woman of science; I believe that there's a logical explanation for everything. There's an order to everything, even things that don't seem to have order. We just haven't figured it out yet. And although the laws of physics may be different in other universes, there will still be laws.

But here, there's nothing to make order out of. There's just… nothing. No order, no rules, no real way to categorise anything. I'm not standing on anything because there's nothing to stand on. I'm not floating through anything because there's nothing to float through. There's not even direction, or sense of direction, and I can't orient myself.

(Caesar grins widely at this point and says, "The enemy gate is down," like he's referencing something.

When I pause my story to look at him, impassive and blank faced under my glasses, he shrugs apologetically, and nods that I should go on.)

There's just… nothing.

No colour - or maybe just no light, because that would stop me from seeing colour, anyway.

And then, just as soon as I've thought it, there are two bright pinpricks of light, like far away stars or two eyes in the dark, staring at me. Then, swirls of blue and purple and pink, like those filtered photos of nebulae. These sudden colours follow a serpentine pattern around the not-space around me. I think *bioluminescent* before I remember I'm most likely in another universe and it's not as though a universe can be alive. I take a moment to frown at myself, because I don't know what a universe can and can't be, frankly.

If I could clear my head, I'm sure I'd be able to think my way out of this. After all, if I'm in another universe, like the experiment was meant to do, then there must be some sort of law or trick or something to help me out of here. But I'm not in my clear head, and I forget my whole train of thought about the characteristics of life being different in different universes, and it doesn't come back until it touches me.

I'm not sure how I know that it's touching me. There's no physical contact or sensation of any kind. I'm just aware that I'm being touched. My entire body feels warmer, somehow, but I shiver anyway, trying to pull away but unsure what I'm even pulling against. It keeps touching me.

It's not entirely unwelcome.

If it speaks, I can't or don't hear it. It's trying to communicate, though, and I want it to. I breathe (how am I breathing, anyway?) in through my nose and out through my mouth. I clear my head. I try to relax. I do relax.

I'm flashing through my old memories. My first day of high school, when I was ten years old. That year, my first panic attack, because I'd put so much pressure on myself. My graduation at fourteen. My first test at university. JuJu and I moving boxes to our tiny flat. Starting up the experiment this morning. There are other memories, too, but these are standouts. I hold on to them. They're so clear it's like I'm reliving them, all the times I was most anxious. There's a lot.

I think this is how the universe is communicating with me. This place is sentient. It's alive. I know it, and I know that it knows me. I stop trying to pull away. I stop trying to figure it out. I relax. It seems to relax, too. It keeps touching me, and I keep my eyes open.

It seems to touch my eyes, and I recoil, but that doesn't stop it. I hear the word *VOID* but that might be in my head. I hold on to it anyway. This is the Void. I understand. It brings up other memories. Times when I raced down the street to JuJu's house because I was mad at my mom or my sister. Times when I was stuck in the nurses office because I'd been panicking again. Times when my dad drove me around because they don't give you a drivers license early just because you're a genius. Times when I needed people.

I understand. The Void needs me.

Now that I've stopped struggling, stopped fighting with my mind for answers, it's not a bad place. It's actually comfortable. Peaceful. It's away from everything else and it's quiet and I feel understood. It's communicating with my memories. I'm not sure how it's doing that - telepathy, maybe. It's not unheard of, in my own universe, so why not here? It doesn't really matter, anyway. The Void cares to be sure I understand. I think it's asking for permission, in its own way.

How can I refuse? I like it here. I feel clearer, cleaner, more myself. It helped me shut my thoughts down, focus on the important things. My emotions take a backseat to my logical thinking - they're still there, of course, but more manageable.

I think the Void is like a child, unsure and nervous and in need of a teacher. And all it needs is my help.

I can help it.

I don't know how, yet, but I am a scientist. I'll come up with something. I have the lab at my disposal, after all. And all the resources that my degree provides for me.

"Whatever you need," I say, aloud.

And then I come back to my own.

"You were gone for ten seconds," the lab assistant says. "You didn't use a failsafe, but I assume you were in some sort of danger to get out that quickly. What did you see?"

I start to turn around, but catch sight of my reflection on some metal on the device. I inch closer, a distant feeling of dread welling up inside of me. My hair is the same - tightly coiled and pulled back in two braids. My dark skin hasn't changed at all. But my eyes - my eyes. They look like galaxies. They look like those filtered pictures of nebulae. They look like the Void.

I know without really thinking about it that my career is over.

It's not that superhumans aren't *allowed* to do important work, not exactly. It's just that there are these expectations of what they can and cannot do. I could finish school— I don't think they can revoke my scholarship— I could even, probably, get some interviews. But once people know that I'm— *more than* human, they could reject me.

Superhumans use their abilities for entertainment. It's why superheroes were popular, with their theatrics and costumes, and it's why, eventually, they fell out of fashion. People got bored.

My career, just barely starting, is over.

"There wasn't much light there," I manage to say. My voice sounds different. Not that it changed, but that it's more level. I'm more aware of myself. I'm more in control. "Can you get me a pair of tinted goggles? My eyes hurt."

She gets me some, and I close my eyes when she comes to pass them to me. I slide them over my face, stand up, and excuse myself.

The world around seems different. It's not, except that I just lost everything.

My breathing quickens. I would've thought being in more control would help these disappear, but apparently not. I duck into a closet and sit against the door, holding my head in my hands. It came on more quickly, it feels bigger.

When I was ten, I hid in an empty classroom in a high school that felt too big for me, my head in my hands, breathing hard. I didn't know what was happening and I didn't know how to make it stop. I learned techniques, breathing patterns and counting, to calm myself down, because I wasn't going to let some small part of my mind prevent me from doing the thing that the rest of it loved.

I try to breathe now, in for seven seconds, out for eight, but it doesn't help.

I'm aware, suddenly, that my mind has expanded. There's more space, it feels like. The anxiety fills every last inch, just like it always did, commandeering my mind to its own use… and I'm pretty sure the Void *is* my mind, now— and that's, that's a lot of space to control.

And the Void— sentient in its own way— has never felt panic like this before. I think that makes it even worse, because it's panicking, too—

I lose that train of thought as the panic takes over. I don't know how long I sit there. A long time. Long enough that I hear people calling out my name.

I keep sitting there until the voices and footsteps have faded. And then I run.

6.

Caesar leans back in his chair when I finish speaking a half-hour later. I hadn't realised how badly I needed to say it all out loud; the version I'd told Xander was much more condensed, barely touching on the 'why' and just glancing over the brief time I spent in the Void. Caesar's eyes are wide, considering.

"So that's what changed your mind about the Caesar Corporation," he says thoughtfully. "You thought that you wouldn't be able to get a job in that industry because of... the Void."

I stay perfectly still, because shrugging and nodding seems like a lot of effort. Xander and Ki are also looking at me with concerned curiosity, their expressions identical with dangerously narrowed eyes, like they'd go fight the entire world for me. I don't doubt that they would.

"I knew that it was going to be an uphill battle," I say, forcing myself to shake my head slightly at the Pae's. "And that even if I was able to continue my research, a lot of it would be... lost. Not mine, anymore. My work was too important to me. I'd rather leave than let anyone else touch it."

"So you left," he says, sinking further into the armchair and looking at me through his eyelashes. "Because your eyes changed colour."

"You saw them," I reply, "It's more than changing colour. People get... drawn in."

He hums in agreement. "It wasn't... the most pleasant feeling."

"It's…" Xander starts, his tongue darting out to lick at his lips. "It's like you're drowning, isn't it? Like you're drowning and you don't even mind."

"Imagine being *in* it," I stress, looking between them. "Imagine *that* asking for your help. Of course you'd give it. I didn't even think about the potential consequences."

Caesar leans forward, resting his elbows on his knees. "I take it there's more to it than your eyes having a, uh, hypnotising quality?"

I nod. "Like I said, my emotions are… sanitised. I still feel them, I know that they exist, but unless they're overwhelming or all-consuming, like panic, then I don't manifest them physically without a lot of effort. Smiling, laughing, crying, yelling… It's all very intentional, when I do it. I have to think about it."

"It only increases her genius factor, cause she doesn't get distracted as easily," Xander says, and Ki rolls her eyes.

"You get used to it, Caesar," she says. "She's more expressive than she thinks she is."

I wonder what she means by that. Is it less that I don't express myself and more that I do so differently than I used to?

"Anything else?" he presses, sounding more excited each second.

"I can go to the Void at will," I reply. "Not physically, I don't think, but… I can go to this other universe in my mind."

"Now that's weird," Xander says, pointing at me with wide eyes. "You go all... blank, and don't hear when we call for you. We have to touch her," he elaborates for Caesar's benefit. "Something about that can bring her back."

"Anything... outward?" he asks, waving a hand vaguely through the air. "Like, you said you weren't superhuman, but obviously people would assume you are. Is there anything you do that affects... the physical world?"

I look at him for a long moment, debating. I've revealed a lot today, especially to a stranger. I know it's illogical, but I'd like to keep just one thing for me. "Does your friend with the numbers affect the physical world?"

He thinks about it for a half-second, then shrugs. "Not directly, I guess."

There's a few heartbeats of silence before Ki stretches her hands up above her head and climbs off the coffee table. "I'm going to visit Sister Atwood," she says to Xander, ruffling his hair. "I'd say that I'll let you kids get to know each other, but I feel like that might be taken care of already. Have fun, there's ice cream in the freezer, no video games on Sunday."

The last part is directed at Xander, who rolls his eyes hugely. She ducks out of the fire escape, waves to us through the window, and disappears.

None of us move for a solid few minutes.

"Can I just ask one more question?" Caesar says to break the silence. When I nod, he continues, "Are you and the Void joined, or are you the Void? Did it already have sentience, or did it gain it once you were there? You're a universe! What the fu-!"

"Don't swear in my mother's house!"

"She's not *here*," Caesar protests, sounding petulant, but at Xander's glare he relents to the point.

Honestly, it's a better reaction than I was expecting. At least he waited for Ki to leave before he started swearing.

"The Void was... something else entirely. Something separate."

"You said it used your memories to communicate with you..."

"I just... felt it call out to me."

"Or were you calling out to it?"

It's suddenly an uncomfortable conversation. I met him less than three hours ago, after all. I think I'm justified in my hesitation. He seems to sense it, and draws back, shifting into a more relaxed posture. "Sorry," he says. "I don't know what protocol is, in this situation. I've never spoken to a *universe* before."

"It's okay," I tell him. "Very few people have."

7.

It's easy to get along with Caesar, after we've both shared these secrets. Xander is ecstatic about the easy friendship the three of us have, asking me painfully obvious questions about what I think of Caesar. We get together a few times in the following week, and spend most of our spare time lounging together in various locations.

Caesar offers to order us food, pay for our movie tickets, and take us shopping. We say no more often than we say yes, but he lights up whenever we agree. It's sort of adorable to see the dimpled smile spread across his freckled face. Caesar smiles often, but they don't seem easy like Xanders, instead almost rehearsed, but I like to see them anyway. When we go out with him, we see cameras and fangirls, so I can't blame him for holding himself like he's being watched. On the rare occasions he gets frustrated with the attention, he only ever curses in Spanish or Greek, because fewer people can understand. I know a little Spanish, from Julia, so I mostly find it endearing.

Sometimes, I'm especially grateful that he can't read my mind. I think I'd spontaneously combust if he could.

"What do you think of him?" Xander asks me, the following Tuesday, collapsing onto the sofa bed next to me. We've been out most of the day, and I've just settled in with my laptop balanced on my legs. Xander's feet on the pillow next to me, his head at my feet, staring at the ceiling with his hands behind his head.

"He seems…" I have to search for the right word. "Genuine."

Xander hums, and when I peek over the top of my laptop, his eyebrows are furrowed and he's almost frowning. I kick his shoulder. "What's up?"

"I think he's planning something. Nothing bad, don't worry. Just… something. I'm not sure what."

"He's planning to reveal his ability to the world," I reply. "You're probably just picking up on tension from that."

"Maybe," he says, but he doesn't sound convinced. "I've known him since I was seven, you know, and we kept in touch as much as teenage boys do while he was in Greece. I feel like I know him pretty well. This seems like it's something more."

"But not something bad?"

"No," he shakes his head slowly. "Just *something*."

"Specific," I quip, shaking my head and focusing my eyes back on my laptop.

Xander heaves a dramatic sigh, bouncing his foot back and forth against his ankle.

"Why are you so worried?" I ask, without taking my eyes off my screen. "If it's not something bad, then surely you don't have anything to be worried about."

"I don't know," he says, shrugging helplessly. "I think he's planning something big that involves us, and I don't know what it is, and I don't like not knowing."

"Keep in mind, you're not the telepath. You're probably getting hung up on nothing. It's like you said— you've known him for years."

"Yeah," he says, after a few heartbeats. "You think he's genuine?"

"I do."

"That's your review? Genuine?" He sounds teasing now, but I can bear it if it gets him out of his funk. "Nothing else?"

"It's a compliment," I tell him, shifting my gaze away from my screen and kicking at his shoulder again. "I haven't known him since he was seven. I've had three days to get to know him, and even if we've spent a few hours together each time, I don't know him all that well. But he seems *genuine*. He seems like a good guy."

"Kind of guy you'd like calling the shots?"

"What do you mean?"

"Do you think he'd be a good leader?" Xander looks thoughtful.

I frown at him. "Now I think you're the one who's up to something."

"Just thinking out loud," he says in a faraway voice. "We used to play knights on the playground. Caesar was always the king. He's… a natural leader. He likes to plan and organise. I think he's planning and organising now, but this time I'm afraid that I'm not his knight, you know?"

"Not really," I reply. Julia and I never played games like that. We watched a James Bond film for the first time when we were eight years old, and after that we liked playing spy games, where she was Bond and I was Q. Once I started high school, we didn't have much time for make-believe, but she was saved as *Bond* in my phone right up until I left. "You're *friends.* If it's important, he'll tell you. That's how it works."

"Are you sure?"

"Whatever he's planning," I say patiently, "if it involves us, he'll tell us. Relax. If you want, you can ask him about it."

Xander hums again. I'm aware of him, but I allow myself to get distracted by the internet. If he has more to say, he'll say it. I'm not entirely sure what he's worried about, or what he's trying to imply, but I'm not too concerned about figuring it out, either. He can't keep a secret to save his life, so I know he'll tell me what's on his mind eventually.

About ten minutes later, he speaks again.

"I think," he says, voice low and raspy, "that he's trying to build some sort of… team. It's like he said, he felt like he should be doing more for superhumans."

"And he came to you, a superhuman."

"Yeah," Xander agrees. "And I think, at first, he genuinely came to me for advice that was it. But then we spent more time together, and he learned more about what I can do, and the fact that you're…"

"A universe," I supply dryly, and Xander nods.

"I think he's imagining, like…"

"Superheroes?"

"Maybe."

Xander's in full-blown crisis mode and I don't really understand why. The guy wanders around at night in a costume jacket with 'Legion' emblazoned on the back, but the minute someone with actual resources is hinting that he *maybe* wants to do something similar, he's freaking out. I place my laptop on the side table and stretch my arms up above my head, considering what to say.

"I guess I don't see what the problem is," I finally tell him, and he sits up to face me properly. "You've been riding the superhero train for months."

Xander huffs and rolls his eyes. "I know."

"Then what's the worry? Explain it to me like I'm dumb."

He laughs at that, like I expected that he would. "The actual, *certified* genius wants me to treat her like she's dumb?"

"I said that once," I say, and despite my monotone, Xander can tell that I'm teasing.

"But it's true though," he returns, lightning-fast. After a moment of consideration, he continues, "I don't know his motivations. Like, I've been 'riding the superhero train'— as you put it— for months, because I want to... help people. I want to use my abilities to make life easier for other people, or at least to try my best too. Going to school at the same time as helping my mom in the shop, that sort of thing."

"Duplicates are useful for that," I agree. "Doesn't explain the crime fighting, though."

Xander shrugs his shoulders up to his ears. "If I have these abilities, then it's a waste not to use them. I mean, I'm nineteen years old, and the rest of my friends have gone off on their missions, but I'm still here. I've been given this ability for a reason, right, and if I *don't*, then…"

I think I know where he's coming from, now. A few months ago, he told me that his favourite parable in the bible is the one about the talents. A group of servants were each given a portion of a lord's money. The first two went out and doubled the money, while the last one buried it in the ground and didn't do anything with it. The first two were praised, while the last one was told he was a disappointment. Personally, I think that's a bit harsh, but I can understand why it resonated with Xander.

"If you don't, then you're burying it," I say, and he beams at me. "What's this have to do with Caesar?"

"The whole point of not burying it is that I'm bettering myself and the world around me, right?" When I offer him a minuscule nod, he continues, "I don't know why Caesar's decided to dig his up."

"I think this metaphor got away from you," I tell him. "And Caesar told you why."

Xander sighs. "It's not that I don't trust him," he says after a moment. "It's just that he's kept it hidden for so long that I don't know if he'll really know what to do with it. And I wonder how people will actually react to him. If they'll trust him."

"Oh," I say, because suddenly this conversation is making a lot more sense. "You've been talking in circles."

"What?"

"You're not worried that he's keeping things from you," I tell him, and wave my hand in his face when he tries to interrupt. "You already worked out what he's planning. And you're not worried about his motivations because you already know what they are. He wants to help people, same as you. He says he wants to help superhumans, and that's probably the main goal, even if he is getting swept up in the idea of a superhero team."

"It's dangerous to get caught up in that—"

"And *that's* what's bothering you."

Xander blinks at me for a few seconds, pursing his lips. When he speaks next, he's sounds just a tiny bit bitter. "You're right."

"I am an actual, *certified* genius," I say, just to get his smile back in place. "You're worried about his safety." To further tease him, I add, "Why don't you ever worry about mine?"

Xander huffs and shakes his head. "Because I know that you're the smartest person in any room."

Somewhere in me or the Void, I soften.

There's a few seconds of silence, and then I ask, "Why don't you worry about your own?"

I'm not sure what answer I'm expecting, but I'm surprised when he shoots me a dangerous looking grin that I've only ever seen on Legion, and he says, "Because I don't need to."

8.

I'm not dumb. As Xander loves to point out, I *know* that I'm an actual, certified genius. I have IQ tests and school results and ten years worth of science notes to prove it. They called me a gifted kid for two years before they realised that *gifted* didn't cut it. And from then on I was called a genius, I was called a prodigy. My mother studied philosophy and my dad worked with his hands. My brother did everything I did, and did it before me, but I did it faster.

So I'm not dumb. I know that Xander is Legion and Legion is Xander. I know that he can create multiple versions of himself, join them all back up, remember everything that every one of them (him?) did. He gets muddled up sometimes; he has memories that conflict and he doesn't always know where he was when. I know that Legion was a name that Xander chose for himself, fifteen-years-old, in whispered conversation with Ava. He still calls her *Acid Spit*, sometimes, affectionately. He's powerful and kind— a careful combination of traits.

Intellectually, I know that Legion is a persona. That Xander is Legion and Legion is Xander.

But Xander is gentle, and wears flowers in his hair.

Legion is deadly, or has the potential to be.

We still go out, every other night, the two of us, and split off in different directions to break up petty fights or help lost kids find their way home. Xander pulls on his mask and becomes Legion. I pull on my oversized sweater and adjust my glasses and I'm still Abyss.

Sometimes, I would envy his secret identity. Since our conversation, I've seen it as something of a burden. He's living two lives; he's being two people. He might not feel the need to worry about himself, but I'm overwhelmed with it. This distinction might ruin him.

"Are you ready?" he asks me, voice low and steady behind his mask. His mouth is hidden and I can't see if he's smiling or not. I wonder if Legion smiles the same way Xander does.

"As I'll ever be," I say in a breath, and we jump down from the fire escape.

9.

"Xander around?"

Caesar is standing on the fire escape, leaning half way into the living room with his hands braced on the windowsill. He's wearing the same red and grey baseball t-shirt he was wearing the day I met him, rolled up around his elbows.

"He's downstairs," I say, "some of us have to work."

Caesar rolls his eyes, but wisely doesn't try to form a comeback. "Are you working?"

"Yes," I reply, but tip my head in invitation for him to come inside anyway.

"What're you working on? Some groundbreaking equations? A piece of tech that will change the way space travel is conceived of?"

I can't help but stare at him as he clambers on the end of the sofa bed and crosses his legs underneath him. My sunglasses hide the movement of my eyes, although I'm not actually sure that, without pupils or irises, someone else would really be able to tell where I was looking anyway. "I'm not a physicist."

"Sure you are," he says, sounding genuinely confused. "You've got a doctorate, you opened a portal to another universe."

"Did you miss the part about me running away?" I ask. "I never finished my doctorate."

Caesar looks just as bewildered as I feel. I thought I'd explained myself well enough, but apparently not. "But you're a genius," he says, and I laugh on a two-second delay.

Smiles come quickly enough, once I decide, but laughter isn't as natural. I have to force myself to laugh. He's looking at me curiously, which he's done often over the past week. It's like he's trying to figure me out. I imagine I'm one of the first people that he's had to.

"I saw your video," I say to him, instead of carrying on. "How's the reaction been?"

"Positive, mostly," he lets out a large, contented sigh. "There were the initial freak outs… the PR department chewed me out a bit. Said I should've gone through them instead of doing it all on my own, but I thought it would feel more authentic this way. I don't want people to think it's some sort of stunt." He bites his lip and picks at the duvet. "Of course, some people think it's a stunt anyway. And there's people guessing about my siblings, which I didn't want. They say that they're fine with it, but I don't know… It's their choice whether they address it or not."

Caesar is always very careful when he talks about his siblings. I'm fairly confident that they also have abilities, but he's never said one way or the other.

"But I've been told that reception is on the whole 'over seventy percent good', so I'm hopeful that it'll all work out," he says, and smiles softly at me. I wonder if he's worried. I wonder if I'm supposed to comfort him. "Did you see Breakthrough Monthly did an article where they claimed they had an 'exclusive' with me? As if the video wasn't public for anyone."

I haven't seen it, but it seems like Caesar finds it funny, so I offer him a tiny smile. "Ridiculous," I say, and he throws his hands up dramatically.

"I know!" After a second or two of light laughter, he sighs again and rests his hands on his knees. "I'd better go down to the shop. Mom wants me to hire Pae's Flowers."

"Big event?"

"Yeah, actually," he replies, breaking in to a wide smile. "They haven't announced it yet, but Charlie and Farah are getting married!"

"Oh, wow," I say, because I'm sure it's what's expected. "Tell them congratulations."

"I will," he says earnestly, and I can see him turning around to his sister and her fiancée and saying 'my friend Abyss says congrats!' even though I don't know them. "They've not set an exact date, but they know they want to be married in six months, so I'm supposed to 'float the idea' to Mrs. Pae and Xander, as if they'll say no."

"That's not a very long engagement," I say, and Caesar rolls his eyes.

"Tell me about it," he says, sliding off the bed. "Mom's beside herself about it. She says there's no time to plan the wedding. And she's worried Charlie is rushing in to it." He puts on a pseudo-feminine voice before he continues, "'You're only twenty-three, dear, I just *worry* about you.'"

"What do you think?"

"Charlie's in love," he says, and he shrugs. "Why wait if you're in love? If you know what the other person is thinking?"

"Well," I say, and I don't bother making my voice lighter, hoping that Caesar will pick up on my tone through my words, "Charlie doesn't know what Farah is thinking. That's your job."

I'm pleased when Caesar grins at me. "That it is. And Farah loves her just as much. I knew she'd say yes even before Charlie knew she was going to ask."

"Best go talk to Ki and Xander," I say, nodding towards the door. "They might be booked."

His eyes widen and he edges towards the door. "I hope not! Mom would kill me! But, hey, before I go downstairs, are you free later? There's someone I want you guys to meet."

I glance at the audio I'm mid-transcribing and try to work out how much longer it'll take me. "I should be," I tell him after a second. "How's three o'clock sound?"

"Perfect," he answers, nodding once. "I'll let Xander know where to meet."

He leaves the door ajar when he disappears. I can hear Ki and Xander serving a few customers, and the thundering of Caesar's feet while he races down the stairs. It's a pleasant sound; I think I'm becoming fond of him.

At three o'clock, Caesar is waiting for us outside of the café he'd told Xander to meet him at, and after we've all said hello, he says we're just waiting for his friend, and then we'll go to a nearby park, because the weather is too nice to sit inside.

While we wait, I eye the gym across the street. It's a lot nicer than mine and slightly more than double the price. The advertisements on the outside boast high-end models of equipment, a pool, and, most enviously, a boxing ring. I'd sigh wistfully if I didn't know that both

Caesar and Xander would immediately jump on it, asking me if I was okay. There are perks to the Void— no involuntary reactions, no sighs, no making my friends worry.

A girl exits the gym and Caesar waves, grinning broadly. This must be the friend he wanted us to meet. She hops across the street without looking and slides up next to him, wrapping him in a one armed hug. She's got her other hand clasped tight around the strap of a red duffle bag, although I don't know why, exactly, she's carrying a duffle when she's wearing what seem to be gym clothes anyway. Her shorts are loose around her upper thighs, black with white piping, and her grey v-neck t-shirt doesn't really hide her red sports bra. She's got long blonde hair in wide, beachy waves draping down her back and over her shoulders, and a smile on her red-painted lips that could rival Xander's best grin.

She bounces on the balls of her feet as she steps away from Caesar and looks at me and Xander, with her eyes narrowed and head head tipped slightly to one side.

Caesar beams and gestures to her. "This is Ace," he says, and she waves by raising her hand and wriggling her fingers through the air.

"I'm his best friend," she informs us, in a voice that seems equal parts teasing and proud. "Xander," she says, pointing at his floral printed t-shirt and raising a brow, "the best, uh, florist in the whole city, according to Cee, but also… it's just a statement of fact. And you must be Abyss."

"Ace," I muse, "you must play cards."

Xander catches on as soon as the sentence is out of my mouth. "Oh! Of course, you're the friend with the numbers and the gambling."

Ace laughs, ducking her head down and covering her mouth with her hand. "That's me," she answers, straightening up. "Ace Jackson, gambler *extraordinaire*." It's a common enough word in English, but she pronounces it like she's speaking French anyway.

Caesar jumps in with a smile that I think is nervous. "Xander is the best florist in the *world*," he says, shooting Ace a look, but she just shrugs. "And Abyss is a phys— a *genius*."

I'm oddly touched that he reworded it, clearly remembering our conversation from that morning. It's sweet that he wants to big us up to his friend, as well. I imagine that he already has been.

Ace looks me up and down. "An astrophysicist," she says decisively.

I wonder how much information she can get from these alleged numbers. I wonder if it makes her psychic, or as good as a mind reader.

"Shall we go to the park, then?" Xander suggests, after a few beats of silence.

We make our way down the street to a tucked-away little park, only a mile each direction. Ace clutches her duffle in one hand the whole way down, bouncing on the balls of her feet whenever we pause. A few times, she opens her mouth, but she doesn't say anything until we're settling down on an ancient picnic bench.

There's a softness to Ace's body. She's clearly physically fit, but she's not skinny or even particularly toned, and her cheeks have an almost baby-fat look to them, despite the fact that she's seventeen. It makes her three years younger than Caesar and Xander, and four younger than me. When I was her age, I was only just starting my doctorate. The mind boggles.

She drops her duffle from her shoulder and it lands with a soft thud on the grass next to us. Caesar takes the seat next to her, and Xander sits across from her. As I slide in across from Caesar and next to Xander, I can't help feeling like we've already found our places— that this is how we'll always be. I don't know where the thought comes from or why, but the idea of the four of us in this particular arrangement feels inevitable. It doesn't trouble me as much as it should.

"Ace is a superhero," Caesar says, after we've warmed ourselves up to conversation. She's relaxed into it, pulling her legs up on the bench to sit cross-legged. When Caesar speaks, she rolls her eyes and bats at him from across the table. "What?" he demands, "you are!"

I ignore Ace's laughing protests in favour of studying Xander's face. He's gone still, a tense line in his shoulders that I've never seen before. I think back to him saying *it's dangerous to get caught up in that* and I think I understand for once. He looks back at me like he can feel me staring and nods sideways as though to say, *see?*

"I gamble for information," Ace is saying when I tune back in. "That's not the same as being a superhero."

"Are people actually willing to gamble for information?" Xander says, and the traces of tension have vanished before I can blink. I glance around the park and find him— the other him, the duplicate— standing by a tree a dozen feet away, his fists curled and his shoulders tight. The duplicates are to Xander as the Void is to me, apparently— taking his emotions and helping him process them.

"Not always," Ace says, and grins sharply. "Sometimes they lie. The numbers help with that. And sometimes I play to lose."

Xander's brow furrows and the duplicate rolls his shoulders and breathes deep. "Why?"

"I hold all the cards," Ace says, like it's obvious. Maybe it is to her. "If I won all the time, no one would play me. If I lose, sometimes, if I'm— if it seems like I'm, uh, giving something up, then people relax. Think I'm harmless."

"But you're not!" Caesar says, throwing his hands up. "You're gathering all this intel and using it against your enemies! You're a superhero!"

I finally tear my eyes away from the duplicate to look at Ace's face when I ask her, "Got many enemies?"

Her face goes blank, even with her smile still fixed in place. "A few. Have you?"

"Not that I know of."

"You should work on finding out," she says, cryptic, and I wonder once again if she's psychic. If she's trying to warn me of something. "You don't want to be caught off guard."

10.

I don't like Ace right away.

Maybe that's rude of me. I liked Caesar within an hour, his quiet assumptions and uncomfortable questions notwithstanding. He inserted himself into my life without asking and he still says things that he shouldn't, asks questions that he has no business knowing the answer to, assumes he's my friend without me ever saying that he is. It's like he believes that if he wants something enough he'll get it, no problem. Maybe it's a side effect of being rich. Or maybe it's just Caesar's unique brand of faith in the universe.

Despite all of that, I liked him straight away. I let him push and prod and poke and I only tell him to stop half of the time. He remains the only person that I've ever seen Xander be even remotely rude to, but it only ever makes him laugh, light and long. Sometimes, he responds to things that Xander or Ki or Ace haven't said aloud and looks adorably confused whenever this happens. When I laugh on a two-second delay, he just laughs with me to make up for it.

I get why Xander says it's dangerous for him to get mixed up in all this superhero business. It's not that Caesar isn't capable— it's that he *is*. He slots easily into our lives, makes decisions out of suggestions, and makes both of us want to be better. If anything ever happened to him, we'd never forgive ourselves. And as a superhero, something will always happen.

Maybe that's why I don't like Ace. Maybe it's because I like Caesar so much, and she's a superhero despite her best protests. Her team may fly under the radar, chasing after some shady company for reasons that I'm still not entirely clear on, but she has a team regardless. Ace might not have a costume or a secret identity, but she has an alias for every occasion and a glint in her eyes that says she's burning alive.

And she's Caesar's best friend. He wants to be like her.

"What do you think will happen when Caesar finds out we've been superheroes this whole time?" Xander asks me, about a month into our tentative acquaintance with Ace.

"Don't you think he knows already? He might not be able to read my mind, but he could look into yours."

Xander shakes his head. "I don't think he has been. He's started asking me about superheroes, you know. What I think it'd be like. If I think it would be worth it."

"If I'm honest, Alexander," I use his lengthened name in some attempt to lighten the ever-heavying mood. "I don't think we'll have to wonder for much longer."

"Why do you say that?"

"It's about Legion," I say turning my laptop around to show him a long article, "And that's *New Perspective* magazine."

"*New Perspective* is writing about me?" Xander says, and there's a note of self-satisfied pride in his voice. He's distracted, however temporarily, from his worry.

He takes my laptop and scans through the article with face-splitting grin. It's not what I would call entirely complimentary. It comments, for instance, on how intimidating Legion can be, with his face hidden and his duplicates behind him. But it also says that he's doing *good*.

"Abs," Xander says, looking up, "they think I'm *good*."

"Of course they do. You are."

He offers a shaky laugh. "I wasn't sure— I mean, it even says right here, people are scared of Legion, but— overall they think I'm doing good!"

"You are," I repeat. I don't think he's really listening to me.

"Man," he says, smiling steadier now. "I always felt like this was what I was meant to be doing. And now I am!"

"You already were."

"Yeah," he agrees, after a beat, "but now it feels real."

"Maybe Caesar feels like this is what he's meant to be doing, too," I muse. "He wants to help superhumans, right? Maybe he thinks this is the best way."

"Why would he think that?"

It hits me after only a half-second of thought. "What's the most important thing for a business?"

"Profit?" Xander guesses.

"How do they get that? How do they get customers?"

He thinks about it for a moment. "Advertising?"

"Exactly! *Visibility*. Caesar wants to make superhumans visible." I straighten up as my excitement builds. "Think about it— C-Corp is one of the highest profile companies out there right now. They have their fingers in all the pies; fashion, technology, energy, scientific research across the board… everyone is looking to them for new breakthroughs. And the Caesar family are celebrities. They've got eyes on them all the time."

"And he just revealed that *he's* superhuman," Xander says slowly, and I can see him coming to the came conclusion that I have. "So not only is he famous, he's going to be CEO."

"That's his play," I nod, "and it has been from the start. I wouldn't be surprised if he'd been thinking of it before… Like, if he wasn't planning to reveal his telepathy after he became CEO anyway. Meeting Ace, realising how some superhumans don't know about their abilities or how to control them or what they can do with them… that just sped up the process."

Xander hums, looking thoughtful. "And because she's a superhero— or superhero-adjacent, like she insists— he thinks that by elevating *her* and *her team*, he can create even more visibility…"

"But Ace is a nobody, and so are her team members. That's not an insult!" I insist when Xander shoots me a disapproving look. "It's a statement of fact. And, beside, Ace relies on being able to hide. She wouldn't go for it. But if Caesar was a superhero, how fast do you think people would flock to superheroes again?"

"So fast!"

"Imagine this: someone popular in business circles but also with young people online reveals that he's a superhuman. Then, he forms a small team of superhumans and gets them costumes and goes out and does good in the world."

"The business circles get to see superheroes as something profitable," Xander says slowly, considering, "because the young people start giving more money to the company."

"And the young people get a hero," I continue, "something they can look up to."

"Ava says the trends are heading this way anyway, but this'll make it go faster. Like when everyone thinks clothing is ugly until some celebrity is seen wearing it," Xander pauses, eyes shining. "You think that's the plan? To bring superheroes back, but to make them stick, so that superhumans have people like them in the public eye?"

"I think so," I say, letting some of the excitement drain out of me and disappear into the further reaches of the Void. "I think it might've helped me, you know... to know what to do."

Xander knows me well enough, after my months of living here, to understand what I mean. Maybe I would've been better equipped, after the accident, if I'd known of superhumans. Maybe Julia would've had other people looking out for her, and her abilities, if there had been other superhumans. He shifts so he's sitting next to me and bumps our shoulders together.

"Who do you miss tonight?" Xander asks, and it jolts me out of my troublesome thoughts.

He asks me this sometimes, when I get in my head and start regretting *leaving*, so abruptly. I don't know if it's to remind me why I left or to help me, eventually, go back, but I'd bet that it's the latter, knowing Xander.

"Tonight," I answer, despite thinking it's obvious, "I miss Julia."

"You could always call her," he says, voice low and steady like Legion's.

"It's been a long time."

"I'm sure she'd answer," Xander says, like he knew her, "I would."

I'm sure she'd answer, too. I wouldn't know what to say.

11.

We arrange to meet Caesar and Ace in an out-of-the-way diner two weeks later, on a Tuesday. I wasn't, initially, thrilled about including Ace in our reveal, but Xander pointed out that she is the only other superhero that Caesar knows. It may help him to have her there. And it's not a bad idea to have a team— Xander wants to save people and I want to figure out who I am now that I am the Void. We may as well have some sort of direction, and the funds to do it right.

As we walk towards the diner, nervously jumping over cracks in the sidewalk and turning our heads as though to make sure that the other is still there, my phone chimes. Ava's sent me a video of a beautiful fabric that looks black at first glance, but shifts to blue and green and pink as she moves the camera.

Ava: *how pretty is this?? for ur costume*

Me: *prfct*

I turn my phone to show Xander and he smiles. "It's like your eyes," he says. "Caesar'll like it."

"Nervous?" I ask, kicking loose gravel.

"He'll be mad, won't he?" Xander sighs, shoves his hands into the pockets of his denim jacket. It's July and nearly blistering, but he insisted on sliding it on anyway. There's a smudge on the inside of the collar that might be his dad's initials, so I don't protest. "That we didn't tell him?"

"Maybe," I admit, because I don't like to lie to Xander. "But… it's like you said. He's a good guy. A good leader. Knights and kings."

It's a familiar joke when he says, "You make it sound like we're playing pretend."

"Aren't we?" I ask, and I'm only half-joking. We come to a halt outside the diner, and we both take steadying breaths.

"Let's go," Xander says, and he sounds like Legion.

Ace sits prettily in a booth near the back, in white jeans and a red crop top. She's got one leg crossed over the other, and she grins sort of wildly when she sees us. It hits me that Ace must have been popular in high school. It also hits me that she's eighteen years old— younger than Caesar and Xander by nearly two years, younger than me by three. No wonder she still has that 'cool-girl' air about her.

"Cee's just getting straws," she says, after greeting us, and gestures to the counter.

The diner is old-school, with checkerboard patterns on the walls and a straight-up jukebox in the corner, playing something smooth and jazzy. The til is fashioned after a classic car, which adds an extra layer of cheese to the place. Caesar is leaning forward with his elbows on the counter top, his baseball tee rolled up, chatting with one of the employees. When he laughs, one of his curls drops down into his eye.

Ace uses her finger to scoop some milkshake on to her finger while she waits for Caesar to return. Xander and I take seats on the opposite side of the booth to her, Xander close to the wall. Caesar will end up next to Ace and across from me, the same way we always are.

When he does slide in to the booth, he hands Ace a bright red straw.

"Thank you," she says cheerily, and then, "They make the best milkshakes here. They're lactose free."

I wrinkle my nose. "That doesn't sound like the best milkshake ever."

"They make lactose versions too," Ace says, wrinkling her nose right back at me and laughing. If there's one thing to act as a point in Ace's favour, it's that she's never once been intimidated by me or the Void. She tosses her hair over her shoulder and rests her elbows on the table.

Caesar leans forward too, tipping his head conspiratorially towards us. "What was it that you wanted to talk to us about, then?"

Xander and I glance at each other, steeling our nerves. And I am nervous; I've grown to like Caesar a lot, and our little unofficial team. I don't want to lose it so soon.

"We've been keeping a secret," I say, because my voice won't shake and Xander's might. I pull my phone out of my pocket and show them the article about Legion. Ace looks curiously at Xander after she scans the headline, then curves her red lips into a tiny one-sided smile. I wonder what the numbers are telling her. Caesar reads the article more closely and then stares hard at Xander for a solid ten seconds. I imagine he must be reading his mind.

"*You're* Legion?" Caesar hisses. At least he's keeping his voice down. "I thought— he's been gaining traction, lately, cropping up in a few different places—"

"I saw a fan account the other day," Ace adds, before taking an obnoxious sounding slurp from her milkshake.

"—and you didn't tell me he was *you*?"

"I'm sort of surprised you hadn't figured it out," Xander says, shrugging awkwardly. "I mean, you know about my ability."

Caesar leans back, folding his arms across his chest. "When I asked you about what you thought of being a superhero, you could've told me then."

Xander and I share another look. He looks down at the table, and I stare across at Caesar. Not that he can tell, exactly, through my sunglasses. "We told you as soon as we were comfortable with it," I say. "It's a big deal, especially for Xander. He's keen to have a secret identity."

Caesar sighs and shakes his head. He still sounds slightly bitter when he says, "Yeah, I guess I understand that."

Ace takes another loud slurp of her milkshake to break the tension. Once we're all looking at her, she says, "There's something you're forgetting, Cee. The, uh—" she glances at the article— "'black-clad sidekick'… and the fact that Abyss keeps saying 'we'."

Xander grabs my phone from the middle of the table and skims through the article. When he finds the line that Ace is talking about, he bursts out laughing, with his leg spasming up and his hands coming up to cover his face. "You're my 'black-clad sidekick'," he says between giggles.

"Once Ava finishes my costume, no one's gonna be saying that." I say, elbowing him in the ribs in an attempt to get him to stop laughing.

"Ava?" Caesar asks.

"Ava Layton," Xander confirms. "She moved here a little after you left. She made my costume and she's working on Abyss' right now."

"So you're a superhero too," Caesar says, looking at me.

I shrug.

"Is it true you can make things disappear into thin air?" Ace asks, and when Xander and I turn to stare at her, she adds, "What? People talk. I've heard rumours. This, uhm, this definitely isn't the first article I've read about Legion... I was seeing these, like, references to you two probably... a month before I met you?"

"And you didn't say anything?" I ask, while Caesar turns to look, baffled, at her.

"Course not," she smiles, "I thought you probably had your reasons. I mean, for all I knew the sunglasses—" she waves a hand in front of her own face— "were meant to be a disguise. Poor attempt, if so."

"It's not," I say, leaning back in my seat. "I wear them when I'm out, too."

Ace shrugs, the epitome of unbothered. "Whatever. Point is, it was your call. But for real, is it true that you can make things disappear into thin air?"

I nod, slowly. "I didn't realise that people noticed."

"Can we have a... demonstration?" She asks, waving her now-empty milkshake glass meaningfully. "I think Caesar's desperate for one."

He does seem to be; his eyes are wide and his lips parted, and he's leaning forward in his seat. It's the one thing that I hadn't told him about when we spoke about the Void. I glance at Xander, who gives me a thumbs up.

There aren't any portals. Julia could open portals, but for me the Void simply seeps out, invisible. I swear sometimes I can see the tiniest specs of something silvery-grey, like space dust, but I think I may be the only one who can. I can just barely see it swirl around the glass.

The the glass vanishes from the table, and I can feel it's weight settling, not-uncomfortably, into the Void.

"Cool," Ace enthuses, waving her hand through the air where the glass should've been.

"Where does it *go*?" Caesar asks, sounding amazed.

I twist my mouth into a sly smile. "It goes into the Void. I can—" I tap the side of my head— "Feel it."

"And she can take it back out!" Xander says, "she's like a cosmic UPS."

I think about it for a half-second, and the glass is back on the table.

Ace picks it up and tosses it gently between her hands. "That's fun," she says, and I feel something in me swell. I think the Void is preening.

"Abs," Caesar says, a few seconds later, and when I look toward him, he's on his phone, undoubtably scouring the internet for articles. "You guys are practically *famous*. Look," he flips his phone around, and Xander and I squish together to scroll through the results. "There's so many articles! Legion and his unnamed sidekick, patrolling the city at night and stopping petty crime."

"Maybe I should get Ava to put my name on the back of my costume like she did for yours," I muse in Xander's direction, skimming through the article as he scrolls, catching sight of a few blurry pictures, clearly off of peoples phones, and, at the very end: *Could superheroes be on the rise again?*

"Wait," Caesar yanks his phone back and starts clicking through photos, dropping it back onto the table when he finds one that's mostly clear. "What is your uniform made of?"

"Uh," Xander says eloquently, "it's a bomber jacket, I think, and Ava stitched the letters on… she made the mask out of plastic and cloth. I usually just wear jogging pants."

"Okay," Caesar says, frowning, "give Ava my number, I want to collaborate on these so that we've actually got… functional designs."

Xander nods, and I see him opening his contacts to text Ava.

"We?" I ask.

Caesar opens his mouth, but nothing comes out but an extended 'uuuuuh' sound. Ace leans back in her seat and laughs. Lowering his phone to the table, Xander smirks. "You haven't actually asked us anything, you know."

"I thought— or, well, I've been thinking," Caesar stutters after a moment of thought, "that it would be good to… form a team of superheroes."

"Why?" I press, and ignore the look that Xander shoots me. It doesn't matter that we figured it out several days ago, I want to hear Caesar say it. I want to know if he's realised it himself.

"Because, well, because of Ace."

Ace looks surprised by this, shooting Caesar a wide-eyed look with her lips parted. "What do you mean 'because of me'?"

"Look," Caesar takes a steadying breath and launches into what I can only assume was his pre-prepared speech; the one he was going to give us, ultimately. "When I met you, Ace, it was a… wake-up call. Superhumans need help— they need people like them around, and accessible, and *visible*. Or invisible, if that's their ability, but in the public eye. There needs to be better education around abilities and how to recognise them, and people with abilities need to have role-models like them. I don't know what it was like in high school here, but we had one unit on superhuman history in Greece."

Ace frowns delicately at this explanation. "I didn't even have that," she remarks, and her eyes glaze over. I imagine she's looking at the numbers, pulling statistics.

"We had about a semester on it," Xander says, and I nod along with him.

"Exactly!" Caesar says, smacking his hand against the table. When a waitress pauses wiping tables to look at us, he blushes lightly and apologises. "People don't know about superhumans. *Superhumans* don't know about superhumans. And as long as superhumans are expected to go into… entertainment, and service industries… as long as superhuman success depends on whether or not superheroes are cool, they still won't."

"So you're solution to that is… to make superheroes cool?" I press, raising an eyebrow (I know, from looking in the mirror, that it will poke out above my glasses, so he can see it).

"It's not ideal," he admits, "but it's *something*. If we make superheroes cool again, people will want to learn more. And, not to sound… I don't know, stuck up, or anything, but my family and I, we're pretty important. If *I'm* a superhero, it'll turn a profit. So we can prove that it's valuable, to have superhumans around."

"Except that the popularity of superheroes is, really, just another aspect of the entertainment industry—"

It's Xander who cuts me off, leaning forward, "It is and it isn't. Ava talks about this sometimes, how superheroes kind of walk a line. Like, on one hand, yes, the surges in popularity are largely because people want to be entertained. But on the other, studies do show that the presence of superheroes in an average sized city in Europe led to people feeling safer."

"Up to thirty-seven percent safer," Ace pipes up, and Xander beams at her.

"Yeah, that! It's like, both? Entertainment and genuine… trust. Interest. It'd probably work well as a transition because of that."

"That's what I thought!" Caesar agrees, "We make superheroes cool, which makes money, which makes corporations start catering to superhumans, which makes more money, which makes people start paying more attention to superhumans as a whole. It's… kind of scummy, I guess, but the world is motivated by money."

"And you're motivated by… what exactly?"

Caesar gives me that look that he sometimes does, startled and kind. I think he must always be, on some level, aware of Ace and Xander and the waitresses and the chefs because of their minds. But he can't see mine, so everything I say catches him off guard. I think he likes it.

"By Ace," he says, nudging her fondly. Then he shakes his head. "By Xander. By *you*. By superhumans in general. I'm lucky," he says, "I'm privileged. My family's importance… sheltered me, I guess. And then I ran into Ace and realised that not everyone had what I had. I had a mom to look up to, someone to teach me about what it means to be superhuman. People need that. I want to be that."

He's got a determined shine in his eyes when he finishes speaking. Xander, of course, is eating it up. I'd be lying if I said I wasn't too. I think maybe he's the leader we've been waiting for. But it's going to be hard, and if he wants to change peoples mind about what superhumans are and can be, I'm not sure that bringing superheroes back is one-hundred percent the way to do it. It seems like pandering.

It seems like playing pretend. But Xander and I have been doing it for months, and it feels a lot better than sitting around. Maybe this could actually help. I think of Julia, again. It would've done her good to have superhumans around. It's for her as much as anything else that I say, "Okay, I'm in."

Caesar's smile is blinding.

12.

Ava squeals when we tell her the news— genuinely squeals in the middle of a church hallway. We frantically shush her just in time for Bishop Flores to round the corner, raising his eyebrows at us while Ava and Xander smile innocently. I just huff.

But she's thrilled, obviously; working for C-Corp is an incredible opportunity. She tells us all about how good it will look for her classes, and on her resumé, and how proud her mom will be. When she meets Caesar, she already has a bunch of sketches to show him, and they sit with their heads together, talking them all through. From what I hear, he pays her well for her work. She doesn't stop smiling for the full month that she works on the designs.

We're all excited to see our costumes. The boys more so than me, I think, but Ace most of all. She's not getting one— her particular brand of superherodom means she spends half her time undercover, so a distinctive costume would be counter-productive— but she sits on a table with her legs swinging back and forth, waiting for the reveal. She keeps chanting, "fashion show, fashion show!"

Legion's doesn't look all that different. He's a martial artist, so anything too restrictive was immediately scrapped. The fabric, however, is tear-proof now, and he'll wear an experimental armour underneath his bomber jacket. "It's new technology," Ava explains before I can even question it, "C-Corp holds the patent, but they aren't using it yet. Legion volunteered. It's supposed to be bulletproof, but it sits much closer to the skin, see?"

The material is tan, only a few shades lighter than Xander's skin. At a glance, I wouldn't even be able to tell he was wearing a top at all. He pulls the jacket on over top, and spins around so we can see the full effect. The *Legion* stitched across his back still seems cheesy to me, but he hadn't wanted to let it go. To finish it off, Ava and the C-Corp designers have developed a new mask with a built-in speaker to make his voice clearer.

Caesar is covered from his toes all the way to his neck in various greys. It looks like one piece when I first look at it, but Ava says that would've been impractical. Ace, who's wearing a little white jumpsuit, agrees they are a pain to get in to. I realise that the decorative gold lines are meant to trick the eye. It's all for style.

The high neckline has two sharp points on either side of his Adam's apple, emphasising when he swallows. Ava's finished the look with a golden circlet that rests around his forehead, half hidden by his dark curls. "We were gonna do it like olive branches," he says, adorably disappointed, "like as a joke 'cause my mom is Greek, and it's funny because Caesars were Roman. Ava said it might be too much."

Before I can think of anything to say, Ace starts nattering to him about how his dad is Mexican, and if they'd honoured one of his parents, they'd have to honour both, and then it really *would* get to be too much. Caesar is laughing when Ava grabs my arm and tugs me behind a curtain to change, his eyes crinkling in the corners and his cheeks dimpled.

"I'm most excited about yours," Ava whispers as she hands me the bundle. I pull on a pair of trousers so black they almost don't look real, made of the same material as Legion's top. They have zipper pockets on either side, deep enough to fit my phone twice, and some extra zippers which are there purely to look cool. The top pulls on easily but fits snug, compressing my chest and covering me up to my neck. The shoes she's provided aren't dissimilar to the ones I wear to the gym, and as soon as they're tied, she hands me a pair of fingerless gloves.

The real star of the show, though, is the cape. It buckles in over my shoulders, and it somehow locks in place so that even when Ava tugs on it with her full force, it doesn't budge. This is where she used the material she sent me the video of, and I'm mesmerised watching it catch the light and change colour as I sway back and forth. It was like my eyes in the video, but in person it really is like the Void.

Once everything is in place, I pull my sunglasses back on and drag my braids forward so they rest on my chest. Then, for good measure, I hug Ava. Her mouth hangs open in blatant shock when I pull back.

Ace 'oohs' and 'aahs' over the cape, clapping her hands together in a way that I would've called mocking if I didn't know her excitement is completely genuine. She steps back to look at the three of us, nudging Ava's shoulder and grinning. "You did good," she says, and Ava flushes, "they look like they coulda stepped out of a history book."

Less than a week after this, we have a press conference. Legion stands stock still next to me, his hands held stiffly behind his back. In profile, I can see the determined set of his jaw, and even with the mask in the way, I can tell that he isn't smiling.

My hands would shake if I didn't have the Void to help with such urges. Thankfully, Caesar does most of the talking. I'm still not used to the way he looks in his costume— uniform, as he and Xander have taken to calling them— a weird contrast of structured materials and flashy gold and his messy, curly hair. Sometimes, when I look at him just right, he really does look like a kid playing dress up, like I joke with Xander. It's… oddly endearing.

He talks about us; our names, our abilities, our team. He doesn't give a straight answer when asked why he decided to form it. My guess is he thinks it would feel disingenuous if he came right out and said that it was to increase visibility for superhumans. My guess is that he's right. Instead, he says, "You already know that Legion and Abyss are out doing good. I thought I'd help them do so on a larger scale."

A reporter asks Legion some questions, which he answers in simple, short sentences. He's kind, because I don't think he knows how not to be, but he's to the point. They only thing they can see of is face are his eyes, which I'm sure they will call 'sincere'.

I'm surprised, even though I shouldn't be, when they turn their questions on me. "What made you join the team?" one man asks.

"Was it the publicity?" another reporter cuts in, earning herself a dirty look from the first. "Many publications have written about Legion, but not very many have mentioned you, and those of us which did didn't have a name to call you."

"Publicity has never been my goal," I say, honestly enough. I'm here because of Xander, and Caesar, and the Void. And, honestly, mostly, because of Julia. She deserved more than she got, and if Caesar succeeds, if this genuinely does help superhumans, then hopefully she'll get everything she deserves. Everything that I couldn't give her with a failed experiment that couldn't even understand what the actual problem was.

I can't say that, though. I can't explain it accurately enough, the way I never really knew what she needed until I was faced with being superhuman myself. Instead, I continue, "I trust these boys, and I trust their motivations."

Things pretty much go back to normal after that. Legion and I go out in the evenings, patrolling around like we used to. The only difference is that, now, people will stop us, point us towards trouble, call out for our help if they see us. Caesar will call us if he catches wind of something bigger, and we'll gather together to chase after it. Sometimes Ace will join, without a costume or any skill in a fight— at least, not compared to me or Xander— just to shout our odds at us. I'd like to be annoyed, but it is helpful to know what might be coming.

I think Ace is Caesar's main informant on danger, anyway. She gambles for rumours and cash and gives Caesar the former. Caesar ropes us in, starting small and getting slowly bigger. We're not law enforcement, but we pull on our uniforms and wait with bated breath for Ace's information to pay off, leaving anonymous tips at local police stations and sticking around to shake their hands afterwards.

Xander does well at press conferences and interviews. He slides his mask in place like a second skin and rolls his shoulders back and answers every question. When he's Legion, he's almost like another person. As Legion gains more attention, the more Xander fades into the background. I'd had the thought before about him hiding in plain sight, and I think it's even more true now; after all, if Xander was a superhero, why would he have a secret identity? Caesar and I don't, and he spends time with us anyway. What would be the point in a double life?

Sometimes I want to ask him about it, but then he smiles freely, and the moment passes. I think about asking later, but he clicks his mask into place and the question dies before it makes it to my mouth.

I don't do so well in interviews. I'm hard to read on the best of days and I think it pisses reporters off. My answers are blunt and to the point, like I always am, but the interviewers don't know me, and they tend to think I'm being bratty or rude. Xander is friendly enough while being Legion even if he's intimidating beneath his mask, and Caesar has been doing interviews like this since he was a child. The world finds it as easy to love them as they find it to turn a critical eye on me.

"They just don't *know* you yet," Xander says, when I quietly broach the subject one evening. "Once they understand you a little better, they'll let up."

"They aren't even trying to get to know me," I point out, but I don't press the issue.

I am, occasionally, stopped in the street. Even when I'm not wearing my uniform, people recognise me and will ask for pictures or videos or, at least once, an autograph on one of my interviews. It hadn't even been for a print magazine— the boy in question must have printed off the webpage. I wonder if he'd planned this. I wonder if this is why Xander wants a secret identity. He's laughing at me off to the side, and nudges me playfully when we resume walking.

Still, I do my best to be accommodating. This does tie in to Caesar's whole thing about visibility and representation, and if people are finding me... interesting or inspiring or intriguing, or whatever, then the least I can do is let them take a picture.

Besides, it's not the most frustrating reaction.

The most frustrating reaction is the people who don't like us.

Superhumans have always been a sore spot in society; I know both first- and second-hand. They'll say it's not that they don't like superhumans, but if they did, there wouldn't be all this *expectation*.

Superhumans don't do sciences or math or business— superhumans go into entertainment or service industries, they use their abilities to make cool special effects or build houses or make sure food is always hot. If they've got a weather-based ability, they might be able to find a cushy job at a news station, or if their ability is something simpler, like super-strength, then they'll find use in trades— carrying bricks or tearing down buildings.

Basically: superhumans don't create, they execute.

It's why I left school, it's why Caesar's dad caused such a stir by marrying a technopath, it's why Ava pretends that she's not a superhuman most of the time. It's easier.

It's why superheroes could fall out of fashion in the first place; they were considered a fashion, a trend. Once they stopped being entertaining, they stopped being supported.

So there are people who are excited by us; by superheroes being back, but there are plenty of people who hate us, too. Caesar talks about my theories on astrophysics, once, mentions that I was on my way to a doctorate, and the next thing I know there's all sorts of talk online about how I'm a menace.

I know why it's important to talk about; getting people to like us and then talking about the things we do outside of being superheroes is kind of the point. I still ask Caesar to be careful about what he mentions, what he says.

"But you're a genius, Abs," he says, frowning and wide-eyed. "You deserve to be recognised for that."

That comment more than makes up for the nasty ones. I resolve to avoid the internet for a while.

Overall, it's a pretty good job. And it is a job, actually— C-Corp is paying me and Xander *wages*. I guess they figure it's a decent investment. I'm certainly not complaining. It's not exactly how I pictured working for the Caesar Corporation, but I'll take it.

We follow Ace's tip-offs, working together to find out if they're accurate and then stopping them if they are. Xander is ruthless when he's Legion, a force to be reckoned with, an army inside a man, and, although I'd never stopped to think about it, Caesar's telepathy means that he's connected to our enemies, helping us predict their next moves. I clear paths by sending things to the Void, watch them disappear in a blink, and I bring them back, when the fighting's done, unharmed.

We settle in; it's routine in its unpredictability, and I find myself anxiously, excitedly awaiting the next phone call, the next tip-off, the next moment where we band together. I haven't felt this clever or this useful since before the Void.

I consider contacting my mom or my brother or Julia. I draft a few emails, wondering what to say or where to start. I type in Julia's phone number, which I memorised in fourth grade, only to hit cancel instead of call. I'm not the person who they used to know, and my heart races and my breath goes short when I think about the fact that, as much as they liked Jenna-Louise, they may not like Abyss. Still, I give myself a pat on the back. It's a start.

So, naturally, everything starts to fall apart around me.

13.

"She calls herself *Jamboree*," Ace says, dropping her bag on Caesar's u-shaped couch and reaching up to untie her ponytail. Her hair is wet and tangled, and it makes me cringe when she starts raking through it with her fingers. "Not sure why yet, but rumour is she's a superhuman, and she's *pissed*. Something to look out for."

We're gathered in Caesar's apartment— although 'apartment' feels too small a word for the top-floor penthouse; two bedrooms, a fully stocked kitchen, a bathroom with a double-size jacuzzi tub. The living room, where we spend most of our time, is almost as big as the Pae's full apartment, or at least it feels that way. Along the west wall, there's a long row of floor-to-ceiling windows, meaning that when we sit on the u-shaped couch, we face a truly spectacular view of the city. The tv is mounted on the north wall, and there's a second couch which faces it, with a long, slim table nestled between the backs of each sofa, dividing the room in two. There's also an oval-shaped table in the middle of the u-shaped couch, which is where we pile the mountains of food we order every time we hang out. My laptop is always moved between the two, carefully looked after.

Ace, seemingly satisfied with her hair— which is definitely still a tangled mess— plops down on the opposite end of the couch to me, next to Caesar. I nudge Xander and he leans back so that I can see everyone easily. Despite the couch being so big, we tend to band together at the base of the u.

"Is that all you've got?" Caesar asks her.

"You know, I didn't sign up to be your, uh… police scanner or whatever," she says, and she tugs on one of his curls. It bounces back into place almost as soon as she lets go, but he still reaches up to it. "Yeah, that's all I've got. *So far.* I'm sure I'll hear more, and I'll tell you when I do."

I watch Caesar muss up his own curls for a second, and manage to mostly ignore the urge to brush them out of his eyes.

We've been doing this for a few months now; I've known Caesar for just over six months and Ace for five and a half. We've been superheroes for three months— or, at least, that's how long we've been superheroes as a team. Xander and I have been at it for nearly a year, and, sometimes, based on things that she says, I think Ace has been doing it for even longer than that. Really, it's only Caesar who's been a superhero for three months, but it still feels like an accomplishment for all of us.

"Nothing new about that drug?" Xander asks, reaching for a fourth slice of pizza. I'm eyeing the spring rolls, but I'll hold off until Ace has eaten something, seeing as she just got here. "What did you say it was called?"

"I've heard a few different names," she replies, leaning forwards to load up a plate with the crab cakes Caesar had fried for her. She completely bypasses all of the takeout, so I don't feel bad about grabbing two more spring rolls. "Hero pills, 4hq… most popular is just 'DNA', though. Rumour is they, uh, give you abilities. I don't really buy it, either, but twenty-something white guys without abilities are eating it up. I guess it probably just, I don't know, makes you *think* you have abilities?"

"Cause that wouldn't cause any problems at all," Xander says, rolling his eyes hugely.

"There's been rumours flying everywhere," Ace continues, nodding at Xander. "You remember that suicide that was on the news a few days ago?"

Caesar and Xander shake their heads, but I nod. Apparently I'm the only one who pays attention to actual news sources, and not Ace's gambling, drunken informants. "Brent Peters, wasn't it? Jumped off a building. They haven't released an autopsy or anything."

"Brett, but yeah," Ace agrees, "word is, DNA was involved in it. That he took a dose and thought he could fly."

There's a heavy silence.

"What would happen if one of us took it?" Caesar muses aloud.

"I'm trying to find out where to buy it." When we all look at her in various states of shock, Ace rolls her eyes at us. "To find out what's actually in it, you dumbasses. And maybe follow the dealer back to the supplier."

"Well, let us know if you find anything," Caesar says, and Ace nods. "About DNA or about Jamboree."

Ace has grown on me, in the months that we've worked together, but I'm still not a huge fan of her methods. Even so, there's nothing official about DNA yet, and I wouldn't even know where to start with Jamboree. I guess this is why people feel safer with superheroes around; Ace's methods might be uncouth, but they're still effective, and she knows things before the rest of us do. I maintain that she's basically psychic, but she only ever rolls her eyes when I mention it.

She's the only one who can go undercover to the dealer, when she finds one— Caesar and I are too recognisable, and no one would believe that Xander's an addict. Still, she doesn't want to go alone, so I hole up in the penthouse while Caesar and Xander follow behind her. After she's bought some of the pills, she's going to bring them back to me for safe keeping— she apparently doesn't trust herself enough to not try them— and Caesar and Xander will follow after the dealer.

She's only been gone about two hours total when she storms into the penthouse, her hair wet and her makeup running. She's wearing well-worn black jeans with rips that aren't stylised, that hang awkwardly around her hips, and a black sweatshirt with holes worked into the thumbs and frayed drawstrings. It's incredibly unlike anything I've ever seen her dressed in; she barely looks like Ace. When she pushes down the sweatshirt's hood to reveal a head of mousey-brown hair, I actually wonder, for a split-second, if she *is* Ace.

"Your hair is brown," I tell her, and she laughs.

"That's because I'm not Ace," she says, then puts on a bored and somehow skittish tone and says, "I'm Eve... I'm just— I'm just looking for a good *high*, man, and... I heard that these pills, uh, 4hq, they give you abilities? That sounds badass, you know, and I could... well, how much?"

I have to admit that I'm impressed. I may have my doubts about her style of superherodom, but she effortlessly slid in and out of the role, and if I'd seen her anywhere else, I'm not entirely sure I would've recognised her— she's holding herself with a hunch, twining her fingers together and shifting her weight every few seconds. Her eyes dart from place to place and never rest long enough to really *see* anything. Her voice takes a different cadence; while Ace does pause, and stumble, and struggle to find the right words, *Eve's* stuttering is done with a completely different inflection.

"I would've thought you'd know the price before you went to meet the dealer," I say, instead of anything about how impressive it all was.

"Yeah," Ace says, shrugging. Her next words are slightly muffled as she tugs the sweatshirt up and over her head, but I can make them out well enough. "But Eve is a nervous wreck."

"Seems like a lot of work," I comment.

"Eve is just a throwaway," she says, and shrugs again. Underneath the sweatshirt, she's wearing a red bandeaux, and she looks significantly more like herself for it. "I probably won't use her again, so I didn't really have to worry about remembering it all. I just needed to be, uhm… believably suspicious. The dealer bought it, and I bought some sick drugs! Here, catch."

She tosses a small plastic bag at me. Inside, there are three little pills that remind me of the vitamins I used to take as a kid. They're green or purple, shaped roughly in a double-helix pattern. "They're really milking the DNA thing, aren't they?"

"Well," she says reasonably, "it is a drug that claims it can, uh, change your DNA, so."

I tip my head in acceptance, and she laughs again.

"I'm gonna go shower. Don't let, you know… scientific curiosity convince you to take one of those." She waves a finger through the air, pointing at me from across the room, and disappears down the hall to the bathroom.

It honestly hadn't occurred to me to take the drug myself. I haven't really tried any substances since the Void. Living with Xander and Ki means that there's never any alcohol around, so I haven't even had a drink. I don't know if I *can* get drunk or high, or if that's another thing that the Void will consume. Maybe, like panic, it wouldn't know what to do with it, and it would end up ten times worse.

Thinking about it, the Void seems like its got a panic disorder of its own. The memories that it pulled to ask me for help all stemmed from panic, and while every other emotion or experience can be or has been desaturated and sanitised, panic only ever gets worse. Like the two of us together are combining forces.

My heart clenches, and, as usual, *thinking* about my anxiety has somehow brought it on. I used to take medication— I had my first panic attack at ten years old, on my third day of high school, but I loved the learning too much to step back— and I saw a therapist somewhat regularly. My mother had insisted on it, but by the time I was starting university, I had cut back the amount of time I spent there. Now, though, there's no prescription to fill and no therapist to see. Even if there was, my brain has fundamentally changed— there's no saying that the medication would work the same.

Since I don't have those tools anymore, I instead try to control my breathing (in for seven counts, out for eight), and count the number of cushions on the sofa.

"Are you okay?" It's Ace, out of the shower and hovering by the side of the couch. I'm about to tell her that I'm fine, and I expect her to believe it— no involuntary actions, after all— when she adds, "You're breathing… carefully."

"I'm fine," I say, trying to swallow the last remnants of my panic.

"It's okay if you're not," she replies. I half-expect her to make some quip about being 'only human', but she doesn't. She just slips into a seat next to me and glances at my computer screen. I focus on the weight of her next to me, take a few more very intentional breaths, and finally manage to shake it off. It wasn't a full-blown attack, thankfully, and Ace doesn't press.

"Found anything?" she asks, when my breath returns to normal. "About Jamboree?"

"There's no pictures, anywhere and so far it all seems like rumour."

"Which *is* what I told you," she says playfully, nudging me.

I sigh and close my laptop, then turn to look at her. "Do you have a brush? Your hair is a mess."

She lets out a long-suffering sigh. "It's all the way in my bag."

I give her a pointed look, and she drags herself across the room to grab her bag, then comes and sits back down next to me. I cringe internally as she tugs the brush through her hair with a sound like separating velcro. "How knotted is it?" I ask in disbelief. "Here, let me —"

I take the brush from her hand and push her shoulder so she turns around, her back to me. I pull my legs up onto the couch and sit cross-legged behind her, carefully brushing her long hair. The brown must've been a temporary dye, because it's back to its normal bright blonde. As I carefully work out all the knots and tangles, I ask, "Have you heard anything else about Jamboree? It's been a couple of weeks."

"Nothing… important. Like, I've heard that she speaks Spanish, and some people think *she's* involved with DNA, but I think that might be, y'know, stereotyping. Racism. She's South American," she clarifies, "Columbian, maybe? So, obviously people are jumping to, uh, blame her. Which is *stupid*, but…"

"My best friend was Columbian," I say, "we liked to watch spy movies and crime shows. She thought that sort of thing was pretty stupid, too."

Ace shrugs. "I never watched those."

"Not even *James Bond*?"

"Nah," she shrugs again, "I was always more into comedies. And dramas. Things with romance. My mom used to tell me stories about soulmates, and I thought they were the greatest thing."

"I can't believe you've never seen *James Bond*," I tell her, shaking my head. "But you do seem like a hopeless romantic."

"Thanks," she says, sounding genuine. "I like ghosts, too, but horrors are kind of boring. I've never found a ghost movie that isn't, like, trying to scare you."

"There's *Casper*," I suggest. "Do you want me to braid it?"

"*Casper* has jump-scares," she says seriously, then turns her head to look over her shoulder. "You want to braid it?"

I nod. "I like braiding hair. It's been a while since I've braided anyone else's."

She gives me a grin that's wider than the offer probably deserves and nods. I start to section her hair. Her hair is very, very different from mine or my moms, and it's thinner than Julia's, but it shouldn't be too hard. I decide I'll pull it into two tight braids, like I do with mine.

"I used to braid my moms hair a lot," I tell her as I begin crossing the strands over each other.

She hums, sounding thoughtful. After a moment, she says, "My sister taught herself how to braid on my hair. When she was... seven or eight, I want to say. She practiced on me and one of those weird doll heads."

"Was she any good?"

"She got better," Ace says fondly. "By the time she was eleven, she was over braiding my hair and only ever did her own. I used to beg her to do it for me before swim meets."

"You're a swimmer?"

"I was," she replies. "Used to be on the team in high school. I was pretty good, too. It forced me to keep my grades up, which I wasn't very good at, and I loved being in the water. I used to be a decent surfer, too."

"You didn't grow up in the city, I take it."

She laughs, tipping her head back, and I flick her again because she made me lose my grip on her hair. After she apologises, she says, "Not a chance. My family lived right near the beach, I spent my entire life in the sand. What about you? Caesar said that you moved here not long ago."

"I lived in a city," I tell her. "Well, more in the outskirts of a city. The suburbs. I raced through school and got my degree at a local college."

"Local college? That doesn't seem like you."

"I was thirteen at the time, so it wouldn't have made sense to go away for school, and my family wouldn't've been able to move with me, so I stayed at home and took to the bus into the more central parts of the city," she hums, and I continue, "I got my masters degree a few weeks before Julia finished high school, and then we both got in to universities near each other, so we moved away together."

"You moved here?"

"No, I didn't come here until after the accident."

"Do you go home much?" she asks, and it feels like a very weighted question, although I'm not sure why.

I take a moment to think, tying off the end of the first braid. "I haven't been home since the accident," I say, slowly. "I mean, I'm not the same person who they knew. I'm, quite literally, a changed woman. I don't think or act or feel the way I used to. I— I can't imagine that they'd want to see me. I can't imagine going back to them."

There's a stretching, heavy silence.

"Do you visit often?" I ask, just to break it.

"Well, my whole family's dead, so."

Shit. I wonder if she's trying to make me feel guilty. If she is, it's working. My hands still in her hair for several seconds before I can convince myself to start moving again. I don't know what I'm supposed to say; 'I'm sorry' feels hollow, and I don't think asking what happened is the right move. I stay quiet, instead.

After a minute, she lets out a long, slow breath. "My godmother— she was supposed to take me in. But… it's such a cheesy backstory, you know, a superhero origin story. It's bullshit, but it's… well, it's what happened. There was a fire, and I'm pretty sure it was meant for me. That company I'm going after, you know. They got stuck in it."

I don't allow myself to shudder, but I think about it.

"My godmother," she says again, "was supposed to take me in. But. I felt… guilty. I couldn't face the idea of being with her, all the time. I was… angry, you know, at the people who did it. So I ran, and I came here, and I met my roommates and Caesar and I got to work. I wonder, sometimes, what my godmother— Mat, her name is— would think of me now. If she'd still… *want* to take me in. So, I get it. I don't — I would kill to see my sister again, my *parents*, and it's driving me crazy that you could see your family but you *don't*, but I get it. I'm sorry, I didn't mean to… dump that on you."

"It's okay," I say, because it is. I finish the second braid and she turns back around, running her hands over it and grinning too widely.

"Thank you," she says, and I'm not sure if she's thanking me for the braids or just for letting her talk about it. I wonder if she's ever really talked about it before. I know that I haven't; sure, I've told Xander and Caesar and Ki about the Void, the story of how it got there, but I don't think I've ever spoken about how much it tore me apart, or how I *felt* to leave behind absolutely everything that I'd had before it.

I've never admitted to being scared to go back. Maybe therapists wouldn't understand, but Ace does, in some small way, or at least she's willing to listen.

The boys arrive a little over an hour after that, when we've moved on to lighter subjects. They scramble over to the couch, climbing over the back of it instead of walking around.

"You found the supplier already?" I ask, and Caesar shakes his head.

With an annoyed huff, Ace asks, "Then why are you here?"

"We found something better," Xander cuts in, practically vibrating in his excitement. He bounces on the couch cushions, grinning widely and a little madly.

Ace and I swap looks and then turn in unison to look at the boys without eyebrows raised.

Caesar stays quiet for a half second longer, like the drama king that he is, before he speaks. He says, "We found Jamboree. And, Abs, she wants to talk to you."

14.

Infinite universes, Julia used to tell me, *Infinite universes, infinite possibilities.* And while I know, logically, that means there is nothing that does not, can not, or could not happen, I never imagined that *this* would be possible.

I figure it out shortly after the three of us load ourselves into the backseat of Caesar's driver's car. (Ace said she didn't want to be involved— her brand of superherodom requires being unrecognisable, and taking down a supervillian would put her on the map. She tells us our odds are good, though, and wishes us luck besides.)

Xander sits in the middle seat, rambling explanations about what they saw. He describes her as an 'illusionist' and I fight the urge to correct him; while I'm confident in my analysis, I don't know for sure. I always want to be right, but this time I'm begging to be wrong.

"They're like, portals, Abs," he continues, and Caesar, next to him, nods eagerly. "Kind of… purple-blue, around the edge, swirling… and then the inside is just, wild. I think she can show you anything that she wants."

Infinite universes, infinite possibilities.

"I wonder why she wants to talk to you," Caesar says thoughtfully. "She was very specific when we spoke to her. It was pretty much immediate, once she saw us."

"What did she say?" I ask, never more grateful for my monotone, for the way that neither my voice or hands shake. I worry that when I see her, I'll panic, but for now I'm relatively detached. The Void stirs, as nervous as me.

"She just saw Caesar and asked where his 'little team' was, and when he shrugged, she laughed and said, 'Tell you what. I'll be waiting. Bring Abyss.' And then she just kind of… left."

Caesar tips his head back to hit the seat. "I don't know how we could've stopped her. She stepped into one of her portals and disappeared."

"She wasn't touching you, then? To show you the portals?" I demand, and the boys shake their heads. "And she… could go through them?"

"Yeah, that's what I just said. Xander thinks she's an illusionist, but I couldn't read her mind after the portal closed, so I don't think it was a trick. Why?" Caesar asks, peering at me from behind Xander's head.

"Just… thinking out loud," I reply, and fall silent.

I can tell without looking that they're curious, but they haven't figured it out yet. Why would they? Even though I've spoken to them about

Julia, and about what she could do, she isn't a part of their lives. *Wasn't* a part of their lives. I retreat into the Void, and tune them out.

The Void welcomes me home. This is the best part of our connection; I just close my eyes and *think* and then I'm here. The colours of it swirl around… not *me*, but whatever semi-physical *thing* it is that represents me here, and I let out a long sigh of relief. Here, my emotions hit me full force, but I can still choose to ignore them, sending them further and further away. I can almost see them, almost touch them. The Void is a physical space, after all, as much as it is my mind.

I'm scared, though, and I let myself feel it, here. I'm scared to see Jamboree. I'm scared that I'll see Julia.

I'm jarred out of it when Xander rests a hand on my arm and says, "Abyss. We're here."

My mind always feels empty and kind of lonely, these days, but it's especially noticeable right after being in the Void.

We're at a basketball court. One of those inner-city ones, with high chain link fence around the outside and graffiti covering the backs of the baskets. At the far end from where we enter stands a tall, skinny girl with long, black hair. She has her back to us, but my heart starts hammering anyway. I know her. I *know her*.

She turns around when she hears us. She's wearing a well-fitted black suit with a bright purple tie, and I remember raiding my brother's closest for his nice shirts so she could wear them and say, 'The name's Bond,' with a cheesy grin she never could keep off her face, 'Julia Bond.'

Because it is, it *is* her, and there's no denying it now. The supervillian Ace has been hearing whispers of is none other than Julia Lago, my best friend. I remember playing dress up with her when we were kids, playing pretend, and that's what it feels like now, all over— she's in her Bond suit and I'm wearing a cape, playing at being a superhero.

I'm a half step behind Caesar and Legion, but her focus narrows in on me anyway. "Abyss," she says, and her voice is familiar but sends a shiver up my spine, "how nice to see you again."

"Julia," I breathe. I can feel panic rising in my chest and my hands shake against my will. Panic; the one thing the Void can't control and the one emotion or experience that I wish I could manage.

She grins at me, and it feels more like she's baring her teeth. "It's *Jamboree*. There's no denying it now."

"Julia?" Caesar asks, looking between her and me. "Abs, is this—?"

"Abs?" she says, cutting him off smoothly. "A nickname of a nickname, cute."

Legion steps forward, fists curled at his sides, but she laughs and opens a portal in front of him. It makes a sound of fanfare as it opens, and I understand, now, where she got her name. When he tries to sidestep, she opens another portal, and then another. She doesn't close any of them. She's significantly more powerful than when I knew her. I wonder when she learned to do all this. It's only been a year. Or, is it a year and half, now?

I stare at her, more grateful than ever for my sunglasses. She can't see where I'm looking. Over her shoulder I see a second Legion, a duplicate, appear. Julia is distracted by the one in front of her; I reach out and pull him back to stand next to me.

Julia laughs. "We're not fighting today, boys."

"Then why did you bring us here?" Caesar demands, but I see his eyes flick to the duplicate behind her. He's buying time as well. I'm still too shell-shocked to speak.

"I just wanted you to see who you're up against," she answers, but she's still staring at me. "You know, the day that I first opened two portals, I was so excited to show you. You came back to the apartment and nearly passed out you were so exhausted, so I decided to wait… then the next day was your big day, so I didn't want to steal your spotlight…"

I don't know if she's expecting a response, but I hope not. I don't know what to say. I feel bile rise in the back of my throat, burning and tight and the shaking in my hands is getting worse and worse, but, at least for the time being, I'm able to keep my breathing in control and my wits about me.

"And then, of course, you were a missing person." She takes another few steps closer to me, then grins wildly. "Found you," she says, and then she sidesteps through a portal as it's still opening.

The portal snaps shut without any fanfare— so the music only comes when they're opening, good to know— and despite knowing that she could be *anywhere* in the multiverse, the three of us look around wildly. *Come on*, I tell myself, *you need to think*. She's gone; and now that the immediate threat is gone, my brain has decided it doesn't need to hold back anymore. Fight or flight— well, I just froze, unable to do anything, too busy staving of the panic to do anything useful, and now that she's *gone* I still can't fight or fly or even *think*.

The anxiety races through me, causing my breath to quicken and my heart to pound even harder against my ribs. I've been holding it off since we got in the car and now it's at risk of exploding out of me. *Come on*, I think, *not now, not now. Think!*

I haven't moved, standing stock still by the three-point-line, forcing my eyes to stay open. Caesar and Legion have moved closer to me; I'm back to back with Legion and Caesar's arm brushes up against mine. Two things I can feel, so what can I see? It's the wrong order, but I need to pull myself out of this panic so we can process and plan—

We all jump when the sound of fanfare starts up again; I want to say that it tears open, but it doesn't— her portals never have. They slide open, smooth, at one with the universe and whatever lies beyond.

"Hey," says Legion's voice, and I jolt. I'd forgotten about the duplicate, and that's who's spoken, from behind Julia. She whirls around, and I reach behind me to grab the original Legion's arm, digging my fingers into his wrist. The duplicate swings at Julia's face.

"You'd hit a girl?" she spits, lunging after him to claw at his face. "That doesn't seem in line with your—" she pauses as she ducks under another swing— "Mormon values."

The Legion I'm gripping on to stiffens, but the one that she's fighting with doesn't even pause. Different brains, different priorities, I guess. I can barely process it anymore— my breath is short and my heart is racing. Everything feels too bright and too loud. I grip Legion's arm even tighter, closing my eyes and shaking my head back and forth.

I lose track of what happens after that, sinking to the ground and pulling my knees to my chest. I know that the original Legion turns around and wraps an arm around me, and I am vaguely aware of the sounds of a fight to the right of me. I hear Caesar's voice a few times, and then, again, the sound of a jamboree.

"She's gone," says the duplicate, more to Caesar than to me. It's silent, then, beautifully silent. I assume the duplicate is gone when

Legion speaks from beside me. "Come on, Abs. Let's get back to the car. Can you walk?"

I nod.

"Okay, then you need to open your eyes."

"How did you—" I start, then shake my head again, give a shaky laugh, and do as he says. I don't know how long, exactly, I've been on the ground, shaking. I wonder if Julia noticed, or if she cared. I used to run to her house if I'd had a panic attack at school and she'd distract me with the newest episode of our favourite show, or she'd ask me to help her with her science homework, and she'd talk my ear off until I forgot what panic even felt like. The idea that— I was having one of the worst attacks of my life, probably in the top ten, and she may not have even cared—

I pause, by the entrance to the court, brace myself against the chain link, and throw up.

15.

The first time I met Xander, I was having a panic attack. The little money I'd taken out when I'd first left had finally run out. A part of me was impressed I'd managed to stretch it for three months, but more of me was terrified that I didn't have anywhere to go. And Xander, when he stumbled across me with my knees pulled up to my chest, immediately sat down, offering platitudes of comfort.

"Hey," I remember him saying, "it's gonna be okay."

"No, it's not!" I snapped, but my shaky breathing meant it didn't carry any heat. "I'm an actual, certified genius… I shouldn't be in this situation."

Xander, being Xander, asked me what situation. The rest is, as they say, history, although I'll never forget the look on Ki Pae's face when we arrived at the apartment and Xander announced that his 'friend Abyss' would be staying with them. He decided we were friends and after not very long it was true. It's the Xander way.

Since then, he's helped me through any panic attack that comes, and he'll teasingly call me an 'actual, certified genius'. If I ever asked him to stop, he absolutely would. But I know him; when he says it, it's to remind me that he's here for me, no matter what's going on in my brain.

Caesar has never seen me panic before.

I'm not ashamed, not exactly— and even if I were, I'm sure the Void would take it and swallow it whole, prevent me from showing it. I mostly just feel vulnerable, if I had to name it. This is *Caesar*, our leader, our friend, and I couldn't keep my head on straight and I'm *smarter than this—*

We've cracked the backseat window so I can feel the wind brush against me. My mouth tastes of stale vomit and my hands are still shaking, just barely. I think I need to move that specific attack from the top ten into the top five. It's been a long time since I've had one so bad I threw up.

"Hey," Xander says from beside me. One hand is clutching on to his mask, the other resting gently on my upper arm. "You doing okay?"

I think about nodding, but then I just shrug.

"Cee is gonna drop us at home, okay? We'll… we all need rest," he nods, once, as if to reaffirm his statement. "We'll deal with this tomorrow."

It's only three o'clock, but I feel like I could sleep for a thousand years. I nod my agreement and Xander squeezes my arm once before letting go. Caesar, on the other side of him, hasn't looked my way since we left the basketball court. He's leaning over his phone, texting. I swallow and look away. I can't help the sickening feeling that I've disappointed him. I don't want to disappoint him; he's our leader, the one who brought us together and got us resources and finds us all the information we need to do our jobs. And more than that, he's our friend. He's my friend. I'm an actual, certified genius. I should be smarter than this. I shouldn't be too panicky to act when we're in stressful situations. I should be able to help.

The car slides to a stop outside Pae's Flowers.

"Go inside," Xander says. "Mom'll look after you. Cee is gonna drop me off somewhere else, and then I'll change and come home, okay?"

I nod again. It makes sense. If he wants a secret identity— and today I'm too tired to dwell on how odd I find that— then Legion probably shouldn't be seen going into Xander Pae's apartment. I wonder why he didn't just send a duplicate out to our meeting, because then it could've just been disappeared, no worries. I'll have to suggest it.

When I climb out of the car and turn to close my door, Caesar looks at me. I can't read his expression, and for a single, heart-stopping second, I think he's going to tell me that I'm kicked out of our team. Instead, he just nods and says, in a small, low voice, "Feel better, Abyss."

Once the car has rounded the corner and is out of sight, I let out a long, slow breath. It's a voluntary motion— although I could rely on the Void to take my emotions and sanitise and stabilise them, there's something comforting it taking the control back. I'll sink into the Void later, evaluate my feelings in a space that no one else can see or touch, but for now I let out a long breath and tug my cape closer around me. It's only when I see someone on the other side of the road pointing me out to their friend that I summon the energy to turn down the alleyway and climb the fire escape, wriggling in through the window and collapsing almost immediately onto the sofa bed.

I should change. I need to brush my teeth and stick my costume in the wash. I need to eat and take a two hour nap, to try to regain the energy that I lost during the attack. I need to shake myself out of this and stop feeling like such a mess. I decide that can wait for five minutes, and I lay, star-fished, on the unmade bed.

I stay on the bed for ten minutes.

I'd stay there longer, but my phone starts vibrating incessantly, and I groan before I pick it up.

ace jackson created the group.

ace jackson added you.

ace: *since cee is being cagey af*

ace: *i made a gc for us to talk in!! how'd it go????*

caesar: *im not being cagey*

xander pae *changed the group name to* ***superkids!***

caesar: *really? superkids?*

xander: *it seems fitting*

ace: *answer the question goddamn it*

me: *x dd wll. hd a pnc atck. bt wr all fne.*

ace: *wtf does that mean*

xander: *'xander did well. i had a panic attack. but we're all fine.'*

ace: *why tf do you type like that*

ace: *ur a genuis*

me: *genius**

ace: *wow.*

ace: *can i ask another question*

me: *ys*

ace: *are you okay??*

I sit up and consider how to answer. I run my tongue over my teeth and cringe. I really, *really* need to brush my teeth. I stretch my arms up above my head until my back pops, and finally convince myself to stand up and trudge to the bathroom. I stare at myself in the mirror.

I really do look like a kid playing dress up. My cape hangs limply over my shoulders. I slide my sunglasses off and rest them on the bathroom counter. Then I undo the clasps for my cape, and drop that onto the tile. *This* looks less like a costume; me, in a black uniform, with my eyes bare so the world can see the Void.

But the world isn't here; it's just me. Pretending to be a superhero, playing dress-up with my friends. Every day, I almost expect a knock on the window, and Caesar's voice saying, 'can Abyss come out to play?'

I'm pretending to be a girl, when I'm a universe. Or maybe I'm pretending to be a universe, when really I'm just a girl. There is one thing I know for sure: I'm an actual, *certified* genius. It's the one thing I can hold on to when everything is spiralling. Another reason I don't mind Xander reminding me.

Maybe I'm pretending for everything else, but I am a genius.

With a sigh, I change into a pair of loose joggers and a university sweater. It's not even the university I went to, I'd just bought it on the open day I went to because I thought it looked cool. All these years later, most of the letters have faded, but it's still the softest thing I own.

I brush my teeth and almost instantly feel better. It's the little things, I guess.

I don't put the sunglasses back on, because I'm going to nap, but I do bring them with me to rest on the table next to my sofa bed. As I sprawl out again, I notice a few new messages have come through to my phone. When I open the chat, it jumps to the oldest new message.

caesar said to **superkids!**: *yeah, abs? how're you doing? let me know if you need anything*

I don't know how to answer that, and the conversation has moved on in the time it took me to freshen up anyway, so I don't say anything. I fall asleep smiling.

16.

When I wake up, it's to the sound of Xander playing video games on the tv. He'd kept the volume muted, which I appreciate, but I still become aware of the click of the buttons on his controller and the small hisses he makes when he gets shot. I can't make out what he's playing from the angle that I'm at, but I can see the way his brow is furrowed in concentration.

I can hear Ki in the kitchen, making dinner, and when I groan and check my phone, I realise I've been sleeping for nearly five hours. "That's gonna make it a bitch to fall asleep tonight," I say, and Xander laughs.

He doesn't pause his game, but he shoots me a quick glances and asks, "Feeling better?"

"Yeah," I say, and I don't even have to lie. Sleep does help. I probably should've eaten something, too, but the point is moot. "I was pretty sure, even before we got there. I should've given you guys a heads up. How are you, though?"

Although it was a duplicate who fought Julia, it does take a toll on him. I've asked him to explain it before, but he seems to struggle for an accurate comparison. "When the duplicates appear," he said to me once, "they are *literally* me. Yeah, they can make choices and react to the world around them without the original- me- being around, but they're still… just me. None of this 'battling for dominance' thing you see on tv. They're just an extension of myself. And when the disappear, I get all of their memories. It's just… *me.* Multiplied."

The present Xander shrugs. "She's not… physically, she's not that strong."

Xander's been doing martial arts since he was six. There aren't very many people who he would think are stronger than him.

He finishes his round or level or whatever it is that he's doing and shuts off his game. He shifts in his chair so that he's facing me, one leg hooked over the arm and his shoulder pressed up against the back. "So, physically, I'm fine. But it… she *knew* who I was. What was it she said? Something about my Mormon values."

"I," I pause, thinking of the word to use, "imagine that she's looked into other universes to figure us out."

"But surely things would be *different* in alternate universes?" Xander asks, his lips parted and his brow furrowed. He's sort of adorable when he's confused.

"Okay," I start, "so if the multiverse exists, which, considering Julia's ability, is a given, then there are infinite possibilities, right?"

"Sure," Xander agrees. "That's my point. In another universe, we wouldn't be the same person."

"Except that *every time* that you make a choice, there's a universe where you made a different one," I explain. "Like, today, you chose to play—" I glance at the open box by the tv— "*Street Fighter*. But there's a universe where you chose… *Mario* instead. And another one where you played *Metroid*, or, I don't know, *Pong*."

Xander looks at his game collection and then back at me. "Sounds boring."

"Well, yeah," I shake my head. "Not every universe is exciting. That's the point, they're *infinite*. So Julia would be able to look at *those* universes, and find out things about you."

"Wait," Xander says, pursing his lips. "Do these other, random, boring universes just spring into existence when we make choices, or do they already exist and then… I don't know, deviate when those choices are made?"

"I think they already exist," I say. "There, uhm. There was this one universe that we used to look at all the time, when we were kids. It seemed pretty identical. I wonder… I wonder what choice separated *us* from *them*."

A few days later, when I rely this same explanation to Caesar, he looks at me curiously, leaning forward in his chair with his elbows on his knees, and asks, "Do you think you've already made it?"

It catches me off guard, but I manage to hide it, squaring my shoulders and staring at him from underneath my sunglasses. He's always so straightforward with his questions, barreling on without thinking of the consequences. It's the way he is with everything— he jumps in without thinking things through. Sometimes it irritates me, but sometimes I'm envious of it.

"I don't know," I reply. "And who says it was a choice that *I* made? Maybe it was just something obvious that we didn't notice."

Caesar leans back, placated, and shrugs. "I haven't really thought about it," he admits, "this whole alternate universe thing. Even when you first told us about it, I wasn't picturing anything like this. But I guess it's like you said. *Infinite.* There's probably a universe where we don't have abilities."

Xander looks taken aback, but then nods. "I hadn't thought of that either. I can't imagine not having the duplicates— they're so much a part of *me*."

"Well," I say, "It wouldn't be a part of *you* there."

I don't have to try to keep the irritation out of my voice— the Void takes it and sanitises it. As helpful as that is, I would still *love* to be in a universe without the Void.

"You'd just have to get on with one body like the rest of us," Caesar teases, and Xander gives an exaggerated shudder.

"I'd rather not," he says, grinning. "They're good for pranks."

My phone goes off before I have to mediate whatever antics that they're going to get up to, which I'm grateful for. I'm even more grateful when I see it's a message from Ace. We've been properly friends since the first time I braided her hair, which has since become a semi-regular occurrence, and texting privately ever since she created the group chat. Our relationship is built mostly on picking at each other, but I do love having her around. Not that I would ever say as much, of course.

ace: *i know ur with the boyz but do you wanna come to the gym with me later???*

me: *we go t dif gms*

ace: *yes im aware we go to dif GYMS (it's literally one letter why r u like this) but i was thinking u should come to my gym now!!*

me: *cnt afrd*

ace: *see that could be afraid or afford*

ace: *but also if i refer you my membership goes to 50% off which is the same u pay now so i could pay the full one and u could just pay me for the 50% price & it all works out the same yeah*

ace: *please i want a gym buddy*

Her gym is a lot nicer. And there's that boxing ring that I totally didn't look up enviously when I'd first met Ace. And if what she's saying is true, then it would be a good deal. If there's one thing you can trust Ace with, it's math. She's right, too— it would be nice to have someone to work out with. I send her my agreement in the form of a simple 'k' which results her sending me three different angry memes. I allow myself to laugh quietly at them and then turn to the boys.

"Are you done acting like idiots?"

There are three duplicates out, one of whom is holding a potted plant for some reason, and Caesar has two fingers pressed to his temple. They don't even look ashamed.

"It's so *weird*," Caesar says, instead of answering my question. "When he's got duplicates out, they can all be thinking different things. But it's not like… they all know that they're part of a whole. It's not like they are different people, or anything. It's *bizarre*, I don't know how to explain it."

One of the Xander's shrugs helpless, palms splayed, while the others laugh. "I'm just a person," he says, "who *happens* to exist across multiple bodies. But I'm still a singular person, and *all of me* knows it."

I guess I can't blame them for trying to understand his ability. And maybe it is a challenge for Caesar as well, I wouldn't know.

Regardless, I shake my head at them and stand, stretching my hands up above my head. "I'm going to meet Ace. You two behave."

Ace tells me, when we're standing opposite each other in the boxing ring, her hair sticking to her sweaty face, my breathing hard, that Caesar once told her that reading minds was less like reading a book and more like watching a film. "Like, uhm, flashes of images, is what he said," she says, propping herself up on her own knees. "Like getting… impressions of things. Connections, associations, you know. Not every one just thinks in words. There's a lot of images and emotions and things. He says I think mostly in French."

"He said he can't read my mind," I tell her, and she glances up at me through her eyelashes.

"Yeah, he told me that," she says with a laugh, although I'm not sure why she finds it so funny, "I think it stresses him out."

We've been doing the 'superhero' thing for nearly six months, gaining more press than we probably would've if we didn't have Caesar on our team. Even Ace has started to get her face in magazines, much to her annoyance. She says it's going to make it that much harder to do her job; she needs to be able to go undercover and if her face is out in the media it'll throw off her whole game. No one has put together that she's a superhero, though, so I think she's complaining for nothing.

"Come on," I say, shaking my head, "Let's go again."

She agrees, and I'm genuinely impressed by her stamina. She doesn't have the technical skill or any boxing experience— swimming and surfing don't translate well to boxing— but she's tougher than she looks. I wonder why she doesn't get involved in the fighting, I think she'd be good at it. She could be valuable, with her numbers and her spirit.

We do two more rounds and afterwards she heads towards the treadmills with no hesitation, and I watch her while she runs a mile. "Not my best time," she admits, "but given everything, I'll take it. Come on, let's go to the pool."

This, too, becomes a regular occurrence in the following weeks. We get together and I braid her hair, and then we go to the gym. It's so *different* from my friendship with Julia. Given everything, I guess I should be happy about that. I *am* happy about that. Ace is Caesar's best friend, and I can trust his judgement, what with his whole mind-reading thing. If she wasn't trustworthy, he wouldn't trust her. It seems very unlikely that she's going to betray us, like Julia betrayed me.

I can't wrap my head around it. Infinite universes, infinite possibilities. I never imagined this, and even if I had, I never would've thought it would be possible in *mine*. She's still, somehow, secretly, my best friend. I can picture her in her neat suit, fighting with Xander and knowing far too much about us, but I am equally aware of her pouring over her media studies work in our shared apartment, stroking my hair after a long day at college, playing board games with me and my family on some random Tuesday. She's been a part of my life since it began. I guess she still is. I just don't like the way it's turning out.

Over the next month and a half, it feels like we're constantly chasing after her, following the leads and rumours that Ace texts the group chat or tells Caesar at their weekly meet-ups. I still feel panic bubble up every time we go to meet Julia-now-Jamboree, but it never boils over. Possibly, it's because we never actually manage to catch up with her, but I like to tell myself it's because I've got a better handle on it now. Sometimes you have to lie to yourself.

At least I don't have another panic attack in front of Caesar. For all his kindness, I still can't help but feel like he thinks I'm weak now. He's seen me send things out into the Void, clearing paths and doing our level best to avoid property damage, but he's also seen me clutching a chain link fence, puking my guts out because I got too anxious to breathe. I never want to be like that around him again.

I wonder what makes him so different from Xander. I guess it's because of how we met. And I live with Xander, so there's no avoiding it. He and his mom took me in and made themselves into an extension of my family. Around Caesar, I have the option to hide it, so I do. I don't want to tarnish his opinion of me.

Ace laughs at me when I attempt to explain it, but won't tell me why. "You'll figure it out," she says, "you're a genius, after all."

I don't get to press her for more because Caesar chooses that moment to walk back into the room, Xander on his heels, both of them carrying way too much food. They'd gone to meet the delivery guy in the lobby because they felt bad making him carry it all. Xander had slotted his mask on, and two duplicates are with him, carrying a couple bags each.

Ace doesn't always join us for these 'team meetings' as she insists (mostly for appearances, I think) she's not part of the team. But she had a free night and some information that might help us out, so she'd agreed to come. "Right," she says, after we've all loaded up plates of food, "I know you've been, like, super focused on this whole Jamboree thing, and I don't blame you. But, uh, DNA is still out on the streets, and we haven't found the supplier."

"I thought there were rumours it *was* Jamboree," Xander says, frowning. "Maybe we should follow up on that."

"I don't think it's Jamboree," Ace says.

At the same time, I say, "I don't think it's Julia."

We glance at each other and smile. We've talked about this before, even if not in so many words. "It's not her style," I say, after a beat. "She hated drug plot-lines."

"Doesn't mean she hated drugs," Caesar points out delicately.

I shake my head at him. "I *know* her."

"Do you still?" He doesn't mean it horribly; I don't think that Caesar has a bad bone in his body. I still have to send a recoil into the Void. She's my best friend. Of course I know her.

He seems to read something from my silence even if he can't read my thoughts. He nods twice. "Okay, so it's not Jamboree. What's the plan, then?"

"I could roll out Eve again," Ace says lightly. "I mean, it'd have to be soon, but you could try trailing a dealer again."

"Why would it have to be soon?" Xander asks around a mouthful of shrimp.

Ace shrugs jerkily. "I'm, uh, I'm going away, undercover. I leave in a few days."

"Following a lead?" I ask, thinking of the very few pieces of information I've wormed out of her about the company she's chasing. She blames them for the death of her family, which I'm not sure I believe, but she did say it was a cliche superhero origin story.

"More like… running from one," she says, shaking her head. "I got close to someone and put myself at risk. I'm gonna head out of the city for a bit, wait for things to calm down."

Caesar is looking at her like she's grown a second head. "Are you okay?"

She gives him a smile that I think must be forced. "Course I am, Cee. It'll be like I wasn't even gone."

He looks at her for a little while longer, probably sifting through her thoughts, and then nods. Ace smiles more genuinely, like they've reached some sort of agreement. "Okay," Caesar says, "we'll try the Eve thing, then. How soon do you think you'll be able to find a dealer?"

"I probably won't be able to go back to the same one," she says, tapping her chin, "but there was another guy I was texting back before all this Jamboree stuff kicked off. I told him that I chickened out, but I bet he'd buy it if I spoke to him again."

We agree to try that, and Ace shoots him a text right then and there. After we devour the food, the boys distract each other playing video games, and I slide a little closer to Ace.

"When do you leave?" I ask.

"Next week, just before Charlie and Farah's wedding," she says softly. "Don't be surprised if you see stuff on the news about me being dead. It's so much harder to disappear completely now that I'm, like, *reported* about. This is why I didn't want to join Caesar's team." She looks around the penthouse, kind of wry. "But… I do like being a part of this."

She sighs, and I don't really know what I'm supposed to say. "You really need to get out, don't you?"

"Yeah," she nods, "I was kind of stupid. The company… I don't know. They're a lot smarter than me. But it'll be okay. I'm okay."

I don't believe her. "How long will you be gone?"

"Not sure," she says, shrugging. "I'll be keeping my eyes open for news. My roommates will let me know when it's safe."

Her roommates are superheroes too, although they fly slightly more under the radar. Sometimes Ace will call them her team, but she's been doing it less and less lately. Actually, I haven't heard anything about her roommates for over a month. Whatever this lead is, it's been isolating her. I'm glad she's finding a way out, even if it seems extreme.

"Guess I won't be able to talk to you, then," I say. I've grown used to her presence in my life, our random texts, braiding her hair, talking about the boys. It'll be hard to not have her around. Is this what Julia felt like, when she realised I wasn't coming back? But I won't turn on Ace— I know it's not her fault. Did Julia know it wasn't mine?

"No, you won't," she replies, and her face is sort of heartbreaking to look at. I guess she'll miss me, too.

"What will I do without my gym buddy?" I ask, to lighten the mood.

The smile she gives me is blinding enough to put Xander's best grin to shame. "Oh, you'll figure out something to, uh, do. You've still got Xander… and Caesar."

I want to ask her what she means by that significant pause, but she's laughing and standing and going over to cover Caesar's eyes. Then he's cursing at her and Xander's screaming in victory and jumping up to dance. I bet she wants to enjoy the last few days she has before she heads out. I can't fault her that. I'll take her to the gym tomorrow and we can punch each other and pointedly not talk about her impending undercover operation.

It hits me that I'm going to miss her.

Maybe I should've spoken to Julia before I left. Maybe if I'd explained what was happening she would've understood why I had to go, like we understand about Ace leaving. Maybe if she'd understood we wouldn't be in this situation, trying desperately to figure out her next move.

It's a lot of maybes. Infinite universes, infinite possibilities. I should probably focus on mine.

17.

Ace does manage to arrange a meet up with the new dealer, and Caesar and Xander follow after him once she's bought a few more pills. She brings them back to me again, but this time she doesn't stick around. She has bags under her eyes and an anxious energy about her, picking at the skin around her nails. I want to ask her again if she's okay, but I think she'll give the same answer. Instead, I surprise her with a gentle hug and wish her luck. She nods at me, barely smiling, and disappears.

I wonder what my family felt like when I left. I think that maybe I should've left a note, or attempted to explain, or something. I think that maybe, if I'd told them everything that happened, they'd have understood.

But I wouldn't have known how to explain it even if I'd tried.

It seems quieter without Ace around, even if she was so often off doing her own thing. Caesar seems more reserved, too. He says he's bad at keeping himself busy. His classes at university aren't frequent from what I can tell, and in the in-between time that he used to spend with Ace, he takes to lounging around the Pae's, or inviting Xander and I to the penthouse.

Xander and Ki work on the flowers for Caesar's sister's wedding, creating extravagant bouquets for her approval. I meet her only once before the wedding, when she comes for a final look at the flowers. She's alone, her fiancée dealing with some sort of catering nightmare, and I'm watching the shop floor for thirty seconds while Xander runs after a customer who forgot their change. His four duplicates were already active in the backroom, so the original had fled without even asking me to keep an eye on things. He's lucky I love him so much.

I would recognise Jocelyn Charlotte Caesar even without her introduction. She's a *Caesar*, after all. After she decided she didn't want to run C-Corp, she went on to become a brilliant photo-journalist. "You must be Abyss! Jocelyn Charlotte," she says, holding a hand out for me to shake. "But you can call me Charlie."

It feels sort of foreign, to call the eldest Caesar sibling by a nickname that, as far as I can tell, is usually reserved for family. But she doesn't seem to think anything of it. She asks after Xander and laughs when I tell her where he went, and when I attempt to make small talk about the wedding she's more than happy to moan about all the stresses. She talks as if I'll be there, despite the fact that when the invitation arrived at the Pae's door, my name wasn't anywhere on it. I don't know how to bring it up politely, so I don't, and I text Caesar about it later.

caesar: *of course you're coming! ur my plus one!!*

I think about pointing out that he never asked me, but I decide against it. It's highly likely that Caesar just assumed I'd know. He's bad for stuff like that. I need a dress. It seems somehow incongruous to wear

149

black to a wedding, and since the entirety of my wardrobe is made up of varying shades of black and grey, it calls for a shopping trip.

I wish Ace was still around. She would love to help me pick out something. Instead, I ask Ava to come with me, and she helps me select something simple in a dark emerald green. It's almost inky, knee-length and flared out from the waist. I'm not sure that it's on par with the level of elegance that's sure to be present at a Caesar wedding, but Ava assures me that I look great. I do take a few pictures in the dressing room to show Ace when she gets back; I'm not sure she'd believe that I dressed up otherwise.

On the day of the wedding, I drive the van for the Pae's, who sit in the back looking after the flowers. We get to the venue (an elegant hotel that I could barely afford to look at under normal circumstances) before any of the guests or either of the brides.

The wedding planner was annoyed when the Pae's expressed that it would be just the two of them setting up the flowers, but he's been accommodating enough about it ever since. "We'll make sure that everything else is set up before you go in," he'd said, "so that you won't be interrupted by any of our staff. Still, I would recommend including us in the set-up. Many hands make light work."

Ki and Xander had shared an ironic smile at that. "We work fast," Xander said, grinning, and that was that.

When we arrive, though, Caesar is bickering with the wedding planner and I can see them both getting more and more frustrated, grinding their jaws together and biting out short replies. As I walk over, I hear Caesar say, "No, I'm more creative than that. I'm a *telepath*. I'll *think* of something much more interesting."

"Cee, what the hell." My voice is its monotone, but Caesar looks chastised anyway. "Don't threaten the wedding planner. He's just doing his job, same as Xander and Ki. They're here by the way," I address the wedding planner, and he nods and heads off to meet them.

"Sorry," Caesar says, looking downcast. "Charlie put a blanket ban on abilities for her wedding, and it's *hard*. Making me irritable."

"I thought you said that Charlie was super understanding about your telepathy?"

"She's the most understanding," he replies, scratching his neck. "I think it must be a big-sibling thing. But even— well, telepathy is one of the harder abilities to be one-hundred-percent okay with, you know? No one likes having someone in their head all the time."

I hum. I've never really thought about it; after all, Caesar can't seem to read my mind, even in the times since our first meeting that's he's attempted it. When I look at him now, head bowed slightly and shoulders up like a protective shell, I can't think of a situation where I wouldn't be okay with it.

Suddenly, I think I understand why Ace laughed when I tried to explain my thoughts on Caesar. It feels juvenile, but I think I have a crush on him. Damn it.

Isn't that a scary thought? He's my friend, my leader, and, possibly above all that on the list of reasons why it would be a terrible idea to ever say anything about it, he's a *Caesar*. One of the most influential families in the world— just look how quickly people flocked to the idea of superheroes.

But he's also just Caesar. My friend. And he's having a rough day, trying to temper his abilities. "Come on," I say, tipping my head in the direction of the back door. "Let's go for a walk."

Caesar lets out a long breath as soon as we get outside, letting his eyes fall shut. It's like he's forcing himself to be at peace. I watch his shoulders settle and his lips curve ever so slightly upwards before he opens his eyes again. "I'm sorry," he says again, and I shrug.

"I don't really care that you threatened the wedding planner," I say. "It's not my wedding. You just seemed… tense. Thought maybe I could distract you."

His tiny smile seems to stretch a little bit wider. "Thank you."

The hotel is just outside of the city, and has a sprawling green space in the back, with short, paved paths worming their way in and around trees and shrubs, with a small man-made lake in the rough middle. I decide to head over to the bridge, bumping my shoulder against Caesar's and pointing towards our destination. He nods his assent, and we head off walking.

"Ace," he stutters, "would let me hang out in her head, in times like this. She didn't like it, really, but it was something grounding."

"You must be missing her." I know I am. She'd know what to say to Caesar right now. I don't know if I'm the best person for this job, no matter how much I like him. Which, given that I only realised that my feelings for him are romantic about twelve seconds ago, is a surprising amount.

He shrugs half-heartedly. "The weirdest thing is people keep giving me their condolences. 'I'm sorry for your loss' and all. Even Charlie. And it's like… Ace isn't *dead.* I'm not mourning my friend. I just miss her, and I can't say anything."

"I wonder what was so extreme that she had to fake her death."

"It's like she said— she got too close to something that she shouldn't have. She was in trouble."

As I have been since she left, I think about the Void. *Got too close to something I shouldn't have?* Check. *In trouble?* Check. *Runaway?* Check. I guess the only thing missing is faking my death. It might have meant that Julia didn't show up. It might have made things easier. Or not.

Caesar is still staring vaguely into space, so I nudge him again and offer him a consolatory smile. "I wish I could offer to let you hang out in my head."

He gives me a full smile this time, something wide that shows his teeth. "Thanks, Abs. I appreciate that."

We make it to the bridge and lean against the railing. Caesar rests his chin on his wrists and stares down at the water. I push my sunglasses further up on my nose and try not to stare at him. He must catch the movement, because he turns to me and says, "I know why you keep your eyes covered day to day, obviously, the Void is sort of… overwhelming. But why do you wear them around your eyes when we're fighting? Surely having the people we go up against be overwhelmed would be a good thing?"

"The Void is… it's a part of me," I admit. "For all that it has its own sentience and personality and whatever else— we're joined. People looking into it feels invasive."

Caesar hums and I get the impression that he doesn't really know what to say, so I keep talking. "I mean… it's impossible to explain. It's like symbiosis, in its own way. The Void takes what it needs from me and gives me what it thinks I need."

"And what did it need from you?"

"I wish I knew *why*," I say, my voice so low it's barely there, and Caesar tips his head closer to me to hear. "But the Void needed *me*. It's like you said, when we first met— I think it was already sentient, but it needed more. It needed... intelligence, movement. It couldn't grow without me. There was nothing *in* the Void to learn from, so it would've stayed the same, in stasis, if I hadn't shown up."

"And when you did, you showed it, however unintentionally, all these things it didn't know about."

"Exactly," I return with a relieved sigh. He understands what I'm saying. "And I think it thought of emotions as... wrong? It saw my anxiety first, because it could relate to that— the idea of not knowing, of being unsure and overwritten— and I think it gave it a bad impression of everything else. So it takes them into itself."

"Which is why there's a delay when it comes to showing your emotion," he says, voice a soft whisper, like mine, "because you have to find it, first."

"Yeah," I say, then smile ruefully. "Like guided meditation every goddamn day of my life."

It coaxes a laugh out of him, which makes me feel, somewhere deep in the Void, very accomplished. We spend the next twenty minutes attempting to skip tiny stones off of the bridge.

"You're the only person I know who wasn't born with their abilities," Caesar says, later, when we've left the bridge and have continued walking in comfortable silence along the rest of the winding paths. "That's why you say you aren't superhuman, right? But, Abs, I think—" he cuts himself off and shrugs, eyes wide and lips parted slightly. "I can't decide for you, of course, but you seem pretty superhuman to me."

"To the outside eye," I agree. "But all of these— abilities, they came from the Void, not from me."

"But you *are* the Void."

"And the Void isn't human," I tell him gently. "So I can't be superhuman."

My breath doesn't catch because that sort of thing doesn't happen to me anymore, but I can feel the Void stir questioningly when he reaches out to brush his fingers over my shoulder. "You seem pretty human to me."

18.

The ceremony itself is quiet. I'm only in attendance because I'm Caesar's date, so I sit squashed between him and his aunt on his father's side. The Pae's are also here, sitting somewhere near the back, and there's a part of me that wishes I was sitting with them, instead. Especially when his aunt leans over to speak to him, and says, "You found yourself a pretty one."

Caesar just smiles and says, "Marta, this is Abyss. She's an astrophysicist and a superhero. Abyss, this is my aunt Marta."

He doesn't tell me anything about her, and she shifts back into her own seat with a scowl. I shift just slightly closer to him and tell myself it's to avoid his aunt and not to push myself physically closer to him. I shouldn't be acting any differently around him now than I was a few days ago. My realisation of romantic feelings cannot change how I act around him. The Void, oddly enough, seems to understand this, and tries to pull this emotion deep into itself. I can feel it taking it in carefully, and although I know that the Void can't get rid of it entirely, I appreciate the sentiment.

Both Charlie and Farah look beautiful, walking towards each other from either side of the alter while processional music plays. Charlie is escorted by her father, William Antonio Caesar the second, and Farah is arm in arm with a woman I assume is her mother. Their vows are traditional, sweet, and they share a chaste kiss at the end, turning around to grin at the congregation.

The reception is, in true Caesar family fashion, an enormous affair. The ballroom— there's really not any other word for the space, as grand as it is— is decorated in the blue and gold of the wedding party, with sweeping sashes of thick, rich fabric draped along the walls and around the tables. There's easily fifty tables with embossed name tags on heavy cream paper, and there's enough space left over for a sprawling dance floor. Charlie and Farah are sitting at a long head table with their parents and bridesmaids, looking radiant and wrapped up in one another. I've never thought about marriage before, but they make it look incredible.

There's a round table near the front of the room where I find my name next to Xander's and Ki's. Caesar's name is also here, as well as his remaining two siblings. Carlos Killian and Elizabeth Marina settle into their seats just as I sit down, chatting animatedly about abilities. When they see me, they grin and hold out their hands for shaking.

Elizabeth tells me to call her Eliza with a roll of her eyes. "Mom is the only one who calls me Elizabeth anymore. I don't know *why*," she huffs and jerks a thumb in Caesar's direction, "she calls him Caesar more often than not, and that's our surname."

"Yeah, but even abuelita calls me Caesar," he says, poking his tongue out at her. "It's 'cause I started doing it younger than you did and it makes it easier to tell me and dad apart."

"Coulda called you Junior," Carlos pipes up. "And Mom calls Charlie *Charlie*, and she started older than Eliza did."

My siblings and parents and friends had all called me Jenny, before the Void. Jenna-Louise Tolbert, but I was Jenny to anyone who mattered. Listening to Caesar bicker with his siblings, I flash back to my brother, Jordan, coming home from school and giving a kindergartener me high fives, saying, "Hey, Jenny. What did you learn today?"

He's an astrophysicist too, last I heard. I did everything that he did and I did it faster, but that's never stopped me from looking up to him. He was ten when I was born, and he'll be thirty-two now. He moved to Scotland when I was thirteen, and I've only seen him a handful of times since then. I wonder how he's doing. Last I heard, he was dating some English girl he met at school. I wonder if I have a niece or nephew out there somewhere.

The homesickness is sudden and overwhelming, and I shove it towards the Void, which takes it gladly and pushes it even further into itself. I tune back into the conversation in time to catch Carlos saying, "Well, Abyss and Caesar are superheroes, which is pretty cool."

I can't quite work out where this thread of conversation came from, but Caesar is laughing next to me, saying, "Maybe you and Eliza could be too, one day."

There's the briefest of silences before Eliza, smirking, asks, "Why, Caesar, did you just out us as superhumans? You've always been so careful to avoid even the implication."

Caesar flushes an adorable pink. "Sorry, I—"

"Don't be stupid, stupid," Carlos says, rolling his eyes. "They're your friends and your team. I trust 'em. I can teleport," he says to me, beaming. "Xander already knows because he hung around our house so much so it's only fair that you know too."

"And I control sound," Eliza adds. "I offered to be the, uh, microphone today, but with Charlie's ban on our abilities it was vetoed right away."

"Why did Charlie put a ban on abilities if you're all superhuman?" I ask, tilting my head to outwardly show my curiosity. "Surely she understands the… difficulty."

"Because of the press," Eliza answers, nodding towards the back of the room. I turn in my seat and am somehow surprised by the sight of a few different journalists and photojournalists. "We're Caesars, and now Farah is too. People care about that, and what with Charlie being a photojournalist herself, she knew there would be people in attendance looking for a scoop. No one *wants* to be covering a wedding— it's just fluff. But if they could find *anything else* to write about…"

She doesn't need to finish the thought, I know exactly what she's getting at. If they used their abilities, they may get caught on camera or have articles written all about them. I remember Caesar being so careful to avoid even the faintest hint that his siblings were superhuman, and wonder if they'll ever want to share it. I wouldn't blame them if they didn't.

We move on to other topics as the meal is served. I'm almost relieved to learn that Caesar's charm is genetic; all of his siblings have an easy way about them, making it easy to get along with them. After the food has been eaten and taken away, Charlie and Farah cut their cake. The music starts up for the first dance, which we all watch in polite silence. Once they've finished and both offered low curtsies, conversation starts up again. I'm not surprised when Xander is the first to stand and the leave the table, called away to dance by one of Farah's bridesmaids. Ki laughs at her son, watching over her glass of sparkling apple juice (the rest of us may be drinking champagne, but the waiters seemed to know to serve the Pae's something non-alcoholic).

Caesar goes next, on his own, to congratulate his sister and spin her around a few times. From my place at the table, I watch her giggle and give him a teasing, sweeping curtsy. The other two Caesar siblings stand up seconds later, rushing at the eldest of them and her new wife. I watch for only a few seconds more before I tear my gaze away. There's a tingle in the back of my neck, like someone is watching me, like something is wrong. It doesn't feel like a panic attack, but it could be my anxiety anyway. I try to breathe deeply, letting my eyes slide shut underneath my sunglasses.

A tap on my shoulder startles me, but thankfully I don't jump. Maybe there are involuntary movements, but I'm still much more in control of my self. I turn towards the touch and watch as the perpetrator slides into Caesar's abandoned seat.

Julia smiles at me, somehow, seemingly, showing all her teeth. She's in a suit again, this time a deep green fabric, and she has a rose pinned to the lapel. Her hand snakes forward to rest on my bare knee. "Hello, Jenny."

19.

"You know," she says conversationally, before I even have a chance to adjust to her presence, "according to the papers I'm a supervillian. I haven't even done anything, Jenny! I'm being labelled 'the bad guy' because I happen to have a bone to pick with the city's darling superheroes. Not fair, is it?"

"You did more than that," I protest, and she fixes me with a hard stare, narrowing her eyes ever so slightly.

"Did I? Or were you fed rumours by a gambling addict with an alcohol problem?" She rolls her eyes hugely. "Oh, sorry. You're not supposed to speak ill of the dead, are you? I'm sorry for your loss, by the way."

I stiffen at the mention of Ace. I wonder what Julia knows— are there other universes where Ace has faked her death? Are those universes similar enough to ours that she knows that Ace is alive? Ace is already running, hiding from one threat, I don't want to add another on top of it.

I ran from one threat and crashed almost directly into another— the Void into Jamboree— and I don't particularly want Ace to experience the same thing.

"So here's what we're going to do, *Abyss*," she says my name in a tone that's dripping with sarcasm, but I suppose that she doesn't think it's my name. "We're going to go on a little trip. Want to see something that's out of this world?"

Her hand moves from my knee to my wrist with lightning speed and precision, dragging me to my feet. I glance across the room and stare hard at Xander, who pauses in his dancing to assess the situation. He doesn't take his eyes from me as he reaches over to hit Caesar on the arm, getting him to turn towards me as well.

Julia tugs my wrist and I'm forced to start walking after her. She guides me closer and closer to the centre of the room. It's going to be a spectacle, I can feel it. I wonder, if I sent her to the Void, would it accept her, or spit her back out? I've never tried to send a *person* in to it before. Aside from me, no one has ever been inside the Void, and I don't think now is a great time to find out how it would feel about that.

She tightens her grip on my arm, digging her fingernails into my pulse point. "Scared, pet?" she says, quirking her lips up into a tiny smirk. "You aren't going to panic on me again, are you?"

Actually, panic hadn't even been on my radar. Still, hearing her make light of my anxiety makes some small part of me curl up and cry. I don't deign her with a response.

I look back towards the boys only to see Xander has disappeared and Eliza is standing next to Caesar. They whisper to each other, and then, in a tone that sounds less like a shout and more like a command, I hear, "Run."

Eliza controls sound— that's what she told me only an hour ago. I imagine she's elevated the volume of his voice so that everyone in the room can hear. Charlie, on the other side of the room, whirls around, mouth open. I imagine she wants to scold Eliza for breaking her one rule, but before she can say anything, Julia rolls her eyes and holds a hand out, opening a portal in the dead centre of the room. The sound of jamboree, of fanfare, fills the space, drowning out the music that the band was playing. When I raise my eyes to them, they've stopped playing and are staring, baffled, at the portal.

"Hey, everyone," Julia says, projecting her voice just enough that everyone can hear. It's quiet enough to hear a pin drop, now that the portal's noise has faded away, and most of the guests are openly staring at Julia anyway. She smiles at them and gives a little wave with the hand that's not holding on to me. "I'm Jamboree. Just want to borrow *Abyss* here, for a bit, hope it's no trouble."

We take a half-step back.

"Run!" Caesar shouts again. The guests seem to listen, finally, pushing past each other in their desperation to get to the doors.

Next to me, Julia rolls her eyes and points to each of the doors in turn, blocking every one of them with a portal. I wonder how long it took her to develop her ability to this stage. I wonder what it would've been like to see it happen. I wish she'd told me, that night, the first night she made two at once.

The guests are stranded, now, in the middle of the ballroom, clutching on to each other and watching Julia with wary expressions. I try once again to wrench my arm out of her grip, but she only responds by reaching across her body to grab me with her other hand, effectively trapping me. I can taste bile in my throat suddenly, but I can't afford to panic again. I swallow it down, and try to think.

"Honestly," Julia huffs, "there's no need to run. Stay, enjoy the reception." She turns her head to look Caesar dead in the eyes. "Try not to miss 'Abs' too much."

He curls his hands into tight fists and races forwards, but Julia tips her chin upwards and a portal opens directly in front of him. I can't see through it, but I hope that he's frozen in place, and isn't stumbling into another universe. As the portal finishes expanding out in front of him, I catch a flicker of movement in the corner of my eye and turn my head, as slowly and subtly as I can, towards it.

One of the portals blocking a door is closing in on itself like a blackhole, leaving a way out exposed. I do a quick count of the remaining portals; there are seven doors still blocked, a portal in front of Caesar, and a final one behind me and Julia. Nine. Can she only open nine portals at once?

"Jamboree!" Caesar shouts, side-stepping the portal. His face is twisted into an unattractive snarl, his brows knit together and his teeth bared. It's a strange picture, with his soft curls and the three-piece wedding tux.

My arm is starting to ache where her hands are gripping it. I need a way out of this. Caesar is still talking, effectively distracting her, so I tune out their conversation and shift my attention to various places around the room.

Charlie and Farah are huddled together on the outskirts of the group, both looking murderous. Why would Julia pick *today*? Why *now*? This must be miserable for them.

That's probably the point. She's been called a supervillian for some time now. She's just trying to live up to the name.

The guests are, comparatively, uninteresting. Until I realise that Ki Pae is standing all on her own, mouth in a tight line. Where's Xander? I scan the group again, just to be sure I haven't missed him, but he's definitely not there.

Oh.

Oh, of course!

Xander has a *secret identity*. He's left so that Legion can come help. But if all the doors are blocked by portals, he won't know how to get in. Even if there is a door that's now *un*-blocked, he won't know that. And it's not as though any of us can text him that crucial information,

can we? I have a feeling that if anyone pulls out a phone, Julia—
Jamboree will make it disappear.

So what do I do? If Legion *was* here, we'd have the element of
surprise and five more bodies, all trained in mixed martial arts. But
how do I let him know how to get here?

Caesar's a telepath. I'm so *stupid*, sometimes.

If Caesar saw the door, he'd be able to tell Legion *telepathically*.

I just need to tell Caesar about the door without alerting Jamboree.
This would be so much easier if he could read my mind. But, of
course, he can't, and I've got one hell of a time limit here; whatever
game Jamboree is playing, she won't be distracted talking to Caesar
for very much longer. I need to come up with something, and fast.

"Cee," I say, letting my voice wobble just a little, to really sell it, "give it
up. It's not worth it."

"Abs?" He's torn away from the argument and instead looks at me. I
feel Julia's grip loosen a minuscule amount, and when I chance a
nervous-looking glance at her, she's wearing a self-satisfied smirk.

"Look around, Caesar," I continue, hoping and praying that he gets
what I'm trying to say. "She's got all these portals out, the doors are
blocked. There's no way for the rest of our team to get in. Think about
it."

"The rest of your team?" Julia laughs, rolling her eyes at us. "There's *one* other member."

I ignore her, focusing on watching Caesar. His eyes are flicking around the room and I see the exact moment that his eyes land on the far door. He looks between it and me. Come on, Caesar, you're clever, you can work it out.

There's a long, silent pause, and then Caesar breaks into a grin. "If you wanna get technical, Jamboree, I guess there's only one other member, but he makes up for it in enthusiasm."

The far door opens, and Legion bursts through. Before Julia can react, I bring my leg up and slam the pointed heel of my shoe into her foot. She lets go of me, startled, and I race over to Caesar, kicking my heels off as I go. I'll be better off barefoot, I think.

The portals around the room flicker out of existence just as I stumble to a halt next to Caesar, who catches me gently.

"You okay?" he asks, tilting his head towards me without taking his eyes of Julia, who's fuming and whirling around, trying to open portals to block each of Legion's approaching bodies. Every time she blocks one, another one appears on the other side of the portal— it creates a rather stunning illusion that there's more than five of him.

I nod, shaking my arm to try to get it to wake up. "I'm going to try something that I've been working on," I tell him, "it may or may not work, and I'd really appreciate it if you wouldn't judge me if it fails."

He shakes his head, sending his curls bouncing against the top of his head. "I would never. What are you going to try?"

I hesitate for a half-second, thinking that this may well be the most terrible decision I've ever come to. But then I decide, damn it all. If Julia is making a million and one terrible decisions, I can get away with making one.

"I'm going to try sending her into the Void."

20.

"Inside of *you*?" Caesar demands. "You said that the Void is a part of you and people *looking* at you is invasive, are you sure you want to send *her* into it?"

I force my shoulders down and back. "Have you got a better plan?"

"Well," he says, and I'm reminded of why *he's* the leader, not me. "It starts with us focusing on getting all the guests out of here while Legion keeps her occupied, and it ends with me sliding into her mind to debilitate her before she can drag you into an alternate universe. How's that sound?"

I scan around the room, where most of the guests are staring, transfixed, at the fight. A few of them have even fished their phones out of pockets and handbags and are obviously recording it. Getting them out of the way before Julia decides to start opening portals around them probably should be our priority. "Fine," I agree. "I'll start getting them out, you get inside her head."

I'm not much of a people-person, but when I wheel around and start manhandling people towards the now-accessible exits, they go along with it easily enough. "What are you standing around for?" I demand, gently shoving on the of the men who's closest to me. "Come out, get out of here!"

Once one person starts moving, the rest seem to follow suit, hastening out of the various doors. Caesar helps too, but he keeps glancing over his shoulder to Julia. Once most of the guests have made their way out of the ballroom, he sighs.

"Slight change of plans," he whispers, and I have to strain to hear him over everyone's movements. "I don't know why, but I can't read her mind. Couldn't last time, either, now that I think about it."

"That's… concerning."

"You're telling me!" His voice takes on a note of panic. I lay a hand on his arm and he stops short to take a breath.

The last of the guests clear out just as I start to talk again. "Okay, so that was plan B. Shall we return to plan A?"

He hesitates, but nods.

I return the gesture and step towards Legion and Jamboree. "Hey, JuJu," I call, and it has the desired effect. She wheels around to look at me. Legion, who must recognise I have a plan, stops dead and takes a half-step back. The duplicates don't disappear, but they mirror the original, watching me carefully, their brows furrowed.

"We aren't kids anymore," Julia says, pursing her lips slightly.

"Are you saying I can't call you JuJu anymore?" I ask, taking another step forwards. "Because, you know, I've always called you that. I hardly ever called you Julia to your face."

"And I've never called *you* Abyss, and yet here we are! And we've got other places to be." As I expected, she lunges forward and grabs my wrist, dragging me forwards as she tears open another portal. But I can feel the Void seep out of me; I can catch sight of tiny, silvery-grey flecks, swirling up and around the two of us.

I'm sending myself *physically* into the Void for the first time since our joining.

I just hope that I'll be able to get back out.

21.

It looks exactly as I remember it— like filtered nebulae. Like space.

I feel it curl up and around me, reaching out to touch my skin and hair and eyes, like it did the first time I was here, asking if I'm okay, taking stock of my emotions and thoughts and memories. We're *joined*; it is me and I am it, and this feels safer than anywhere else, especially with Julia hovering a short distance away, eyes blown wide and hands curled into fists.

"What did you *do*?" she demands.

The Void does not like that she's here. *I* don't like that she's here, but the Void seems to pull away from her, as much as it can, even more uncomfortable than me somehow.

"You're in the Void," I tell her, taking my sunglasses off and tucking them into the neckline of my dress.

"The *what*?" she asks, and I can see her struggling to find her orientation whenever she looks away from me. I don't know if direction exists in the Void, in the same way that it does on Earth. I just don't try to orient myself. The Void has me.

"The Void," I repeat. "Stop squirming, you're pissing it off."

"Oh," she says with a shaky laugh. "The Void is *alive*, okay."

I shrug, waiting her for her to stop moving. "It *is* my mind, you know. Of course it's alive."

"So you mean that I'm pissing *you* off."

I shake my head. Wrapped up in the Void, it's easier to move and feel and express. Where my emotions usually feel separate, tempered, wrapped-in-cotton, when I'm physically here, I can sense them completely, and my body moves involuntarily, subconsciously. It's odd, after so long spent controlling it all. The Void seems thrilled by it.

"We're connected," I admit, and something pink-purple-blue swirls around my head. The Void is agreeing with me. "But still individual. It's a universe, I'm a universe. I'm a scientist, it's a scientist. Still, it likes you less than I do."

Julia frowns. I remember how overwhelmed I felt when I first arrived here, but also the eery sense of calm. Julia doesn't seem to be experiencing the Void in the same way, which should be unsurprising. It clearly doesn't like her.

"You're my best friend," I say, and Julia freezes for a half second before looking down. "But this— what you're doing, this is crazy! I just don't understand *why*!"

Julia's head snaps back up, glaring at me. "You don't understand *why*? *You* don't understand? You may be a genius, Jenny, but you're such an idiot."

Before I can open my mouth to protest, Julia is throwing a hand out and opening another portal in front of me. My head pounds with a sudden headache— of *course*, the portal is both in front of and inside me— and I flinch downwards, cradling my head but knowing that it's no use. It *hurts*, ten times as bad as any regular headache.

The Void, naturally, doesn't like it either, wrapping itself around me in its desperation. I hadn't even thought that she could hurt me here. Surely I should have the upper hand in my own mind? I'd felt *safe* here—

I'd felt safe here. Complete.

I don't have time to be thinking about this.

The portal is still open, and the dull pounding in my head doesn't seem likely to subside any time soon. I have to pull myself together. Julia still looks disoriented when she comes around the side of the portal, but she's managing it much better now. I raise my head and stare into the portal.

"What's through there?"

"Another universe."

"Which one?"

Julia sighs, looking at me with simpering pity. "Can't you guess?"

When we were kids, JuJu and I would lay on my bed, staring up at the ceiling. She would grip my hand and show me the universes that she could see, showing me, time and time again, different versions of ourselves.

Back then, she couldn't open them in clear view, and if she ever accidentally let go of my hand, the portal would vanish from my sight. She couldn't go through them, as far as I knew, and she definitely couldn't open more than one at a time. But I still thought it was the coolest thing ever. We'd huddle together and watch different universes and talk about what-if's just to see them appear in front of us. Sometimes it sucked, being able to see the could've-beens (when Julia's eighth grade boyfriend broke up with her, for example, and she obsessively watched a universe where he *didn't* for two weeks), but mostly it was exciting.

There were some universes that we returned to time and time again.

Like this one.

I don't need to ask where we are, when we go through the portal. I recognise it. This is our apartment. Or, I suppose more accurately, the apartment that would've been.

We'd moved in together, scraping by with student loans and part-time work. I was nearly killing myself with my course-load, but determined to get my doctorate quickly, so I could start working. Julia worked at the coffee shop across the street and would barely have time to eat between that and her media classes; the apartment was always a mess as a result, and that much seems consistent across the universes.

There are a few differences, of course. There's a framed doctorate hanging above the kitchen table, for example. "She got it," I whisper, oddly moved.

We'd watched this version of ourselves move almost in tandem to our own lives. We used to make guesses about what would make this universe different from ours— as far as we could tell, it was completely identical, to the point that on occasion, we'd be staring at them while they were staring back at us, and we'd wave to each other.

But we were kids, and we must have missed something.

"They have dampeners in this universe." Julia says softly from behind me. "Not just rumours of ones, like in ours, but something that people can use on the daily. Some of them target specific abilities— especially abilities like telepathy."

That explains why Caesar couldn't get into her head. I turn back to look at her. My sunglasses are still off, so I force her to confront the

Void when she meets my eyes and see her baulk. After a half second, I put them back on, more out of habit than anything. "So that's what makes it different?"

"You'd think," she says, and doesn't elaborate.

I imagine this version of me struggling with new and all-consuming abilities, being able to switch them off with the click of a button. I don't know if that's how dampeners work or not, but I can dream. Maybe that's how she managed to get her doctorate still. It's funny how one tiny thing can make all the difference in the world.

"Why are we here?"

Julia looks at me, and for a second she looks bone tired. I can make out heavy, dark bags underneath her eyes, giving her a somewhat hollow appearance. Her lips curve downwards, and when she next speaks, her voice is low and sad, almost choked. "You don't get it, do you? I was kidding earlier, but you really *are* an idiot."

A portal opens up beneath my feet, and I'm literally crashing into a wedding.

22.

It's Legion who manages to catch me, easing me into a slow descent. Thankfully, the portal on this end hadn't been opened too high up, and all he does is guide me to the ground so I don't land on my face. The floor is cool against my bare feet.

My shoes are still abandoned a few feet away, and I debate going to put them back on. But if Julia does follow after me I'd rather not be tied down with high heels.

"Are you okay?" Legion asks, one hand still steady on my arm.

"Where's Jamboree? What happened?"

I nod to Legion and turn to Caesar. "We went to the Void. She opened a portal."

I debate whether or not to talk about the pain that caused, but ultimately I do, filling them in on everything that happened. They both look at me with concern, but after I assure them that I'm fine, they nod their acceptance and let the subject drop.

We've barely finished our discussion when another portal opens and Jamboree is back in front of us, strolling out of it with her head held high. The achy, tired expression that I'd seen just minutes before is completely gone, replaced with something pinched and angry.

"Jamb—" Caesar starts, stepping towards her, but she shoves him out of the way, her narrow focus fixed on me. Legion creates three duplicates all at once and they appear in formation ahead of me, two on either side and one in front.

"I really don't care about you, boys," Jamboree says, glaring hard. All of the duplicates straighten up in near-unison, pulling themselves into fighting positions. Jamboree rolls her eyes. "Okay, well, you asked for it."

It happens very quickly: she reaches behind her back, pushing her suit up, and before we have time to blink, she's whipping her hand back out, wrapped around the handle of a gun. She takes aim on one of the duplicates and fires.

The duplicate vanishes, but I see the original stumble beside me, hand coming to rest over his heart as though he expects it to be in pain. Outside the ballroom doors, I can hear the guests murmurs of shock and concern. Jamboree aims again, but before she can fire, Caesar is on her, pushing her arm upwards as it discharges and grabbing at her wrist in an attempt to stop her from firing again. They grapple with the weapon for a few tense moments, but Jamboree pulls away victorious, pressing the barrel against his forehead.

Think, think, think!

Caesar has both of his hands in the air beside his head, one slightly closer to her, like he may try to take the gun, but she doesn't budge. Legion creates a duplicate on the other side of her, probably planning some sort of ambush, but Jamboree opens a portal beneath his feet after barely glancing at him. The duplicate disappears before it's even gone all the way through the portal.

Think, think, think!

I'm being dumb again, I realise, too caught up in my worry for the boys and guests and the wedding to think things through logically. I don't really want to be in possession of any sort of gun, but it seems sensible that I take it into the Void.

It's gone before Jamboree even realises what's happening. I always imagine that they disappear with a *pop*, but the Void takes things silently. She rounds on me and stalks forward, and for a split second I worry that she's going to pull a second, secret gun on me. But she doesn't. Instead, she rails me across the face with a rather solid punch.

I probably should've seen that coming.

She moves to swing again, and I throw my arm up to block it. She goes low, for my stomach, and I pull backwards, out of the way. It's like boxing— I haven't ever fought seriously as boxing was basically just exercise for me, and Julia never boxed with me, but I try to convince myself that it's the same thing.

She follows me back, and from there it's a plethora of swings and misses, swings and blocks. After probably less than a minute, she growls in frustration and brings her knee up to my stomach. I double over at the unexpected movement and she brings her fists down against my back. I groan, trying to pull myself up.

Legion is already on her by the time I recover a few heartbeats later. He must have been waiting for an opening. He has her hands pulled behind her back and she's struggling against him, trying to rush forwards to me, pushing one shoulder forward and then the other.

The movement draws my eye to the rose pinned to her lapel. I hadn't payed it much mind before, but now I see something small and metallic hidden behind it. The dampener.

I reach forward and pull the rose out, then pull the device off of the back of it. It's lighter than I thought it would be. I feel like I could crush it between my fingers.

"Come on, Jamboree," I sigh, "you're better than this!"

She looks at me levelly, one side of her mouth curling up into a snarl. "I thought you were, too."

Nee-naw, nee-naw!

Sirens. I suppose I shouldn't be surprised by someone calling the police, especially after the gunshots. Jamboree makes another attempt to escape Legion's grip, and then falls immediately unconscious.

"You got rid of the dampener," Caesar says, when the two of us turn to look at him. "So I could get inside her head. I thought this was the best way to make sure she didn't use another portal."

It makes sense. Legion scoops her up into his arms, and we make our way to the ballroom entrance just as the police throw open the door. Caesar is the one to speak for us, as always. "Jamboree attacked the wedding. We managed to subdue her."

Legion nods towards his arms, and I can bet that he's wearing a sly smile underneath his mask.

"The guests heard gunshots," one of the officers says, casting his eyes around for the weapon.

"Oh," I say, and I point to the floor, where I've just placed it. "Sorry. I took it."

My ability isn't super well known to the public— they don't know, for instance, what the Void is. They do know that my eyes have a somewhat hypnotic quality and that I can make things disappear and reappear at will. The officers nod, and one of them picks up the weapon with gloved hands.

We exit the ballroom, Legion still holding Jamboree in his arms, and the guests all murmur excitedly at the sight of us fresh from a battle. Caesar and I are still in our wedding clothes, looking disheveled, while Legion wears his uniform and mask, looking well put together. There's a news van as well, and a reporter stands to one side, narrating everything they know.

"And it looks as though the rumours are true," she says, and gestures for her cameraman to zoom in closer on us. "It appears that Legion is holding the supervillian Jamboree in his arms— she seems to be unconscious. Caesar! Abyss! Care to comment on the events today?"

Caesar smiles politely at them and shakes his head. "We need to regroup and discuss everything that we know before we feel comfortable making any sort of official statement. Rest assured, we'll share by the end of the night."

The journalist seems appeased; it's probably a nicer 'no' the the typical 'no comment' and brush off she'd get elsewhere. Caesar's got press experience. I offer her a tiny, forced smile.

Legion is helping an officer load Jamboree into the back of a police car, and as soon as she is safely closed in, he waves to Caesar and I and disappears.

I hadn't even noticed the original slip away, but this is a sensible decision. I scan around the crowd and see Xander slip quietly out of

185

one of the doors and rush immediately to his mom's side. They discuss something that I can't hear from this distance, and then the guests shift, and I lose sight of them.

Charlie, unsurprisingly, rushes over to us as the police cars drive away. She first tells the journalist to leave, calmly and politely explaining that she doesn't really want her wedding broadcast live, thank you very much. The journalist, visibly disgruntled, stalks off, her cameraman following behind. "You're both okay?" she asks, once they're safely out of earshot. When we nod, she continues. "Thank you both. And Legion too, when you see him next."

A wave of guilt ripples through the Void. If I hadn't been here, Jamboree wouldn't have shown up. I say as much, and Charlie waves a hand. "I'd rather you were here, where you had backup and people to call the police, than you being attacked when you were alone. And I know you can hold your own, but there's safety in numbers. And, look, now she's been arrested, and maybe this will be the last we see of her."

Only if the rumours are true, I want to say. Only if there really *are* holding cells lined with dampeners. I'm still holding the one that I pulled off of Jamboree's rose, and I bring it up to eye-level to examine. It's small and round, with a pin on the back like a broach. It's warm to the touch, and has a minuscule green light on the bottom, most likely to show that it's turned on.

"Hey, Charlie... Sorry— I guess I shouldn't assume. But the rest of your siblings have abilities, so I imagine that you do too?" When she nods her confirmation, I hold the dampener out to her. "Do you mind holding this on for a second? And then try to use your ability?"

She frowns, but agrees, and takes it from me. She snaps the fingers of her other hand. A small fire appears on the tip of her finger, which she blows out. "Any help?"

"Maybe," I tip my head to the side. "Cee, can you read her mind at the moment?"

He shakes his head almost immediately. "No. I can't."

"It's targeting telepathy, then. That explains why she could use her own abilities while still blocking yours." I purse my lips. "I bet a dampener like this would be very popular in a universe where there were lots of telepaths. Or even just one exceptionally powerful and important one."

I look pointedly at Caesar, to see him pale as he understands what I mean. "Not a universe I want to see," he mutters, and I shake my head.

"It's *this* universe," I say, taking the dampener back from Charlie to wave in his face. "So we can't let this exist."

I drop it on the ground and go to crush it with my foot before I realise that I forgot to put my shoes back on. Caesar does the honours himself.

23.

We get word later that night that Jamboree escaped custody. We're all lounging in Caesar's apartment after the reception finally finished, in much more comfortable clothes, when the phone rings. Caesar comes back from answering it with a sour expression. "She came to before they got to the station and created a portal down the middle of the police car," he tells us. "Cut it in half right in the middle of the street. I guess she wanted to make a point."

I groan and tip my head back against the couch. "So she's gone then. Again."

It's another month before she makes another appearance, and it's very brief. We see it on the news— someone recorded her on their cell camera opening a portal in a back alley by a corner store. She's spotted again two weeks after that, wandering around a museum. There's only pictures from that, but as it was Ava who saw her, we get them direct. Another three weeks after that, Xander sees her hovering across the street from Pae's Flowers while he's working. She catches his eye and waves at him before she disappears.

Just because Jamboree isn't around doesn't mean that there's no excitement in our lives. We celebrate Xander's birthday in March. He's twenty, now, and I joke that I feel *ancient* at twenty-two. Caesar, who turned twenty in October, laughs with me.

Xander spends most of his time looking after the flower shop. Caesar has another semester at university, bogged down with homework and exams. I settle in to the apartment and reopen my old notes from my doctorate, reading through it all and wondering if it's worth trying to pick it back up.

I google my brother just to see what he's working on. He's still an astrophysicist, and I read through some of his work, feeling a smile grow across my face. I wonder what he'd make of *me*, of the Void. He'd probably call me a dumbass for how I went about conducting my experiment, but I don't really mind. I think I'd just like to speak to him. Or any of my family, but I always felt that he understood me better than my mom or dad.

I start drafting an email, and get as far as *Dear Jordan* before I realise I don't really know what I want to say.

I spend time in the Void, too. It feels safe every time. I'd said *whatever you need* when it joined with me, and I don't think I've been keeping my end of the bargain. I try to understand it better. I try to remember that as separate as we are, we're still one and the same. I am the Void, and the Void is me. I am Abyss.

I feel much more sure of that, now.

We celebrate with Caesar when he finishes his last exam of the year sometime in June. He takes us to this fancy steakhouse, even though we'd tried to insist that we treat him, given the occasion, but he waves us off and says he wants to thank us for the last year.

"Has it really been a year?" Xander marvels, and Caesar nods.

"Right around there, anyway. And we've been superheroes for like… ten months."

Ten months? It feels so much longer than that.

We all have our normal lives, of course, but that doesn't mean that we aren't still following up on tips and rumours, stopping petty crime. We do a few press conferences, and slowly but surely the questions about Jamboree fade. I doubt we've seen the last of her, but I'm glad for the reprieve anyway.

A friend of Xander's comes back from something he calls a mission and describes as a two-year service where they teach people about the church when Caesar asks. I've been listening to Xander and Ava plan a welcome home party for a few weeks now. "All of their stories include Zoram," I tell Caesar, shortly after we've been invited to the party. "He's the essential third member of their group."

"And he's dying to meet you!" Ava enthuses. "He's barely believed us when we've talked about you two."

There isn't a word that describes Zoram better than 'steady'. He's a little reserved, which fits with the impression I'd gathered from Xander and Ava, but he's genuinely excited to meet us and makes fast friends with Caesar.

After that, the summer is spent torn between amusement parks and beach days and the occasional battle in the middle of the city. We get to lounge in Caesar's penthouse, taking advantage of his air conditioning, whilst we plan our patrol routes. I turn twenty-three in the beginning of August, and the boys make a big fuss over me. I feel myself smiling, and there's barely a delay.

There are a few more new reports of deaths related to DNA, but we're no closer to sussing that out than we were six months ago. Caesar thinks that Ace would have better luck with it. I miss her. The gym feels quiet without her there to banter with. It's been five months since she left, and there's still no word from her. I wonder when she'll feel like it's safe to come home.

I'm starting to think that it's safe for me to go home.

It's not until late August that we see Jamboree again.

But she makes it count.

24.

There are nine massive portals open in city centre. Each portal is easily double the height of a stoplight and as wide as the street. They open simultaneously, grinding traffic to a halt, although not before a few cars drive through. There's immediate panic, and I'm glad that the three of us were nearby in a small cafe.

The city centre is in ruins by the time we arrive. The portals are closing and opening all over the place, cutting buildings in half and displacing huge pieces of concrete. It's a Saturday, so thankfully most of these office buildings will be empty, but my stomach still churns at the thought. There's a shopping district only a few blocks away— is she affecting *there* too?

I can't actually see her, even now that we're in the main street. I don't know what I expected; maybe for her to be elevated on top of some huge building, in the centre of it all, orchestrating her portals like a conductor. But she's no where in sight.

"Okay," Caesar says, taking control of the situation easily, "Jamboree isn't somewhere we can see, so we should focus on getting people out of the way. Directing traffic, that sort of thing."

"I'm sure there'll be police here soon to do that," Legion says. "I called them on the way over."

Caesar nods. "She'll likely have replaced her dampener, so I won't be able to feel her out telepathically. Legion, it makes sense for you to be out there guiding people. You can cover more ground."

Legion nods, and three duplicates appear, and the four bodies scatter, running off in different directions. He must already have one out somewhere, because normally there are five of him.

"I'm going to stick in Legion's head," Caesar says to me. "Heads. I'll have eyes all over the place, that way. If he needs backup, I'll go to him."

"You might be safer away from here," I say gently. He is the only one without any sort of combat training, no matter how good he's got on-the-job. "You'd still be able to be in his head."

"But I wouldn't be able to help," he says, and then adds, as if it's the most important thing in the world, "and I wouldn't know where you were."

"And what is it that you want me to be doing?"

He hesitates for a half-second. "Only if you're happy to… but I think we could use some bait. We need to draw Jamboree out!" he says, in a voice that goes up at the end despite trying to sound reasonable. "She's come after you every time."

He makes a compelling argument. I nod my agreement. I'll need height. I'll need to make sure that she can see me, from wherever she is. I scan around for an appropriate place, and my eyes land on the obvious choice.

The C-Corp tower is the second-tallest on the street, and the only building that remains completely untouched by portals. "Can you get me inside?" I ask Caesar, pointing. He follows my finger and then looks back at me, brows knit in clear confusion.

"I need to get to the roof."

He nods, and we begin to pick our way through the rubble, pausing occasionally to help people to their feet and point to the nearest Legion, who takes over guiding them somewhere safe. The portals are still opening and closing, spitting concrete and metal out of the sky or sideways into the trees and street-lamps. A few times we have to jump or shove each other out of the way, and once I grab the back of Caesar's uniform and drag him backwards before he races directly into an opening portal.

The fanfare-music that accompanies each portal is nearly deafening. I wish Eliza was here to mute it for us, and when I say as much to Caesar, he laughs and says he'll give her a call.

It's a poor attempt at humour, but we'll take what we can get, given the situation.

We do finally make it to the C-Corp tower, and Caesar uses his fingerprint to open the front door. He ushers me inside, giving me directions to the nearest elevator. "Abs," he says, when I turn to go. "Good luck. And… I'm sorry. I know she's your friend."

I lift a shoulder, somewhat helpless. "I have other friends."

The tower is eerie, when it's just me. I make my way to the elevator, which plays a totally incongruous melody as I ride it up to the top floor. From there, I race across the empty offices and tear up a hidden flight of stairs to the roof. The door is, naturally, locked, but I send the deadbolt to the Void and push my way onto the roof without any trouble.

The sound of the portals nearly sends me reeling after the dead-silence of the offices.

I go to the edge of the roof and brace my hands against the ledge, staring down at the chaos below. The portals are getting bigger and bigger, with the largest ending at nearly my eye level.

I'm pushed off the building.

I barely have time to scream before I'm rolling through a new portal landing, back on the C-Corp roof. I breathe hard for a few seconds before I'm lifting my gaze up to meet Jamboree's dark eyes.

"You're so *predictable*," she whines, raking a hand through her hair. "Used to make fun of *me* for being a Caesar family fangirl, but look at you now."

The portals stop suddenly, all at once. I see a few more buildings topple, hear screams distantly. But then it's just us and the wind whipping around our faces. For a blissful second, nothing happens, and I manage to drag myself to my feet.

I shouldn't have bothered— C-Corp, the only building still untouched, starts to tip forwards, towards the street. There must be a portal, or maybe many, tearing it apart, but I can't see for sure. I stumble, losing my balance again. Jamboree steadies me, holding my shoulders to keep my standing straight.

"Don't worry," she says, "I'm not gonna kill you."

"Why not?" I wonder aloud. "It'd make more sense! You're the one who always picked apart supervillian's plans in movies!"

"Yeah," she says, shrugging hugely. The roof has come to a rest in the middle of the street, positioned like a boxing ring. I try not to wonder if anyone is crushed beneath it. "But back then I was *Bond*. And you were *Q* and we were on the *same team*."

"Why aren't we still?" I demand.

She just glares at me. "Excellent question."

There's a tense silence for the next several seconds. Jamboree huffs, rolls her eyes hugely, and shoves me away with all her force. Before I can react, she's opening portals. I hear the fanfare and it takes me longer than it should to process what's happening.

The portals are opening *inside* me. Not in the Void, not in the form of a pounding headache, but inside me, ripping through my stomach and thighs and neck, sending me throughout the multiverse in parts. I don't realise I'm screaming until I'm suddenly *not*, in too much pain to even think about, scattered across eight or nine universes, barely holding together— I think it's my connection to the Void that means I can.

Jamboree is screaming too, fury wound in her features. Like a child, she stomps her foot and lets the portals close. I drop down— I'd been suspended in the air?— and struggle to catch my breath with my face pressed against the cool concrete.

"You *abandoned* me!" Jamboree shouts, finally comprehensible, but I'm too busy trying to make sure I'm all in one piece to really listen. "All that talk about helping me, loving me, wanting to explore other universes—"

I can feel the Void calling out to me; it's worried, it doesn't know what's going on, and it wants to make sure I'm okay. It wants me to come into it, so it can be sure that I'm safe. I shakily push myself to my knees, telling it, *not yet.* I glare up at Jamboree, lip curling into a snarl, and point to the streets below us. "Since when is this what you want?! I mean, if our families could see you now—"

I barely get the thought out before she's slapping me across the face, hard enough to sting. I take another set of shaky, shallow breaths, but I don't look back up at her.

"Scared, pet?" she crones, and the square is overwhelmed again with the sound of fanfare.

The Void is getting more and more insistent, like a constant itch at the back of my skull, and I want to tell it to *shut up*, that I *can't*, that I need to focus on this. I want to look around and make sure that everyone is safe, but I just don't have the energy. I stay on my knees in front of Jamboree, head bowed, breathing hard.

And then the Void is joined by another presence. Something unfamiliar— is that *Caesar*?

Initially, the Void doesn't seem to like this either, but I can feel it relax when we realise, simultaneously, that it's Caesar, our friend. He seems to be struggling, searching for something that he can't quite grasp.

Void Calling, I think in his general direction.

It's a part of me, a physical space that's also my mind. It's got its own rules, its own plane of existence. It's still calling, dragging me into it, refusing to let me stay. Caesar must have a plan. I need him to understand, I need him to follow. When he thinks of my mind, I wonder, does he think of the Void? Does he realise that to read my *mind*, he must also read a *universe*?

Come on, Caesar. Come to the Void, Caesar.

And he does.

25.

I let the Void drag me into itself, although I'm not entirely sure if it's physical or not. Caesar isn't here physically, at least, but I can feel him, feel the Void's cautious reaction. He looks around, poking and prodding and spreading, getting used to the feeling of my mind.

It doesn't feel like a human mind, something in him murmurs. I wonder if I'm picking up on his thoughts or if he's actively trying to communicate. I'll have to ask him later.

It's not a human mind, I remind him, fond at his naivety. *It's a universe*.

You're a universe, he repeats back to me.

I can hear him quite clearly, now, as though he's speaking in my ear. He says, "I wasn't going to be able to get up to you, so this seemed like the next best thing. I'm going to try to dispel the pain, okay? I'm going to try to make it go away. Can you take on Jamboree, if I do that?"

I think I nod. The Void lets me seep back into reality.

I'm still aware of Caesar's presence— it's comforting, actually, to use his borrowed strength. As I push myself to my feet, I look down to the ground and see him, propped up against a loose piece of concrete, a red-headed girl by his side. I can't see him super clearly from this angle, but it looks like his eyes are squeezed shut.

Focus, Abs! he says from inside my head, and I whirl around to face Jamboree. She's got her back to me, staring out over the city centre. There aren't any more open portals, thankfully. I can hear sirens, and when I turn towards the sound, there're both police cars and ambulances pulling to abrupt stops behind mountains of concrete and trees. It looks a wreck.

"Jamboree!"

"Abyss." She sounds tired, her voice flat. She turns on her heel to face me, and her expression is blank. "You know… I'm starting to get real sick of having the same conversation with you every time we speak. We used to talk about all sorts of things. Now it's always 'why are you doing this?'—" she mimics me with a high pitched voice— "followed by me *telling you* and you being too dense to actually understand. Or maybe you're being wilfully ignorant."

I bristle at the accusation.

"'Oh,'" she says, and the simpering, high-pitched voice is back, "'I'm *Abyss*, and I'm a goddamn *genius* superhero, the Caesar Corporation is practically *gagging* for me, and I've got two hot boys wrapped around my pinky finger.' Please! You've got it all, Jenna-Louise. Why do you even bother trying to understand me, huh? What's the point?"

"You were Bond," I say, lifting a shoulder into a shrug. Caesar's still keeping the pain at bay, which I'm endlessly grateful for. "I was Q, we were on the same team. I want to know why we stopped."

She huffs, looking up and away from me. "You left. You left, and you didn't even look back. It's not that complicated."

I want to say, *if it's not that complicated, then maybe you're overreacting?* but I manage to stop myself. I feel like it would only make things worse.

Caesar laughs— I can feel it in my head. It's... surprisingly welcome.

"Explain it to me like I'm dumb," I say, desperate.

She laughs, cold and hard. "No thanks. You're a *genius*, after all. You can figure it out on your own, or you can go to hell. Or both. See if I care."

I can't believe this. "You've just torn apart three city blocks! It's pretty damn obvious that you care, Jamboree! Just *explain* it to me! I want to help! You're my best friend!"

"Oh yeah?" she says, raising both her eyebrows. "Then why are you calling me Jamboree?"

I pull back, my blood going cold.

"Tell you what. I'll put it all back," she gestures wildly around. "If you can tell me *why*."

"Why *what*?" I demand, but she just looks at me sharply. "Why I left? Don't you *know*? I was scared! I was terrified. I tried— I tried to open a portal to another universe and what I got was the Void, half-sentient and almost-alive and it needed me and I agreed, and I was scared. I panicked in a supply closet and I left without thinking. I didn't think. I should've—"

I break off, unsure what exactly I should've done. It must show on my face, because Jamboree just shakes her head and opens a portal in front of her with some finality. "Some apology. I'll try to put it back," she takes one step into the portal. "You'll still need C-Corp money for repairs though."

She's gone before I can even finish blinking.

26.

There's no clear way down, so I end up going back down the same stairs I'd come up to get on the roof in the first place, go down to the lowest floor that I can before the building abruptly stops, and then open a window. I climb out and only have to jump a few feet.

Caesar wraps me in a hug as soon as I'm on the ground. The red-head who was with him is, on closer inspection, Ace. She hugs me as well, and I end up leaning into her more than I probably should. Caesar's been doing well in 'turning off' the pain, but I can feel it slowly seeping back in. Ace wraps an arm around my waist to support me, and I lean heavily across her shoulders.

"Where's Legion?" I ask Caesar, and watch him pale.

"I don't know—"

Jamboree must've already cleared some of the rubble that was blocking the ambulance, because we see two zoom past in rapid succession. After only a few moments, we hear someone shout, "over here!" and we head off towards the sound.

As we round a corner around some particularly nasty destruction, I get a sinking feeling in my chest before we can even see anything. There are three paramedics all talking rapidly to each other. One is checking over the scene. Another is digging around in the back of an ambulance.

We inch closer, careful not to interrupt. There's only one person in this particular area, a young guy, sprawled across the ground as though he fell from a great height. Given the desperation of the paramedics, I have a very bad feeling that he's not going to make it.

Well done, Julia! You've killed someone now.

It's possible she's killed people before, with all of her antics, but I've never witnessed it before. My stomach twists. I curve in towards Ace, who strokes my side soothingly.

Caesar gasps beside me, then chokes out a strangled noise. Ace stiffens, her motions stopping suddenly and completely.

I lift my head only a fraction, but it's enough.

The man on the ground is Xander.

They must've removed his mask as part of the first aid, because it's been cut up and discarded around his head— I'd forgotten that only his fingerprint could undo the latch. His eyes are open and staring out at nothing, a pool of red seeping out from behind his skull, matting his hair.

There are other injuries, but I can't bring myself to tear my eyes away from his face. I'm sickly fascinated, despite the churn in my stomach. *Xander*. He was always so worried about Caesar, about me. Why didn't he worry about himself? What was it he'd said to me? *Because I don't need to.*

"Maybe it's a duplicate," Caesar chokes out, barely audible.

I shake my head, as much as it pains me. "Remember when Jamboree shot one? It just disappeared, he—"

The paramedics suddenly become aware of us, looking at us sharply. When they see me leaning heavily across Ace's shoulders, one approaches me and asks if I'm injured. "Not physically," I answer, barely able to meet their eyes when Xander is laying *right there*. "I'm just in a lot of pain."

Caesar looks over at me, and I can practically see the guilt writing itself into his features. I want to tell him not to worry, but I can't seem to find the words. The Void is calling out to me again, but I can't imagine answering it right now.

The paramedic takes my arm and lifts my weight from Ace, guiding me towards the ambulance, where they sit me down and start checking me over. I'm given pain medication and a shock blanket. Ace comes to stand next to me, staring into space.

I say thickly, "He's my brother."

"I know," she says, and pushes herself up to sit next to me and wrap me in a one armed hug. "I know, Abyss."

She ends up leaving as more paramedics start to move around, saying she's going to go check in in other areas, and get her roommates down to help with clean-up and press. She squeezes me one last time before she goes, and I watch her walk over to where Caesar is standing, looking more in shock than I feel, and touch his arm. He nods at whatever she says, and in a few moments he's over standing in front of me.

"I was supposed to be in his head," he says, and I don't know what to say to that. He was in mine, instead. I imagine that took all of his concentration.

"Maybe you should get out of mine."

He looks at me sharply, but then his shoulders seem to deflate and he nods. I don't want him getting all wrapped up in my emotions as well as his own— that can't possibly be good for him.

I reach out for his hand and squeeze it gently in my own. He laces our fingers, and we press our shoulders together, borrowing each others strength.

27.

Caesar takes me back to his penthouse to shower. He gives me a pair of leggings that must've belonged to Ace and a sweatshirt that smells of his cologne. It's cosy enough, even if I do have to slip back into my dirty socks and the boots from my uniform.

None of us were supposed to *die*. We were kids, we were dressing up in costumes and playing pretend. It wasn't supposed to be *real*.

Except that it was, wasn't it? Xander had always believed one-hundred-percent in what we were doing. I was the one who'd always said it felt like playing pretend, and he'd teased me about it because he knew what we were doing was real. Is real. It's not like I can stop now.

I'm *Abyss*. I'm a universe wrapped up in a girl and all the things I've defined myself by are, cumulatively, things that make me a superhero. It's who I am, now. Xander wouldn't want me to give up on all of that. And Jamboree is still out there. Whatever it is that she's trying to say, I need to figure it out. We need to figure it out.

When I re-enter the living room, Caesar is staring out of the floor-to-ceiling windows. It's summer, so despite the later hour, the sun is still up. It doesn't seem right. It seems like things should've gone dark.

"I have to tell his mom," I say, and even though my voice is quiet, it still cuts through the silence. He turns his head over his shoulder and lifts one corner of his mouth into a tiniest, saddest smile I've ever seen.

"Do you what me to come with you?"

I shake my head. "No, you should stay here and rest."

He looks back out the window. I make my way over to him and tug him into a tight hug. He wraps his arms around me, and we stay there for several long moments.

"I'll see you soon," I promise, and he nods. "Take care of yourself."

His driver is waiting for me downstairs. When I look at him oddly, he explains that Caesar called him and asked him to give me a ride to Pae's Flowers. It sounds much nicer than getting a taxi, so I climb into the car and sit quietly while we zip through the city.

I thank him when we arrive, and stare at the display in the window until he drives away. Xander had done he window-dressings just two days ago. Now he'll never do them again.

I choke, force myself to turn away, and climb the fire escape.

Ki Pae is sitting on the sofa-bed, staring wide-eyed at the TV. I barely have to glance to see that it's a news report of city centre. Her head whips around when she hears me come in. "Abyss!" she says, and her relief is palatable. "Where's Xander—?"

I can feel tears in my eyes. The Void can't take this from me, even though I can feel it trying. I shake my head twice, open my mouth, and close it again. Forcing myself to swallow, I say, "I'm sorry."

Her hand comes to her mouth and she's crying before I can say anything else. I hover awkwardly in front of the window, unsure what to do or say next. She holds her hands out to me after a second, and I nearly throw myself across the room and onto the bed next to her. She wraps her arms tightly around me and stokes down my back. I can feel the sobs that wrack through her body. The news is still playing, detailing damages and injuries. I reach blindly for the remote to turn it off.

We sit in the new silence, holding on to each other desperately, and sob until all of our tears are dried up.

Ki falls asleep shortly thereafter, but I can't sleep. The hospital had called and told Ki what had happened; it was arbitrary. He'd fallen. He'd been on top of one of the buildings that Jamboree destroyed, and he'd been thrown from the roof and onto the concrete. He'd cracked his skull and been dead almost immediately.

Dead. He's dead.

Ki shifts next to me. I stare at her, wondering if I should rouse her and take her to her own bed. I decide against it— she needs the rest. She deserves the rest.

They're extensions of my family; Ki is like a second mom, and Xander was another brother. I miss him. I miss the rest of my family. I miss my mom, and my dad. I miss my brother. I reach for my laptop, moving carefully and slowly so I don't wake Ki.

I think it's time to reach out again. I open my email, and type softly, one key at a time.

Dear Jordan,

There's so much to tell you.

Part Two: Caesar

28.

"Caesar!"

It's a familiar voice, albeit one that I haven't heard in a long time. Six whole months, actually, but I'd remember my best friend's voice anywhere. I turn towards the sound, searching for a face that I recognise. I hear pounding footsteps over the otherwise quiet concrete, but my eyes just can't seem to find her.

And then Abyss screams, bloodcurdling, high pitched and full of agony. I suddenly realise that I've never heard her scream before; she's always been deathly silent when suffering or in pain. I whirl around without any hesitation, abandoning my search for my friend in favour of staring up at Abyss, where she and Jamboree are elevated on a piece of building that was once the C-Corp roof. She's suspended in mid-air, twin braids flailing in the wind, mouth open even as the scream breaks off. It's like she's gasping for air, unable to make even the most simple, primal of noises. It takes my brain a second too long to process the reason behind the shriek in the first place, and when it finally catches up to my eyes, I wish it hadn't.

There are portals, Jamboree's portals, swirling, purply-blue things, opening and closing around Abyss. But, no, not around Abyss. Inside her, poking out of her stomach, wrapping through her arms, twisting in her head. It's as though Jamboree is channeling every universe she can think of straight into Abyss' body. Abyss' mouth is still open, screaming silently. My legs feel suddenly weak, and I lurch forward into a dry heave. There's nothing around to brace myself on. I take a few fumbling steps forward, off-balance.

In seconds, there are hands wrapping around my arm, holding me up. "What's going on?"

I turn towards the voice, trying to steady myself against it. It takes me a half-second to realise that it's Ace. She looks different, now, which makes sense, given that I haven't seen her in nearly six months. I blink, a few times, taking her in. "Your hair is red," I say, because that's the most obvious change.

She rolls her eyes at me, slowly pulling me towards a large chuck of cement and iron. Probably, originally, a piece of a building. She props me up against it, and after another brief round of dry heaving, I turn back to stare at Abyss. The portals have disappeared, and she's fallen, crumpled, onto the pseudo-platform Jamboree had created. I can see her sucking in heavy, deep breaths, even from this distance. Ace, next to me, curses, taking in the same sight.

"You know," she quips, "I was hoping for a welcome home party."

I barely have time to huff a laugh before Jamboree starts shouting comprehensible words, rather than whatever wordless nonsense she'd been screaming before. She stalks towards Abyss, glowering. "You abandoned me!" she yells, her hands curled into fists. "All that talk about helping me, loving me, wanting to explore other universes —"

Abyss shakily pushes herself up onto her knees, breathing hard as she glares up at Jamboree. I can't hear what she says, but whatever it is, it's the wrong thing. Jamboree sneers, and slaps Abyss across the face. Ace lets out an animalistic growl, and I instinctually reach out to hold her back, as though she has to ability to make it up to the top of the platform.

Abyss doesn't lift her eyes back up to Jamboree, which I almost think is an undeserved kindness. Jamboree deserves to stare directly into the Void, and to experience its full wrath. Abyss doesn't let her.

"Scared, pet?" Jamboree says.

Ace nudges me, and I tear my eyes away from the scene to look at her. Her eyes have the glazed over, glossy look that means she's looking at the numbers. "Jamboree is wearing a dampener- ninety-three percent probability. Without being able to get into her head, your chances of success drop down to nineteen percent. Since when are *dampeners* a thing?"

I forgot that she wasn't here for Charlie's wedding. Before I can answer, she's shaking her head and continuing, "It's, uh, targeting telepathy exclusively— seventy-one percent— but maybe if I get up there I can distract her long enough to knock it loose."

"Ace," I cut in, "you said it's targeting telepathy, right? What about Abyss' abilities, can it stop those?"

"I thought you couldn't—"

"Life or death, A, what are my chances?"

She seems to realise what I'm planning at the same time I do. Her vision clears long enough to look at me in surprise, then clouds over again. She mumbles a long list of numbers to herself, none of which I have any hope of understanding, even if I could see the numbers myself. "I sure hope you know what you're doing," she says. "Because the odds are pretty fifty-fifty, right now."

It's not the most encouraging thing to hear, but I have to run with it.

I stare back up at Abyss, willing myself to focus.

I stare at her. Jamboree takes another few steps forward, says something that I can't hear. Abyss half-grins, still looking down and away from Jamboree. The fingers on her left hand are twitching. I imagine she's still in pain— having universes ripped through her can't be an experience that is easily processed or moved on from. I wish I was up there, able to put my body between her and Jamboree.

I stare at her. She doesn't say anything, even as Jamboree continues to goad and glower, pacing forwards and backwards. Abyss, from my limited vantage point, looks like she's a little bit out of it, swaying slightly in the wind, eyes blinking shut for longer and longer periods of time. Jamboree must know every single way to destroy her. The twitching in her left hand gets more erratic. I watch her take a huge, shaky breath. Jamboree doesn't even pause. I can't imagine any universe where they were ever friends.

I stare at her.

I become her.

Entering her mind is an all-consuming feat. There is first stillness, and then pain. Unbearable pain, shooting through every part of her body, every single part of my brain registering the sensations that she, herself, is too far gone to feel. Distantly, I'm aware of myself screaming, of Ace's soothing motions and noises, but I can't do anything to stop it, or I risk losing this already fragile connection to Abyss' mind. I've never been able to read her thoughts; there was always, simply, vague, misty nothingness where human thoughts went, sometimes the briefest, fleeting notion or idea. Here, forcing myself into it, clinging to it, I still am getting nothing.

Except…

There's this unfamiliar feeling. Some sort of distant call that I don't know how to answer. A tug, a gentle nudge, encouraging and all-encompassing. I don't know what it is. I don't have a word for it.

Void Calling.

That's what she calls it, this unnamable emotion, this unending feeling. It's the very foremost thought, the only thing I've ever been able to read. The fact that she's capable of coherent thought at all surprises me.

It's the Void. That's what's maintaining her coherency; keeping her safe, stopping the pain. It calls her into it, and now, being in her head, it's the only thing that I can feel, too. *Come on, Caesar.*

Abyss must sense my presence; it's like she's hoping that I'll figure it all out.

How?

The Void is a part of her mind. It's a part of her, and, in many ways, the most important part of her. When I try to read her mind, do I ever think of the Void? Do I remember that's she's different?

I pick up on the meaning of her thoughts easily enough. I always knew her mind would travel at a mile a minute, lightyears ahead of where I would be. She's not explaining herself fully, but why would she? This is her mind, her thoughts, and she's not a telepath, she's not used to focusing her thoughts to be understood by others. It's hard enough to read it anyway. I could be missing things.

I'm still screaming, still, somewhere, outside of her head, outside of mine, experiencing every bit of pain that her body is.

Come to the Void, Caesar, she thinks, but she's getting more and more distant.

I try to focus, I try to follow the thread of her, the call of the Void, but it's much harder than she made it sound. The Void is a universe, one with its own rules, and for whatever reason it chose Abyss. Maybe it won't want me in it. This whole experience is so beyond surreal. I always knew Abyss' mind would be unlike any other that I'd experience. I never thought it would be like this.

I don't have the words to describe the Void. I'm very suddenly aware of Abyss' emotions, her current whirlwind of thoughts. It hits me like a sucker punch, the realisation that this is part of Abyss I've been neglecting. By thinking of her as only a part, instead of as a whole, I was missing out on so much of her. But it's almost overwhelming; so many new things all at once. It doesn't feel like a human mind.

It's not a human mind, Abyss reminds me gently. *It's a universe.*

You're a universe, I repeat, awestruck.

29.

Less than half an hour after Abyss leaves my penthouse, Ace is knocking on my door. I have about a million questions for her; how her stint undercover went, what her plans are now, if she wants to keep the red hair. She pushes her way into the house without so much as a 'hello' and stands, in the centre of my entrance way, with her hands on her hips. I open my mouth to say something, but she cuts me off before I can start.

"Let's get you cleaned up," she says, assertive, and I suddenly remember that I'm still wearing my uniform. It's sticky with sweat. My hair is slick against my forehead, and my muscles ache even when I'm standing still. I hadn't even been thinking about it in my haste to get Abyss somewhere safe and away from the press which was sure to appear, but I can feel the bone-deep exhaustion now.

I don't move. Ace smiles at me, pulling her lips in to make an understanding line. She takes one of my hands and leads me towards the bathroom. She's not dragging me, exactly, but the pressure of her hand on mine is enough to get me following dumbly after her.

I sit on the toilet seat while she runs a bath. I'd been so concerned with Abyss that the reality hadn't settled in, but now, with her gone, I can feel it catching, heavy, in my chest. Ace doesn't speak until the bath is full, and then she turns off the taps. The lack of white noise is what finally gets me to speak.

"Xander's gone," I say, looking at her through my lashes, unsurprised to see wetness clinging to them.

Ace reaches out and squeezes my hands in hers. "I know, honey."

She turns her back while I strip down and sink into the bath. I hadn't noticed her adding bubbles, but I'm glad that they're there. She takes my place on the toilet seat and props her feet up on the edge of the bathtub. I suddenly can't remember what she was wearing when she ran to meet me during the battle. Whatever it was, she's not wearing it now. She's clean, her hair washed and pulled into a high ponytail, wearing a pair of leggings and a t-shirt tied up above her bellybutton. I don't know how she had the time.

I sink further into the bath, the water settling around the line of my lips. I want to find something to say, something to break the heavy silence. I can't think of anything.

After a while, Ace throws a cloth at me. It lands in the water with a lacklustre *plop*. "Just laying under the water won't get you clean," she says.

I mechanically scrub at my arms and legs, the back of my neck. I disappear under the water to scrub at my head, but I don't bother using any shampoo. Ace doesn't comment.

When I move to get out of the bath, Ace leaves the room. She knocks a few minutes later, and after I inform her that I'm decent, she slips inside with a pile of clean clothes. A pair of jeans, a baseball tee. A clean pair of boxers. Any other time, I'd flush at the idea that Ace had been through my underwear drawer, but I can't find the energy to care. She leaves the room again as I get dressed, but she's only standing outside the door when I step back outside.

"What do you want?" she says, her voice kind. "Do you want to sleep, or should we try to stay up?"

I'm exhausted in an all-encompassing way, but I don't want to go to sleep. I'm afraid that all I'll have in visions of Xander's lifeless body; twisted, contorted. He'd fallen off that structure with no one around to see it happen, cracking his head open on the rough pavement below. We'd been distracted, and Xander had died alone. I can still see his eyes…

Ace is waiting patiently for a response. Thinking about it, I'm actually sort of surprised at her suggestions. I know how she reacted when she lost her family, and it wasn't something as simple as staying up with a friend. "I don't want to sleep," I say, my voice sounding small and distant even to my own ears. "I don't want to sleep, A, I don't want to sleep."

She nods, takes my hand again, and we go to the living room. My couch, the one facing the windows, offers a great view of the city, especially at night. I collapse into a seat, my legs finally giving way after the intensity of the day. Ace takes the spot next to me, leaning her head against my shoulder and pulling her feet up under her thighs. I wrap an arm around her, stroking up and down her bare arm just to remind me that I'm not alone.

"He was all alone," I whisper. "We should've been there."

Ace doesn't try to tell me otherwise. "I know it's hard, Cee," she does say, staring straight ahead. "It's gonna be hard for a long, long time. But you were trying to do the right thing. The, uhm, priority had to be stopping Jamboree."

"Xander was trying to help with that," I shift, uncomfortably. "And we *left* him."

Ace is quiet for a long time, and I almost think she's not going to say anything at all. I stare out the window and worry my bottom lip between my teeth. She pulls away from me. "When Riley died," she starts, and in her mind I see flashes of a young girl, barely twelve, and then burning, red hot fire. It's the starkness of the word 'died' that gets to me. I haven't been able to think of Xander like that yet. "I blamed myself. For months— years. You can't do that, Caesar. You can't, it'll tear you apart."

I stare over at her, trace the tension in her body like it's a line. Her trainers, flat against the hardwood floor, her knees at a ninety degree angle, back straight as a rod. Her hair is red, and it's just as off-putting as it was earlier. Red, red, red. Like Xander was, when we found him.

Ace turns her head towards me, her eyes wide and pleading. She's been down this path before, and it didn't lead her anywhere good. I know her and Xander weren't the closest ever, but I have to wonder if she's forcing herself to stay on the strait and narrow this time around. "Caesar," she says, and I've never heard her so serious. "Caesar, honey, I know it means nothing, but I'm sorry. I'm so sorry."

I can feel hot tears pricking at my eyes again. I close my eyes and let them pour out through the gaps between my eyelids. "How—" I swallow, and have to start again. "Is this what it's like all the time?"

I can't see it, but I'm sure that Ace shakes her head. She's physically expressive, like that. "No," she says quietly, "not all the time."

"How did you get over it?"

Ace offers a bitter, startled laugh, just one split-second noise. "I'm not over it, Caesar. But I'm… used to it."

It's not very comforting, but it's honest.

I stare out the large windows as the city sinks into nighttime. The last rays of brilliant orange give way to inky blue, and I let out a long sigh. Ace leans back towards me, offering quiet comfort, and her hand finds its way into my curls, smoothing them out and, as they inevitably spring back into place, smoothing them again and again and again.

"Are you going to keep your hair red?" I ask, because it's the least emotional of my many questions about her absence. I need to talk about something, anything else, and her hair is as good a topic as any.

"Hell no," her voice is full of feeling, close to disgust, but still quiet, soothing to listen to. "I hate it *so* much! You know, I was so damn paranoid that I touched up my roots every morning, just in case. I wanted it to look as natural as possible. But I'm so sick of it now, I could shave it all off. As soon as I can, I'm going to strip the dye." She pauses, for a long moment. "I was going to ask Abyss if she'd braid it again. I missed that."

"I'm sure she did as well," I say, but I don't really know. The relationship that Ace and Abyss have has always confused me; it seems like its two parts in-fighting and one part nattering at each other. "I'm sure she'd do it, if you asked."

Ace hums. "I'll probably stop by their house tomorrow, anyway."

It sounds like a good idea, but I'm trying to avoid that particular subject. "Did you miss anything about me, while you were gone?" I ask instead, trying to infuse some joviality into my voice, some sort of teasing sound.

Even if I'm not one-hundred-percent successful, Ace responds in kind. "Nope," she says, popping the 'p' sound. "Not one thing. You're not my *best friend* or anything."

"I'm truly hurt," I reply, fighting a yawn. I still don't want to sleep, but it's becoming harder and harder to fight. Ace has continued playing with my hair, but, upon noticing my attempts to stifling a yawn, carefully slides her hand down my eyes to force them closed.

"I'm kidding," she says, softly. "I missed a lot about you."

"Like what?"

"Everything," she says, and I can hear the smile in her voice. "Every curl and freckle and each of your eyes."

The flashes of memory I catch from her tell me she used to say the same to her sister all the time. Riley, a curly-haired, freckly twelve year old with big brown eyes. Riley, who is dead. Like Xander. I want to say something, anything, but I can't find the energy to open my mouth. She's still keeping my eyes closed, and I shift as though I'm going to pull away, just to hear what she'll say.

She sighs, gently, through her nose. "Get some rest, Caesar. I'm not going anywhere."

"Promise?" My voice sounds small to my own ears.

"Promise," she says, and I'm already half-asleep.

30.

When I wake up, Ace has shifted away from me, and is curled up on the corner of the couch with her head tucked into the crook of her own elbow. She doesn't stir as I stand up and patter over to the kitchen. I wonder if she's been home for a significant amount of time since getting back, or if the first thing she did was join us on the battlefield, shower, come to me.

I pour us matching bowls of sugary cereal, but hesitate over the milk. She hasn't been around, so I haven't been ordering lactose-free stuff. I sigh, put everything away, and wander back to the living room empty-handed. Ace is still asleep. I wonder when she fell asleep. I wonder if she'd hate me if I woke her up.

I don't have to worry about it. She blinks awake, on edge for a second too long before she remembers where she is. *Penthouse.* I don't mean to read her mind— sometimes I just catch waves of thought without intending to.

"Morning," she says, "You been up long?"

I shake my head. "I don't have any lactose-free milk."

"Weren't you expecting me?" Her voice is light, teasing, because of course I wasn't. "Let's go to the diner instead."

We take the elevator all the way down to the bottom floor in silence. Not uncomfortable, but sticky with sleep that's not quite shaken off. Ace catches sight of herself in the mirror and balks. I wonder if she ever got used to the way she looks like this, because she doesn't look like herself; bare-faced, slouched. I watch as she straightens up, reties her ponytail. It doesn't help.

The diner is a fifteen-minute walk from my house, and it's also where Ace and I first met, that year and a half ago. Man, it feels longer than that. We'd got warm drinks together (black coffee for me and lavender tea for her), after she'd finished panicking, and pancakes and eggs and sausages. It's become 'our' place, sort of, somewhere that I'll always associate with her, even if I come here with other people.

A waitress pours our drinks within seconds of us sitting down, and Ace smiles brightly up at the waitress, although she makes no move to pick it up. "Aw, it's good to be back. No where in the world makes tea like you do, Nani."

"It's good to have you back. No one in the world tips as well as you do." Nani shakes her head fondly. "I didn't recognise you with the red hair. News got it wrong, huh? Kept saying you were dead."

"Well, I was. Until last night."

The waitress smiles again, rests a hand on Ace's shoulder briefly, and walks away with a wave at me. "Just last night?" I repeat. "Have you been home at all?"

"Course," Ace shrugs. "I had to shower and everything, didn't I? My roommates understand, though. They've been helping with clean-up and helping, uh, civilians find their way around."

Her voice goes up slightly on 'civilians' like she's not quite sure it's the right word to use. My heart swells. Her roommates are among her best friends (she has a lot of those). The fact that she, after being away from them for six months, still came to help me, leaves me torn between pleased and aching.

We order pancakes that come in stacks a mile high and coat them in half a bottle of syrup each. As we eat, Ace fills the time chatting about anything and everything she can think of. A book she read that she hated, the article about me on SuperTrooper, the fact that she finally sat down and watched some Star Trek, because she decided that Adelina- her undercover persona- loved it. She says she liked the new movies better. I think that's blasphemy, but I'm grateful that she's filling the silence and doesn't expect me to speak.

We finish eating, pay, leave a generous tip. Ace's tea went cold, but I'd had three cups of coffee. Nani waves at us as we walk out, and I give her my best smile. "Hasn't it reached the news, yet? Don't they know?"

"It has," Ace nods, "but they aren't reporting that *Legion* died."

"Why not?"

"Because the paramedics aren't speaking about it," she explains, voice low, gentle. "I may have threatened them, a little, but it's working. Plus, confidentiality. By the time that reporters got there, he was just… Xander. The news reports are about Xander. And, even if people know that he does the flowers for your family's events, or that you played with him when you were kids, they don't, uhm, they don't necessarily know that you're friends."

She's still speaking in present tense. I wonder if this is affecting her more than I realised. She thinks mostly in French, so it's hard for me to tell without being more invasive. Ace has made it clear how she feels about that. With a sigh, she says, "I've got to go, Cee. Don't be alone today, okay? Go see your family, visit a park with lots of people. Just don't be alone."

I nod, and Ace squeezes my arm one more time before disappearing down the street, towards the Pae's apartment. Mrs Pae's apartment. The breakfast we just ate churns uncomfortably in my stomach. Xander doesn't live there anymore.

I square my shoulders and walk back to my building. There are a few people who point, a few teenage girls who snap pictures, but, thankfully, no one tries to talk to me. I'm still exhausted in a way that sleep can't quite shake. I think about what Ace said, about me needing company. As far as I know, Mom and Dad are in Greece, visiting mom's family. Carlos, the youngest of us, will be with them. Charlie, my elder sister, the oldest, is in Monaco with her wife. That leaves Eliza, middle-child like me, who's a half-hours drive away, and always has gummy bears in a bowl on the living room table.

I pull out my phone to call my driver, Aaron, but pause when I realise that I have an unread text from Abyss.

Abs-tract: *thx fr lst nite. hop ur ok. <3 u*

It's the most affectionate Abyss has ever been. It's not that I'm surprised by it, really, I know that we're friends and we care about each other, but she's never said it aloud before. Or typed it, I guess. I give myself a little shake. It's just an emoji, and not even a proper one.

I text back:

Me: *Np. Always here if you need me or a place to stay. Hope you're okay. Love you too.*

31.

Aaron has this unique ability to avoid all traffic and traffic lights. I don't know if he's superhuman (he's certainly never said) or if he just has chronically good luck, but we arrive at my childhood home, where Eliza's staying, in twenty-five minutes. He tips his hat at me as I open the left backseat door, such a stereotype, and says that he'll pick me up again whenever I'm ready.

Eliza opens the door on the first ring. "I heard you coming," she says, ushering me in.

Elizabeth Marina Caesar has the ability to control sound. It sounds a lot less impressive than it is; she can make things louder or quieter, turn sound waves into blasts of pure noise, or, if she really tries, even move at the speed of sound. When we were growing up, she used to 'turn us down' when we were annoying her. I can't count the number of times she 'muted' Mom when they were arguing. She spent more time grounded than otherwise as a young teenager.

She's only seventeen, now, but she starts university in a few weeks, and had wanted to arrive a little beforehand to get used to the environment. She's been living here for nearly two months. My parents had hesitated at first, but then I reminded them that I was only eighteen when I moved into my penthouse, and that I'd be sure to visit her at least once a week. Eliza and I have always been close — closer than I am with any of my other siblings, anyway— so she didn't mind the stipulation.

She's staying in the house we used to live in. It still smells like home; wood varnish and old books, ink and pine. The pine is new, actually. Eliza's burning candles.

"Did you hear about the fire in Monaco?" she asks me as she straightens up from re-lighting a candle.

"Anywhere near where Charlie is staying?"

"Same hotel," Eliza says, biting back a grin. We hold eye-contact for only a millisecond before we dissolve into giggles. "I'm sure she's fine."

I nod, the ghost of a smile still on my face. Then I remember why I came here and feel a pang of guilt at the idea that I could be laughing so soon afterwards. Eliza seems to catch the shift in my mood. "I heard about Xander," she says, sinking in the loveseat. I half-collapse into the armchair and nod mutely. "Do you want to talk about it?"

"I don't know," I sigh. "I want to talk about *him*, but I'm not so sure about... *it*."

Eliza nods. "I'll make some tea. Then you can tell me all about him."

She heads off into the kitchen. I take the opportunity to stare around the space. It's been relatively untouched since the day we left; cleaners stop by, obviously, to maintain it, but otherwise, it's exactly as I remember it. The floor-to-ceiling bookshelves on the leftmost wall, the bay window giving way to the luxurious green garden. The seating is all olive green, suede, and more comfortable than sitting on a cloud, and the wood is all rich red-toned mahogany. The table, which sits low to the ground and doesn't quite make it to my knees when I'm sitting down, is as large as a billiards table, and has a railroad map from the nineteen-thirties carved into the wood. It's covered with a thick sheet of glass (my mother had it custom made to fit, to modernise the table), and, in the centre, just as I suspected, is a ceramic bowl full of gummy bears.

Eliza arrives with two piping hot mugs of tea and a handful of rocks. *Crystals*. She's been really into crystal healing lately, it's her new passion— spending hours researching different meanings and uses, scattering different stones around the house. She's thinking of starting to grow herbs in the garden, seeing if that helps as well, and maybe investing in a psychic, if she can find one with good reviews. Which shouldn't be hard, in the city, but it's proving difficult to find one who isn't just a quack.

"Get out of my head, Caesar, I can feel your judgement," she sets down the tea without coasters (Mom would be furious, but I don't point it out) and sits back down on the loveseat. "It's harmless, you know. And besides, I think it does help, even if it's only just the power of positive thinking, or whatever." She fixes me with a withering glare. "Which you should know all about, Mr. Telepath."

I roll my eyes, but gesture to the crystals and the tea. "Go on, then, explain it to me."

She lights up, excitedly placing the stones in a line in front of my mug. "Okay, so this is Onyx—" she holds up an inky black stone— "which is supposed to, uh, provide personal strength. And this one is rose quartz—" a pale pink stone, rough, with some jagged edges— "and it's for soothing loss and promoting peace. *This* one is raw, which is supposed to make it more potent. Finally," she pauses and holds up the last piece, a greenish-blue stone about the size of my thumb. "This is amazonite. It helps to dispel grief. And the tea is chamomile. It's *calming*."

She says it all with a sense of assurance that I couldn't hope to obtain. I guess if these rocks are giving my sister some sort of peace, I can't knock them too much. I pick up the tea and take a long swallow. It settles, warm, in my stomach. Maybe it does help.

"I remember a little about Xander," she says, bringing her teacup to her mouth. "He was always nice to me and Carlos, even though we were so much younger. Remember how he used to rope you in to playing with us? He let me be a knight with him, and we saved Carlos from the witches."

"He didn't like the idea of slaying a dragon," I recall, "so our kingdom was always being attacked by witches and wizards and things, 'cause people made the *choice* to be evil, but a dragon was probably just looking for food or something."

"God, that's so like him," Eliza laughs. "He was always going after the bad guys."

"Yeah." I frown, pulling my eyebrows together. "He was."

We're quiet for what feels like an eternity. I sip my tea and stare at Eliza's rocks. Soothing loss, dispelling grief; as if. Xander is gone.

He's gone, and there's nothing I can do about it. Take that, you dumb rocks.

Eliza smiles at me for a heartbeat too long, and I start to feel uncomfortable. I'm not the one people should be pouring their sympathy on to. I should be helping Abyss and Mrs. Pae, not hovering around my sister's house, accepting pity.

"I'm sorry, Caesar," she says, "I can't imagine what it's like to be you right now."

My discomfort must show on my face, because she finishes her tea faster than is humanly possible (she is superhuman, after all, and although people don't appreciate it as being 'fast' the speed of sound is pretty damn impressive) and stands up. "All right," she says, clapping her hands together. "You don't get to feel… guilty. It's written all over your face. May I remind you that you have the coolest job in the world? I know it's got to be hard right now, but, at the end of the day, you're *helping people*. You should've heard what they were saying on the news. People care about you."

"People don't *know* me," I protest. "They'll see it on the news, or they'll read a script, and it'll tug at the heartstrings a little, and then, guess what, they'll move on with their lives!"

"It was your friend," she says, voice growing louder. I'm never sure if she's yelling, or just amplifying "It was Abyss!"

Abyss was on the news? *When*?

Eliza smirks at my obviously evident confusion. "It was like an hour ago, some reporter caught her leaving the flower shop. They asked her if she was passing the news on to Xander's mom— I guess that's the trouble with you two not having secret identities, it's a hell of a lot easier to find you— and she said that she was. They asked who she was texting and she said *you*."

Abs-tract: *thx fr lst nite. hop ur ok. <3 u*

I got a that text from Abyss about an hour and a half ago. If she'd left just after Ace arrived— and she wouldn't have left a second before, not a chance she'd leave Mrs Pae alone, not today— and the reporters were already there, then it would make sense. Not that Eliza has any reason to lie about it, anyway.

Eliza is still talking. "My point is, *William*," and now I know I'm in trouble, if she's calling me by that name, "you have no reason to feel guilty. You saved lives. You lost someone. You're allowed to mourn."

"Am I?"

The question is out of my mouth before I can stop it. My voice is quiet, low, deeper than usual and thick with some emotion that I don't want to name. Grief, I know it's grief. I can feel tears prickling at my eyes again, and Eliza coos, comes over to squeeze her way on to the armchair and wrap her arms around me. She's so young, so fragile. I wrap around her up in a big hug, cry into her shoulder.

"He's gone," I say, and then, "he's dead."

The word feels heavy on my tongue.

Hours later, when I leave my childhood home, I feel lighter. Eliza had let me cry my guts out onto her new shirt, stroking my back and whispering assurances that it was all going to be okay, and that it wasn't my fault. I'm still not sure I believe her, but it did help to be with family.

I think I made her promise to never become a superhero.

But I can admit that Ace was right— as awful as confronting it all was, as wrung out as I feel after crying for that long, it would have been a million times worse to go through that on my own. I pull out my phone to text a thank you.

Me: *U were right; needed company today. Hope ur ok too.*

Ace-thetics: *im always right. stay safe cee :)*

I call Aaron for pickup, and as I move to put my phone back in my pocket, I feel it buzz. Assuming it's Ace again, I roll my eyes as I click to answer it.

Abs-tract: *ki sys u shd com fr din tmrrw*

It takes me a half-second longer than it should to realise that she's talking about Ki Pae, Xander's mom. The idea makes my heart stop and my blood run cold.

Me: *I don't know if I'm ready to see her.*

Abs-tract: *sh dsnt blm u*

Abs-tract: *i dnt blm u*

Me: *I blame me, though. I was supposed to be in his head. I should've been there. I should've been with him. He shouldn't have been alone, Abs…*

Abs-tract: *d u blm me?*

Me: *What? No!*

Abs-tract: *i dd th sm thngs u dd. blm me to thn*

Me: *U were being attacked by jamboree*

Abs-tract: *So were you.*

I stare at the text until Aaron pulls up, but I still don't have an answer for it. She used proper grammar, and spelt out the word 'you' for once in her life. I climb into the backseat and say that I want to go to home. Aaron salutes and starts to drive.

I stare out the window. I *was* being attacked by Jamboree, it's true. But Xander was trying to help with that, trying to stop her just as much as we were. Still, I appreciate what Abyss is trying to do. As we pull up to the building twenty-two minutes later, I finally reply, and even then it's nothing special. I can't think of anything that would properly convey how much she means to me in this moment, so I just say:

Me: *<3*

32.

The funeral is held one week later at the local LDS church.

It's the same one that he and his mother went to every Sunday, and the same one that he invited me to a few times when we were kids. And it's the same one he went to for YSA activities on Tuesday nights, which he also invited me to. I knew that his religion was important to him, and he wanted to share it simply because it made him happy. It's surreal, and depressing, to think that I'm finally going to his church, and it's because he's dead.

I'd picked up Abyss and Mrs. Pae, the three of us sitting side by side in the back of the car. It was the least I could do, I said. The only car Mrs. Pae has is the van that the flower shop uses, and Abyss told me that she was struggling with anything work related, lately.

Oddly, at least to me, we're not the first to arrive at the building. There's three other cars there when we pull up, and men in suits come over to shake Mrs. Pae's hand and offer condolences. I'm surprised when one of them greets Abyss by name and shakes her hand as well.

"I… go with them, sometimes," she whispers to me when he turns away. "I don't believe it, exactly, but it's still nice. That's the bishop, Bishop Flores."

When we head inside, Abyss walks with her head facing straight forwards. Her sunglasses hide her eyes, which makes hiding her emotions a little easier, I suppose. That and the whole 'Void' thing, which, even after seeing, I still don't really understand. Still, she's handling it all remarkably well, outwardly. She almost always wears all black, but this conservative black dress isn't a standard Abyss outfit- especially not with the yellow rose pinned the front, right over where her heart rests inside her.

Yellow roses. Friendship. Maybe it's common knowledge, but I only know because Xander told me. I have a feeling that's the one reason Abyss knows, too.

Mrs Pae is a little ways ahead with the group of men, wearing a black skirt and jacket, but a light yellow shirt. Black seems traditional, appropriate, but there's a lot of people here wearing not-black too. I wonder if that's normal for this religion. I guess it must be, because no one seems to be pointing it out, or even thinking about it.

Mrs. Pae has her head down, her hands folded against her chest. No one has tried to get her to speak yet, and I'm thankful for it on her behalf. I can't even bring myself to give her head a cursory glance, but I know that anyone trying to talk to her would break her. I think anyone trying to talk to me would break me, and Xander wasn't my son.

There're a lot of chairs set up in the chapel. They make a vaguely horseshoe shape, with a section at the front which I assume is meant to be for family, and a larger section at the back for everyone else. But Xander's extended family are all in Korea, and they didn't know him, not really, so it's unlikely that any of them specifically made the trip. He didn't have any siblings, and his dad died long before he did. There is only one family member here for him today.

Mrs. Pae reaches out, her arm spreading out and back. I don't know who exactly she's reaching for, but Abyss meets her in the middle and takes her hand. Mrs. Pae pulls her in, presses her to her side. Abyss lets herself be hugged, and even wraps an arm around Mrs. Pae. They make their way to the family section, and I'm left standing stupidly in the middle of the room, wondering where to go. And then Abyss turns around, and I assume she's trying to catch my eye, but it's always hard to tell with the sunglasses on (and she told me to get out of her head the day that Xander died, and I haven't gone back since), and jerks her head to tell me to come on.

I go, and I take a seat next to her.

Ava Layton arrives with her family shortly after, and she races over to Mrs. Pae. I flinch instinctually, but all she does is rest a hand against Mrs. Pae's shoulder, and Mrs. Pae covers said hand with her own for a moment. Ava takes the seat on the other side of Mrs. Pae, and her family settles in next to her.

I remember Xander saying that he thought their families sort of collectively believed that he and Ava would still end up married, and how Ava being superhuman made them all the more determined. Xander rolled his eyes when he said it, blowing his bangs up and away from his face. He went on to say something about how Ava was his best friend, and as good as family, and that he was so glad to have her in his life, but he'd never, ever marry her. I'd asked Ava about it, once, and she'd laughed in my face and said 'good, I don't want to marry him either.'

But she and her family sit with Mrs. Pae and I can't help but peek into their heads. I think Ava's parents are grieving their daughter's lost future, a little bit, even though they're mostly mourning Xander. Her mother thinks he was good, and her father's thoughts are a neat echo. Ava's mind is in chaos, jumping from one memory to another almost too quickly for me to keep up.

I expand my reach, brush across the top of everyone's thoughts. The room is filling up quickly; there's Zoram, and who I presume is his family, and a few other boys and girls who seem to be roughly the same age. They're all thinking about the time Xander taught their lesson when they were fourteen, and he told the story of Ammon and the Arms with more ferocity than anyone they'd ever heard. I guess they must be reminiscing together. I don't know the story, but it's familiar to them. There's a notable edge of grief to their thoughts; the memories tainted with something bittersweet.

There's an older couple who are traumatised by the fact they outlived him; a man only a few years older than me who's already crying at the thought that Xander won't ever teach again; a few families who gather together and remember Xander playing with the kids after church and youth activities when he was growing up—

At this rate, they'll need to pull out more chairs.

It's not just people from church, either, although they do make up the majority. Most of Ace's roommates have made the trip as well, all dressed more formally than I've ever seen them. I catch Ace's eye, and she waves, offers a tight smile. She's worried that her skirt is too short to be considered funeral-appropriate, but it's the best she has. I wave back.

There's a few people I recognise from the photos around Xander's room— school friends, I assume. The guy who he helped at the flower shop two weeks ago, who he'd had a familiarity with that went beyond flowers. A stranger who stands near the back of the room and doesn't speak to anyone.

All these people who Xander touched, in some way, who he loved and who loved him in return. All of them are thinking of Xander, to some extent, are remembering him and missing him and aching for him, and I'm remembering him and missing him and aching for him myself, and on behalf of all these people—

Abyss has her hand on mine, and I tear away from everyone in room and focus on her. She'd got her head titled just so to look up at me. I realise suddenly that I'm crying; there are sticky, wet tears clinging to my face and eyelashes. I have to blink a few times before I can properly see her.

"Come on," she says, a murmur that I can barely hear. "Stay with me."

I look at her quizzically, and she huffs, moves her head in a motion that I think implies she's rolling her eyes. "Stay in my head."

She'd told me to get out, last week, and I had. But she's offering it again. I ask her if she's sure before I accept, and I enter the blissful quiet and serene of the Void.

It's hard to explain what the Void is— all I know for sure is that Abyss and the Void are one and the same. I've only seen it the once, and I have to take a few moments to get used to it. It's distinctly not a human mind, but it's still full up with memories and emotions and Abyss is *unbearably* sad. It's showing outwardly, now that I can see her face more clearly, with tear tracks peeking out from under her glasses, and her mind is, like everyone else in the room, focused on Xander. But the Void distills it, at least for me. I'm sure Abyss is feeling it all, overwhelmingly, unbearably, but for me, an outsider, it feels almost numb. It's exactly what I need, so I'm not taken in by everyone else's thoughts and emotions. I think Abyss knew that. It's nice, to be known.

I hear my name, the short, light whisper of 'Caesar!' and I turn to see my mother and father, along with my youngest sibling, Carlos, approaching me. They'd been in Greece. I didn't know that they were coming.

My mother comes and sits down next to me, threading our arms together and pressing a kiss to my temple. Carlos and Eliza, the latter of which they must have been staying with, take the two seats directly behind us. Eliza claps me on the shoulder, and Carlos immediately begins to fiddle with the program.

"I didn't— I didn't know you were coming," I say, looking between my mother and my siblings.

"Of course we came," my mother says, like it's the most obvious thing in the world. "Xander meant a lot to us. Charlie and Farah are on their way, too."

I blink a few times. Charlie and her wife, Farah, had been staying in Monaco, some sort of couples getaway for their six-month anniversary. The idea that the two of them would fly back for this makes me want to cry. I love my family so much; I'm struck with the thought that Mrs. Pae doesn't have any. I glance over, and see that her arm is still linked with Abyss's.

Shortly thereafter, Bishop Flores, takes the podium— *pulpit*, according to Abyss' thoughts— and introduces himself.

We stand for the procession; Mrs. Pae sobs into her hand, and Ava and Abyss both take an arm and physically support her. I think that Mrs. Pae might really fall over without them. I think I might fall over, honestly. There's a coffin, and Xander is inside it, and he's dead. He's been dead for a little over a week. Today, we're going to bury him.

The coffin is set almost directly in front of us; I can't tear my eyes away. I stare at the flowers and wonder if they're what Xander would've picked. And then I notice the type of flower and can't hold back a small laugh.

Abyss turns to look at me oddly, and I smile as I send the thought her way. *Hydrangeas.* Xander's least favourite.

I see the moment that Abyss gets it, because she looks at the flowers, then back at me, and then she's laughing too. It's all in her mind, in the Void, and it's short-lived, but I decide to count it anyway. *Heartlessness*, she thinks. *Heartlessness, that's what they mean.*

Given how much love is in this room, it seems incredibly incongruous. Ironic. I have to stop myself from laughing. Abyss turns her head to glance at me and immediately looks away. I feel the Void sucking her amusement away, to stop anything showing on her face, her version of biting back a smile.

She and Ava don't let go of Mrs. Pae even after we sit down. I can't blame them.

There's a program that I haven't looked at, so I pick it up and flip through. Talks and songs. I've never been to a funeral before; I wonder if this is typical, or just a this-religion thing. Someone goes up the pulpit to say a prayer, so I mimic everyone around me and bow my head. It's sweet, but tearful. I guess that's to be expected. I'm hit with another wave of gratitude to Abyss for letting me hide in her head; I don't want to be picking up random waves of peoples thoughts or emotions.

Brother Flores introduces Ava Layton, and I watch as she removes herself from Mrs. Pae's grip and heads up to the pulpit herself. I hadn't even registered that she was giving one of the talks.

"Sun-Young Alexander Pae," she starts, her eyes misty but her voice strong. "We all called him Xander, but to some of us—" she looks significantly at me and Abyss— "he was also called something else. It's with permission from his mother that I tell you something many of you already suspected, and a few of you already knew." I see her eyes skip over to where Zoram is sitting, but he doesn't look up. "Xander Pae was Legion."

A few murmurs break out across the room, and Ava lets them. Bishop Flores, who's sitting just behind her, looks up at her sharply. I wonder if he knew. I wonder if he's worried.

"I don't tell you this to shock you," she says, once the quiet is restored. "I tell you this because Xander loved people. He *loved* everyone in this room. I've never known anyone like him— I doubt," here, her voice shakes, just slightly, only momentarily, "I will ever meet anyone like him again. If you want an example of Christlike love, he was it. Legion was considered by many to be ruthless, dangerous. A force to be reckoned with. I wonder if your opinions will change, now that you know he was Xander Pae. Xander Pae, who worked at the flower shop and came to Mutual with roses in his hair."

A few of the boys sitting near Zoram break into startled, amused laughter.

"Xander Pae," Ava continues, "who danced like no one was watching and also made sure to ask someone lonely to dance when slow songs came on."

The girls are smiling watery smiles and squeezing each others hands.

"Xander Pae," she looks, again, at me and Abyss, "who wanted to change the world in whatever small way he possibly could, and did so by fighting against evil with his friends."

There're some half-hidden looks shot our way. People here must've known that Xander was friends with superheroes— neither Abyss or I have secret identities— but I wonder how many of them came to the logical conclusion. I'm sure some of them joked about it, laughing it off as an impossibility. I wonder how much it annoyed Xander, to be underestimated like that.

I guess I'll never know.

The rest of her talk takes a much more religious tone, but mostly, it's a memorial. She reminisces with the congregation, recounts his stories, and, tearfully, finishes with, "I know Xander is safe, now, and has been welcomed home. And," she looks at Mrs. Pae, who smiles tearfully up at her, "I know his dad is there, waiting for him. Xander was a good man."

She flees the pulpit after saying 'amen' and races back to her seat. Mrs. Pae opens an arm for her, and Ava settles in with her head against her shoulder. Bishop Flores introduces the next speaker, who turns out to be a middle-aged man who introduces himself as Xander's YSA leader. I nudge Abyss' mind and she returns with a flurry of memories; sitting in lessons or at bowling alleys with this guy leading a group of people all around our age.

I barely pay attention to his talk. It's nothing against him, but he doesn't have the vocal cadence that Ava does, and I'm stuck on the fact that the people who are speaking at this funeral are connected to Xander through his youth. He was younger than me by a couple of months, only twenty years old.

Abyss reaches out and takes my hand in hers. Without thinking, I thread our fingers together and squeeze. *It sucks,* she thinks, bluntly. I nearly laugh at the understatement.

It really sucks, she thinks again, staring at the coffin.

The current speaker finishes, steps down, and I watch as Zoram walks up to say a closing prayer. He doesn't cross his arms like other people do, but braces himself against the pulpit, his dark fingers curled around the edges. He offers a prayer with careful, slow words, and he doesn't cry. Afterwards, as people start to stand and talk again, he comes over to us.

He shakes my hand as Abyss helps Mrs. Pae to her feet. Ava's eyes flick between Mrs. Pae and Zoram until she finally stands besides him. We form a vaguely circular shape. Zoram releases my hand and I let it fall back to my side. Abyss brushes the back of her hand against mine.

"Xander never specifically told me he was Legion," he says, still in that careful, slow voice of his. He always seemed so mellow, a calming influence to Xander and Ava. "But I knew about his ability, so I put two and two together. Especially after I met you and Abyss. If he was going to go," Zoram licks his lips, "he would've wanted to go doing something he believed in."

"And he believed in being a superhero?" I ask wryly, and to my surprise, Zoram and Ava both nod.

"He thought it was… important," Ava smiles. "He didn't go on a mission because he felt that he had another way to serve— his ability. He always wanted to help people."

"He prayed about it a lot." We're all startled when Mrs. Pae speaks. She looks at us with fond exasperation. "I am able to talk, you know. My son has… passed on, but I can still talk. He prayed about it a lot. He felt that this was where he was supposed to be. So do I."

I notice the use of present tense and feel tension I didn't know I was holding bleed out of my spine. Abyss grabs my hand and gives a short squeeze, as though to say: *see? I told you she didn't blame us*.

At the graveside, it's just Mrs. Pae, Abyss, the Laytons, and my family. It's a much more sombre affair. I'd never thought about how morbid it is to drive bodies around from place to place so that people can stare at a coffin and cry. Mrs. Pae is going to have dinner with the Laytons, so she hugs me and Abyss goodbye after Abyss shuffles awkwardly and says she'd rather not go. I tell Mrs. Pae that I'll take her home.

My family hover around for a little while after that. My mom wraps me in a backbreaking hug. I'm sure she had the same realisation that I did; Xander was even younger than me.

My dad is chatting with Abyss a few steps away. Mom follows my gaze and smiles brightly despite the situation. "She's a brilliant girl, isn't she?"

"Yeah," I say, "a genius."

"I didn't just mean her intellect." I'm not sure what to make of that, so I stay quiet until she speaks again. "We're staying at the house with Eliza for a few more days, if you need us. Dad is going to be staying longer for some work stuff. I think he's going to do some more training with you, but don't worry too much if you're not up for it. You're more than welcome to come stay with us tonight, if you want."

I look at Abyss again. "I think I'm okay tonight, Mom. But let's go out for dinner before you and Carlos head home, okay? How about Thursday?"

We set a date and time, and I agree, after she pesters a little bit, to invite Abyss along as well. They pile into their car, leaving me and Abyss alone at the entrance to the graveyard.

"Mexican?" I ask.

"I know you are," she says lightly, and the humour of it catches me off guard.

"Mexican food?" I clarify, grinning. "We could go back to mine, watch some comedy specials."

I'm still in her head, so I can see the moment that she brightens and decides to agree, just a split second before she nods. I should probably leave the Void, leave her, but I don't really want to. Still, I let out a mental sigh and pull, slowly, carefully away. She looks at me oddly, and I shrug.

"I figured you wouldn't want me hanging out in there forever," I apologise. Without actively trying to be in her head, I can't get anything, not even a slight wave of thought, so I'm confused at her stiff shouldered shrug.

"Yeah," she agrees, voice level. "Probably not."

33.

It's three days after the funeral and Abyss hasn't left my couch for anything other than grabbing food from delivery guys. I don't mind; I haven't moved very much either. After the second day, Mrs. Pae had stopped by with a bag of clothes and Abyss' laptop, so now she's sectioned off a portion of my couch for her work, curling up to type away.

I ask, "what are you working on?"

"We need to decide what we're going to do about Jamboree," she answers, pushing her hands under her glasses to rub at her eyes. "She's not going away forever, and I want to make sure that we're ready when she comes back."

I flash back to the portals opening in and around Abyss. It makes me shudder, to remember that pain. And Jamboree had left through another portal shortly afterwards. I have no idea where she could've gone, but I assume it's out of this universe. Why would she hang around here, when she has the entire multiverse at her fingertips? Especially when she knows there are people looking for her?

Abyss was her friend, once, and I do think that some part of her still is. I'll have to defer to her on this. "Any ideas on how she'll come back? Or when?"

Abyss shakes her head. "She's changed a lot. I don't know what she's going to be like now. I didn't even know she could enter portals… When I knew her, she could only watch through them."

She sounds the same as she always does; level and monotone. Sometimes, she'll imbue some texture into her voice, but not often— it takes a lot out of her, to pull them out of the Void. She explained it, once, as her emotions having somewhere else to go, and apologised if it made her seem cold. She doesn't seem cold to me, not anymore — she just seems like Abyss.

"Did she have a favourite?"

"Back then," Abyss says, tipping her head towards me, "we were just kids, really. The universe she showed me most was this alternate version of us… It's where she took me at your sister's wedding. The one with the dampeners. I think it's… diverged a lot, but I couldn't tell you exactly how. And I have no idea if she'd go there on her own."

I have to wonder what we're missing. "You can't think of anything else?"

Even in her monotone, I can tell she's annoyed when she replies, "Even if I could, I have no idea if it's possible for us to go there without Jamboree's portals."

"But it could give us insight into what she's planning," I point out, then immediately throw my hands up as Abyss purses her lips. "I'm sorry, I know it's not your fault. I'm just…"

I think of Xander (red, red, red) and shake myself. If I can convince myself that was entirely Jamboree's fault, and if I can help stop

Jamboree for good, then maybe I can move on from all of that. If not, I think the guilt of it is going to eat me alive.

Abyss shrugs, dropping down against the couch cushions and stretching her legs out so her feet brush against my thigh. I look away. I know she's just trying her best. I know we both want to stop Jamboree. I just wish we had *something* to go off of, and we don't. Xander is dead, and we don't have anything to avenge him with.

Vengeance was never Xander's style. He'd probably be ashamed that it was my first course of action. If I'd been the one to die, he would've wanted to stop Jamboree, not for revenge, but so that no one else got hurt.

But I'm not Xander. I'm selfish, I know.

"Maybe…" Abyss' voice is small, "Maybe you could take a look?"

My startled expression must show on my face, because Abyss immediately looks away. It's not that I wouldn't do it, or even that I don't want to, but I can't help my surprise at the suggestion. I was grateful when she offered her mind at the funeral, but this is something else all together. This is a moment when it's unnecessary, and she's still inviting me in.

"I could," I reply, slowly, "if you're sure you're happy for me to."

Abyss looks back to me. I don't process the fact that she's moving until her glasses are off.

It's easy to get sucked in, easy to feel half-hypnotised by her eyes. There's a reason she keeps them covered by thick, tinted sunglasses. The reason is this: if they aren't, people don't look away. The Void is dangerous, or at least that's what Abyss always says, and on the few occasions that I've looked directly into it, or *been* in it, I've understood why.

I feel hollow, empty in my stomach. Confusion worms its way to the forefront of my thoughts, and then an unnamable nervousness. The Void sucks me in and leaves me without so much as a goodbye.

And 'I get lost in her eyes' is supposed to be a cliché.

"I'm okay with it if you are," she says. I can't take my eyes off of hers.

"My mind to your mind," I quip. The Void welcomes me. Abyss welcomes me. *My thoughts to your thoughts.*

As it was at the funeral, the Void is filled with an eery calm. I can feel Abyss' thoughts drifting by but they aren't overwhelming. I know if I reach out, I could grab at them, turn them into something concrete and maybe even begin to understand them. If I look, I'm sure I can find her memories, shuffle through them like Ace shuffles her cards. Abyss' mind is more organised than most; presumably, it's a side effect of being a universe.

But it's *more* than just her mind— it's something physical, something concrete, that exists outside of firing neurones. When I read someones mind, normally, I get impressions, flashes of memory. Most people don't *think* in perfectly constructed sentences; it's more flashes of images or fragments of language or a series of seemingly random connections that can be hard to follow. Here, I can see what I can only describe as a landscape, although that's not entirely the correct word. The entire place is lit up in swirling masses of colours, like space dust. It's like I really have sunk into Abyss' eyes.

It is not a human mind.

I watch thoughts and emotions (there aren't words to describe how I 'see' these things, but I do; I physically see them, because they, somehow, impossibly, exist in this physical space) dance around me. It's beautiful. It's incredible. It's eery and calm and *perfect*. This is Abyss, and I am blown away.

Abyss smiles, maybe laughs; normally I'd say such things aren't quite possible inside someone's head, but the rules are different here. There's an entire universe laid out at my feet— or my mind— and it's taking every ounce of my self-control to stay where I am, to go only where I'm invited.

Is it always like this, for you?

In answer, I get a series of impressions in quick succession. She's unemotional in her day to day life because all of her emotions come here. She's able to focus so singularly because all other thoughts come here. She feels the Void call out to her, a unique emotion she thinks of as 'Void Calling', but she isn't always here. It's only when her conscious mind comes here that it's like this.

What's it like otherwise?

Quiet; a science lab with all the lights off, only the occasional beep of a machine, with no one to see the reason.

When she's here, this is her truest self.

She's letting me see her truest self; the self she's only just begun to accept. It almost makes me want to cry.

Where are your memories?

I don't know if we'll have to physically travel, here. I'm still vaguely aware of my body, sitting on my couch, hand in hand with Abyss, but it's distant, unimportant. I feel like I could walk, here, to get from place to place, physical manifestation of thought to physical manifestation of thought. We do, sort of. Our bodies aren't here, but some sort of indication of our minds are, or must be. I can't see her, but I'm aware of her beside me.

Her memories are stored near some swirl of sky-blue (although it seems odd to apply the word 'sky' to a place which has no sky). I feel her nudge me towards it.

Think about Jamboree.

I immediately regret saying it when I'm overwhelmed with ideas-images-impressions of Jamboree; portals opening through Abyss' body, screeching accusations of abandonment. I relive, from Abyss' perspective, the moment that Jamboree slapped her across the face, and come away from the memory shaking, spitting mad.

I need a moment; I pull back, ever so slightly, and see Abyss' questioning confusion twist around me. I send a wave of reassurance back. I just need to think, and to do that I need to be at least partially removed from her mind, from this situation.

And just like that, I know what will help me sort through these memories. Something with less negative associations, something removed, at least partially, from this situation.

Abs, think about JuJu.

It makes all the difference. Impressions appear from when they were just kids. Jamboree— Julia Lago, then— is softer here.

Each memory blends seamlessly into the next, and I watch Jamboree grow up, come in to herself. Abyss goes to high school when they're ten years old, but at night she and Jamboree watch cartoons and child-oriented television. Sleepovers when they're a little too old to be calling them 'sleepovers'. A bedroom that must be Abyss' covered in posters with science puns and pictures of the two friends. Jamboree, laughing. Julia, crying. She fails science in Freshman year, the same year that Abyss starts the second year of her physics degree, but they only grow closer for it. They study together, Abyss talking a mile-a-minute about things I have no hope of understanding.

"Jenna-Louise," she says, "you're brilliant!"

"There must be a universe where I'm not."

A giggle. They're laying on Abyss' bed. Black bedspread, but colourful throw pillows.

"A universe where you're not brilliant isn't a universe I want to see."

"Show me."

"Never."

"Show me something else, then. Our favourite."

They join hands, and Jamboree- Julia- waves a hand to open a portal. I wonder if Abyss could only see the portals if they were physically linked, back then. I see, through her eyes, the familiar oval swirl (not a tear or a fold or a wrinkle, but something far more natural, a space in-between the multiverse) and feel, through her heart, a sense of mystified awe (not fear or fear or fear, but something warm and heartfelt).

And, through the portal, some alternate version of the same girls, laying on that same bed, chatting aimlessly, shoving at each other. *Those* girls existed in a universe almost parallel. *Those* girls would make different decisions in the future, but they hadn't yet. This is the universe that Abyss talked about.

Do you wonder about them now?

Always, the answer comes. She wonders about them always, wonders what decisions they made that branched them away from our timeline. She wonders if, maybe, that other her doesn't have her connection to the Void. If that other her didn't lose her best friend and her life's work in one fell swoop. If that other her met Xander, met me, if we were friends enough without her abilities.

I can't imagine a universe where I don't want to be your friend.

Hope, overwhelming, blinding hope, a joyful exuberance that consumes the Void, consumes her mind. Abyss is *happy*, overwhelmed with the emotion. It rubs off on me. I almost feel dizzy.

My phone rings.

I'm startled out of our connection; it doesn't sever easily, as I was much deeper in her mind than I ever am with most people, but I drag myself away, back into my own mind. Abyss lets go of my hand quickly, and it feels cold at the sudden absence.

"It's my mom," I say, apologetic. I could stay in her mind forever, easily. Instead, I watch her nod, and answer my phone.

"Caesar," Mom snaps, "where on Earth are you?"

I have to bite back a smile at the wording. I picture saying 'I wasn't on *Earth*, Mom, I was busy in another universe, and if you don't mind, I'd really like to go back to it.' But she wouldn't understand that — despite being superhuman, my family doesn't really 'get' my telepathy, and, as much as I love them, I doubt they'd 'get' the Void, either. I hardly get it.

I ask, "What do you mean?"

"Dinner, Caesar, remember?"

It's Thursday. I'd forgotten. Mom made reservations at a fancy restaurant only a few minutes away, for my convenience. I glance at Abyss, who, hearing the conversation, is standing and digging through the clothes Mrs. Pae brought her. "Right, sorry," I say, stalling for time. "I was just… helping Abs get ready. She's never been before, and doesn't know what to wear. We'll be there soon, I promise."

"We can only stall the waiters for so long, you know," she says, but I know she's not really annoyed. Mentioning Abyss has that effect on my parents. I think they like her more than they like me, sometimes. "Hurry, okay?"

"Okay," I agree. "We'll rush."

34.

Abyss really doesn't know what to wear. She only owns one dress— the black one she wore to Xander's funeral— and it's laying in a crumpled heap on the floor where she discarded it as soon as she got other clothes. But she does have a forest green sweater. It's cashmere, soft to the touch when I brush against her arm. She pairs it with some dark trousers and a pair of sleek lace-up boots. As I change into slacks and a button-down, she picks at her go-to braids. "I need to get them redone," she moans. "But it's kind of a pain. My mom and I used to do them for each other, but now it's like, I've got to find someone."

I'm still tying my tie as we board the elevator and ride it down to the ground floor.

"No driver today?" Abyss asks when we exit the building, eyebrows raised.

"It's only a two minute walk away."

"You told your mom you were helping me get ready. Will she buy it if we show up on foot? We would've have walked from Pae's Flowers to here."

I blink. It hadn't hit me that my mom would assume we weren't in my penthouse. I suddenly remember that Abyss doesn't live there, no matter how used to her presence I've gotten. It's only been three days.

"They'll already be inside," I say, but I'm not sure. "They won't notice."

Thankfully, when we arrive at the restaurant, a little out of breath from power walking, I'm right. We spend a few seconds levelling out our breathing before I open the door for her, and we slip inside. I barely have time to open my mouth before the hostess is smiling at me. "Caesar," she says warmly. I try to remember if I've seen her before, when I've been here. "Your family is already seated. If you give me one moment, I'll take you over there—"

She's cut on when Eliza comes around the corner and ambushes me in a hug. I stumble backwards, but wrap her into a hug anyway. "How long were you standing there?"

"Long enough. I've gotten good at making myself completely silent," she replies, then catches sight of Abyss over my shoulder. She laughs, and then, whispers (or at least suppresses the sound), "Mom's gonna have a field day."

As I pull away, I must look confused, because she points at my tie and glances significantly at Abyss. "You match."

I look down. I hadn't even realised I'd picked a green tie, almost the exact same colour as Abyss' sweater. I wonder if Abyss noticed, or what she thought about it.

Eliza waves for us to follow her to the table, and I smile apologetically at the hostess. Abyss thanks her as she walks past to join me, and the hostess smiles at her in return. I wait for Abyss to catch up, and she falls into step beside me. Eliza grins at Abyss over her shoulder. "So, you excited? I think half the reason Mom pushed so hard for this dinner was because Dad wants to interrogate your genius."

Abyss shrugs. "I'm sure it's just because they miss being together as a family."

"Then why didn't they push for Charlie and Farah to be here, too?"

"Are they not here?" I ask, surprised. "I thought they'd stay."

"Yeah, we thought so too," Eliza brushes it off, "but they only came down for— you know. They've gone off back to Monaco. I guess we can't blame them *too* much. It is their 'anniversary' trip."

Abyss is quiet, so I reach out to brush the back of my hand against hers. She turns to face me, but she's unreadable behind her glasses. I wish I could slip back into her mind. I wish I could stay there. She lifts the very corners of her mouth into a tiny, knowing smile, and for a moment I feel bare, open, like she's the telepath.

Our moment, if you can call it that, is broken by my Mom squealing and coming around the table to greet us. Eliza has taken her seat, but Abyss and I didn't move fast enough, and now Mom is holding her arms open for a hug. I oblige her. "Hi, Mom."

She smiles at me and moves over to hug Abyss. Abyss returns it, but I can see a slight stiffness in her. After a moment, my Mom seems to clock on and pulls away, patting her shoulder gently instead. Abyss smiles gratefully. We take our seats at the table, and I'm unsurprised to see that Abyss' seat is right next to my dad.

William Antonio Caesar II. Current CEO of the Caesar Corporation and a genius in his own right, my dad has spent the last twenty-eight years (since he married my mom) changing the game for superhumans. Back in the day— like, the seventies or something— it was nearly impossible for superhumans to get work outside the service or entertainment industries. We were novelties, I guess, and we brought in good money. Circuses could be more outrageous when you had people who could fly or talk to animals; special effects could be nearly obsolete if you had people who could control fire or water or lightning.

By '85, things were already starting to change, but there were still expectations that meant superhumans struggled to find work in quote-unquote intellectual areas. When my dad, an already prominent figure because of his dad's company, married my mom, who never hid away from her ability, in the nineties, it was some sort of big scandal. My grandpa had a lot of thoughts on that, but he was already sort of crazy, so they mostly just ignored it.

My mom's a technopath, which means she can control any technology. The Caesar Corporation *makes* technology, or at least researches it intensively. Mom applied for a job there, and that's how my parents met. I think it's crazy that someone who could literally control technology was all but barred from working with it, and so did my dad. From then on, he fought to change that.

With my mom beside him, they've definitely helped. It's still not a perfect world, and I know lots of superhumans still feel like they have no choices, but it's better than it was. I think the resurgence of superheroes will really help with that. There were loads of superheroes in the sixties, but it fell out of fashion pretty suddenly. I think the fact that they're— *we're*— back is helping along the idea that we should have different, varied jobs.

Dad loves Abyss. They've only ever met briefly, but he thinks she's absolutely amazing. I think he admires her brilliance, and he definitely wants to offer her a job.

"Abyss!" He greets her, shaking her hand. I wonder if he ever contacted her, like he said he was going to, or if he's just going to take this as an opportunity to speak with her. "It's good to see you. Now, my lovely wife will have to forgive me for talking business at the dinner table, but I do want to have a quick conversation with you, if you're amenable."

Abyss nods, and I try to pay attention but Mom steals my attention away. "How's school going?"

I don't really have the heart to tell her that I haven't gone all week. If I did, I'm sure she'd understand; I've just lost someone, and I've been grieving, but I don't really want her sympathetic looks, either. It's only the first week of classes, anyway, so I don't feel bad telling her that it's going well, and that I've mostly been reading the syllabuses.

"I'm glad to hear it," she smiles. "I know that your dad was very excited that at least one of his children decided to pursue business.

He really wanted one of you to take over the company." She shoots pointed looks and Eliza and Carlos, but I know she's not actually mad. I'm sure she and Dad would be disappointed if none of us had wanted to take the company, but I did. Mostly because I didn't know what else I'd do. Charlie always loved writing and journalism, Eliza's wanted to teach since she was eleven, and Carlos doesn't really have that much ambition, but he's started some video making thing online, and it seems to be going well for him. I never really had anything that called out to me like they do, so I decided to follow in Dad's footsteps.

The condition on any of us getting the company was that we had to attend business school, and then work in various different departments, taking orders and responsibilities from others, and learning about the company from the bottom up. I worked a summer job in the mailroom when I was sixteen. I was a secretary last year. I'm not sure what's next, exactly, but that's okay. I'm busy enough as-is.

"I'm a long way from taking over the company, Mána," I reply, and she smiles fondly at me. "I've not even finished school. Speaking of, aren't we all so excited for Eliza to start school?"

Carlos laughs, elbows her playfully. "Oh yeah," he says, "taking her in for her first day of kindergarten is going to be *emotional*."

Eliza rolls her eyes at him. With three years difference between them, Carlos Killian is only fifteen years old. He's hyperactive and never stops moving, which is only compounded by the fact that he can teleport. There's an empty chair on Eliza's other side, next to me, which I had to assume is for him, so he can bounce between seats.

Mom shushes him. "We *are* very excited, Elizabeth, dear," she says, reaching across to squeeze her hand. "Teaching is a noble profession, and learning is the foundation of it."

"Thanks, Mom," Eliza says, although it sounds a little bit exasperated.

Mom's just trying to be supportive, and she's worried that she's growing distant from her daughters. With Charlie spending most of her time travelling with Farah and Eliza moving back here, she's equal parts excited and terrified for them. And she *misses* them, so much. Misses the whole family, really, all of us being together. It's not just her daughters she's watching grow up, after all— she misses me, too, and worries for my safety every waking moment. The funeral was like looking to her future, she may not have long left with any of us. It's why she's so glad to be—

"You're moving back?" I ask, a little louder than I intended to.

I startled Dad and Abyss out of their conversation. Eliza looks sharply between Mom and Dad. I'm still staring at Mom, waiting for her to say *something*.

"Sometimes," she says, sounding pleasantly exhausted. "I forget we have a telepath in the family."

"We're moving back?" Carlos asks. He sounds startled and out of breath. He was only eight when we went to Greece, and he's always liked routine. "Since *when*? What about my school or my friends?"

She sighs, gestures for him to come closer. He disappears and abruptly reappears in the empty seat, so he's between Eliza and Mom. It's subtle enough that no one else in the restaurant will notice. "Nothing has been decided yet. Your brother jumps to conclusions."

I want to say 'you can't lie in your mind!' but before I can, Abyss reaches over and places her hand on my thigh. I turn to her and she shakes her head incrementally. She's right; Mom is trying to soothe Carlos, and anything I have to say will only make it worse.

"We've just been thinking about it, over the past few days," Mom continues, and in her mind I sense the unspoken *since the funeral*. "Eliza and Caesar both live here, and Farah's family, too, so Charlie is bound to be here often enough. It might make sense to come back."

"You're worried Caesar's gonna die," Carlos says bluntly. "If he's gonna, it won't make any difference where we live."

"Carlos," Dad warns, an uncomfortable sternness in is voice. Dad never yelled growing up, but he got tough, hard as stone, when he needed us to listen. I feel my stomach tighten, suddenly guilty— I shouldn't have said anything, I shouldn't have read Mom's mind. I didn't even mean to, it just sort of happened; human minds are like an open book— or a billboard that I can't *help* reading. It's just there, and before I know it I've processed it.

The tension at the table is suddenly very high, and when a young waiter arrives to take our orders, we're all very stiff. The poor guy must realise something is off, because he jots them all down without much talk and bolts as soon as we're done. Abyss' hand is still resting on my thigh, and I think it's as much for her benefit as it is for mine.

"I shouldn't have said anything," I finally mumble. "I was just— surprised."

Dad's eyes soften marginally. "I know, William, but…"

He doesn't have to say it. "I shouldn't've been in her head, I know."

Eliza's eyes widen. I wonder if this is the first time she's seen me actually get in trouble for it. Carlos looks between Mom and me for a few seconds before appearing back in the seat next to me. Abyss turns her head slowly to face my dad. I wish I could see inside her head; I don't want her to think less of him because of this— he doesn't mean anything by it, and, in all honesty, I should be better about controlling it.

I've always known things that I shouldn't. From the time I was nine years old I was privy to private thoughts and communications. I haven't been surprised by a birthday present in eleven years. It's always frustrated Dad, a little bit.

Dad looks around the table, meeting the hard eyes of my siblings. "I know you can't help it," he says, quiet. I glance at Eliza, and I'm pretty sure she's dialling down the volume of our table. "I don't mean to imply that you shouldn't… ever read people's minds. I just don't think it's right to broadcast people's secrets."

"It was hardly a secret," Eliza spits. "It was something that effects all of us, which, hopefully, you would've discussed with us tonight. Caesar's reaction was the same mine would've been if you'd said it out loud. He just gets there faster."

Mom places a hand on Eliza's again, then turns to look at Dad. "You don't get it," she reminds him, "you just *don't*. I know that you try. You've been trying for thirty years, and I love you for it. But you don't understand. Being superhuman isn't something that you can shut off… Even right now, I can feel the hum of my phone, or the cash machines, or the waiters devices. Charlie is always drawn to an open flame."

"When you used to take us for drives," Carlos adds, "I felt trapped. I said I was claustrophobic, but really it was that it was too slow. I need things to be fast."

Eliza nods her agreement. "And I need noise. All the time. I feel really weird when it's dead quiet. It's why exams are always so hard for me."

I lick my lips, watching Dad for any sort of outward reaction and carefully avoiding slipping into his mind. It's not the first time we've had this conversation; although, it is the first time that the rest of the family has been involved. I wonder if, hearing that other superhumans also can't shut it off, he'll finally understand that I don't do it to be rude.

"I wasn't born superhuman," Abyss says, catching my dad off guard. The rest of the table as well, judging by the way all their eyes snap to her. "It didn't develop naturally. It happened in a lab, because for all my genius I can be incredibly stupid sometimes. But even for me," she's looking at my dad, and he seems the slightest bit intimidated by the blankness of her stare with the glasses in the way. "It's not something I can slip away from. For the rest of my life, I will be different, because of my abilities."

Her hand slides away from me before I can stop it. "I'm sorry, this is a family matter."

She moves to stand up, despite protests from my mom and me. It's Dad's voice that finally gets her to still. "Thank you, Abyss," he says, and she sinks slowly back into the chair. "You're all right, of course, I don't get it. William has tried to explain it to me more times than I can count. I misunderstood the way that your abilities worked, and for that I apologise. You should be able to feel comfortable with yourself and your ability, especially around your family."

I nod at him, and watch gratefully as my siblings relax. I know my dad loves me, and more than that I know he's trying. Every parent struggles to understand their child, I think, and Dad has the added disadvantage of children who are superhuman. But I appreciate the effort, and I appreciate my family coming to my defence.

"Love you, Dad," I say, and the tension starts to diffuse as we move on to different topics.

The rest of the dinner passes with far less excitement. We talk about the company, and Eliza's schooling, and Carlos's videos. Abyss talks a little about her old studies, which she says she misses more than anything. Maybe I can do something to help her finally get her doctorate. It's an idea worth revisiting.

When we stand to say our goodbyes, Dad takes me aside and speaks in a whisper. "I am sorry," he says, "You'd think after eleven years of overheard thoughts I'd know better, but I'm still learning. It shouldn't be your job to teach me."

"I know you're trying," I smile, because it's the most honest thing to say. "That counts for a lot."

We rejoin the group and head out of the restaurant. I text Aaron that I'll need a ride to Pae's Flowers before I go home, and he responds that he'll be here promptly. Mom *does* make a fuss over my tie matching Abyss' sweater, just as Eliza predicted she would, but, thankfully, Abyss doesn't seem to hear. She's busy talking to Carlos and Dad about the company, as far as I can tell. The valet brings my dad's car around within seconds, and my family disappears shortly after.

Abyss and I stand on the quiet sidewalk, the cool air brushing past us.

"Your dad offered me a job," she says, voice low as though she doesn't want to disturb the soft night. I'm unsurprised by this announcement, and only hum in recognition. "I applied for the Caesar Corporation once. It was my dream job, then."

"And now?"

Abyss lifts one shoulder, lets out a sigh. "I don't know. After the Void — my work wasn't something I could easily continue on with. I never finished my doctorate. I never applied to any job. I met Xander, I met you. I was doing other things."

"Your work is still important to you," I say, brushing my hand against hers again. I find it comforting, to know that she's there, less than an arms reach away.

Abyss sighs again, leans against me. "It is," she allows. "But I studied astrophysics because of JuJu. I wanted to see other worlds, prove that alternate universes exist. I wanted to help her. It seems a bit late for that, now."

I think of Jamboree, slapping her across the face, opening portals through her body.

"I didn't know you studied it because of her," I whisper. "I thought you studied it because of you."

"She was my best friend," Abyss says, and she takes my hand. "I did study it because of me."

35.

I haven't been to Pae's Flowers since three days before Xander...
passed, and I can't help but think it looks dimmer, now. The flowers
in the window seem to be wilting without him there to care for them,
and maybe it's just the dark, but the sign feels desaturated, less
grand. Pae's Flowers was always such a bright spot in this city. It
feels *wrong* to see it going dark.

I follow Abyss out of the car to say goodbye. She invites me in.

Mrs. Pae is asleep already, judging by the lack of light. Abyss unfolds
the sofa bed as quietly as she can, gestures for me to sit, and
disappears to the bathroom to change into a pair of leggings. The
sofa-bed sags slightly beneath my weight. I wonder if Abyss will
move into Xander's room, eventually. I wonder if that room has been
touched, lately.

When she comes back, she stretches out across the sofa-bed, laying
down and staring up at the ceiling. I lay down next to her. It feels odd,
being in Xander's home without him here. I understand why Abyss
has been staying at mine, but I worry about Mrs. Pae. She's been
alone. I've been keeping Abyss to myself.

She takes her glasses off, setting them on the coffee table. I roll on to
my side to face her, and she mirrors me, her eyes closed.

"Hey," I say, and my voice breaks the quiet as gently as possible.

Her eyes open, and I allow myself to *feel* them, for a few moments. They don't feel so all-consuming, so dangerously lonely. Not anymore. I've seen the Void beyond these tiny fragments, and now her eyes are just her eyes. She blinks languidly at me, mouth curved into a half-smile.

"Why do you call it the Void?" I ask. I'm hyper-aware of the space between us, and of how easy it would be to reach out and take her hand or brush her hair from her face. "There's so much there."

Abyss hums, lets her eyes slide closed again. "There wasn't much there when I first saw it. There wasn't much there before me."

The Void is her and she is the Void. It has its own sentience and its own set of rules, but without Abyss, it was a space of nothingness. Abyss is a genius, a beauty, a universe.

I watch her as she falls asleep.

36.

I'm jolted awake by a knock on the window. The lights are on now, and Mrs. Pae is in the kitchen. Abyss is sitting next to me. Her glasses are back on, making it impossible to tell whether or not she was looking at me. I feel a bit silly, laying on the sofa-bed in my rumpled dinner clothes.

"I didn't mean to fall asleep," I say thickly, my mouth dry and sticky.

Abyss smirks. "Don't worry, I assured Mrs. Pae that your virtue is still intact."

I hadn't even thought of that. Suddenly mortified, I cover my face with my hands. I don't know everything about her religion, but I know that's not something they're okay with. The idea that Mrs. Pae might've thought that I had sex in her house without her knowing makes me wish that *I* had a connection to the Void, so it could swallow me up.

Abyss laughs at my expression and swings her legs off the sofa-bed when the knocking at the window sounds again. The fire escape is the main point of entry when people don't want to go through the flower shop. I remember slipping in and out of the window as a twelve-year-old, and then, just last year, sitting with Xander, looking out at the city with hot chocolates in our hands. When I finally uncover my eyes and look, I'm surprised to see Ace standing there.

Abyss lets her in, and doesn't seem concerned.

"What are you doing here?" I ask.

She eyes my wrinkled, day-old clothes and raises an eyebrow. "I could ask you the same question," she teases, tossing a wink in Abyss' direction.

Abyss doesn't take the bait. "I asked her to come," she says. "We really need to hammer out a plan for Jamboree, and I want her to check the odds."

Ace shoots me double finger guns and grins.

I don't know how exactly Abyss conveys that she's rolling her eyes, but both Ace and I catch the meaning. I laugh, and Ace says, "Rude."

She comes and sits next to me on the sofa-bed while Abyss stays standing, pacing back and forth in front of us. "The first question is, how do we find her?"

"Seems pretty impossible to me," Ace says. When the person who can literally see probability is saying the odds aren't working for us, we know we're screwed. "Even if we knew where she was, she'd be outside of the universe. We wouldn't know how to *find* her."

Abyss scowls. "Don't be so negative."

"I'm being realistic," Ace counters. I'm somewhat inclined to agree with her.

Mrs. Pae enters the room with a tray of drinks and breaks whatever weird silence had fallen by handing them out. Herbal tea for herself and Abyss, hot chocolate for me and Ace.

"Not tea?" I ask her, gesturing to her cup. For as long as I've known her, she's preferred lavender tea to almost anything else. Besides maybe tequila.

"Not anymore," she answers, shrugging and not meeting my eyes. "Hot chocolate is much more, uh… comforting. And Ki makes the best stuff in the world."

Mrs. Pae laughs (I wonder when Ace started calling her 'Ki'), and surprises me by sinking into the loveseat to join our conversation. I suppose she has even more reason than the rest of us to want Jamboree stopped. Abyss nods at her, takes a long sip of her own tea, and launches right back in to talking.

"Even if we can't find her, knowing where she is might lead to our next step," Abyss cuts in. "Caesar said last night that he thought it might give us insight."

Ace and Mrs. Pae look at me, and I give a little wave.

"Let's figure out where she's gone, and we can go from there." Abyss sighs. "I hate not having a plan, but this is all we have to go off of."

For a few moments, there's nothing but the sounds of us slurping on our drinks and clinking our fingernails against our mugs to break the heavy silence. Abyss is visibly frustrated; she's chewing on the edges of her fingers. Before I can say anything, Ace grabs her arm and says, softly but firmly, "Braid my hair?"

Abyss sighs, long-suffering, but nods. Ace shifts to sit cross-legged and Abyss kneels behind her on the sofa-bed, combing through her hair with her fingers. I guess this was their *thing*, something private that I've never seen before. I knew that Abs used to braid her hair— Ace would always excitedly show it off, running her hands underneath them and saying "Isn't Abyss the *best*?"— but I've never been in the room before.

Abyss concentrates on her hair. She brushes through Ace's blonde locks with her fingers, detangling her perpetually-messy hair, and then she starts separating it out into sections. Ace hums and closes her eyes. It feels strangely personal, like Mrs. Pae and I are intruding on some secret ritual. Abyss is even *smiling*, albeit only slightly.

I've wondered if maybe Ace is an empath, as well, with how good she is at reading people. But she's just a people-person, and good at knowing what her friends need. I'm overwhelmingly grateful for it, as I watch Abyss ease into the familiar motion.

"I think our only option," Ace says, when Abyss is too engrossed in the activity to abruptly pull away, "is to kill her."

I look at her sharply. She meets my eyes unapologetically.

Abyss' hand still for a moment, but she takes a breath and continues braiding. Mrs. Pae doesn't make any noise, but when I glance towards her, her mouth is parted and her eyes wet.

"Think about it," Ace says, "She can create portals *anywhere* and disappear off to places outside the universe. Even if we lock her up, she'll be able to escape off to who knows where, and then come back. Prison isn't really an option for her. If we don't kill her, she'll always be able to come back."

"I don't think murder is the solution," Mrs. Pae says gently. Ace's eyes narrow in response.

"It's not murder, at this point," she retorts. "It's self-defence. It's, uhm… preservation."

My stomach drops. She's right, of course, that Jamboree would always be able to escape, and to come back. Based on what I've seen so far, I doubt that she's ever going to give up. She tore our city centre apart. What else could she do?

Abyss ties off the first braid, the mini-elastic she'd nabbed from the side table snapping loudly. "I'm not going to kill her. I don't know *what* I'm going to do, but I'm not going to kill her. She was my best friend."

Her voice doesn't crack, but I react as though it did, reaching out to squeeze her arm. I've seen her and Jamboree, laying in a bedroom from years ago, talking with a comfortable fondness and familiarity.

A universe where you aren't brilliant isn't one I want to see.

Ace softens, too. She has a million best friends and she'd stop at nothing to save them— she knows that Abyss considered Xander her best friend, too, and now she's lost him. Damn, the things she'd do if she'd lost *her* best friend... But she understands that Abyss' reactions are different. She understands that Abyss wants to keep at least one of her best friends alive.

Ace glances at me, and I pull myself out of her head.

"Okay," she relents, but she doesn't sound pleased about it. "I guess we should worry about finding her, first, anyway. Any bright ideas of what she might do next?"

What was it that Abyss had said to Jamboree, right before she got slapped? Ace and I had been on the ground, hadn't heard, but I'd relived the experience while I was in Abyss' head only yesterday. It was something dangerous, something that had aimed to hurt, at least some...

"If our families could see you now..." I whisper.

Abyss startles. "What?"

"That's what you said to her," I say, gaining confidence in my barely-formed theory. "You said 'if our families could see you now', and she slapped you."

"Damnit," Abyss curses, then follows it up with much more colourful language.

Mrs. Pae frowns at her. "Do you think she'd go after them? Do you think she'd go after her own *family*?"

"I don't know," Abyss says. "She wasn't ever especially close with her family. Not that they hated each other or anything, just that they weren't close. I don't know if she could separate them from herself enough to go after them…"

"It's the only lead we've got," I say. "Where do they live?"

Abyss rattles of an address from memory while she ties off Ace's second braid. "They live just down the road from us. If she goes after her own family, with my family just down the road, then it'd be easy enough to kill two birds with one stone."

Ace's mouth curls into a disgusted snarl. "I can't imagine going after your own *family*."

I think about Charlie, Eliza, Carlos. I think about Mom and Dad. I think about the dinner last night, and the ways we all try and fail to understand and support each other and the way we rush to each other's defence. I can't imagine hurting any of them, no matter how much they may piss me off sometimes.

"I wasn't close to my family either. I'm fifteen years younger than my brother." Abyss says wryly, "I was something of a surprise."

Ace shakes her head. "I can't imagine not being close to your family. I would've done anything for my sister."

"I still love them," Abyss defends. "And I suppose I was closer with my parents than Julia was with hers— we spent more time at my house, anyway."

"It's an idea," I say. "How do the odds look, Ace?"

Her eyes go unfocused and her mouth moves almost imperceptibly as she runs through the numbers. "Not bad," she answers after a couple of seconds. "We're on the right track as far as what she's doing… and it's over fifty for success in stopping her. I say you should go for it. It's as good a plan as anyway we'll come up with."

"Over fifty aren't the best odds," Mrs. Pae points out, her quiet voice cutting through all of us like a cold knife. I shiver under her fearful gaze. She's just lost her son. Will it ruin her to lose us to?

Ace picks at the end of one of her braids. She'd stripped the red from her hair, but it's still not quite its usual blonde. "Over fifty is better than under fifty. They're more likely to win than to lose."

"You won't come with us?" Abyss asks, and Ace shakes her head.

"I can't leave again, not so soon," she says. "I need to be myself, for a little while. Besides, I'd just get in your way. I'm not built for the fight scenes."

"You're more of a fighter than anyone I know," I tell her, and she replies with a crystal laugh.

"Ah, but I'm not very good at it." She says, "The odds drop if I'm there. Not by a lot, but I'd rather give you the best possible chances."

"How much do they drop?"

"Zero-point-zero-three," she says, then shrugs. "Like I said, I'd rather give you the best possible odds. Also, don't leave for another week."

I gesture to my own head. "D'you mind…?"

The numbers won't mean anything to me, even if I look at them through her eyes and from inside her head. She's the only person on earth who can understand them, but I want to see them anyway. It always calms my nerves.

She nods, and I slip inside.

I do love looking at the world through someone else's eyes. It's always weird, seeing my own face from an outsiders perspective, but once I make her aware of my presence with a gentle nudge, she looks away from me, and starts looking at the numbers. They're always there, floating around her vision like letters in an alphabet soup— to use her own thoughts on the matter— but it's only when she tries that she sees them properly, sees them in a way that makes them make any sort of sense.

Her thought process towards seeing the numbers is vague, too vague for me to follow, but it makes sense to her subconscious, and they've never been wrong yet.

I leave her mind easily.

"All right," I say, nodding a few times. "We'll go in a week."

37.

Xander has been dead for three weeks.

It hits me, sometimes, the absence of him. It's little things; the fact that the *superkids* group text is still one of my top five most recent chats, or the space on my sofa, between Abyss and I, where he used to sit when we strategised, or the empty van parked outside the flower shop, collecting dust.

Abyss starts driving the van for Mrs. Pae and I start sitting closer and closer to Abyss while we plan. I haven't found a solution for the group text problem, yet.

Abyss spends most nights in my penthouse, now. We blame it on strategy meetings going long, on planning taking us well in to the night, but I think it's just that we don't want to be apart. I've gotten used to her presence; the ever-growing pile of clothes in the spare room, the toothbrush in the main bathroom, and, most importantly, her, sitting cross-legged on the sofa, her laptop balanced on her legs and her head tilted, welcoming, towards me.

Sometimes, I think I can feel that inexplicable emotion that was rattling around her head the first time I managed to read it. *Void Calling*.

But I'm not connected to the Void— I can't slip inside it, I can't answer it's call the way Abyss can. And besides, I don't really think it's the Void calling out to me. I think it's *me*, looking at Abyss and wanting that closeness, again. She trusted me with her mind, and I would give anything for her to trust me with it again.

She hasn't brought it up since, and neither have I.

We have other things to focus on, so I try to shove this unnamable emotion out of my head. It's hard, when Abyss is less than an arms reach away every evening and every morning I send her off as my driver takes her to Pae's Flowers.

The secret is out, now. Ever since Ava revealed Legion's identity at the funeral, there's been rumours flying around, reporters at the flower shop. People would've figured it out eventually, I'm sure. Legion disappearing the same day that Xander died would be proof enough, and even with the mask, it's easy enough for people to see the similarities in their appearance. His appearance.

Abyss drives the van, delivers flowers. I try to fill my days.

I take Eliza and Carlos around the city, showing them all my favourite places. Carlos goes back to Greece with Mom, looking relieved. If they do decide to move back, at least he'll have time to adjust to it. I'm grateful on his behalf.

In the airport, Mom makes me promise to be careful. She's thinking of Xander. I don't have to read her mind to know— I'm thinking about him too. Dad claps me on the shoulder, guides me back out to the car. He's staying, for a while, on business. Mom told me that, but I'd forgotten.

"Do you still want the company?" he asks me, and looks relieved when I nod. "There'll be work for you to do, soon. During your break. I'll email you."

University. Classes. I'd almost forgotten about them. I really should go to some classes, but I'm finding it difficult to muster up the energy. At least it's only my second year, and it's only the middle of September. I've got plenty of time to scrape my grades back up to an acceptable standard.

I go to the history museum. It's been years since I've been and it's nice to be back. I used to want to be an archeologist, after I watched every single Indiana Jones movie in a row. I outgrew that particular ambition, but the love for history remained.

Me: *Theres a new interactive exhibit ab ancient romans. remind me to show u the part where u can dress up as a caesar*

Abs-tract: *i thnk thts fr kds cee*

I have to resist the urge to get fully into costume to send her a picture. Instead, I wait until I get to the section on British history, and send her a picture of myself wearing a plastic golden crown.

Abs-tract: *cute*

Keeping myself busy is pretty much my only goal, and I'm not very good at it. I end up bored, in my penthouse, rewatching *Star Trek* and *Buffy*. I text Ace and Abyss and, sometimes, hover over the type box in my chat with Xander. I wish I could talk to him. He'd have ideas

294

about Jamboree. They might not be different ideas from mine, but we could still talk them out, and he'd infuse me with confidence. He was good at that.

Ace comes by, two days before we leave for Jamboree's parents house. She sprawls out on my couch like she owns it, legs hooked over the arm and head laid back against the cushions, looking up at me through wide blue eyes.

"You nervous?" she asks, her tongue poking out from between her teeth in a playful grin.

It seems tonally inconsistent, and draws me up short. "What?"

"To meet Abyss' parents," she elaborates, as though that clarifies anything.

"First, we're going to Jamboree's parents house, not Abs'," I say, frowning. "And secondly, why would that make me nervous?"

Ace waves a hand through the air at my first point, huffing, and grins even wider at my second. "You mean you haven't figured it out yet?"

I blink at her a few times, not sure how to feel about what she's implying. She laughs at my expression, rolling over on to her stomach and propping her chin on her hands. "I'm sorry, I guess I shouldn't assume. You *do* love her, don't you?"

Void Calling.

"Of course I do," I say, shaking my head. "I love you, too."

She laughs at me, reaches out to pull on one of my curls. It bounces back into shape and I scrape it behind my ear. It's not quite long enough to stay put.

"You're avoiding the question," she says to me, and I shrug. I'm not ready to think about it. Thankfully, Ace doesn't press. I'm sure it will come up again, later, but for now she lets me be, choosing instead to pick up a few controllers from the living room table and wave them in front of my face until I'm agreeing to play video games with her. She's not very good, but after a few rounds, she's content to watch me play against strangers online.

She wears the headset and provides running commentary to my opponents. Sitting on the floor in front of the couch, with Ace, elevated, cross-legged behind me, I can hear strangers laughing at her jokes and naivety towards the game. She doesn't seem to mind.

But the day does come for Abyss and I to leave. I spend the night before at the flower shop, because Mrs. Pae had said she wanted to see us off. She puts me up in Xander's room, tutting about how Abyss and I won't be sharing a bed in her house.

His room is impersonal. The vase on his nightstand that is usually filled with various bouquets has been taken away. The desk has been freshly dusted, everything cleared away into cardboard boxes, stacked by the door. His dresser is closed— I don't think I've ever seen those drawers pushed completely shut— and his bedsheets freshly washed.

It's cold, empty. Like the room itself has died.

Mrs. Pae stares. "I've only been able to do… small amounts at a time. Ace has helped. I will have to donate things, soon. But I find it hard to get rid of them." Her voice is tight and small. "They're all I have left of him, Caesar."

I wrap an arm around her. She covers her face in her hands and presses herself against my chest. She feels frail. She hasn't been eating well.

I drop my overnight bag on the bed and usher her out of the room. Abyss is waiting for us in the kitchen, pulling a glass tray out of the oven. She offers me a tiny smile as I guide Mrs. Pae to her seat, before I step in to help serve up plates of food.

"Some people from church brought her freezer meals," Abyss says to me, low enough that Mrs. Pae can't hear. "I've been reheating them for her before I leave for your place."

I nod, find a spatula, and start serving the casserole up on to three plates. We sit around the rectangular table— Mrs. Pae at the head, Abyss and I across from each other. I angle my body away from the empty chair on the other end and Abyss mirrors my body language. Mrs. Pae, however, can still see the place where Xander would've sat.

Regardless, she bows her head and offers a blessing on the food (a Mormon thing that had caught me off guard as a kid and still startles me now). We dig in. It's not the best food in the world and it certainly doesn't hold a candle to Mrs. Pae's cooking. I watch her push the food around her plate and resist the urge to reach into her mind.

I have no guarantee that my presence there would be helpful to her, and I think seeing and understanding her grief first hand would ruin me. I glance to Xander's empty chair and let out a long breath. I don't know how helpful the offer will be, but I feel compelled to make it anyway. "Do you want to talk about it?"

Mrs. Pae lets out a startled, watery laugh. "You're very sweet, Caesar," she says, and squeezes my arm. "I meant what I said at the… funeral. He felt that this was what he was meant to be doing. I agreed with him. I worried about him— every day." She looks at Abyss, at me. "I worry about you two, as well. You were his best friends."

I look down at the table, lay my hand on top of hers, which is still resting on my arm. I've been so caught up— my own grief, Abyss, Jamboree— I hadn't made enough time to look after her. I resolve to fix that, going forward.

"Abyss," Mrs. Pae continues, and her voice dips lower, serious and sad. "My girl. I know you have a family, a mother, but you've been here with me, with Xander, and you've come to be like a daughter to me."

Abyss bows her head and reaches out to Mrs. Pae, palms up. She looks meek. I have never seen her ask for anything so obviously as she is asking for affection now. Mrs. Pae releases me and takes Abyss' hands in her own.

I feel as though I'm imposing when Abyss speaks. Her voice is low and thick, an outward show of emotion that is uncommon enough to draw me to her while simultaneously making me want to look away.

She whispers, "I'm different, now, than I was, and I've accepted who I am, what the Void has made me. I *am* Abyss. I'm happy. My family didn't know. I didn't know how to explain. I'm still trying to tell my brother, and I haven't spoken to my parents yet. But..." her voice catches, breath sharp. "You are like a second mother, and you've never rejected me. Xander was another brother, more than a best friend. You two gave me a second family when I couldn't bring myself to see my first one."

Mrs. Pae is crying. I stand, begin clearing the dishes and they seem to take no notice of me. They hold each others hands over the kitchen table, caught up in a moment that I shouldn't intrude on. I stay in the kitchen. The rushing water that fills the sink disguises their talking as white noise, and I allow the mindless task of washing dishes to distract my thoughts.

Xander has been dead for three weeks.

The absence of him is in every waking hour, and I think it always will be.
38.

Abyss has a new air about her by the time we wake up the next morning. She seems steadier, somehow, and I wonder what she and Mrs. Pae spoke about late into the night. I could hear their voices, through the door, as I lay awake in Xander's room, but hadn't been able to make out words. Just as well.

I hadn't been able to sleep. I'd fallen into some sort of doze, but my mind wouldn't shut off entirely, and all I could think of was *this is Xander's bed and he's not here to sleep in it*. I wished I could've talked to Abyss and Mrs. Pae about it, but I didn't want to intrude on their private, family mourning. Xander was my best friend, but I couldn't consider him a brother. Mrs. Pae means a lot to me, but I can't consider her a mother. She and Abyss have a unique relationship, and a unique right to mourn.

I don't have that right. I was supposed to be with him, and I wasn't.

Abyss seems to notice something is off about me, but she thankfully doesn't say anything until we've already hugged Mrs. Pae goodbye and climbed into the backseat of the car. The separation is up, as it always is when we're on superhero business, dividing us from Aaron. He's said he prefers not to know.

Abyss brushes her fingers against the back of my hand to get my attention. As if she has to try to get my attention. I think I'm always aware of her, on some level. "Are you okay?" she asks me, and I shrug. She takes her glasses off and puts them in her shirt pocket, fixing me with a stare. "Talk to me, Cee."

I let out a long breath. "I feel like I've failed him."

It doesn't seem to be the problem she's expecting. She blinks her nebulous eyes at me a few times, waiting for an elaboration I don't know how to give.

"I'm just…" I sigh, scrape a hand down my face. "I was supposed to be with him. He's *dead*."

"That's not your fault."

"Maybe, maybe not," I say, shrugging up to my ears. "I just keep thinking of how he'd react, if the roles were reversed. He wouldn't be out for vengeance, he'd look out for my family, he'd…"

"You're not Xander, Cee," she says, softly. "He wouldn't… he wouldn't expect you to react the same way he would."

I think of him, alone, falling; laying dead on the concrete for twenty minutes before anyone found him. I wish I'd been there, I wish I'd been able to do something. I wish I knew what to do *now*. Everything is so sticky and complicated, catching me off guard. I look away, staring out the window.

"Caesar," she says, reaching out and laying a hand on top of mine, holding on the middle seat. I turn to look at her, and she's smiling just slightly. "He was one of your best friends," she continues. "You're allowed to *feel*."

Our hands stay, joined, on the middle seat, and I try to take her advice.

39.

It's nearly twenty-one hours between Pae's Flowers and the street that Abyss and Jamboree grew up on, and we're trying to drive it as straight-through as we can. Once we leave the city lines, I feel like a weird weight has been lifted. It's good to get away, sometimes, I guess. It's good to be doing something, again.

Abyss and I fill the silence with long conversation about her work. I can't really keep up with it, but   I love to watch her expression light up as she explains her studies, her thesis. Her face always falls when she talks about getting her doctorate, which I suppose I can understand. She left before she could finish it.

"I wish I had a lab," she says, sounding surprisingly wistful. I don't know if she's gotten more outwardly expressive or if I've just gotten better at noticing the little ways she always has been, but I like it nonetheless.

"I could get you one."

Abyss laughs, and it startles a smile out of me. Her eyes crinkle around the corners when she smiles, something I never could've noticed with her glasses covering them. "I'm sure you could," she says, "and I'm sure your dad's job offer comes with a wonderfully well stocked one."

"I mean it," is all I say before we're pulling into a drive-through for greasy takeout, and the conversation naturally progresses on to some other topic.

We sit in probably unsafe positions with seatbelts twisted around our arms to face each other as we eat. Abyss takes a picture of me with ketchup on my face and, when she thinks I'm not looking, sets it as my new contact picture. I retaliate by taking one of my own— her eyes, wide with humour, mouth smiling wide around a french fry. It might be the nicest picture in the world.

Later, full and tired, we shift until we're both slouched in our seats and staring out the sunroof. Night is falling, and we can just about see the stars.

"Nice to get out of the city," I say softly, and Abyss hums in agreement.

I knock on the separation, and Aaron slides it open to speak to me. I ask him to pull over so we can all get some rest, and he nods. The car slows to a stop on the side of the road, and after we all stumble out to stretch our legs, I decide to take the opportunity to take the middle seat. Abyss beats me to it, and settles in with her back resting against my side, her legs stretched out on the spare seat. Without thinking about it, I end up with my arm wrapped around her, her hand in mine.

"Do you think I should take the job?" she asks me, and when I glance at her, her eyes are closed.

I smile at the sight of her, and feel my stomach go hollow and my heart pick up.

I say, "I think you could do incredible things in and for this world if you had the resources, and that the job could give you those resources. I think that you should do whatever makes you happy."

I think that I love her.

Or maybe I know it.

40.

We spend the rest of the road trip lounging in a comfortable, sleepy state. It's probably not the best way to prepare to face our mortal enemy, but it's what we do. We talk, sometimes, idly, about next to nothing. Mostly we just lap up each others company.

A few times, I think of asking about the Void. *Void Calling. Love.* I want to know if the Void reaches out to me, too. I want to know if she loves me, too.

The moment always passes.

We arrive at the street she grew up on at a quarter-past-noon on the day after we left. The street is shockingly normal— I don't know what exactly I expected, but somehow the sight of green front yards, sectioned windows, and children's bicycles surprises me. Beside me, Abyss' breath catches, and I follow her gaze to a house a few down the row. It's covered in blue panelling and has two evenly spaced windows on either side of a red door.

This must be her childhood house.

"D'you want to…" I start, but she's already walking towards it. When she realises I'm not beside her, she turns back, extends a hand. I take it, and she leads me up the front steps.

She rings the bell. I can hear Ace's voice in the back of my head. *Are you nervous? To meet Abyss' parents?*

Judging by how tightly her hand is squeezing mine, I'm willing to bet that she's pretty nervous too. We wait together for the door to open, a palpable energy simmering between us. Nothing can prepare us for what's behind that door.

When it opens, it reveals a tall guy who's far too young to be Abyss' dad. The similarities are still plentiful— the guy has the same nose as Abyss, the same texture to his hair. His eyes are warm, dark brown. I imagine this the colour that Abyss' were, back when she was Jenna-Louise. The man must be her brother; there's no other explanation for it. Abyss releases my hand and stands awkwardly beside me.

He says, slowly, lowly, almost too quiet to hear, "Jenna-Louise? Jenny?"

Jenny.

I have to bite back a smile at the nickname. It's so easy to imagine a young Abyss, hair up in two bunches before she started to braid it, working hard on some experiment or another, or maybe some homework. I imagine her tongue poking out of the corner of her mouth, a stereotype of concentration.

Abyss has yet to confirm or deny her brothers assumption, so I reach over and brush the back of my hand against hers. "Jordan," she whispers. "What are you doing here?"

"I'm visiting Mom and Dad," her brother— Jordan— replies. "Someone's got to."

Abyss looks down. I take her hand on impulse, and she links our fingers together. For the first time, Jordan seems to notice me. His gaze flicks over me and settles, hard, against my face.

"Well," he says, turning back to Abyss. "And least you were among high-class company."

I think that's probably meant to be an insult.

Abyss stiffens and raises her head again. "This is Caesar," she says, and maybe it's just me projecting, but her voice sounds hard and defensive. "He's my *friend*."

I can't help the tiny surge of pride at her tone. She's glad to call me her friend, I can tell. I squeeze her hand in a silent show of support. Jordan hums.

"Yeah," he says, "he's *the* Caesar."

Abyss makes a motion with her head that I know means she's rolling her eyes and pushes past her brother into the house. I follow after her, ignoring Jordans's gaze. In the main room, on the couch, sits an older woman. I think she must be Abyss' mother. She's got a certain elegance about her, a sense of self-assurance that is visible even simply sitting in her own house. She's reading Kant when we walk in.

"Who was that?" she asks, glancing up at us for a split second before realising that we're not Jordan. I watch as her mouth goes somewhat comically wide and she drops the book on to the side table. She rises and walks over to us, resting her hands on Abyss' face. Abyss seems to melt, ever so slightly, into the touch. Her mother blinks back tears. "My baby," she says.

Once again, I feel like I'm intruding into Abyss' family life. I let go of her hand and take a step back to give them space. Her mother wraps her into a hug and Abyss' arms slide easily around her neck. I turn away to give them privacy.

Jordan is right beside me, looking at me thoughtfully as he leans against the wall.

"We thought she might be with you," he says, nodding vaguely towards Abyss. "When we saw Abyss on the news, we were pretty sure she was our Jenna-Louise. We thought about contacting you, to try to find out if she was alright. Mom said that there was no way you'd reply."

"I would've," I say truthfully. If someone had called me claiming to be Abyss' family, I would've followed up immediately.

Jordan hums again, disbelieving. "She's been emailing me, over the past, I don't know... three weeks." Even without looking in to his mind I can sense the concern. "Hasn't told me everything, yet."

It may not be a question, but I answer it anyway. "I think she'd rather tell you herself."

"How'd she end up with you?" Jordan asks, and I try not to dwell on the typical implications of 'end up with'. I'm sure that's not what he means.

"We had a mutual friend," I reply, swallowing thickly. I wonder how closely they follow Abyss' life. I wonder if they know that he's gone.

When Jordan's gaze softens, I deduce that they do. "Was he a good friend to her?"

But of course, he doesn't care about me. Why would he? Abyss is his sister, and there are a million mysteries attached to her. "She lived with him and his mom," I tell him. "They looked after her. He… he was an incredibly good person, and I've never met someone who knew him, and didn't come away from the relationship *better*."

Jordan nods thoughtfully. Abyss and her mom pull away from each other. Her mom is crying.

"My baby," her mom repeats. "What happened to you?"

"Too many things," Abyss replies in a whisper. "I missed you."

"You can't imagine how much I missed you."

Abyss lets out a choked sound. I'm about to turn away again, but she seems to gather herself, and reaches out for me. I step closer, and her hand rests on my arm, above the crook of my elbow. "Mom, this is my friend," she says, and I swoop in to introduce myself.

"William Antonio Caesar," I say, extending a hand. "The Third, but you can just call me Caesar."

Her mom, unlike Jordan, doesn't eye me warily. She just shakes my hand and smiles warmly at me. "Caesar. A bit of a pernicious name, don't you think? To call yourself a king."

"It's my surname," I defend lightly, but, thinking of Ace, add: "But I do have a friend who reminds me of my place. She always tells that an *ace* is stronger than a king."

Abyss laughs, without the typical two-second delay. It makes me grin. Her mother looks between us curiously. "Your friend has the right idea," she says, releasing my hand. "I'm Meghan Giles-Tolbert. I'm sure you understand, Caesar, that I'd like to talk to my daughter—"

"He can stay," Abyss says hurriedly. "Please, Mom. We need to talk to you, too."

Jordan shakes his head, but excuses himself. "Talk to them, Mom," he says, waving a hand almost dismissively. "Jessie needs my help, anyway."

From the corner of my eye I see Abyss mouth 'Jessie' to herself.

"His daughter," her mom supplies. "She's two."

Abyss takes my hand again. I can tell that this knowledge shakes her. "I've only— it's been three years, already?"

"Yes, already," her mom snaps, her first show of anger. "Jordan says you've been emailing him bits and pieces, but no straight answers, and now that I know you're *alive*, I'd rather like to know what's kept you away for three years. And take those ridiculous glasses off. You're *inside*, for heavens sake."

I barely have the time to say *don't* before Abyss' mom is reaching over and pulling the glasses off. Abyss doesn't have time to stop her. Maybe this *is* the fastest way to explain.

Abyss stares at her mother, unblinking. Wordlessly, she hands Abyss the sunglasses back, looking dazed.

Abyss says, "we have a lot to talk about."

And her mother nods.

41.

"You remember Julia Lago," Abyss starts, and her mother arcs an eyebrow at her. Of course she remembers *Julia Lago*, her daughter's best friend. It is, in my opinion, an interesting place to start. "Do you know what she's up to now?"

"I assume," she replies, somewhat dryly, "this is you trying to break the news that she's a super-villain now? We do watch the news, Jenna-Louise, and we especially pay attention to *you*."

Abyss bristles. I wish I could reach out and take her hand, but we're sitting on two separate armchairs, facing the couch that her parents are sitting on. "Do you know *why* she does what she does now?" she asks, voice tight.

Her father had come in a few minutes after we had, done a double-take, a triple-take, and started crying. When Abyss said she needed to talk to them both, he'd excused himself to wash his face of the grime he collected at work— I learn that he works as a mechanic. He'd barely spared me a glance, but Abyss said his eyes went wide because he saw me, not because of her. I think that's a definite lie.

To him, her mother says, "She thinks we don't know what our daughter and her friends have been up to."

"I'm trying to rely a warning," Abyss says, voice flat, in the emotionless tone I've learned means she's feeling too much, and the Void is taking it all. "And to tell you why I ran. If you'd just listen—"

Her parents eyes bore into her with such intensity that even I shift under the gaze, and it's not directed at me. She stills, lets out a long breath.

"Do you know *why* Julia is a super-villain, now?" she repeats.

"Is that really important?" her father asks. "I just want to know that you're safe, looked after. I just want my baby girl back, sweetie."

"You can't have that," Abyss says. I know the matter-of-fact tone comes from the Void, but her parents don't, and they freeze. The tension is thick, making the air feel gummy. If Abyss hadn't seemed so insistent that I be allowed to stay, I'd excuse myself. After several seconds, Abyss continues, "I just mean… I'm not coming home. I'm different, now, I'm not the daughter you knew."

"Everyone is different," her mother says softly. "We all are."

"You don't understand. I'm not even human anymore."

"I know," her father interjects. "You're superhuman."

"Abs…" I say, angling my body towards her and letting my hand, palm up, dangle off the chair. It's an unsubtle offer. Damn it, I'm hopeless.

Her mothers eyes fixate on me. "Her name is Jenna-Louise."

"My name is Abyss," she says, and she takes my hand. "I'm *not Jenna-Louise anymore*, that's what I'm trying to tell you. I need you to listen. And," she adds, "I need you to stop talking to Caesar like that."

Her parents' mouths click shut, looking at their daughter with new eyes. I find myself reaching out to their minds and I'm unsurprised to find lingering worry, and, deeper, buried, feelings of betrayal. They're confused, and hurt, and they're worried about their daughter. Images of Abyss' childhood flash by, and her father especially can't seem to differentiate between the little girl in his memories, and the woman sitting in front of him.

I pull back, pull away. Just because I perceive human minds as billboards advertising thoughts and opinions doesn't mean that those aren't private things. I always understood my dad's concern about it and even agreed with him most of the time. Her father is staring at me. I wonder if he was aware of my presence there. I look away.

Abyss recounts the story. Jamboree's ability, how Abyss wanted to prove it was real. The experiment, the Void joining her.

"I knew," she says, staring directly at her enraptured parents, "that my life would never be the same. I'd just become superhuman. My work was *over*. It wouldn't be taken seriously anymore. Everything I'd worked for my entire life was everything I couldn't have anymore. I was one year away from a doctorate, and I knew that even if I got it, finding work in my chosen field would be nigh impossible."

She continues; she talks about how she panicked, and ran. She talks about living day to day for a while, until meeting Xander. How eight months after that, she met me. How Jamboree found her.

"I think she felt betrayed," Abyss says softly, looking at her hands, folded on her lap. "I can understand that. But in the same way that I'm not the daughter you knew, I'm not the best friend she knew. The Void changed me, fundamentally. I'm not human. I'm the Void. I'm Abyss."

"She's a universe," I say, and I'm sure I sound just as awestruck as I felt the first time I fully realised it. Abyss smiles at me, just slightly. Her parents glance between us, and I shift uncomfortably in my seat.

"The point is," she says, "we came here because we think that she's going to come *here*, after you and her parents."

"Why do you think that?" her dad asks, and I'm overwhelmingly grateful that he doesn't sound anything other than genuinely curious. "Has she said something?"

Abyss and I trade looks, and I know that it's my turn to talk now. I've been staying carefully silent, knowing that, up until this point, it was a family matter. Now, with the conversation shifting to the superhero business, Abyss is turning to me as the leader.

"Jamboree is obviously incredibly influenced and motivated by her emotions," I start. They mentally flinch at my use of *Jamboree*. "Abyss… made a comment about what your families would think of her, if they could see her now. Obviously," I add, with a sidelong look to Abyss. "We underestimated how easily you'd recognise them."

"Of course we recognise her," her mother says softly. "She's our daughter."

I decide to let Abyss work that one out with her family at her own pace. "Anyway, we figure that Jamboree will come here, possibly after both of your families, either as bait, or to prove to Abyss that she doesn't care."

"So, really, you don't have any proof that this is even a possibility?" Abyss' mother raises her eyebrows at me. I shift in my seat again.

"That friend I mentioned, she can… see probability." It's the way that she's always described it anyway. I always called it 'underdeveloped future-probability cognition', which has only ever made her laugh. "We get her to triple check our odds, and she says that we're right."

Well, she'd said we were 'on the right track', which is about as good as it gets when all we were going off of was guesses.

Abyss' parents look at each other, and back at us. "Let's get the Lago's over," her father says. "We'll explain everything, and hash out a plan."

42.

The Lago's are more open to conversation. They make almost as big a fuss over Abyss as her own parents did, so I keep my distance. It seems the best course of action, until Jamboree's father pulls me to one side.

"I don't pretend to understand my daughters motivations," he says, his voice low enough that no one else can hear. "But I know that she was hurt by Jenna-Louise's disappearance. They'd been inseparable growing up, they lived together, they told each other everything. I made many mistakes as a father— but the worst was not believing her ability was what she said it was. I thought she was an illusionist. We all did, except Jenna-Louise. Jenny trusted her, and set out to prove us all wrong. When she left…"

I don't have to go into his head to fill in the blanks. Jamboree had lost everything; the one person who fully believed in her abilities.

He continues, "If I know my daughter at all, then I think all of this is some plea for her best friend back. She was lonely, I think, and once she realised… once she knew that the reason she left was because she was *also* superhuman… nothing could've hurt her more. They could've bonded even further. I wonder what would be different if they had."

Realisation dawns and I clap a hand to my mouth. Jamboree's father looks at me, and I can't force myself to speak, so I just prod at his head to speed along the realisation process. He stares at me, and if he can sense my interference, he doesn't let on.

"Julia can see that."

Damn it, no wonder she's so angry at us for just existing. The universe that she took Abyss to, at Charlie's wedding— the universe that they used to watch together. Is that a universe without the experiment, like Abyss had hypothesised, or is it just a universe where she *didn't leave*?

My hand is still over my mouth, I'm still staring wide eyed at Jamboree's father, when Abyss comes to stand next to me. She rests her fingertips against my upper arm to get my attention, tipping her head to indicate that I share.

Without really thinking about it, I reach into her head and dump all of my thoughts and realisations from the last thirty seconds. It's bound to be an overwhelming mess, but Abyss barely flinches at my intrusion into her head. In fact, I swear I see a wave of happiness roll by, before the inevitable shock of confusion.

"You think…" she says slowly, and I can see her mentally sorting through my thoughts. I hear her quiet 'oh' within her head before it's vocalised.

"Yeah," I say, finally managing to talk aloud again. My hand drops down to my side, and Abyss takes hold of it after a split-seconds thought. It feels very intentional.

I hadn't even thought about it, but it had been so incredibly easy to read her mind this time around; no deep explanation or exploration required. I guess it's because I'm more aware of the Void now, and I know how to read her.

Like before, I don't want to leave her mind. As though she can sense this, she squeezes my hand, and I'm sent a wave of *welcome*. I glance at her (*how often am I welcome, will you ever want me to leave, when you say that I'm welcome here what does that mean to you*) and promptly table that discussion for another time. Abyss just smirks at me, the barest lift of the lips that no one else seems to catch.

And speaking of everyone else, there's a newfound awkward tension settling over the room. I'd forgotten how many people were now in this room; two sets of parents, and Abyss' brother and niece. I feel my face heat up, and I scratch at the back of my neck.

Abyss' mother, at least, only looks amused. "What just happened, there?" she asks, and I kind of want to sink in to the floor and die.

Thankfully, Abyss has always been smarter than me. These people have no idea that I've never really done anything like that with my telepathy; they don't know how... intimate whatever-that-was was.

Abyss, recovering swiftly, says, "He was just sharing some information. It's… faster, especially when we're working."

She's not wrong— it would be useful to use that particular skill when we're on the job. The way she says it, though, so casually, like it's something that's a habit, that we don't even think about anymore… It makes me a little wistful.

When did I become such a sap?

"We," I gesture between myself and Jamboree's father, "think we figured out Jamboree's motivation. It feels like a missing piece of the puzzle, even if it doesn't really help us form a plan. It just makes things a bit easier to understand."

We explain what we mean; Abyss and I keep cutting each other off as our thoughts run in to each other, until I finally have to admit that it isn't productive, and pull myself out of her mind. The families have similar reactions to the rest of us; shock, and guilt.

Abyss is radiating guilt. I want to tell her she has no reason to be, but, in this one instance, I can sort of see where Jamboree is coming from. Not the 'destroy-whole-city-blocks' or the 'killing-and-or-hurting-my-closest-friends' thing, because there's no justification for that, but I would be hurt too. I can understand why Jamboree felt abandoned.

Clearly, Abyss can too. I reach out a hand for her, but she doesn't take it. I try not to feel disappointed by that. Casually holding each other's hands has become a part of my life over the past few weeks, and it's strangely hurtful to be rejected.

Or maybe not so strangely. I do love her, after all.

I keep trying to table that revelation for another time, but it sneaks up on me at inconvenient moments. She's trying to convince her parents and the Lago's to leave home for a few weeks, and I should probably be focusing on that conversation, but all I can think about is how nice it was to share my thoughts with her. I've always been able to read people's thoughts. No one has ever read mine before.

She glances over her shoulder at me and lets out a tiny huff of air. Shaking myself, I step forward to stand next to her. "We're trying to help," I say, attempting to smooth out any protests. "She knows where you live, and even if we may not know exactly what she's planning, we can be pretty sure that she's planning to come here. To keep you safe, we want to keep you away. Please. I'll pay for everything, you'll be well looked after."

Abyss smiles at me, and I can't help but return it with a sure to be dopey grin.

Then her brother coughs and says, "heel."

Abyss turns to face him more quickly than I've ever seen her move. "What's going on?" she snaps, pointing at her brother. "You've been nothing but snappy and rude to Caesar. What the hell is your problem?"

Jordan makes a face like he'd just bitten down on a lemon, but then he shakes his head. "You've got a Caesar ordering you around, Jenny. Every few seconds you look at him like you're asking for permission, all of your superhero gear is C-Corp branded… you can't blame us for thinking you've been bought."

I shift awkwardly from one foot to the other, staring between Jordan and Abyss' mom. I feel like I should say something, but I don't really know what I possibly could. Abyss looks back to me, and I shrug helplessly.

She says, "You know how much he's helped me, Jordan. I've *told* you. He's more than his money."

Jordan looks at me and raises his eyebrows. "Could've fooled me."

Abyss opens her mouth to say something else, but to my surprise, Jamboree's father steps in. "That's enough. We're all tense. There's been a lot of new information today, and we're stressed and confused, but we're all adults. They're offering us safety, and I personally think it'd be best to take it." Here, he pauses and sucks in a long breath. "I love my daughter, but I don't trust her to make the right decision right now."

Abyss' mother sighs, and reaches out for her daughter. "Has he really helped you that much?"

Abyss nods twice. "He's a good guy, Mom. He's my *friend*."

Again, I feel my heart swell at that. I'm her friend, and she thinks I'm good. I'm her friend, and she'll defend me. I'm her *friend*, and that seems to be enough to get her family to relax. At least for now; I'm sure this is an argument that we'll rehash in the future. Jordan shoots me a distrustful look as they disperse to grab overnight bags, but when I smile nervously at him, he at least attempts to return it.

It's only a few minutes later that the six of them are standing in front of us, each carrying bags (even Jessie, who's wearing a Dora the Explorer backpack). I call them a taxi and send them to a nearby hotel, and after we send them off, I call the hotel and book three adjoining rooms over the phone. The receptionist seems frustrated at having to organise this on such short notice, but there's very little that Caesar money can't buy.

I understand the concerns that Abyss' family has.

"I didn't... buy you, did I? Or Xander?"

Abyss smiles at me, and maybe it's just me, but she seems amused and a little fond. "Nah," she replies. "You've never been anything but decent. I think we got a pretty good deal. I mean, C-Corp tech and resources *and* a great team leader? What's there to complain about?"

43.

We stay in Abyss' childhood home. She doesn't seem to feel weird about it, although she doesn't go look in what would've been her bedroom. That's fair enough— if it were me, I wouldn't want to look either.

There's no guarantee that Jamboree will appear tonight, even if we did follow Ace's advice. As she keeps reminding us, she's not a psychic. So we decide to prepare for both outcomes: we change into our uniforms, and we order what might be a literal ton of food.

We're playfully arguing over a box of pad Thai when Abyss relents, leans back, and smiles softly at me. Her glasses are off. She'd taken them off almost as soon as everyone else had left. I try not to read into that.

"You really worry about it, don't you?"

"What?"

"If Xander and I are only your friends because of your money," she clarifies. "If the only reason I like you is because of all this." She gestures to the food spread out across the living room table, and then to her own uniform.

Truth is, I had thought of it before. Not about Xander, not really. He and I were friends before either of us understood how different our lives were, and my family all but adopted his family into ours. But even still, when I first started thinking about this superhero thing, and I reignited our friendship through a series of fancy lunches, I'd heard his mother's voice rattling around his head: *I almost think you're taking advantage.*

"Maybe sometimes," I admit. "Or at least that… I'm not the person you think I am. That maybe I really *am* bribing you. And on top of that, I've got *telepathy*, maybe I'm messing around in your heads without even thinking about it!"

"William," she says, and it sounds softer and nicer coming from her than from my own family. "You couldn't even read my mind until three weeks ago. I've been your friend for almost a year. I don't think you need to worry about *that*."

That's a fair point, actually. It does calm me down a little.

"And as for the money thing," Abyss continues before I can even think of anything to say, "it *is* nice that someone in our group has access to all of this… stuff. We wouldn't be the team that we are without your money. But if you think for one second that Xander would've agreed to this team if he didn't genuinely like you, if you think that I would've let you boss me around, without honestly believing in you as a person, then you're even dumber than I thought."

"Well," I say, emphasising the vowel sound to distract from my flushed cheeks. "We can't all be geniuses."

She elbows me. "Maybe not."

It's quiet for a few moments; me digging into my pad Thai, Abyss picking at a spicy meat pizza. It's companionable, and leaves plenty of room for my thoughts. It's easy, spending time with her. It always has been, even if I didn't realise it before.

We used to have Xander settled in between us, and very rarely was it just the two of us together. The thought sends a ripple of nausea through me. If he were here, this might not be happening, but I've grown used to brushing knees with Abyss when we sit side-by-side.

He's been gone less than a month. We used to see each other every day. Does it make me horrible— I think it might make me horrible— to be getting used to his absence? It feels like it's been eons. It doesn't feel like it's been long enough.

Abyss puts down her pizza crust— she never eats them, much to my annoyance (the crust is the *best part*)— and shifts ever so slightly closer to me, resting her head on my shoulder. My hand stills with chopsticks halfway out of the box, my eyes close. She doesn't seem to notice, or, if she does, she has the grace not to say anything.

I rest the takeaway box on my knees and lean back against the couch, careful not to disturb Abyss. I chance a glance at her and find her eyes wide open. I can never tell what direction she's looking unless she's looking at me. She's not looking at me currently, but that's okay. In fact, it would be a lot harder to ask her what I'm about to if she was.

"Abyss—"

I'm cut off by the front door opening. Lightning fast, Abyss is on her feet, and I follow a few steps behind, shoving my takeaway box on the table before I'm able to stand by her side. She's pushed her glasses back down over her eyes, and her face returns to its typical blank, unreadable expression. I try to school mine in to something similar, but I'm sure my nervousness is plenty visible. I can feel my heart pounding against my ribcage and my hands are never still when I'm worried. Without my realising, they've started tapping against my thigh.

Jamboree strolls into the room. She moves languidly, panther-like, her long arms swaying in time with her steps. Her straight dark hair falls in a perfect curtain around her face, sleek and well-styled. I'm distracted by her hands— her fingernails are painted a pretty pink, but I've seen those same hands rip universes open, tear portals through Abyss, cause Xander's death.

She laughs when she sees us, her head tipping back, and raises one of those deadly hands to cover her mouth. I'm somehow unsurprised by this reaction.

"Oh," she says, once she's calmed down a little. "I guess I should've known— there aren't that many universes where you don't come here."

Abyss and I stay silent, as though by some unspoken agreement. I hope that Jamboree doesn't act so much as a cliché as to start monologuing, but, in all honesty, I wouldn't put it past her. She's dramatic like that.

"I think you're forgetting how well I know you, Jenna-Louise," she says, and Abyss, next to me, straightens up, tense. "You said something about our families and I reacted poorly, so of course you'd... *extrapolate* that I'd be coming here from that tiny bit of information. You call yourself a scientist."

"You came here, didn't you?" Abyss quips.

Jamboree tuts, and I have to resist the urge to scream at her. I curl my hands into fists and dig my fingernails against my palms, the pressure reminding me to stay still. The movement must catch Jamboree's eyes, though, because her gaze snaps to me, and she smirks as though she's amused.

"Ay," she laughs, "¿No eres guapo?"

"Sí," I reply shortly. "*Muy* guapo, mucho gracias."

Jamboree's eyes sparkle in amusement. "You know, I used to collect magazines with you in them. Read all about the languages you spoke. I loved that you spoke Spanish, like me. Dreamt about getting to talk to you."

"Muérete," I spit. She smirks at me and returns her attention to Abyss.

Abyss is still stone silent, face blank and body unmoving. Her gloved hands slowly curl into fists as Jamboree scans her up and down. "Oh, Jenny," Jamboree drawls. "You don't scare me."

"Oh, JuJu," Abyss replies, perfectly matching Jamboree's tone. "I think you're forgetting how well I know you."

For the first time since entering the room, the humour in Jamboree's face falters. Her eyes go wide and her mouth parts as though she's going to speak. It's only for a moment, for a heartbeat, and then she regains her composure, curling her lips into a cruel smirk.

"Know me?" she says, stepping forwards until she's toe-to-toe with Abyss. "Jenny, you haven't seen me for three years. You don't *know* who I am, anymore."

"Well, then," Abyss replies, unflinching, "I guess we should get re-acquainted."

And she punches Jamboree in the gut.

I jolt backwards, out of the way of Jamboree's stumbling body. Her eyes are wide, but she recovers quickly, finding her footing and bringing her fists up. I try to slip into her head, but she must have gotten a new dampener, because all I get is static, white noise. Somehow aware of my attempt to get in, she smirks at me.

While she's distracted, Abyss darts forward and hits her again in the stomach. Abyss is a boxer, and I watch her settle in to some sort of rhythm, ducking underneath Jamboree's arms when she lashes out, reaching for Abyss' hair. Abyss, ducked low beneath Jamboree's flailing arms, hooks her hand behind her knee and pulls. She stumbles forward, and Abyss rolls out of the way, leaving the hard floor open to catch Jamboree. Her head smacks against the ground, and she groans.

Abyss straightens up, dusts off her arms, readjusts her glasses. Jamboree pushes herself to her feet.

Then lunges at me.

I grab each of her arms and hold her still in front of me. I'm not particularly strong. I'm not a good fighter. Jamboree stills anyway. She glares at me, dark eyes burning. At this negligible distance, I can already see slight swelling where her head hit the floor. Her long hair is mussed, and although we haven't been going at this long, she's breathing hard.

"You've crossed every single line," I tell her. "You've killed people!"

"I haven't killed anyone!"

"Legion is dead because of *you.*"

She seems to falter at this, if only just a little. When Abyss opens her mouth to speak, Jamboree narrows her eyes again, any trace of concern vanishing in an instant.

"I can see why she likes you," she mocks, "Guapo *y* fuerte."

The sound of fanfare— of *jamboree*— shouldn't surprise me, but it does.

I hear Abyss shout my name, and then I'm falling.

44.

I fall through the portal feet-first, but the orientation is off, and I end up landing flat on my back in a grassy field. Jamboree stands over me but turns away as she brushes off. I stay on the ground, winded, sucking in deep breaths.

I hear another portal start to open and force myself to my feet, grabbing her wrist and squeezing. She attempts to shake me off, but I only hold tighter. I'm not letting her go anywhere without me. I'm not staying in some other universe.

"Take me back."

She laughs, throwing her head back and sending her long black hair cascading down her spine. She'd be beautiful girl, if not for everything she's done.

"Take me back," I say again, trying to sound forceful and failing. I still haven't fully caught my breath. Inter-dimensional travel can take a lot out of a person.

"I thought you were supposed to be the *leader*. You're not very commanding, you know."

She's my only way home. I can't let her leave me here— I'd be stuck. Probably forever. My internal monologue descends into mindless cursing, and I have to fight the urge to sink back to the grass.

Jamboree continues, "You aren't the brains of the operation, are you? That's Abyss. And Legion was the only one of you who could actually *fight*. You're not exactly the strongest team in the world. And if *you're* the leader, then we're all screwed."

I bristle at the comment, and, using my grip on her wrist as leverage, spin her around to face me. She spits on me, wrenching her wrist from my grip and gesturing to the side, tearing open a portal. She sidesteps through, and I chase after her, barely making it before the portal closes.

The sky is purple here, and I have no way of knowing if it's only because of the time of day. We're on a crowded city street, the bustling people barely noticing our appearance. I almost lose Jamboree, but I catch sight of her velvet suit jacket as she worms through the crowd and dart off after her. We pass by a bus stuck in stand-still traffic, and I do a double take when I notice the advertisement on the side shows Abyss, smiling, deep brown eyes wide.

"Wha—?"

"It's another universe, dumbass," Jamboree says, and I jump. I hadn't realised she'd noticed me following her. "Here, the Tolbert's are the most influential family in the world, and the Caesar's are just ordinary."

"Am I a genius here, then?"

Jamboree snorts. "You haven't got a clue, have you? You're no one, Caesar. Your name means *nothing* here. No money, no influence, and, no, you're not a genius. Anywhere we go—" she jerks her head to the bus— "that's her job. Here, you aren't *anything*."

A universe where you aren't brilliant isn't one I want to see.

Caesar is more than his money.

Am I, Abyss? What can I do, stranded in another universe, with a meaningless name and three bank cards for accounts that don't exist? I'm not a fighter, I'm not a genius. I've spent so long in the public eye that I barely know who to be without it. It's been about balance my entire life— not letting anyone get too close, not telling anyone too much about myself, because they could use it against me.

Abyss, Ace, *Xander*, they're exceptions to the rule, but even then— I pulled them into the public eye, didn't I? Have I shared anything with any of them that I didn't also, eventually, tell the world? Have I let any of them in on anything truly personal?

Without my money, without my name, without my team, who am I?

Jamboree shakes her head, smirking. I haven't answered. I don't have an answer.

We fall through another portal, and this time I land on my feet. The trees around us seem to whisper at our arrival. I wonder if it's the wind, or if trees really do talk wherever we are.

"So many universes," she says, picking at her nails, "where you're no one."

No one? Nothing?

She stalks forward and I step backwards until my back is flush against a tree. She smirks at my continued silence.

She's forgetting something important. *I'm* forgetting something important.

I'm a telepath.

Take away everything else. What am I?

I'm Mexican, I'm Greek, I'm my father's son and my mother's child. I'm a good brother to all my siblings. I'm a best friend, a confidant, a leader. I'm a history buff and a science fiction nerd. I'm a *telepath*.

Jamboree is still wearing a dampener on the breast of her jacket; obviously, she hasn't forgotten it entirely, but she clearly underestimates it, and underestimates me.

"I've got a few things going for me," I tell her, and I've been silent for too long for it to have any impact— but that's what I'm counting on.

She starts to laugh, cackling like a hyena. I watch her, waiting for the moment when she— yes, she tips her head back, eyes sliding closed as she laughs at me. I reach forward, wrapping my fingers around the dampener and pulling hard, while using my other hand to shove her out of my personal space.

She stumbles backwards caught off guard. For all her talk, she's not much of a fighter either. The dampener stays with me, popping away from the pin back. She notices immediately, of course. She may not be a genius, but she's not a complete idiot.

"You're right," I tell her, dropping the dampener and grinding it under my heel, "I'm not that much of a fighter. And I'm definitely not the 'brains of the operation.' But…"

I slide into her mind.

I have easy access to them.

Her mind is chaotic, filled up with a few too many thoughts, song lyrics and book quotes and— huh, she likes Star Trek too— floor plans.

336

Floor plans? On closer inspection, I recognise the layout as the penthouse. She does her research, clearly, and I recoil at the thought of her studying our home. She's got memories in her head of herself, in third person, snippets of other universes that she's watched or visited. And— oh, it's the first time she opened a portal.

"Get out of my head!"

"Hey," I say, suddenly curious, still sifting through her memories (the portal appears in a bathroom, still half-shared even if the other occupant hasn't been home in a few days— swirling, silver-blue-purple-green, at one with the universes— and she *can't wait* to tell Jenna-Louise—), "Think of Abyss."

Jamboree's thoughts turning instantly vicious. Flashes of black glasses, of curled fists, of— Xander, with his arm slung around her while they laugh— me, kicking at her feet while we walk— Mrs. Pae, stroking her cheek and smiling— everything tainted, bitter, angry. HAVE YOU SEEN THIS GIRL? on sheet after sheet of paper, spitting out of a printer. *Abandoned*, Jamboree thinks, *left behind.*

A different universe, but the same two girls: Jamboree and Abyss, Julia and Jenna-Louise, curled up on a couch, talking in low voices about what to do now. I see Abyss' eyes, nebulous, and how she ducks her head and laughs at one of Jamboree's suggestions.

Another version: the two of them sobbing in a bathroom, Abyss pressing her palms roughly against her eyes, Jamboree talking in low, soothing tones, playing with her hair.

Another: shaky fingers dialling a familiar number and speaking all in a rush about experiments gone wrong and the voice on the other end promising to be there in a heartbeat.

And another: Abyss reaching out to Jamboree for a hug—

And another: Jamboree in the room when the experiment fails, racing to Abyss—

And another: they sit, with others I don't recognise, clearly on some sort of team—

I push myself away from the tree, stepping carefully closer to her. She sniffs, going for dismissive, but I catch sight of watery eyes before she turns away from me. "Get out of my head, Caesar," she says, weakly, quiet, and I do. It doesn't take much. It was volatile from the get-go.

"Jamb— Julia," I start, but she whips her head around and cuts me off.

Her eyes don't look watery, now, they're burning. She shoves me back, shaking her head furiously, grinding her teeth together. "Every universe," she half-growls, "every universe but mine."

I want to say, 'have you considered, maybe, talking to her about this, instead of turning super-villain and trying to kill her and her friends?' but I don't get the chance, because Jamboree is lurching forwards again, shoving my shoulders and sending me stumbling.

"You tell her what you saw," she tips her head forward at an angle that casts her eyes in shadow, dons a smirk that shows off her sharp teeth. "I want the guilt to eat her alive."

"Yeah? She's not the one who killed someone," I say, stepping forward so we're toe-to-toe. I think I see something pained flicker across her face. "Legion is dead because of you. I want the guilt of *that* to eat you alive."

And then she pushes me again, and I fall backwards through another portal.

45.

I land flat on my back on Abyss' parent's living room floor.

"Caesar!"

Abyss is immediately in my line of sight, hovering over me. She's got her phone pressed to her ear, her free hand resting on my arm. I want to assure her that I'm alright, but landing hard on my back has knocked the wind right out of me. Again. I try to catch my breath, and focus on Abyss' words.

"No, no," she's saying into the phone. "I think he's fine. Just catching his breath. Is this really what you meant when you said the odds were good?"

Ace, then, and Abyss is close enough to me that I can hear her response through the phone. "I said the odds were over fifty, not that they were *good*."

"Well, you didn't mention anything about Caesar getting sent to an alternate universe," Abyss gripes, her lips pursed into a minuscule scowl I'm fairly confident no one else would've noticed.

"You didn't ask for specifics!" Ace huffs. "So I didn't get the numbers to break it down that much."

I sit up, finally breathing normally, and gesture for Abyss to hand me the phone. "Ace," I say, as soon as I have it in my hand. "In the future, when we're dealing with Jamboree, factor in the very real threat of *being sent to a different universe.*"

"I gave you what you asked for!" she protests.

I roll my eyes and wrap up the conversation by assuring her that, yes, I'm okay, and, no, we don't blame her *or* the numbers. I hang up, and turn to see Abyss, worrying her bottom lip between her teeth. I reach a hand out to her, and she takes it, threading our fingers together.

"You disappeared. You could've been anywhere," she says, then shakes her head. "What happened? Did she say anything?"

Abyss will avoid calling her 'Jamboree' if she can help it. I think of all those other universes where she may have called her Jamboree, but in different contexts, for different reasons. I shake my head. "Nothing important," I reply. Abyss doesn't look convinced, but she nods anyway.

After a beat, I add, "let's go home."

She nods again.

46.

Abyss spreads her arms wide as we walk back into the penthouse, dropping her bag off of her fingertips so it hits the floor with a soft thud. The sofa welcomes her into its comfortable embrace, and she sinks into it gratefully. She grins at me, and gestures for me to join.

As I drop my bag next to hers and place my keys in their dish, she says, "It's good to be home."

"Yeah," I reply, making my way over to sink into the place next to her. "Yeah, it definitely is."

She positions her arm so it's behind my head, threading her fingers through the curls at the nape of my neck, over and over. I sigh at the touch, leaning in to it and feeling myself relax.

Her family had been frustrated when we'd announced that we were leaving again. Her brother had sighed, long and hard, her father had stroked her hair, smiled, and her mother had wrapped her up in a giant hug. Abyss had returned these affections, but explained that she needed to go home.

Even without telepathy, I would've been able to feel her parents heartbreak just from their expressions. I think they understood it, though. But I would be distraught if Abyss had decided to stay, just as they were when she decided to go. That's what happens when you love someone, I think. You can understand them, but it still hurts.

Abyss had saved all of their contact details, promised to actually call, promised to visit. Then she linked her arm through mine, and we left. Climbed into the backseat and taken off. Abyss had slept most of the way, her head resting on my shoulder.

Her fingers continue to play with my curls, and I feel myself sink in to a blissful sleep.

When I wake up, we're laying out on the wide couch, Abyss tucked into my side with her head to my chest, her feet tucked under my calf. I've got one arm draped over my stomach, brushing against her side.

"Hey," I whisper, "bed will be more comfortable."

We brush our teeth side by side. I scrub at my face, change out of my jeans and into a pair of loose sweatpants. Abyss finds a pair of leggings in amongst her things, so she changes too. We crawl into the bed, and without really thinking about it, we end up in the centre, in much the same position we'd woken up in.

I, personally, feel a little bit more awake now. Abyss, who keeps idly kicking at the covers, seems to be as well. I laugh lightly, and after a few seconds so does she.

"You were going to say something," she says, voice barely above a whisper. "Before Julia showed up, you seemed like you were going to say something important."

It takes me a second to remember. It was nearly two days ago, in my defence. When I do, I make a quiet sound of realisation and debate on whether or not to say anything. She nudges me expectantly. My thumb strokes up and down against her side.

"I was just—" I cut myself off with a shaky breath. "I was thinking about the Void. About *you*. About your mind."

"Good things?" she asks lightly, but I can feel her tense under my hand.

"Very good things," I clarify, resting my chin on the top of her head. She relaxes almost immediately. I like that she trusts me that much, that my word is all it takes. "When I was sending you my thoughts, I didn't send you something specific. I just opened my mind to you, and you understood my mess of thoughts."

"It was easy," she says, "I know you, it was easy."

I smile up at the ceiling. "I've never done something like that before. Opened my mind to someone, let them… you could've dug through all my memories. You're— you're welcome to dig through my memories, if you want. I've seen yours, it's only fair."

She huffs a quiet laugh, her breath ticking my chest through my t-shirt. "I bet you offer that to all the girls," she teases.

"No," I reply, even though I know she didn't expect an answer. "Just you."

"Why?"

I'm sure she can feel my heart rate pick up, so I take several long breaths to try to calm it down. I should tell her, I should *absolutely* tell her. It's on the tip of my tongue: *I love you, I love you, I love you—* but she shifts, her braids tickling against my arm. I've gotten used to this closeness. I trust her with all of me. I've never let anyone close enough to see me at my most personal, at my most private. But I'd let her stay in my head forever, if she wanted.

"Because you're my friend," I say. "Because I am endlessly fascinated by you."

47.

"You *what*."

"I told her," I repeat, shaking my head at Ace's laughter. "That I'm 'endlessly fascinated' by her."

Ace only laughs louder at that, pulling her hands up to cover her smile, and I bury my face in my arms, groaning. I hear Nani place our drinks— Ace is back to drinking tea, although it's peppermint now— on the table, and glance up to smile at her. She grins in return, patting me sympathetically on the arm.

Thankfully, the diner is pretty quiet. Early afternoon isn't peak greasy breakfast food time, unless your names are Ace and Caesar, in which case, apparently every time of day is greasy breakfast food time.

"How long have you loved her?" Ace asks me as I straighten up to start drinking my coffee, arms folded on the table with one manicured nail resting against her bottom lip.

She's cut her hair short around her jaw recently. It makes her look older. She looks happier than I've seen her in a long time. I thought this over-performance of herself would fade away after a few months of her being back, but it seems like this is her new identity. It's better than the red hair and high-necked blouses. Ace has always been more of a short skirts and fishnets sort of girl.

Her eyes widen slightly, and she pushes her head forward in some sort of curious nod; I realise that I haven't actually answered her question.

"Sorry," I say, "I got distracted... you just seem really good, these days. I'm happy for you."

Ace smiles, a unique expression where one corner of her mouth goes up slightly higher than the other, and her eyes squint just a little. "I'm happy for me, too. But you're avoiding the question. How long have you loved her?"

"What do you mean?" I ask, playing dumb. Ace doesn't humour me. She just rolls her eyes, drops her hand from her face and onto the table. I'm hit with a rush of fondness for her, just from this simple expression. She stares to the side of us, seemingly watching passers-by out the window. But I can see the way her eyes go all unfocused. I resist the urge to slip into her head and watch whatever numbers are flying through her vision. She's said she doesn't like it very much when I do that.

But she won't look back at me or even say a single word until I answer her question. "I don't know," I finally answer. "Since I met her?"

"That's not how love works," Ace says, turning back to face me and almost immediately reaching out to pull one of my curls. It bounces back into shape as soon as she lets go. I huff, pushing my hair out of my face. "Come on, Cee," she sighs, "When did you know?"

"Why does it matter?"

"Because," she smiles again, teasing, "I want to be able to pull this story out at your wedding."

I shake my head again, raking a hand through my hair. "What wedding?"

"It's, uhm, bound to happen eventually," she says, but I can tell there was some other word she wanted to use. Her brow always furrows together into a tiny scowl when she can't think of the right word to use. It's something she's always struggled with. I wish I could help, but I don't understand the French that she thinks in.

 "I doubt that. She's too good for me."

"Oh, please," Ace flicks her hand dismissively through the air. "She loves you, too."

I don't ask her how she knows that. If she knows that. Instead, I pause a little longer and try to think of a more honest answer to her question. She's right, people don't fall in love at first sight, not in real life. I lick my lips, bounce my leg. Ace, to her credit, doesn't try to rush me. "Long enough," I say. "Long enough to know it's for real. D'you remember... that last fight against Jamboree?" Ace nods, her red-painted lips forming a delicate frown. It looks like a performance of sadness, but I know it's genuine. "It was that day. While I was in her head, properly, for the first time."

"When you understood her," Ace breathes, and I nod. Sometimes, Ace just gets me, and I'm more glad that ever that I met her. "Caesar, that might be the most romantic thing I've ever heard you say."

"Is it romantic that I had to know her, in her entirety, before I loved her?"

Ace shrugs, pushes a stray hair behind her ear. "I dunno. I think you probably loved her before then. You *cared* about her, anyway, and you guys were always, like, looking at each other and stuff. There was *definitely* some kind of attraction, and she was your friend. If you ask me, that's what love *is*. And when you understood her, that was, uhm... something else. Something that made everything else make sense."

Her explanation makes as much sense as anything else.

Before I can think of anything more to say, Ace is giggling, a hand coming up to ineffectively cover her mouth.

"What?" I ask, already grinning.

"It's just..." she giggles again. "You're in love with a universe."

When she says it like that, it is pretty funny.

"It's like, it's like… Boy-meets-girl? Nah, boy-meets-universe." I say, joining her in laughter.

I feel lighter for having shared these thoughts with *somebody*, and when Ace goes to take a drink from her tea and, when overcome with another giggle, spits some over on the table, I'm overcome with a fondness for her. She reaches for napkins to clean up her spill, cheeks flushed red with embarrassment, worried that Nani saw.

I lean back in my seat, feeling the laughter subside. "Hey," I say, and she looks up as she drops the dirty napkins to the side. "You're my best friend."

I say it seriously, because I don't think I've told her enough. She smiles at me- not her typical cheesy grin, but a real, soft smile that doesn't show her teeth.

"You're mine, too," she says, equally serious. "I don't know where or, uh, who I'd be if I hadn't met you. You helped me so much, and I'm so glad that you're in life, Cee."

"You've helped me more," I reply, and when she waves a hand dismissively through the air, I continue, "No, seriously, your friendship has done me so much good. Without you, I wouldn't be doing what I'm doing, I wouldn't have this team, I wouldn't— I don't know. You mean so much to me, A."

"Back at ya," she says, and then she's grinning again. "If only it were as easy to tell someone that you love them as it is to say that."

"It's just so *different* with Abyss."

"I know," she says, sinking down in her seat and flicking her hand dramatically. "*Romance*! It makes everything so much more complicated."

"Are you having romantic woes?" I ask, brow furrowing. She hasn't mentioned anyone since before she went undercover.

"Woes!" she laughs. "There is this guy. I met him while I was undercover, and when it came time to come home, I told him the truth. Before you say anything," she says in a rush, because I had already opened my mouth, "I *know* that was risky, but I trust him. A lot. We've... stayed close."

"You love him?" I ask, because, well, turnaround's fair play.

She sighs, and I watch her eyes trail distractedly to the window. "Yeah," she says, after a moment. "Yeah, a lot."

"How'd he take the whole 'I'm not who I said I was' thing?"

"Surprisingly well," she admits, smiling at the memory. I see flashes of a smirk, some rolling eyes, before I pull myself away.

"Tell me about him?"

She smiles wider, and starts to talk.

48.

The two weeks after my chat with Ace seem to fly by without my consent.

It's not that I'm busy, really. I force myself to go to classes, shaking off the fog that's been in my head and start actually actively learning things. I make a point to speak to to my professors, to apologise and explain. Most of them are understanding. They'd seen what happened on the news. Still, I'd missed a good portion of the first month, which mostly means that I have to play catch up on the introductory stuff. I drag myself to the library after classes, studying, making notes.

I get home late pretty much every night. Abyss mostly gives up the pretence of living with Mrs. Pae, although she does spent a handful of nights there over the fortnight. Mostly, she'll arrive at the penthouse either shortly before or after me, and we'll get food (sometimes, we attempt to cook— it turns out that even thinking of it as chemistry doesn't help Abyss, and I run out of recipes I can confidently make after four nights) and curl up to watch comedy specials or science fiction shows. Abyss is always aware of which comedians have new specials, and I rope her into watching *Star Trek* and *Buffy* with me, too.

Sometimes, we talk about Jamboree, and what we're going to do about her. I do end up telling Abyss what she'd said, and she goes quiet for nearly twenty minutes, before sighing, and setting her shoulders. We agree to leave it for now. Jamboree seems desperate for attention, and I have no doubt that she'll make herself known sooner or later.

I don't even really notice the time passing until I open the penthouse door to shouts of 'SURPRISE!' and the sound of a party popper.

As I shake confetti out of my hair, I do a quick head count. Abyss, who's standing with an elbow resting on Ace's shoulder (she's holding the party popper, grinning a little crazily). Judging by the fresh braids tied in Ace's hair, I'd say they probably spent yesterday together, planning this. My family, bar Carlos, who'll still be in school; Mrs. Pae, Ava Layton arm-in-arm with Zoram, and a bunch of Ace's roommates — at least five of them, but there may be more hanging around. They've even managed to invite people from my classes at university, although I'm glad to see they've curated the guest list. No one who'll film this. No one who'll use it for their own gain.

"Is it the nineteenth already?" I ask, closing the door and allowing myself to be wrapped up in hugs from my family. Charlie and Eliza come at me from both sides, ruffling my hair and pinching at my cheeks.

Abyss smiles in answer to my question. "You've been all wrapped up in stuff, so I thought it'd be nice to do something for you."

"She just needed my decorating, uh… expertise," Ace adds with a bright laugh, half-tackling me in a big hug, "Happy birthday, Cee!"

When I finally disentangle myself from her and look around the penthouse, I'm unsurprised that Ace had a hand in the decorating. They've covered an entire wall in mis-matched birthday banners, there's twenty-one 'it's a boy!' balloons placed randomly around the living room, and there's confetti covering almost every surface, including the couch.

"I tried to stop her," Abyss stage whispers to me, smiling, "but apparently if you give Ace a balloon, she goes power-mad."

"I can hear you!" Ace says back in a sing-song. "And I don't care!"

My mom and Mrs. Pae come over to me once I'm sitting down on the couch, trying not to think about the confetti clean up later. My mom wraps an arm around me, and Mrs. Pae affectionately pats my knee.

"Happy birthday, William," my mom says, and I roll my eyes at the use of my given name. "Don't you roll your eyes at me, young man. It's your birthday, and I'm your mother. I'm allowed to call you by the name I gave you."

Mrs. Pae snorts, but when we look at her, her eyes are faraway and watery. "Xander was the same way. It was *always* Xander. Never Alex or Alexander. Sun-Young was okay, but he called himself Xander."

My mom laughs fondly, squeezing Mrs. Pae's shoulder. "I called him Alex once, and the look on his face…"

I smirk at the memory, remembering the distinct curl on Xander's lip as he debated between correcting my mom and letting it go in an effort to be polite. In the end, I'd rolled my eyes at my mom and said, pointedly, "Xander, let's go upstairs."

We were just kids then, and it was before I told him about my telepathy. We would've been about ten, maybe eleven. I glance around the room, and smile bitterly to myself. How times change.

As though she can sense my shift in mood, Abyss looks up and locks eyes with me at the exact moment I turn to look at her. She's chatting with Ava and Zoram, but she pauses, seemingly mid-sentence, to smile. I see Ava follow her gaze and grin, winking knowingly at me. I flush, and look down.

Mrs. Pae and my mom have moved on to talking about flowers, which doesn't surprise me. My mom needs to order about a million marigolds. I push myself up and away from the conversation, sliding next to Ace at a drinks table.

"Nothing alcoholic," she says, handing me a plastic cup full of something orange. "At least, not until we kick the adults out."

I take a sip. Orange soda. "Maybe I don't want anything alcoholic."

"It's your twenty-first," she says. "Of course you want a drink. You're legal and everything. Your dad offered to bring whiskey, but whiskey is gross, so I told him you weren't keen to drink on a school night. But don't worry, I've brought some of my favourites for later."

"You're only nineteen," I point out, raising an eyebrow at her. "You're one to talk about me being 'legal'."

She shrugs, unconcerned. "Bars, clubs, and casinos are necessary in my, uh… specific brand of superherodom. I've obviously had a drink."

It's a go-to excuse, one I've heard more than once. I worry about her, sometimes, but she does seem to be getting better. Maybe her months undercover helped; I don't know. I wrap one arm around her shoulders and squeeze. She laughs, and pushes me off of her.

"Go on, *mingle*. It's your birthday. Go bug your sisters, or hit on Abyss, or *something*."

I smirk at her and pointedly stay exactly where I am, sipping on my orange soda. "Is that guy around?"

Ace doesn't play dumb, just waves a hand vaguely next to her. "Oh, he's around somewhere."

"Have you told him yet? That you love him?"

"Have you told Abyss yet? That you love her?" She parrots, staring hard at me over the rim of her own cup. "It's your birthday, so I'm not going to call you a hypocrite, but…"

"You just called me a hypocrite, pretty much."

"Good," she says, "then we understand each other."

We chat for a few minutes longer, making conversation about my schooling, her thoughts about going back to finish high school.

"You *could* just get a GED," I say. "It's just one test then."

"Yeah," she says, sighing. "But I *liked* high school."

"You're a bizarre creature, Ace," I reply in a deadpan, and she laughs. This time, when she shoves me away, I actually go, tossing her a wave over my shoulder.

I do go bug my sisters; trying to convince Charlie to light my birthday candles with her abilities, telling Eliza to mute anyone who decides to sing Happy Birthday. Charlie's wife, Farah, joins me, ribbing into them until they both relent. I chat to my dad about what work he wants me doing at the company now that I'm back into my routine at school. I avoid Ava and her teasing smiles, chat to Ace's roommates. A bunch of them are superheroes too, although on a smaller scale than me and Abyss, but they've got a lot more going on than I realised.

As promised, once the adults leave, Ace cracks out some bottles and starts mixing cocktails. She hands me the first one, shouting about my first legal drink. We pass out more drinks and start playing loud music.

Ava and Zoram, who don't drink, excuse themselves around midnight, hugging me goodbye and wishing me a happy birthday.

The rest of us end up sprawled out in my living room, passing each other drinks as requested and, on occasion, getting up to dance to our favourite songs. Ace dances the most, alternating between dragging me to my feet, or getting her roommates to bounce around with her. She's not drunk, but she's happy, giggling and talking to the air.

I decide to kick them all out at three-thirty, ordering taxis for everyone. I get more hugs, claps on the back, and birthday wishes as they all file out. I breathe a happy sigh as the door finally closes behind them. Abyss grins at me, and holds out one final surprise: a cupcake from my favourite sweet shop. It has a sugary crown placed on top, and my name written on it in red syrup.

"Happy birthday, William Antonio Caesar the Third," she says, her voice tired but full of good humour.

"Thank you, Abyss," I reply, holding my arms out for a hug. She places the cupcake on the kitchen counter before she wraps her arms around my waist, resting her head against my chest. I breathe slowly.

Tell her, something inside me that sounds suspiciously like Ace whispers. And the words are on the tip of my tongue: *I love you, I love you, I love you.*

I open my mouth, but before I can say anything, she's letting out a tired sigh and saying, "let's get some rest. You've got school tomorrow."

49.

When we wake up the next morning, closer to midday than is actually an acceptable time to wake up, I decide to eat my cupcake for breakfast. As I'm licking off the creamy frosting, Abyss stares at me for a long moment, chewing on a bite of a protein bar, before she speaks.

"They had Halloween cupcakes," she says, voice scratchy from overuse the night before. "It made me think of Xander… Halloween was his favourite."

My stomach drops a little, and I place the cupcake back on the counter. "It's only eleven days away. There'll be trick-or-treaters, probably. I had loads last year."

"You live in the nicest penthouse in the city," she says, shaking her head. "Of course you did."

I lick some loose frosting from the corner of my lip. "Well, sucks to be them. I'm not going to be here this year."

Her brow furrows. "Why not?"

"I'm not allowed to host anymore," I reply, grinning. "I spilled a bottle of wine and then knocked over some of the candles while trying to clean it up, which went about as well as you'd expect. Plus, according to dad, I didn't have enough food, and Carlos said my decorating was horrible. So we're celebrating at the main house this year. Now that Eliza lives there, we don't have to worry as much about cleaners and things, so mom's arranging it all."

"Celebrating…?" Abyss trails off, and then seems to realise what I'm talking about. "Día de Muertos?"

I nod, not having realised she didn't know. "Yeah," I shrug. "We usually spend the whole three days together, but Carlos is still in school, so he can't miss that much. And once you factor in travel, it does take a while."

"Can't he teleport?" Abyss asks.

"Not over oceans," I say, shaking my head. "Or at least, he's tried it once and came back soaking wet, so we figured it was best to leave it alone. He does hate flying though. He hates how slow it is."

"Huh," she replies, and even without reading her mind, I can see the gears turning in her head. I grin at her, and pick my cupcake back up, finishing it in two bites.

"You're invited," I say, and she snaps out of her thoughts to look at me. "I mean, you can come, if you want, to be distracted from all the Halloween stuff. And because… I'd like you to be there. If you want."

Abyss smiles softly at me, and shakes her head. "Of course I'll come."

"Good," I say, and I'm surprised by how relieved that makes me feel. "Good, I'm glad."

Abyss shakes her head again, finishes off her protein bar, and heads towards the door.

"Where are you going?" I ask, pressing my palms onto the counter behind me and leaning back into my shoulders. I realise she's wearing her workout clothes: black leggings and a dark grey short sleeved top.

She grins at me over her shoulder. "I'm going to go punch Ace. Repeatedly. You can come, if you want."

I decide that I do. It sounds more appealing than going to school hungover, and I only have one class today anyway. I don't know how Abyss is managing to be so composed— I wonder if the Void has something to do with it. I follow along a few steps behind her as she leads the way to the gym, with whatever the Abyss-equivalent of a 'spring in her step' is. She looks purposeful. I watch her twin braids bounce against her back, and my steps match the rhythm.

The gym is clean, well-maintained. I don't know why, but whenever Abyss spoke about boxing, I always pictured dingy, underground rings with a vaguely yellow tint, like the grimy casinos Ace used to drag me to. But Abyss' gym is well lit, with long mirrored walls, and high-end equipment. Ace is waiting by the boxing ring, leaning against the ropes and playing on her phone. She's wearing bright red leggings with a black sports bra. Her hair is still in the braids that Abyss had done, twin ones that mean they almost match.

Ace smirks as she sees us approaching, scanning me up and down. She thinks I look a mess, with my curls matted and my eyes still sort of bleary and unfocused.

"How are you both avoiding hangovers?" I whine, and they laugh at me.

"I didn't drink very much," Ace says, which is a lie, but she's got a hell of an alcohol tolerance, so I guess I'll give it to her.

Abyss answers, simply, "the Void," which sounds about right.

They step into the ring, and I drop down on to a low bench just outside of it. They launch in to it without any preamble, which doesn't really surprise me. Their friendship still confuses me.

Ace and Abyss shoot insults at each other as they swing, dodge, and bounce around the ring. I can tell, even without experience, that they aren't actually fighting. There's too much rhythm and balance; it's a workout, not actual training.

The patten slips, switches into something slightly more like a real fight, but I'm sure that they aren't putting any real force into it. They knock each other on the arms a little bit, and once Ace has to take a breather after Abyss slips, just slightly, and catches her in the ribs, but otherwise they're smiling and laughing, even as they scoff and tease.

They're both covered in a thin sheen of sweat by the time they step out of the ring about fifteen minutes later. Wordlessly, they move on to punching bags (Abyss) and treadmills (Ace). I hover somewhere in the middle for a few seconds, until Ace rolls her eyes and waves me towards Abyss with a shooing motion.

I find another seat and watch Abyss. After a few minutes of harsh swinging at the bag, she turns to me, breathing hard. "You look like an idiot," she says, "sitting around at a gym. You could work out, you know."

I ignore her. "Do you ever get weird looks for wearing sunglasses at the gym?"

She ignores me right back. I take it as a yes.

Eventually, I get bored watching the two girls go from exercise to exercise, and go to a cafe across the street to drink strong black coffee and scroll through my emails. They join me about forty-five minutes later, at half-past two. They both get protein heavy salads, but when Ace orders a strong, peppermint tea, Abyss gets a green smoothie.

"Always trying to show me up," Ace says to Abyss as they take their seats. I try not to flush when Abyss sits next to me and Ace slides in across from us.

Abyss scoffs. "Not my fault you put that crap into your body."

I look defensively at my coffee. "I'm on your side here, A. She was judging me for not working out earlier."

"Abs? Judgemental? Shocker," Ace replies, eyes dancing. Abyss shakes her head, and both Ace and I understand it as her rolling her eyes. "But, uh, she does have a point, Cee. Hanging around a gym watching two girls work out is a little weird."

I pick an1 edamame bean out of her salad and toss it towards her face. It bounces off her cheek.

As soon as she's finished her salad, she's jumping to her feet. "I'm out. I need to shower, and then I've got some cards to play tonight."

"For a case, or are you just gambling?" I ask, because as far as I know she's not got anything superhero related going on.

"You wound me," she says, smirking. "It's not really gambling if I know I'm going to win."

I sort of want to protest that, but it's an old argument, and Ace is already heading out the door, waving at us over her shoulder. After she's gone, Abyss and I spend the afternoon together. We go bowling and eat terrible, terrible nachos. It's almost like a date.

The next few weeks pass mostly without note, although I do notice Abyss' proper toothbrush showing up in my bathroom, rather than the plain guest one she had been using. I decide not to comment on it.

Halloween decorations have been cropping up all over the place, but Abyss and I do our best to avoid it. Mrs. Pae puts up a Halloween display in the flower shop window, all orange daises and black roses, with paper bats stuck along the edges of the window. There's a tiny little gravestone, near the front, which reads: *In Loving Memory: Pae Sun-Young.* It seems to help her, but it makes me sick to look at.

I try my best to ignore it as Abyss and I make our way into the shop.

Mrs. Pae smiles at us, her eyes bright and wide. She steps away from the counter to give us both hugs, stroking Abyss' back and ruffling my hair. "Long time," she says, playfully admonishing Abyss, who simply smiles and hugs her again.

"We're here to pick up the marigolds," she says, and Mrs. Pae nods.

"I figured. Your driver is here?" she addresses me.

I nod, and she pats my cheek on the way to get the flowers. I try to avoiding looking at the Halloween display, positioning myself with my back to it. There's something itching at the back of my mind. Abyss looks at me curiously, and, not for the first time, I wonder if she can read my mind.

"I've visited his grave," I say, by way of explanation. "The display reminded me."

Abyss nods thoughtfully. "Isn't visiting the graves a part of Día de Muertos?" When I nod, she continues, "We'll go see him then. Leave some flowers for him, he'd appreciate that."

He would, actually, and for more than just the flowers. He loved hearing about other people's traditions and beliefs. "Okay," I say, and it helps settle my rattled nerves.

Mrs. Pae walks back out with the flowers, and Abyss and I each take an armful to carry back to the car. There's a picture frame tucked into one of the boxes. "For the ofrenda," she says to me, kissing my cheek. My throat feels suddenly tight, and all I can do is nod. She squeezes my arm, and moves away to chat to Abyss while I compose myself.

Abyss and I pile back into the car, settling the huge bundles of flowers petals on our laps. "You ready?" I ask her, voice serious but with a playful expression.

She fixes me with a mock serious look, before dramatically putting her sunglasses back on. "As I'll ever be."

We're still giggling when the car starts moving.

50.

Eliza opens the door before we have to figure out how to knock with our arms full of flowers. "I heard you coming," she says, which is what I already suspected. She leads us through to the living room, where my mom and dad are still finishing off the decorations. Dad takes the flowers from Abyss and I, and I immediately collapse onto the sofa.

Eliza looks Abyss up and down, frowning. "Charlie!" she shouts, and my eldest sister appears, following Eliza's gaze to Abyss.

"Oh, that won't do," Charlie agrees, and I don't even have a chance to think about what they're talking about before Charlie continues. "All black? Really? I know this is a day of the dead, but it's not a *funeral*."

Personally, I think that's a poor choice of words, given that the last time that Abyss saw Charlie was at a funeral, but no one else seems to catch it. I think I'm just hyper-sensitive to Xander's absence today. I might not be celebrating Halloween, but it still is Halloween, and it was his favourite.

"I always wear all black." Abyss protests dryly.

"That's not true," I comment, holding up a finger. "You sometimes wear varying shades of grey."

"I've seen you wearing green, once or twice," my mom says, grinning teasingly at Abyss as she makes her way over to me. My dad is still fussing with the marigolds, oblivious to the conversation. Abyss huffs and looks at me, as though asking for help. I shrug. I can't do anything to stop my sisters.

"It's a *celebration*," Eliza says, and before anyone can say anything else, she's grabbing Abyss by the wrist and dragging her upstairs, Charlie following close behind.

After a few seconds of silence, I turn my head towards my mom without taking my eyes off of the stairs. It's eerily silent, but I blame Eliza for that. "Should I go rescue her?"

"Something tells me that Abyss can handle them," Mom replies, "maybe even better than you can."

"No," I disagree. "*Definitely* better than I can."

We laugh, and after a beat I ask, "Where's Carlos?"

"In the kitchen. Farah is teaching him to make bread," she smiles, "apparently he's really good at kneading. Keeps his hands busy, so he's not jumping around so much."

Dad finally finishes setting up the ofrenda, and takes a seat next to Mom. "How are you Caesar?" he asks, but I'm distracted, staring at the ofrenda with wide eyes.

I push myself up off the sofa and make my way over to it. There's the usual pictures; Dad's family tree, my grandparents on my mom's side. Farah must've added one of her dad, too, because the smiling black man doesn't look like anyone but her. But, there, in the corner, is the picture frame that Mrs. Pae gave me. It's one of those ones that holds two pictures. I recognise them immediately.

The one on the left shows Legion— mask on, eyes burning, almost frighteningly determined looking. The one on the right is Xander— holding the mask in his hand, leaning forward from laughter. I don't remember what got him laughing, but I remember sending the photos to our group text a few hours after I took them. I remember Abyss responding with 'the duality of man' (although, of course, she spelt it *th duo of mn*).

Mom comes over to stand behind me. "Wow," she breathes. "That's... the entirety of him."

"Yeah," I say in a whisper. "Legion and Xander."

"We asked Ki if she would be okay with it," Dad says, like he's not sure he did the right thing. "We thought it might be important to you. To... make sure he could come back, if he wanted. To make sure he was remembered. I'm glad she did allow it."

I open my mouth to say something, but I'm not sure what. It *is* important to me, but I'd hesitated to suggest it, unsure if it would be disrespectful to Xander's own religious beliefs. But Mrs. Pae had given me- us- the photos, and I couldn't be more grateful to see him there.

I rush at my dad with a hug when I can't think of anything to say, and my mom shakes my curls gently with her fingers. Carlos appears in the room with a pop, startling us all into breaking away from each other.

"I got bored waiting for the bread to rise," he says, "so I thought I'd scare you. I wouldn't have if I'd realised you were having a *moment*."

I laugh, and move to shove him, but his teleportation has always been faster than me, and he appears, grinning, on the sofa. A few minutes later, Farah comes into the room, drying her hands on a tea-towel. "Where's Charlie?" she asks, and as if on cue, the missing three girls descend down the stairs.

"Presenting: celebration-ready Abyss!" Eliza projects, and Charlie sets off a few tiny, contained sparks from her fingertips.

Abyss is still wearing her black trousers, but instead of her black turtle neck, she's on one of Eliza's white off-the-shoulder tops. They've threaded marigolds through her braids, which I'm sure she'll be annoyed about in the morning, but it creates quite a striking image. She's smiling too, however faintly, even as she complains.

"They made me try on six different tops," she says, "this was the least offensive."

Eliza makes a dismissive noise, and everyone laughs. If my laughter starts a beat too late, a little caught up in the sight of Abyss wearing *white*, then no one comments on it. Abyss comes to sit down next to me, and lifts her feet to tuck them underneath her like she does when we're at home.

I wrap an arm loosely around her shoulders, relishing in the fact that none of my family points it out, in the fact that she sinks into me without thinking. We turn on some music and chat, swapping stories of the people on the ofrenda, starting with my great-great-grandmother and stories that I've heard a hundred times, and ending with Farah's dad, who I'd never met. There's food, so much food, and Carlos excuses himself to go put the raised bread in the oven, and fifty-minutes later we're tearing into bread that hasn't had time to cool. The candles flicker and cast dancing shadows across the walls when the sun sinks low, which, naturally, causes Charlie to jump up and announce that it's time to dance, pulling her wife up after her.

Farah, giggling, goes, and after only a few seconds, Mom and Dad stand as well, twirling around the room and laughing. Eliza and Carlos bounce around more than they dance; Eliza raises the volume of the music and Carlos teleports across the room every few seconds, in time to the beat. After a few minutes, it's impossible to resist the urge, and I hold out a hand to Abyss. She doesn't know how to dance, but that's okay. We spin and jump around anyway, one hand in hers and the other low on her back.

"We should go to Mexico next year," Dad says, after we've all gotten tired and disheveled. "We could visit your aunt, and it would be nice to share the day with other families."

"I'm sure there are other Mexican families in the city," Charlie says, laughing, "but it would be nice to escape to the sun."

I hum my agreement, squeezing Abyss' shoulder. "Have you ever been to Mexico?" I ask her, and she shakes her head.

"Well, maybe when I was little. For the beach, I don't really remember. It would've been before I started high school... I would've been too busy after that. And it might have been somewhere else."

It takes me a second to remember that she started high school at ten years old. "I'll have to take you sometime."

She just grins at me, a proper grin that shows her teeth, an expression that I don't think I've ever seen. It almost knocks the breath out of me, to see her so free and open. I thread our fingers together, and she squeezes my hand playfully.

Maybe it's the wine we've been drinking, the music, the laughter, but I finally (finally!) manage to open my mouth.

"I love you," I say. It comes out easier than I expected it to. I want to say it again and again and again, just so that she knows.

Her grin softens into a smile, "I love you, too."

"I mean," I say, because I need to be sure that she understands, that she knows what's going on in my head. "I'm, like, I'm *in* love you with."

"And I'm *in* love with you, too."

I think she's making fun of me. Her voice is teasing, lighthearted. I'm not sure she understands the gravity of the situation.

"I mean," I say, because if I don't clarify that we're on the same page, I think I'm going to go crazy in the next five minutes. "I want to have you in my life, forever, and I want to do things like buy you a lab without it being weird and come home and have you there- or on your way there, because we think of the same place as home. I want to… I want to be able to see in your mind, to see the world the way you see it, and pretend I understand all the science stuff you talk about. I want you to be in my mind, and to have access to everything that no one else can. I want… to be with you. Because I'm in love with you."

Abyss squeezes my hand again, runs a hand through my hair. I forget that there's anyone else in the room. Her legs are draped over mine, and she's smiling, softly. "Caesar," she says, and her voice is low and warm, "did you really think I didn't want the same?"

"How long?"

"Long enough," she replies. "I mean, I've all but moved in to your house, Cee. We've slept in the same bed for at least a week, plus a handful of nights before then. I let you into my head. How much more obvious did I need to be?"

I flush, and look down at our linked hands, focusing on nothing but the points of contact between us: her legs across mine, her fingers in my hair. We've been close like this for weeks, linked together. None of my family had commented when I wrapped my arm around her. Mrs. Pae seemed unsurprised to find that Abyss was at my house. Ace had asked me, weeks ago, if I was nervous to meet her family.

"Apparently my big brother is dumb as hell," Carlos says, and I snap back to reality; aware, suddenly, of my entire family in the room.

"Yeah," Abyss agrees, but her smile is fond and *she loves me too*. "That doesn't surprise me."

Charlie pours us all another glass of wine ("To celebrate," she says, winking, and Eliza adds, "I knew she'd need to be celebration-ready!") and my mother teases me, my father rolls his eyes. When my family is finally distracted, I turn my head so I'm close to Abyss' ear.

"Move in with me," I whisper, and she laughs.

"Haven't I already?"

"Make it official," I say, and I grin when she giggles. "Get the rest of your things."

51.

As promised, Abyss and I go to Xander's grave with some of the flowers. He's buried in a different graveyard to my family, and to Farah's dad, so after leaving flowers for my dad's parents, we all split off to different places. The night air is cool, but not uncomfortable, even in the cemetery.

Xander's grave is still the newest. Abyss places the flowers down and sits cross-legged in the grass. I sink down next to her, and wonder what to say.

"Have you visited him before?"

"A few times. He was a brother to me. I told him everything. I didn't want to stop. Guess what, Alexander?" I'd forgotten she used to call him that, and it makes me smile. I can picture his huff of false annoyance perfectly. "Caesar finally told me he loves me."

"Hey!" I protest, laughing. "I've been a wreck about it for weeks."

"And I've been waiting for you to realise for months," she teases, elbowing me. "I think I win."

We're quiet for a few minutes, listening to the wind and the faint sounds of cars whizzing down the street. Abyss rests her cheek on my shoulder, and I press my nose to the top of her head.

"Do you think he'd be happy for us?" I ask.

She hums. "I think he is."

52.

Ace-thetics: *rumour has it u and abyss are in ~love~*

Me: *how could u possibly know that already*

Ace-thetics: *i have my ways*

Ace-thetics: *mainly abyss told me at the gym this morning*

Ace-thetics: *proud of you boo*

Me: *never call me boo again*

Ace-thetics: *okay honey*

Abyss moves in the next day. It doesn't take long; she's been staying in the Pae's living room for nearly two years, but it's not as though she had a lot of space for things. Plus, and I grin when she points it out, anything that's super important gets sent to the Void and retrieved when she needs it. Most of her clothes were already at my house, her toothbrush, her laptop.

Honestly, I can't believe I didn't notice it before.

We hang her clothes in my closet, stack her books on the bedside table. We clean, and organise, and find all the places where her things slot naturally next to mine. It's like this space was made for us to share, and I just never realised.

At night, we sink into bed, next to each other, like we have been for at least a week, and I don't feel the need to overthink the way her head tucks against my chest or the way my hand rests on her hip. It just *is* and it's *nice*.

I start saying 'I love you' every morning, just because I can, and I don't need to be afraid anymore. I begin to stop thinking of time in terms of how long Xander's been gone and start thinking of it in terms of how long Abyss has known that I love her. It's been two months and change since the last time I heard Xander laugh, but it's been a week since Abyss said she loved me.

Nothing else changes, not really; we're pretty much the same as we've always been. I go to school and do my best to not fail my classes. Abyss drives the van for Pae's Flower's and debates back and forth on a job at the Caesar Corporation. We talk about Jamboree, sometimes, throw theories back and forth like kids playing hot potato, try to decide if it's worth attempting to contact her.

"Maybe all she needs is an apology," Abyss says one day, when we're laying in bed in the early hours of the morning. A sitcom is playing on my laptop, balanced on her legs, but the volume is low, and we're not really paying attention. "You said… every universe but this one. Maybe I should've… maybe I need to say that I'm sorry."

"Are you?"

"Sometimes."

"You know," I say, after a few seconds of thought, as the credits start to roll. "All the universes I saw in her head… She said 'every universe but mine', but there wasn't a single universe that I saw where you weren't… *you*. Where you weren't Abyss."

"Oh, that's comforting," she snorts. "I always end up connected to the Void, that's cool."

"I mean, it is," I say, rolling my eyes at her flippancy. "Like, is there one Void, or are there lots? Are you sort of 'connected' to your counterparts in other universes? But that's not the point I was making," I continue in a rush, when she frowns and opens her mouth like she's about to start hypothesising. "In ever universe she looked at, you were still a genius."

A universe where you aren't brilliant isn't one I want to see.

"Oh," Abyss says, her voice barely above a whisper.

Jamboree clearly still cares about Abyss, on some level. Maybe all she really needs is an apology, but Abyss is the one who would have to give it. I can't do it for her, as much as I'd like to take that burden off of her shoulders.

I try to imagine a universe where Ace turned evil and the only way I could think to stop her was to apologise to her. I try to imagine if Ace was somehow, tangentially, responsible for Xander's death, and try to picture what it would be like to apologise to *her* for it all. I don't know if I could bring myself to do it.

But even now, Jamboree just wants her best friend. I can understand that, too.

53.

I do follow through, and I get Abyss a lab.

It's been two weeks since Día de Muertos when I take her to the space I've found. I wanted it close to the penthouse, so she could go over there whenever she wanted, but also far enough away that it was very much her own space. It's bigger than strictly necessary, but I'd wanted to show off.

She wanders around the lab, excitedly running her hands over every piece of equipment and every long table. She turns back to me and takes my hands, beaming. I'll never get over how beautiful her smile is.

She drags me over to a table and pushes me onto one of the stools. "Caesar," she says, with laughter in her voice. "Marry me."

I laugh, but squeeze her hands. "I take it you like it?"

"Absolutely," she replies, looking around the room with something that I can only describe as awe. I want to be in her head, I want to see the room through her eyes. "I have a *lab* again, Cee, I can do my work again! I don't even know what I'm going to do first."

"Whatever you want," I say, smiling at her enthusiasm.

"Whatever I want?" she repeats. I straighten up, looking at her curiously. "You know, you said something… a while back, but then also when you told me you loved me."

"I did?"

"Yes." She takes a few steps and sits down on the stool next to mine. I pivot around to face her. "You said that I was free to dig through your memories. You said you wanted me to be in your head. Does that offer still stand?"

I thought I'd have to be the one to bring it up again. "Of course," I nod. "What's mine is yours, and all that."

"Caesar," she whispers, reaching out and tucking a curl behind my ear. Her hand stays, pressed against my jaw, for a few seconds. "It's your mind. Are you sure that's something you want to share?"

"I've read your mind. It's only fair."

"You asked me for permission, too," she points out, and I have to concede that. "Besides, you read everyone's mind. Has anyone ever read yours?"

I shake my head slowly, and she squeezes my hand again. "No one but you," I whisper. "Abyss, you're the only one I want to read it. I want it to be something you can... see, whenever you want. What's mine is yours."

"You mean that?"

I nod, more serious than I've ever been. It feels heavier than a marriage proposal, a confession of love. It's me: laid out bare and wanting. It's offering up my mind to be picked through and questioned; consumed and spit back up if she doesn't like the taste. But I mean it. I want her to see all of me.

"Well," she says, "then I want you to be in my mind all the time, too. I want it to be yours, too."

"What?" I breathe.

The lab lights are only half on, the machines still dark and unused. There's empty spaces in the room, because it's not quite finished, and things are still missing. The high ceiling is cavernous in the low light. It's like my thoughts are echoing off the ceiling and back to me: *what do you mean?*

Abyss slides her glasses off her face and I'm faced with the Void, all-consuming and never ending, and a smile that shows her teeth. "You heard me."

"You can't mean that," I protest, my voice coming out a hoarse whisper. No one ever means that. I flash through: Ace telling me to get out of her head; Eliza saying she can feel my judgement; my dad telling me off for seeing my mom's thoughts. No one wants me in their heard all of the time.

"So you can mean it, but I can't?" she says, and thankfully her voice is light. "I like having you there, Caesar. It... kept me sane when there were portals tearing through my body, it helped me sort through my memories and face down Julia versus Jamboree, it... it's comforting, having you there."

"You like it?" I say, my eyes wide, an aching, startling need taking me over. I wasn't tired a moment ago, but now I swear that I can feel black bags underneath my eyes. My lips are parted, just so, slick where my tongue has darted out to lick them. She strokes a hand through my hair, slow, gentle, like she did on Día de Muertos, making soothing noises. "You mean that?"

"Caesar," she says, and her voice is low and warm. "Did you really think I didn't want the same things?"

I have to laugh at that, but it comes out nervous and shaky. "You really mean that," I say, and I'm sure my voice is awe-filled. "You really do want these things."

"Do you need to read my mind, to be sure?" she suggests playfully, and I laugh again, a little steadier. "Because it's open to you, Cee, it's open to you if you want it."

"Of course I do," I whisper. "I'm not used to it being offered."

"Well, get used to it," she whispers back. "I love you."

"I love you too," I say, and I slip inside her mind.

54.

I don't know how to go about creating a permanent link. It's never been something that I've needed to do before. But after spending almost an entire day in the lab, sifting through each other's memories and sending images and impressions back and forth, it's clear that it's something we both want, so I set about trying to make it happen.

"It can't impede your other telepathy," is her first stipulation. "You need to be able to read other people's minds still, or you won't feel like yourself."

She's right, and I know she's right, but her mind could keep my occupied for years to come. Still, I try to accommodate for the eventuality that I'll want to see into other people's minds too. I go for lunch with Ace, holding the thread that attaches my mind to Abyss', and try to read her thoughts. She's thinking about ghosts, which is typical of her.

Abyss says it gave her a headache trying to keep our thoughts straight. "I want the connection open," she says, "but I can't have the constant stream. I'm sure there's a way."

Abyss is treating it like some big experiment, which makes me laugh, bubbling over with excitement and anticipation. Even though the connection isn't perfect, it's not yet settled into something we can carry around with us, it's still something.

When we're alone in our penthouse, when the rest of the world isn't around, I re-open the connection and we slot into each other easily.

Even when we're in other rooms, doing separate things, we're aware of each other, a tiny thread that means I can find my way to her, to her head, without any trouble at all.

I'm constantly aware of her. Sometimes, she's exploring my memories or my ideas, but usually, she's settled just away from the forefront of my mind, content to exist in the same space as me. Sometimes, I sink far enough into the Void that I'm not entirely sure what I'm seeing, or how to put it into words, but usually, I settle down between her thoughts and her emotions and let them roll over me.

The first time I manage to read someone's mind without Abyss catching any of their thoughts, the first time we're together and separate at the same time, I take her out for dinner at a fancy steakhouse that I know she'll love. It's been three weeks since I told her I loved her, and three weeks since she said she loved me, too.

"I love you," I say, because I can, and she grins at me.

"I love you, too," she replies. "I have for a long time. You know, Ace says we're soulmates."

"Ace says a lot of things," I reply, but I kick at her feet underneath the table so she knows I'm not being serious. "What do you think?"

"I don't believe in soulmates," she says after a few seconds of thought. "But I can't imagine anyone but you."

My grin so wide my face might split in half. I'm not a poet, but if I were, I'd say she was responsible for all the stars and the moon.

As though she can read my thoughts— and, she can! She can read my thoughts! She's aware of every thought that I have, every single wish and worry and want— she scoffs, and squeezes my hand across the table.

I can't imagine anyone but her, either.

It's not that we don't have our secrets; there are things we keep to ourselves, painted over with caution tape and 'do not enter' signs. Most of these things are things that aren't ours to tell, the secrets that our friends have trusted us with. We talk about it, sometimes, and we trust each other enough not to pry. Abyss sends hers to the farthest reaches of the Void, the places that I can't go without really, really trying, and I lock mine away.

There are some thoughts I send there before they can even fully form. There are some things I want to surprise her with. I think she'd understand.

55.

I meet Ace for a late breakfast on a Tuesday morning a month after I told Abyss that I love her. We've been existing in this shared headspace for a little over a week, and it's something that's still a novelty, even as it becomes more and more normal. It's something that I never want to lose.

I try to explain it all to Ace, and she looks at me funny, and says, "To each their own, I guess."

"It's amazing, A," I say, half-sighing. "You don't even know."

"I can tell that it means a lot to you," she allows, and she smiles at me, a traditional Ace grin. "I'm proud of you, you know."

It's not a teasing remark, not like the text she'd sent me the day after. It seems so genuine, so real, and I have to ask, "What for?"

She rocks her hand in the air in a see-saw motion. "I say this with love," she starts, "but you've never been the most... open of people. I'm just... I'm happy for you, Cee. You let yourself fall in love, and you told her, and you've trusted her with... you. With who you are. I'm impressed, and I'm glad that you're happy."

"She's it for me," I say, laying my hands palm-up on the table. Ace looks at me curiously, setting her tea down and placing her hands in a mirror of mine.

"You sure, buddy?"

I know she's only asking because she's my best friend, and she'll worry about me no matter what (she's genuine in her concern, thinking about all the ways this could go horrible wrong— she's been a cynic for a long time, and it's a hard pattern to break, but she wants me to be as happy as I can be), but the question makes me bristle anyway.

"Yeah, I'm sure," I reply, maybe a tiny bit snappish. She throws her hands up defensively. "She's it for me," I repeat, softer. "I can't picture anyone but her in my future. I want to try, Ace. I want to assume she's it for me, and work off of that assumption. Have you ever felt like that?"

She tips her head, and it occurs to me that I'd probably know if she'd felt that way. But without going into her head— a temptation that's getting easier to resist when I can feel Abyss' presence without trying — I have no way of confirming, and she surprises me by nodding. She's not looking at me, instead staring at the empty table next to us with a soft smile.

"I get it," she says. "I've... I've had that feeling. Just, be careful? Promise me you'll be careful."

"I will," I say, but I don't think I have anything to worry about. Abyss has shared her mind with me; if normal minds are like billboards in the city, Abyss' is all of Times Square. I can see it, all the time, and I know I have nothing to worry about. "She says you called us 'soulmates'," I tease.

"Yeah, well, you know me," she waves a hand through the air. "I'm dramatic like that. You're good for each other."

Nani arrives to take our orders, and seems unsurprised when we order the exact same thing we always do. She rolls her eyes at us, but smiles fondly. Ace giggles at the expression, and the humour stays in her face when she turns back to me after Nani disappears.

"How long have you loved her?" she asks me, and I flash back to having this same conversation not so many weeks ago. I think my answer has changed, though.

"Since I met her," I answer, "I had this feeling, like I needed to know her better. And once I did start getting to know her, every scrape of information was the most important thing to me. I think I've been falling for her since I met her. I've loved her for ever, Ace. It's just… different, now."

"Better?"

"No," I say, shaking my head. "It's just different. A different sort of love, but just as good."

"You've really fallen for her, haven't you?"

I can't help my dopey grin or overly enthusiastic nod. "I've got her something. Do you want to see?"

Ace shrugs, but she's grinning ear to ear. "Oh, go on then."

I reach under the table and pull out the box, pushing it across the table for her inspection. She opens it, and I watch her jaw go slack with some satisfaction. "Oh my God, Caesar," she says. "It's beautiful, but—"

Something on Abyss' side of the connection starts pulling taught, like a cord stretched *just* beyond its capacity. I feel it being pulled tighter and tighter, and I slip further into her head to find that it's her anxiety, just in time for it to snap, and the floodgates to open. It's an overwhelming surge of panic, and I feel like a drowning man. Panic, I remember her saying, is the one thing that the Void doesn't pallet well, and it's especially awful in stark contrast to her otherwise easily controlled and discarded emotions.

She hasn't had an attack in the time since we've formed the connection; I can't remember her having one in months. I wonder, gasping back to myself, if this is how it always feels. If it's always so overwhelming.

Ace is looking at me, expression etched with concern.

"Sorry," I say, gesturing vaguely at the side of my head and hoping she understands. "Abyss…"

"It's okay," she says, pushing the box back towards me and watching me stand up. "Call me if you need me."

I mumble an agreement, hoping that it's not the sort of problem that requires Ace's assistance. I move away from our booth, and she gently catches me by the wrist. "And, Caesar?" she smiles, even if it is tinged with worry. "Good luck."

I manage a grin despite my worry, and I nod again before racing out the door.

The city is calm, unbothered. I run all the way home.

56.

Abyss is still shaking by the time I get inside, sitting on the sofa and staring at her silent phone where it rests on the table, looking like it might come alive and try to eat her. I sink down next to her, greet her softly, and rest a hand against her lower back.

She curves into the touch, bundling herself up by my side, her head finding its home against my chest. She breathes heavily against me, and I stroke circles against her back, gentle and slow. Slowly, her breathing levels out to keep time with my heartbeat.

"Want to talk about it?" I ask, once she's gathered herself.

"Phone call," she murmurs. "Probably just someone being a dick, but it… it sounded *so much* like him. I couldn't…"

Like him?

"Do you want me to call whoever it was back, give them a piece of my mind?" I ask, and she rolls her eyes. "I could threaten to sue."

"If you want to," she replies. "I won't stop you."

I pick up the phone and hit redial. Abyss stays curled into my side, her ear directly over my heartbeat. I continue to draw circles with my fingers.

"Good morning," says a voice on the other end of the line, followed by a name of a hospital a handful of hours outside of the city. "How shall I direct your call?"

"Hi," I say, suddenly confused. Abyss, sensing my mood shift either through my mind or my heart, looks up at me curiously. "I just received a phone call from this number?"

"Give me just one moment," the voices says, and the line goes dead for several long minutes. Abyss goes from confused to worried and back again, but I try to focus on my hand on her back, as though that has any effect on the situation.

"Hello?" the voice asks. "Are you still there?"

"Yes," I confirm.

"Excellent. Do you mind confirming your name for me?"

"My name is William Antonio Caesar the Third," I answer, looking down at the top of Abyss' head. "But I'm calling from the phone of Abyss Tolbert."

"Ah," the voice says. "Let me just transfer your call to the correct room."

There's a brief delay as my call is re-directed. I have to wonder who on earth was calling Abyss from a hospital.

"Hello? Abyss?" the voice sounds desperate, shaky. "Oh my gosh, I'm so glad you called back."

I nearly drop the phone in shock, but I manage to keep hold of it. I can feel my heart rate pick up, and Abyss extracts herself from my arm to look at me dead on, worry clear in her features. I reach my hand out to her. She takes it, and it seems to help.

"Hello?" the voice says again, and now, more than anything, it just sounds familiar.

"Xander?" I croak out.

"Caesar?" he replies. "Where's Abyss? What's going on?"

"I could ask you the same thing, man."

"What do you mean?"

"Sun-Young Alexander Pae," I whisper. "You're supposed to be dead."

Part Three: Legion

57.

"Legion!"

The panicked shouting cuts through everything else, even the wind whistling in my ears. Someone can see me, and is shouting for me, and I'm about to die. Let me tell you, death by falling? Not how I thought I'd end up going. Also, it sucks.

Because the thing is, I can see the ground racing towards me, hear people shouting my name, and feel my stomach churning as the realisation sets in: I am going to die.

I'm not scared of death, not exactly. I think I've lived a pretty good life — I've stuck to the strait and narrow. I've tried to leave everyone I meet better than they were when I met them. I poured my heart and soul into the little things and always tried to choose the right. And I have my faith.

It's not that I'm scared of death. It's that someone watched me fall and called out for me, and they're going to see me die.

Abyss and Caesar and my mom— I'm going to die, and they'll have to deal with that.

It's kind of my own fault, anyway. I'd sent a duplicate on a YSA trip with Ava and Zoram, thinking it was best of the original was here, in case Jamboree or someone showed up. Maybe if I'd just said that I couldn't go, if I'd had another duplicate here with me, I wouldn't be falling to my death right now.

But I didn't and I don't, and the ground is getting awfully close.

58.

"Sun-Young Alexander Pae," Caesar says on the other end of the phone. "You're supposed to be dead."

I keep replaying that part of our conversation, over and over. When I'd woken up in a hospital, alone in a room with four beds, feeling completely, one-hundred-percent fine, my first thought had been to call my mom. There wasn't— still isn't, actually— a phone in my room, so I'd pressed a button that seemed likely to get a nurse's attention, and when she'd raced into the room, the shock was obvious, etched into the lift of her perfect brows.

"You're awake!" she'd exclaimed.

Then there'd been tests, and paperwork, and *more* tests, and *more* paperwork, and they couldn't find anything wrong with me. Right as rain, the doctors said, looking more and more puzzled as time went on.

A coma, they said. For three months, they said.

"Can I call my mom?" I'd asked, and when that call had gone through to voicemail, I assumed she was working and called Abyss instead. Abyss would be sitting on the sofa-bed, probably on her laptop, and she'd run downstairs to get my mom and then they'd come get me. Instead, Abyss said, "This isn't funny," with a distinct note of panic, and hung up almost immediately.

And then Caesar called.

"Sun-Young Alexander Pae, you're supposed to be dead."

They're coming to get me. I'm not in the city, instead tucked into some small out-of-the-way hospital in a town a few hours out, where the YSA convention was held. I remember stopping for greasy fast food, deciding to park instead of braving the drive-through. Ava and Zoram were re-hitting it off (although why it took them so long, when they've clearly been pining for each other since we were seventeen is beyond me) and I'd slipped away when they were distracted to go sit on a patch of grass outside and enjoy the last of the August heat.

I don't remember much after that, and I certainly don't remember dying.

I keep trying to remember dying.

I haven't told any of the doctors about what Caesar said. I haven't told any of the doctors that I'm actually Legion. Sometimes I catch them looking at me like I'm a puzzle to put together. One of the nurses, a pretty boy with green, hooded eyes, breathes "Xander Pae," when he sees it written on my chart, and then looks at me like he knows me. I furrow my brow and he shakes his head with some sort of knowing smile.

I think if I told these people how much I try to remember dying, they'd make me go to some sort of counselling. As it is, I sit in my hospital bed, waiting for Caesar and Abyss to arrive and take me home, wracking my brains for how this all happened. I know it's pointless.

Supposed to be dead. I'm supposed to be dead.

How does that happen? If I'm *dead*, then how am I here?

If I let my mind wander, I start thinking about the fact that this body is a duplicate, and the fact that duplicates never could create *more* duplicates—

I don't let my mind wander. I try to remember dying, instead.

If I can remember dying, then I must be the original, and there's some big misunderstanding or miscommunication that Abyss will explain. If I can remember dying, then everything will be okay.

59.

Caesar and Abyss aren't speaking when the nurse escorts me downstairs, but they're standing very close together, head tipped towards each other. I think I see their hands joined. Before I can get a closer look, Abyss is turning towards me and bringing both her hands up to cover her mouth. I give an awkward little wave.

She comes and wraps me up in a tight hug. She's only hugged me once before, on the day she moved in with me and my mom. I hug her back, leaning down so my chin is buried in the crook of her neck. Caesar, over her shoulder, is staring at me like he's seen a ghost. I guess he has. I look down at where my hands are pressing into Abyss' back, half-expecting them to be invisible.

"You're real," she says, pulling away, and the monotone of her voice has lifted, slightly, leaving the sentence coming out almost breathy and relieved. That's almost as off-putting as Caesar's uneasy expression.

"I'm real," I say, scratching the back of my neck. "Very much *not* dead. Where's my mom?"

Caesar and Abyss share a quick look. He says, "We... didn't know if we could trust that you were real. We thought it would be best if we didn't tell your mom until we were sure."

"You didn't tell her?" I demand, narrowing my eyes. "She's my *mom*, Caesar! She thinks I've been dead for three months and you didn't tell her that I wasn't?"

"We had to make sure. If it were me," he says, keeping his voice level and sounding far too reasonable for me to continue being angry, "would you tell my family? Without making sure it was true first?"

I huff, but he's right.

There's somehow even more paperwork, but before I know it I'm standing outside again, staring up at the sky and breathing the crisp winter air in through my nose. It wasn't even September last time I blinked, and now it's somehow late November. I know how it happened, but I simultaneously don't know how it happened.

We climb in to the back seat. Abyss takes my spot in the middle, and doesn't seem to think anything of it until she turns to look at me as I climb in after her. I guess they got used to me not being around. Why wouldn't they?

I stare out of the window. Abyss and Caesar don't say anything for a long time.

"Xander?" Abyss says my name like it's a question. I whirl my head around sharply. "Do you need anything?"

I'm about to say no— I don't want them worrying about me— but my stomach chooses that exact moment to growl obnoxiously . Reluctantly, I say, "I could go for a milkshake."

Abyss nods, and Caesar leans forward to speak to his driver and direct him to some fast food place.

"A chocolate one, please. And some fries."

Caesar relays my order to Aaron as we pull up the the drive through. Within minutes, I'm holding a chocolate milkshake and some crispy fries. Caesar looks at me like I'm mental when I pop the lid off the milkshake and start dipping the fries in it. I can almost pretend it's like old times.

Old times. They were just *times* for me. Months have passed and things have changed and I was dead. I still can't remember dying.

After I'm through half of the fries, I pause, wipe my mouth on the back of my hand, and ask, "So, what happened, then?"

They don't even look at each other. I count, and they're quiet for about a minute.

"Jamboree… she attacked again," Abyss says. "City centre. It's still a wreck, but she at least tried to put it back."

"Put it back?"

"There were portals," Caesar clarifies. "Everywhere. She was tearing buildings apart with them. It was awful. You were— helping. Guiding people away, that sort of thing. I was supposed to be in your heads, monitoring…"

He cringes, and I can practically taste the guilt radiating off of him. There's silence for another few moments.

"And?" I question, over-pronouncing the syllable.

Caesar shakes himself a little, and Abyss continues. "Jamboree attacked me, which went about as well as it has every other time—" Caesar snorts and makes to interject, but Abyss plows on— "And Caesar made the call to get into my head to help. As you can probably imagine, it took a lot out of him. He wasn't in your head, we didn't know where you were—"

"Wait," I hold up a hand to pause her speaking. "He *was* in your head, though? He could read your mind?"

"Since then, yes," Abyss nods, and Caesar, over her shoulder, grins blindingly. "The point is that we didn't find out until— after. You were on top of a building, scouting, we think, and one of the portals ripped it apart, and you... fell."

I close my eyes and try to picture it. I try to remember it.

"We..." Caesar sounds kind of choked now. "Abyss and Ace and I, that is, we found you after. You were just... laying there. And we... we *mourned* you, Xander. You have to understand that. There was a funeral. You were buried. Everyone knows that you're dead."

"What did you do about Legion?" I ask, thinking that someone must have picked up on that disappearance. I wonder if anyone put two and two together, or if Caesar and Abyss came up with a sensible cover story.

This time, they do share a look, Abyss twisting around to face him and Caesar looking at her with wide eyes. "We thought you were dead," Caesar says slowly. "We had no way of knowing that you'd come back."

"What are you saying?"

Abyss reaches out to rest a hand on my upper arm. "Ava talked to your mom. She spoke at the funeral, and she told people about who you were. Are."

"She told—!"

"*We thought you were dead*," Abyss repeats, more forceful than I've ever heard her. "Ava thought it would be the best way to mourn you and honour you and your mom agreed. It was a touching speech and she shared it because she's your friend, and she wanted you to be remembered for every part of you."

My jaw clicks shut.

I'm still fuming, but I'll do it silently now. I never did find the words to explain to anyone why I wanted a secret identity so badly. I'm still not sure I can find them now, and it's too late. I swallow thickly. I may not be dead, but Legion is. The one thing that I always insisted on— they couldn't leave it alone, could they? Now everyone knows that Xander Pae and Legion are one and the same.

It's ruined.

I try to remember dying, and I can't. They had a body to bury. *This* body is a duplicate.

I shake my head, and look back out the window. My milkshake melts.

60.

Ace is in my house when we arrive. I can see her the through the window when we clamber up the fire escape, sitting on Abyss' sofa bed— which is, oddly, folded in— holding a bowl of popcorn. Her head snaps up when she sees us, and she holds up a hand to us. Caesar stops moving. Frustrated, I bounce in place. I just want to see my mom. She thinks I'm *dead*.

Ace crawls through the window and joins us on the fire escape. It creeks dangerously.

"Welcome back to the land of the living," Ace says dryly, lips quirked into a half smile. I try to mirror it, but I can't seem to. She tip her head downwards for a moment, before looking over her shoulder into the house. "Your mom is downstairs. I take it you haven't seen her yet?"

"No, I haven't, now let me—"

Caesar keeps me from jerking forwards with a hand on my elbow. He couldn't hold me back if he tried, but he's my friend, and he's *trying* to help, so I still anyway. Bitterly.

"She's had it rough, Xander," Ace says, like she has any authority to speak about my mom. "If you waltz in out of no where, she'll freak out. Wouldn't you?"

I want to say that I *am* freaking out, but I don't think it would make any difference. "I have to tell her I'm back," I say, forcing my voice to be steady. "I can't just not tell her."

"That's not what we're saying, Xander," Abyss cuts in. "We're just trying to think *how* is best to tell her."

I've had enough. "I'm her *son*. Let me tell her."

I push past Caesar more aggressively than is probably necessary and climb through the window into my house. There's something *wrong* about the space that I can't quite put my finger on, but I don't dwell on it, choosing instead to go for the door and leads down to the flower shop. I race down the stairs and hover somewhere around the third step. Mom's put out the Christmas display in the window. It's nearly December, so it makes sense, but it was still August the last time I was here.

The smell hits me first; warm and damp and, obviously, floral. The smell of soil, and the plant food we've used for years and years. Mom's perfume— sweet and familiar, wafting around the store like it always does.

And my mom is standing with her back to me, serving a customer, who pays for a bouquet and laughs at something she's said. His gaze flits upwards as he does so, and his eyes land on me. My heart pounds, because now he has a *reason* to recognise me, and he clearly does.

I want to wave for him to be quiet, but this whole situation is my fault. I should've listened to my friends. They were probably right to try to plan this out.

My mom turns around, and she screams.

"Mom!" I shout, frantically waving my arms. "Mom, Mom, calm down, it's only me!"

"You're—"

Yeah, I definitely should've listened to my friends.

"I promise it's me, Mom, I'm so sorry," I say all in a rush, thundering down the last few steps and coming to an awkward stop in front of her. The customer frowns at the display and, with a final wave, exits the stop, shoving his phone into his back pocket.

She brings her hand up to my face, cupping my jaw to make sure that I'm real. Her other hand rests on her mouth, covering a hiccuping gasp. Her eyes take on a glassy sheen, and I'm sure that mine do as well.

"Xander!" someone shouts admonishingly from the top of the stairs, and I turn to see Ace chasing after me, followed closely by Caesar and Abyss. "Ki— we wanted to…"

She trails off when she catches sight of my mom's awed expression, bowing her head like a chastised child. "We just wanted to warm you up to the idea. So it wasn't… y'know. Such a shock."

"It would've been a shock regardless," Abyss says, and I can practically hear her eye roll, despite the monotone. I've always been able to tell when she's rolling her eyes. Ace can pick up on it too, and turns to stick her tongue out at Abyss.

"Xander," My mom says, her voice cracking, and I turn back around to pull her into a tight hug, whispering assurances. "I love you," she says, and then re-iterates in Korean.

I murmur it back to her, in both languages, and she squeezes me again before letting go.

"So this is real?" she asks, addressing the others. Her eyes are still glassy, but she's got a familiar determined look in her eye. "No tricks? No Jamboree?"

Does she think that I'm from another universe? I suppose it's a sensible conclusion to reach, but it makes my heart ache regardless.

"Real," Caesar says, softly. "No Jamboree. No tricks."

My mom nods, squeezing my hand between both of hers.

"I had a duplicate out," I tell her, in a whisper that everyone can hear. "For the— the convention, with Zoram and Ava. I guess… If I'd had to guess, I would've thought the duplicates would've… disappeared, you know?"

She nods. "We thought the same. Ava— she was devastated. It was on the news, she saw it, and then… she said you were gone. She said she couldn't find you."

"I'd snuck out," I say, forcing myself to laugh even as my throat starts to close up. "I'd gone outside to get away from them for a bit. I didn't realise I'd left my wallet and my phone on the table. They must have — assumed that I'd disappeared. And when my things were still there… why— why would they have looked?"

"Your ID was with them," Abyss says, her voice soft. I can tell she's still putting the pieces together.

I crack a shaky smile. "That's why you're an actual, certified genius."

"When they found you," Caesar says, and I realise he has a hand around Abyss' shoulders, fingers curled near her collar bone. "They wouldn't have been able to identify you. That's why we didn't know until you woke up."

I nod, squeeze my eyes shut, and cry.

My mom wraps herself back around me, and I can feel her tears as they settle in my hair. My mom is shorter than me, but I've curled down so far that she's able to press her lips shakily to my forehead, cradling me like I'm a kid.

I can hear my friends leave, calling soft goodbyes to me and my mom. Ace goes first, sounding awkward— she's usually so empathetic, so I find that surprising. Caesar and Abyss head out together. I wonder where Abyss is going.

My mom lets go of me only for as long as it takes her to flip the sign to 'closed' and lock the door, and then we head back upstairs. I'm still hit by the wrong feeling while we stand in the living room, although I can't really place what's different. Abyss' bed is folded away into a sofa, and my mom and I sit down together.

She can't seem to take her eyes off of me. I can't blame her for it; I can't take my eyes off of her, either.

61.

Here's something they don't teach you in school: how to tell people that you're not dead.

Ace tries to help, a little. When she faked her death, and came back, all she did was hold a small press conferencing explain that it was important that she disappeared completely. She was annoyed about, I know, annoyed at how it turned a spotlight on her. I'm annoyed at the spotlight too.

"How did you going back to being... yknow. You?"

Ace just shrugs, a little helpless. "It's harder, now. To fly under the radar. But... I'm always gonna be *me*, no matter what."

There is a difference in our situations, though. Ace faked her death. I did not.

I actually died, and there was funeral attended by... a lot of people, actually. More than I would've guessed. Reporters, too, because my death was the first, and thankfully only, one caused by Jamboree. Plus, Caesar and Abyss were there, which made it worth their while.

There was a recording on everything Ava said. I find shots from the video of the procession— of my coffin. *My* coffin. I'm morbidly curious enough to keep watching. That body, I can't help thinking, is decaying the ground. This body will likely disappear when it dies.

I shiver, and rewind the clip.

Abyss reaches out and stills my hand, closing her laptop. We're sitting on her bed in the living room, our legs stretched out long, shoulder to shoulder. "You don't need to keep watching this," she says, and even with her glasses in the way, I know she's staring at me, and if she had human eyes they'd be filled with concern.

I don't say 'yes I do,' but I think it. I just drop the subject, and, later, when I'm alone in my room, I search up the clips myself, and watch them until I fall asleep.

We tell Ava and Zoram first. My mom and I have them over and tell them far more carefully than I showed my mom. Zoram takes it better than Ava, who bursts almost immediately into guilty tears. "We should've looked," she says, hiccuping. "I should've looked more, and maybe we would've known."

Zoram looks at me with a steady expression. I've known him longer than I've known Caesar. I don't really know how his mission changed him— my mom always says that they leave as boys and return as men— but I know that he's my best and oldest friend. When he says, "I'm sorry, pip," I can't find it in me to be offended.

They wouldn't have thought to look. Roles reversed, I'm not sure I would've thought to look. I can't be hurt.

I still am.

For the next three days, I don't leave the apartment. We slowly spread the news to trusted people. The Caesars, of course, are among the first to know. Charlie makes a show of leaving her camera downstairs when she comes in, but all it does is make me laugh. I know she wouldn't sell this story unless I let her, and when she comes over to hug me and kiss my cheek, I still flush.

Charlie was my first ever crush— she's three years older than Caesar and I, and when I met them on the playground as a seven year old, she played pirates with us, and had really pretty hair, and she could do the monkey bars. I thought she was the coolest person ever. Now, as she cups my face and says she's so glad I'm okay, I still kind of think it.

Her wife sits next to us and clears her throat pointedly. When I look over at Farah, she's wearing a teasing grin. Charlie does pull away from me anyway, and leans up against Farah with a contented expression.

"Sorry," I say to Farah, trying to put on one of my 'trademark' grins. Abyss said once that if she ever saw me without a smile, she'd worry the world was ending. I've had similar comments through my life. These days, smiles are hard to come by, and I do feel a little bit like the world is ending. It seems to work on the two women though, as they both mirror it before I can even say my next few words. "Charlie's a charmer. She won my heart when I was only a boy…"

"Don't be dramatic," Charlie says with an eye roll, and in response I pretend to swoon, with a hand to my heart.

"Well, she grew up to be a lesbian, so I don't think I have any competition," Farah teases, "No offence, Xander. You're a very handsome boy."

I reply from my position sprawled out on the currently folded sofa bed. "I think it's the 'boy' part that's the killer."

The rest of the family chooses that exact moment to arrive. Mrs. Caesar— who's insisted my whole life that I call her Helena— wraps me up in a hug so tight that it could rival my mom's. Mr. Caesar— who never told me to call him William— claps me affectionately on the shoulder. Eliza gives me a little wave and smile, while Carlos pops up behind me to tackle my back. I pretend to heave under the weight.

They're all excited that I'm back, and our time together manages to coax a few genuine smiles out of me. As I watch my mom and Mrs. Caesar talk in a tucked away corner of the room, I remember that I wasn't the only one to gain friends from the Caesar family. I remember the two of them sitting together while I played with the Caesar kids, talking about learning English and moving across the world— their circumstances may have been completely different, but they bonded over the familiar struggles, and they'd been friends ever since. I think they stayed in closer contact than Caesar and I did, when they moved away.

I was only two when my family moved here, and by the time we'd met the Caesar's I'd already settled in well enough. I went to school and church and made friends, but my mom was still struggling. My dad too, I think, although he died when I was still young enough that I didn't think to ask him about it. The Caesars gave them friends, and I couldn't be more grateful.

"Your mom came to Caesar's birthday," Eliza says next to me, and by the time I've turned to look at her, I can't hear anyone else, and I'd bet that they can't hear us, either. Her ability was always helpful for sharing secrets, although this doesn't seem like it should be one. "She gave us photos of you, as well, for the ofrenda. So you could come visit us, if you wanted. Didn't bank on…"

She trails off and waves her hand at me. I shrug. "I wouldn't have either."

"Are you doin' okay, Xander? You keep… staring. At all of us, but your mom especially."

"I'm fine," I say with a smile I hope doesn't look forced. "I'm just adjusting, is all. A lot feels different, but I wasn't gone all that long."

I don't think she buys it. "We care about you, Xander. You know you can come to us if you need anything, right?"

I nod, and the sound in the room races back to me like I've just taken off noise-cancelling headphones. Eliza wanders off. I look around for Caesar and Abyss, only to find that they haven't arrived yet. They'd said they were following up on a lead about Jamboree, looking apologetic. I waved them off. It was my choice to stay in the apartment.

Still, it does seem like it's taking them longer than it should. When I voice this, Carlos snickers and replies, "They probably got distracted making out or something."

Although Farah attempts to mask her laugh, Charlie doesn't. "You may have another wedding to plan soon, Mom."

"As long as it's not a shotgun wedding," Mrs. Caesar replies, with a fond smile and an eye roll.

"Uh, what?" I say to the room at large, and everyone shares hasty looks and avoids my eyes. "Are Cee and Abs, like…"

My mum rests a hand on the back of my neck and squeezes gently. "They've been together for a little over a month now, yes."

"Only 'officially'," Eliza elaborates. "I think Cee's been in love with her since he met her, practically. And she was already living with him, so, really, it was more him being oblivious than anything, you know? Like, they were totally already together, Caesar just didn't realise."

"But Abyss lives *here*," I say, gesturing to the sofa bed. "She's been here every night since I— uh, got back."

There's an awkward silence. I take a breath and sit down. Abyss *has* been staying here. But when I look around more closely now, I finally work out what's felt *off* about it since I've been back. Most of her personal items are stored away in the Void for easy access, but her laptop usually rests on the side table, charging. It's no where in sight.

The sofa bed was folded away when I first came in, when normally she wouldn't bother.

Her favourite mug, too, the one that Mom made her tea in when her anxiety got bad, is missing from the kitchen, now that I think about it. The miniature Newton's Cradle I'd gifted her for her birthday isn't on the TV stand. All these little marks she'd left on the house are gone, subtle enough that I hadn't noticed until it was pointed out.

She's living at Caesar's. She's living *with* Caesar. Because they're in a relationship.

I try to drum up some enthusiasm for the development. It *is* good, and I *am* happy for them.

I just wonder how it happened. Caesar's been in love with her since he met her, Eliza says. Even I'd noticed his curiosity about her. Has Abyss felt the same? She'd confessed, once, that she was interested in him, but never that it had developed further. If, despite them only being 'officially' together for a little over a month, they decided to live together, they must feel pretty confident about it.

And they didn't tell me.

And I *didn't* notice, *couldn't* notice, while it was happening, because I was too busy being dead.

Caesar and Abyss.

I was only gone three months.

There's something sharp and white-hot hissing in my stomach. Anger. I try to swallow it, shove it into the box labelled 'Legion' and ignore it, like I always do. Did. Anger went to Legion; all the stinging, rough emotions did.

But now, there is no Legion who can take my negative emotions and turn them into power. There's just me. There's just Xander Pae.

I think I understand what Abyss used to say about 'playing pretend', because none of this feels real. Maybe I was playing pretend when I dressed up as Legion and sought out crime and made a name for myself, but this— being *Xander*, putting on a smile— feels more fake than that ever did.

Still, I keep trying to manage it somehow, forcing myself to ignore the tightening coil in my gut. How do people manage to keep all of their thoughts and emotions in one head? I know I used to, before my abilities manifested, but I can't seem to remember it. I've always been able to physically compartmentalise.

Then again, maybe I am still okay at it, if I'm able to, for the most part, ignore that I don't have my abilities anymore.

I don't have my abilities anymore.

Legion doesn't exist anymore.

Something in me snaps like a rubber band pulled too far. I stand up. No one is looking at me anymore, moving on into their own conversations. I slide open the window and step on the fire escape just in time for Caesar and Abyss to arrive at the bottom of the steps. They are, of course, surprised to see me.

"Xander!" Caesar says, grinning up at me. "Are my siblings driving you crazy?"

"Something like that," I grind out. "Were you ever gonna tell me?"

They realise immediately what I mean. They look at each other and then to me. Abyss says, "Eventually. We didn't want to shock you with too much at once."

"Mission accomplished, I guess." I'm snappish, now, almost snarling, my nose scrunched. "Instead I get 'shocked' with a different life changing thing every twelve seconds, but I guess that *is* better, huh? Better than my *best friends*— allegedly— sitting me down and talking me through it all? But, no, I guess I'm, what? Traumatised? Weak, or something?"

"Xander—" Abyss starts, but I shrug, race down the steps with my shoulders squared, and push between them.

I pause when I'm a few steps away, looking backwards just enough that they'll be able to see me roll my eyes. "Oh, and *congratulations*. I'm hearing wedding bells already."

62.

I feel like a dick. Correction: I am a dick. The only thing more dickish than what I said is the fact that I've followed it up by sneaking into the city centre construction site and climbing up the building that, I'm told, I died on. If Mom knew I was here, she'd be worried sick. As would Caesar, or Abyss, or any of my friends. So, yeah: I'm a dick.

I groan and drop my forehead onto my hands, which are resting on a metal railing. The building isn't even fully finished being repaired yet and it's definitely dangerous to be up here, alone, when no one knows where I am.

I've already died here once. What is it that they say about lightning? I feel like that probably applies with this too. Or not. Who knows? This is uncharted territory, I'm pretty sure. And I doubt there's anyone who shares my abilities who'd want to test it out with me. "Hey," I say to no one, "Wanna lose your powers? You won't *die*— except, you know, four-fifths of you will be dead!"

I look down, over the edge of the building, and feel queazy. I don't remember dying. Well, I guess I sort-of remember that time that Jamboree shot me— standing in three different places, staring at a bullet with no time to react beyond that. The duplicate vanished without any command, and my hand went instinctually to my stomach, expecting it to come away bloody. I saw the bullet racing towards me, but I have two other angles of that same event. It gets confusing. Got confusing.

I guess I won't have to be confused by multiple contradictory memories anymore. Silver lining!

I don't remember dying on this building, hurtling through the air. I only ever got memories from duplicates after they disappeared, not before, like they were reabsorbed into me, or something. Into *him*? This body has never created or vanished duplicates, so maybe I'm someone brand new. Probably not. I don't feel brand new, anyway. I feel very, very old.

Was I scared? I must have been. I'm scared *now*. How could I possibly be fine about *dying*, but scared to live?

I keep staring at the ground. I know this is the building I fell from, but I have no idea where I landed. It could've been anywhere. It's probably unhealthy to want to find it, and sit there, and see if there's some small fragment of me left over. They don't make therapists for this.

"You're not supposed to be up here," comes a voice from behind me and a little to the left. I turn around, greeted by the sight of a pretty woman, about twice my age, with auburn hair cut in a messy bob that looks like she did it herself. She's wearing a pair of coveralls and a safety vest.

I must stare at her for a second too long, because her expressions softens around the corners of her eyes and mouth, and she adds, "What's your name?"

"Alex," I say after a moments thought. I don't want to *lie*, after all, and both Xander and Sun-Young are recognisable enough now, based on my googling.

"Well, Alex. I'm Mat. You're still not supposed to be up here."

"Sorry," I say, waving a hand across the view. "It's… it's coming along nicely?"

Her expression shifts again, into something light and amused. Her mouth quirks into a tiny smirk. "Yes, it is. That Jamboree girl did a lot of damage. C-Corp is funding it all, of course. Insurance doesn't cover psycho supervillian portals. Why would it? Never been a problem before."

"Psycho?"

Mat raises her eyebrows at me and pointedly scans the city centre. "Yes, because this just screams 'mental and emotional stability'."

She has a point. Jamboree *killed* me. Or at least four-fifths of me. Her motivations are still unclear despite numerous conversations. I've always seen the good in everyone. I'm finding it hard to see the good in her.

"I guess I agree." The words feel heavy and sticky on my tongue. "That— that Legion guy died, didn't he?"

"You been living under a rock, kid?" Mat asks, shaking her head. "Yeah. It's a shame, you know. He was my favourite."

"Really? Why?"

She shrugs, staring at some point over my shoulder while she thinks. "He always seemed... *good*. Not that the others don't, of course. He just encapsulated it most, I think. Like he was a good influence. Sort of person I'd like my goddaughters to spend their time with. Like, wow, he could fight, and he was dangerous, *ruthless* — you should look up the footage — but even before his secret identity came out, he just always had this air about him. He knew what he was doing was the right thing."

"No, he didn't," I say before I can stop myself.

"What?"

"Uh," I reply eloquently. "I mean, all these, uh, superheroes, they're just kids. My age. I don't know what I'm doing, so I doubt that they do."

"Maybe you're right," she says, her eyes narrowed as she looks at me. I feel like an old vase up for auction. "But at least they were trying."

"I think they're just dressing up and playing pretend," I say, thinking back to when I'd joke about it with Abyss. She always called our uniforms 'costumes' and told me and Caesar that we looked like we'd come out of science fiction shows. "They don't think about the consequences. Think they're above it."

"Well," Mat says, and something in the way she comes closer to me makes me think that she's pitying me. Maybe she can tell that I'm upset. Maybe she can tell that I'm a wreck, that I don't mean what I'm saying, that I'm looking for a fight. She doesn't give it to me. She just shrugs, rests her forearms on the same bit of metal railing that I'd been leaning on a few minutes prior. "Even if they didn't believe in the consequences *before*, I'm sure that they're thinking about them now."

"I lost my abilities," I burst out. I haven't told anyone. I hadn't really acknowledged it until today. I need to tell someone, and it comes out without me fully intending it. I don't think it really counts, telling someone who doesn't know me. Mat looks at me curiously. "I, uhm. There was an accident, and it damaged— me. I used to be... I used to want to be like them, you know? And now I can't."

She looks at me again. I get the impression that there's something she wants to say, but when she finally opens her mouth, the only thing that comes out is, "I'm sorry."

I shrug jerkily. "Me, too."

We stand in silence for a few minutes, staring out over the city centre. I'm tempted to ask if she knows anything about where Legion was found, but my stomach churns and I think it might be giving away too much.

My phone buzzes unexpectedly, twice in rapid succession.

abs said to **superkids!**: *x whr r u*

caesarean said to **superkids!**: *ur mom is getting worried*

I think that Caesar could find me pretty easily, if he wanted to. He could spread his mind out across the city and pinpoint my exact location from my thoughts. I know he can do it. He was supposed to be in my head on the day that I died, but he wasn't. Things might have been different, then.

I shouldn't be angry at him, but I am. It's not his fault that Abyss needed his help more. It's not Abyss' fault for needing help. It's not Ava's fault that she didn't look for me, either. It's not Ace's fault for trusting the numbers when they said I was 100% done for. It's not *anyone's fault*, and that's the real kicker. I died, and there's no one to blame.

you said to **superkids!**: *safe. dw.*

There's no one to blame, and yet I'm blaming everyone. Up to and including myself.

Mat speaks again when she sees me typing. "You really aren't supposed to be up here, you know. Come on, I'll escort you back down."

I nod mutely, and follow her.

63.

By the time I convince myself to go home, it's dark. The fire escape creeks in the same places it always does, the real reason I could never sneak out. Mom knew all about my superhero escapades, even before Abyss came along and joined me. She used to say she prayed for me every night, worried sick but certain that I was doing the right thing. I was certain, too, and then I died.

She's waiting in the living room, on the sofa-bed that until recently I thought of as Abyss'. After my outburst, I'm sure she's gone back to Caesar's penthouse. Her penthouse? Their penthouse? It makes me a little guilty, regardless. Mom pats the space next to her, and I go without a word.

"Pae Sun-Young," she says, and I know I'm in trouble, "You should know better than this."

"I know," I say, voice low and thick. "I know, I'm sorry. It's just— it's all so much."

The anger doesn't disappear from the line of her mouth, but it softens. "That doesn't give you the right to run off. You scared me."

The guilt intensifies. I died, and I'm making it all about me. Mom had to cope with that, and now that I'm back, she's probably petrified to lose me again. "I'm sorry," I say again. "I missed so much time. So much has changed, and I didn't even have the chance to know about it. I mean— Caesar and Abyss? Who would've thought?"

"Everyone," Mom replies, smiling just a little. "Even if the two of them were oblivious, I would have thought you'd pick up on it. You're their best friend. Abyss calls you her brother, sometimes."

I swallow, looking away. I'm such a dick. "I didn't… neither of them ever said. And then I wasn't… around to see it while it was happening. I'm not shocked, I just… I don't know. It's just another thing I missed. Like, Ava's start-of-term art show, Caesar's birthday party, Halloween. This is just… bigger, I guess. But everything I missed feels big."

She sighs, and presses her hand gently to my knee, squeezing twice. "It's got to be hard for you. I'm sorry."

"Don't be," I say, trying to shrug it off.

"You're my *son*, Xander," she says, somehow both a reprimand and a reassurance. "You're my only son. I love you, and I'm sorry."

"I love you, too," I say, turning back to face her and pulling her into a tight hug. "And I'm sorry, too."

It's late, and she tells me to go to bed. I promise that I will, and then wait for her bedroom door to close before I flick the TV on. I mute the volume before it has a chance to fully load, and swap the source to one of my consoles. The Street Fighter menu plays. I select Zangief, my favourite. It's mindless, but just bright and colourful enough to keep me distracted, even though I only button-mash tonight.

I don't want to go to sleep. When I lay alone in the dark and quiet, all I can think about is caskets, and I've thought about death too much today. I focus on the screen instead, flashes of orange and blue, and pixelated characters throwing punches. I play round after round, and fall asleep with the controller still in my hand.

Jolting awake only a few hours later, I'm greeted by the sight of Jamboree and a closing portal. The noise of it must have woken me, and before anything else I glance towards Mom's closed door. When Jamboree opens her mouth to speak, I scramble up to slam a hand over her mouth, holding my breath for several seconds while I wait to see if Mom will wake up. Just because she knows what it is that I do — *did*— doesn't mean she'd be okay with me bringing it home.

Scowling, Jamboree shoves my arm away from her face and arcs an eyebrow at me.

I glare back. "Abyss doesn't live here anymore."

She glances around the room with exaggerated surprise. "Clearly."

There's a tense few seconds where neither of us speak. She's got her arms folded in front of her chest, still wearing her signature two-piece suit. It's three in the morning. Like a sensible person, I'm wearing sweatpants and a floral t-shirt. I shouldn't feel under dressed— this is, after all, a late night attack. Presumably. Actually, we've just been hanging around looking at each other for quite a while now.

My eyes narrow. "What do you want?"

She shrugs, not meeting my eyes. It's like she's trying to play this off casually, but I think I can see a tension in her shoulders. It's dark, and I don't know her well, so I can't say for sure, but it seems like it. "Just wanted to see if this universe is like all the others." She gestures flippantly at my chest. "Not dead, so. See you later."

Before I can even attempt to process what she meant by all that, she's opening another portal, and she's gone.

I blink at the darkness, breathing hard. Nothing happened, but I feel short of breath anyway. And, really, *why* did nothing happen? What was that conversation even about?

A problem for tomorrow me. I go back to sleep.

64.

I make it a point, the next time I see them, to apologise to Abyss and Caesar and offer them a much more sincere congratulations. I am happy for them. I think it's great. Abyss beams— actually *beams*— when I tell them this, and then I don't have the heart to tell her about Jamboree's weird behaviour. Caesar looks at me nervously and says, "You really don't mind?"

"Why would I mind?" I ask, confused. "I know I was acting like a dick, but I really am happy for you. You're my best friends, and if you're happy, I'm happy."

His shoulders relax, and Abyss playfully jabs him in the side. They go quiet again, for a few seconds, then Caesar laughs and shakes his head. When he looks back at me again, he's smiling.

I text Ava about it, later, because as happy as I am for them, it is still a little weird. And the fact that Mom said anyone with eyes could see it coming left me feeling a little bit out of sorts.

acid spit: *i didn't like, *know* know, but i knew, you know?*

me: *not really*

acid spit: *yeah, you do! like with me and zoram before his mission or how i knew ab you and jessica before you did or when you liked that dumbie parker for a while*

acid spit: *it was an unspoken thing*

me: *so everyone just knew ab cee and abs?*

acid spit: *everyone but them, honestly*

I've been back from the dead for a little over a week when the the news breaks. The video was posted the same day I got home, but only gained traction over the past few days, and it's only after eight days that it actually makes the news. It's me, standing on the stairs, looking down at Mom with wide eyes, her short black hair all that's visible of her. When they play it on the news, I listen to myself saying "Mom! Mom, Mom, calm down, it's only me!"

Mom recognises the poster from his profile picture— the customer who was the only other person in the store that day— and tells me that he's not welcome in Pae's Flowers anymore. That's all well and good, but it doesn't change the fact that the video is out there.

With it, the conspiracies start. There's all sorts of theories about where I was and what I was doing, about if I really died or if it was all fake, about if Legion was *really* little old Xander Pae or if that was all for attention. If I want to stay ahead of this, I'll have to address it, and soon, which I really didn't want to do. I wanted to live in a comfortable bubble of obscurity for a little while longer.

I miss being *Legion*. I miss having *him* and having *me*, and that extra layer of safety draped over me. It wasn't why I wanted a secret identity, at least at first, but it was a nice bonus. No one payed attention to Xander Pae, even if he was friends with superheroes. I could blend, when I wanted to. Now I can't, and I really want to.

I still don't leave the house, and I won't until I come up with a plan of action. I stay on the couch, kicking my feet and playing old video games. Caesar comes by a few times to play with me. He's not very good at Metroid, which is my current favourite, so we play co-op on first person shooters and occasionally switch over to Mario when we want a break. Abyss visits too— I'm still trying to wrap my head around that. When she sits with us on the sofa bed (rarely unfolded, these days) it's because she's visiting, not because she lives here. She and Caesar aren't particularly physically affectionate, but he'll look over his shoulder at her at random intervals, and sometimes she'll card her fingers through his hair when she stands to get food or help Mom.

I do feel kind of silly for not noticing it sooner.

Ava and Zoram come over whenever they can. Ava still has school to go to, and Zoram is working at a restaurant while he sorts out his applications. They can't be around as much as they used to. Before his mission, before her university, we'd be over at each others houses almost non-stop. I have great memories of dragging my duvet out on to the fire escape and making a pile of pillows for the three of us to sit with hot chocolate and popcorn. It was different than sitting in the living room, if only by three feet, and that made it special.

Other friends reach out to Mom, asking if it's true, if I'm alive. Slowly, they all come by too. Most of my friends from Young Mens are out on missions, but some of them have come home. Some of them were back in time for the funeral. The girls I knew from the same age group make a day of it, all of them showing up together on a Wednesday evening, piled into three different cars.

Bishop Flores stops by, citing meetings in the area, but he looks at me with concern when he extends his hand. "Xander," he greets with a nod.

I shake his hand. "Bishop."

"How are you doing?"

I shrug, finding it difficult to meet his eyes. "As well as can be expected."

Of course, no one has ever been in the situation, so there really isn't a 'to be expected'. I think Bishop Flores knows it, even if he doesn't say. Instead, he just nods. "If you ever need to talk, just let me know."

"Will do," I say, and I try to mean it.

I spend every day exhausted. Each conversation I have with my friends leaves me feeling drained and tired. It doesn't help that I'm still not sleeping. I lay in my bed tossing and turning for hours when I bother to go to bed at all. Usually, I wait for Mom to go to bed and then I sit up in the living room doing anything I can to distract myself. I watch a lot of late night tv, level up in every video game I own, and read a bunch of books I pull from the shelves at random.

I pass out on the couch more often than not, and wake up early in the morning, jolted awake by dreams of falling through the sky.

I still haven't told anyone other than that construction worker, Mat, that I lost my abilities. It's another complication to the whole 'proving that I really am Legion' thing. I don't have abilities anymore. Maybe I'm not Legion anymore.

Gosh, that makes my stomach turn.

I keep coming back to my conversation with Jamboree. *Just wanted to see if this universe is like all the others*, she'd said, *Not dead, so.*

Does that mean that it is or isn't like the other universes? If it *is*, how does other-me cope? I could really use the pointers. I almost wish I could call her up and ask her to show me. I have a feeling that, even if I could, she'd laugh in my face.

65.

I put Legion's uniform on methodically. I always have. The trousers first, and then the top. I tie the boots before I slide my arms into the jacket, and I finish by clicking the mask in place. It covers my eyebrows, curves over my cheekbones, finishes right along my jaw. The speaker sits right over my mouth, amplifying and modifying my voice. I guess I don't need it modified anymore, if everyone knows who I am.

I look in my bedroom mirror, and for the first time I feel like a kid in a costume.

I was going to go out tonight, patrol around, try to feel normal again. I hadn't told anyone, not even Caesar and Abyss, because I was trying to do it for me. Looking at myself in the mirror, I don't think I can stomach it. I'm not superhuman anymore. I'm not a super*hero* anymore.

I'm not Legion anymore.

66.

"People keep coming to the shop to try to get pictures of me," I complain to Charlie on the phone one day, about three weeks since I've come home. I'm using the old landline Mom keeps hooked up, tugging at the spiralled cord as I speak. I could've used my phone, but Mom's been plugging it in downstairs for music, and I don't want to bother her. Charlie's been calling somewhat regularly, checking in like she's *my* big sister. She and Farah have been fantastic about that, looking out for me without it ever feeling patronising or pitiful.

"Bet the actual customers love that," she quips.

"I've been relegated to stockroom duty," I moan, dropping my head back against the couch cushions. "I have to hide in with the flowers, or else I'm upstairs, scheduling."

"I didn't think you'd mind hiding with the flowers."

I have to relent on that point. "Okay, I don't mind that so much. But I'm going crazy, Charlie. I've filled the entire apartment with plants."

"You're telling me it wasn't already filled?" she says, aghast. "Last time I was there, there wasn't a surface left uncovered."

"Yeah, I've just about doubled them," I push a vine out of my face as I speak. "I have nothing better to do. I can't even do my job! They're relentless. I'm getting cabin fever all cooped up. I don't want to just... go out into the world, though, you know? Like, I'm worried that they'll just keep following, trying to get pictures without giving me a break."

445

Charlie's quiet for a moment. "What if we did a photoshoot?"

"What?"

"Yeah, like, we could take a bunch of pictures. Just me and you, so it'd be more comfortable, and then we publish them all in one go. I'd sell them to a good magazine— maybe New Perspective, they were always kind to you in their articles— and that would satisfy the need for photos. It wouldn't stop the press all together, but they'd probably ease up once public curiosity did."

"That," I say, sitting back up and whipping myself in the face with another vine. "Sounds awesome."

"Okay," she says, "I'll come by tomorrow."

When I hang up, I'm in a better mood than I have been for weeks.

I'm still smiling to myself when Mom serves up dinner that night. We're having kimchi on rice, my very favourite, and my mouth is watering just at the sight of it. We load plates and sit at the square table, opposite each other.

"I haven't seen Ace in a while," she says, sounding kind of sad. Now that she mentions it, I haven't either. All of my other friends have crashed into our house in various states of excitement, but I haven't seen Ace since the week I came back. Granted, she and I were never all that close; she was Caesar's best friend, Abyss' gym buddy, but we'd never clicked on any special level. Still, when everyone else is coming by, and she isn't, it's notable.

"Me either," I say. "I'm sure she's just busy. I mean, she's only been back in the city for, what? Four months? She's probably catching up on everything that she's missed."

Mom shakes her head. "I don't think so. She spent a lot of time here, while you... before you came back."

Huh. It's news to me. I make a mental note to go check in with her. Maybe tomorrow, after my photoshoot. I tell Mom about it almost as soon as we've finished blessing the food, and although she doesn't say it, I know she's as relieved as I am to have a plan to get rid of the press. It hasn't been great for business.

Charlie comes by before lunch, and we sit eating peanut butter sandwiches while she talks me through her 'vision'. She's a photojournalist— which she's always assured me, her voice full of playful disgust— is different from a regular photographer. She won't stage it, won't fix me up or pose me. Instead, I'll just do everything that I've been doing anyway, and she'll chronicle it. I shrug, willing to go along with almost anything she suggests.

I clear away plates while she gets her camera ready. Then I just do what I normally do; I pull on an apron and wander around the stockroom. I fill out order forms, purchase office supplies online, occasionally poke my head out onto the shop floor.

Charlie Caesar's presence has a weird effect on press and paparazzi; on one hand, they'd love to photograph her, as she is one of the Caesar kids, but on the other, they respect her as a photographer and a journalist, and they don't want to step on her toes. As it is, there aren't as many cameras pointing through our window just for her being here, and even less once they put together that she's shooting me.

"You know what I should do," I joke to her, "is make a really big deal about press passes. All over my internet presence: 'press pass only, we will be checking'. And then I could only send one to you."

She rolls her eyes at me, but she's smiling, and that makes me smile, too. She lifts the camera and catches it before it drops.

She takes some more pictures when I inevitably retreat upstairs. I'm only sitting on the couch, surrounding by plants and flowers, balancing a notebook on my legs while I make brief phone calls about orders. When I say who's calling, I don't say my name anymore.

The more calls I make and notes I take, the more frustrated I get. My favourite part of my job was talking to people. I like getting to know our customers and slowly discovering the perfect flowers for them, laughing with them, making their days a little bright. Ever since I died, I haven't been able to in the same way. People want to ask all about me, and I don't know what to tell them.

I can feel my shoulders getting tighter, my voice getting clipped, and I don't know how to stop it. Smiles used to come easy enough— even when I was getting frustrated, I could send out a duplicate to deal with it, so no one would ever catch on. Abyss said 'If I see you without a smile, I'll think the world is ending'. She was joking, I know she was joking, but I liked that that was my reputation. I could separate it out, and be sure that I always put my best foot forward.

Not that people never saw me in different moods. Mom definitely did, sometimes looking between several different bodies to suss out what the problem was. Caesar was always aware when I had other bodies out, his telepathy making him, on some level, knowledgable about the people who were around him. Abyss lived with me, as good as family, used to my contemplative moods, and seeing me send fear and anger away to other bodies the same way that she sent everything into the Void.

But I could control who saw it and when— people knew me as happy, and I always was.

These days, I don't have that same level of control. I know that there are ways to do it without other bodies— obviously. I'm not the only person who can control their facial expressions. But that was how *I* did it, and it's killing me to lose it.

After about an hour, Charlie seems to catch on to my increasingly sour mood. She tips her head like she's not one-hundred-percent sure how to deal with it, and then stands, ruffles my hair like I've seen her do to Caesar and Carlos, and tells me she has enough to work with. She says she'll go out through the flower shop, to say goodbye to my mom.

449

Before she heads down the stairs, I catch her by the door. "Charlie, wait. I just... I wanted to say thanks. You've been really good to me."

"Of course," she says, shrugging like it's nothing. "When we met you, I was nine years old and liked being 'in charge' — as much as I could be with bodyguards looking after us. But then you walked up to Cee and I, with a blinding smile, and asked to play, and it was... I don't know, Xander. It was just good. We've always cared about you and your family, and I care about you."

I open my mouth to reciprocate, but she shrugs again and says, "Let me tell you a secret. When I say you playing pirates with my kid brother, letting him be the Captain because you knew it would make him happy... I thought you were the coolest person ever."

My mouth snaps shut.

She laughs. "I still kind of think it, you know."

I'm glad someone does.

I go back to the sofa and, after standing mutely for only a few seconds, I pick up the notebook and throw it across the room. It collides with the wall, scuffing the paint. Looking upwards at the popcorn ceiling, I let out a frustrated scream, then rake my fingers through my hair hard enough to hurt and drop my head back down. On impulse, I kick the coffee table in front of me and, when I miscalculate and slam my shin into the top, I stumble backwards, lifting my leg to clutch at it.

Of course, this is the exact moment that the tell-tale sound of fanfare fills the living room.

I trip over the loveseat and crash onto the floor. I can't help but scream again, dropping my leg out of my hands and bringing them up to cover my face.

"Smooth," Jamboree says, and when I drop my hands, she's looking down at me with an eyebrow raised.

I scramble to my feet. "What are you doing here?"

I'd half convinced myself that our previous conversation was a dream, but when she shifts her gaze away from mine to stare at the blank wall, instead, I have a feeling that it was real. Not that it explains why she's here again. "Can't I just drop by to say hello?" she tries, and it just about sounds sarcastic.

"No."

"Fair enough," she says, and she shrugs, but offers no further explanation.

I died fighting her. I died trying to save people from her temper tantrum with still undefined causes. I died, because she couldn't stop thinking about herself for ten seconds and realise that people were in danger. We stand, on opposite sides of the coffee table, for several seconds. Then I dart around it, grab her wrist, and drag her out of the open window, onto the fire escape, and the up onto the roof.

It's cold outside. We're only a week away from Christmas, and the air is biting against my bare arms. Jamboree is wearing more layers than me, as she's in her usual suit. As soon as we stop moving, she wrenches her wrist away from me and takes two steps back. "What was that for?"

"Are you here to fight me, Jamboree?" I demand. "Are you here to kill me?"

"No!"

I step closer to her. "Fight me, Jamboree." When she makes no move, I straighten up and say it again. "Fight me!"

I can see her gaze harden, and her jaw set. "Xander—"

I take a swing at her, almost wildly, and she steps back, leaning into her shoulders to dodge it. When I take aim again, she ducks, skittering backwards, and when I follow, she kicks a leg out to trip me, and I stumble over it, but I don't fall. Grunting, I chase after her, catching her by the arm and yanking her back towards me. She slams her heel into my toes, knocks her head backwards and barely misses my nose. The force shoves my lip back against my teeth, and I can feel it split.

She shakes herself free while I'm distracted, and I summon up a duplicate to catch her while I catch my breath.

I freeze, and raise my head.

There is no duplicate, and Jamboree is heaving her own ragged breaths a few steps away. There is no duplicate.

She stalks towards me while I'm still frozen, and punches me across the face, then hooks her foot around the back of my legs and drags me to my knees. She looks mussed; her hair messy around her face, her jacket rumpled, but I'm the one who's on my knees with a bloodied face. I'm well and truly beaten.

There was no duplicate.

She looks down at me, still breathing hard. Her hand is in my face a second later, like she's offering to help me up. When I don't do anything for a moment, she waves it impatiently.

I take her hand, and she pulls me to my feet.

"What do you *want*, Jamboree?"

She shrugs, staring past me and into the city.

A sudden burst of wind makes me shiver. She takes several steps backwards, opening a portal behind her. I don't make any move to stop her. "You should get some ice on your lip," she says, and walks backwards through her portal.

I stay on the roof for two full minutes before I go take her advice.

67.

I spend the next two days in bed, getting out only to eat and use the bathroom. My lip is swollen, although not as badly as I thought it might be. I mostly avoid Mom's questions, shrugging and offering non-committal grunts. I don't allow anyone to come over, just texting 'busy' to anyone who asks. In response, my friends have been bombarding me with text and phone calls, so I'm not surprised when I roll over, around noon on the third day, to see a list of messages a mile long.

acid spit: *are you sure you're okay???*

caesarean: *you know you can ask if you need anything*

abs: *ur mm is cllng me. tlk to hr. or us.*

caesarean said to **superkids!:** *we're worried about you x*

abs said to **superkids!:** *wht d u nd?*

zozoram: *hey man. hope you're feeling better. if you want to hang out, just let me know.*

I can't bring myself to read any further than that. I throw my phone back on the nightstand and grab my other pillow, slamming it over my face. Zoram never texts anyone. Ava used to complain about it all the time. If *he's* texting me, then I know this has gone too far.

But then again, *I* went too far.

I struck first. I went after her. I don't know why, exactly, she came to my house, but she didn't attack me. I'm the one who dragged her onto the roof and fought her. I wish I could say I was out of control— but I wasn't. I knew what I was doing. Blinded by anger, white-hot and dangerous, I'd let myself react violently when it wasn't at all necessary.

When you sign up for martial arts, they talk a lot about how it's only for self-defence, how you should only use it when absolutely necessary. Some of my teachers spoke about balance and inner peace and whatever else. It worked, sometimes, kept me steady on my feet even when I felt like the rug was being pulled out from under me. It usually didn't. I've always been violent. It's part of why no one guessed that I was Legion, because *he* took all of my violent urges, all of my negativity, and I was allowed to be kindhearted and gentle.

The last time I lashed out like that, it was shortly after Dad died. We knew it was coming; he was sick, and working with numbered days. He was so dopey with pain meds that I'm not even sure that he noticed dying. Afterwards, I went to a nearby skate park and got in a fight with some boys from a different school. My stomach was in knots, and they'd barely said two words to me before I was on them. I was outnumbered, and I ended up tearing away, the sound of my feet pounding against the concrete drowned out by the pulse I could feel in my ears. I sat underneath the fire escape when I got home, my knees pulled up to my chest, sobbing.

That's when the first duplicate appeared, and things got easier.

I threw myself into martial arts, paying attention to their lectures about emotions and stability for the first time. I took up meditation. The more I looked at myself, the more duplicates I was able to create.

It's always been a balancing act, like juggling spinning plates, but I used to have more hands.

I don't know what I'm doing.

I'm so angry, all the time, and every little thing sends me spiralling. It's terrifying. I'm terrified.

Legion was supposed to be the one dealing with this. He took all of this away, and dealt with it, and worked it out, and I got to hang back, telling customers the meanings of the flowers they were looking at. Abyss asked me about my secret identity I don't know how many times, and even once she stopped asking, I know she was curious. I never had the words to explain it, but I think I do now.

I was scared (I'm still scared) of my potential to be dangerous. I've always loved people as easily as breathing, and the idea that I could be something that people feared left me petrified. I wanted Legion to be separate, I wanted Xander to have the freedom to be his own person.

I've been Legion for nearly four years now; since before I met Abyss, before Caesar, before Jamboree. I've seen how people freeze when they see him, not knowing who's behind the mask. The way they seem wary, even after our press conferences, even after we announced who we were and what we hoped to do.

But I've also seen the way people look at *Xander*. They look at me in my Sunday best, floral tie and navy blue jacket, and they think that I'm no one. That I need protecting. I was at Charlie's wedding, and then I wasn't and *Legion* was, and no one thought that maybe we were one and the same. Caesar knew about my abilities, and knew about Legion, and still didn't put two and two together.

I hated it, I hated how Legion was feared and Xander was underestimated, and I always knew, somehow, that I couldn't have the best of both worlds. Eventually, keeping them so completely separate wouldn't be an option anymore. I knew that.

But it makes me so, so *angry* that it wasn't even my choice. I didn't have a chance to think about it, to decide how I wanted to merge the two. I was Xander and Legion, two different people, almost, and now four-fifths of me are dead, and I don't know how to re-strike that balance, or if it's even possible.

I don't respond to any of the texts, but I do force myself to get out of bed. We need groceries, and Mom has been working so, so hard. It's the least I can do. I pull out an old and faded grey hoodie, put in some headphones, and head out. I still feel like I'm dead while I walk through the aisles, but at least I'm amongst the living.

"Xander!"

I can hear the voice over my headphones, so I pop one out and turn towards the call.

"Oh, hey, Bishop," I reply when I catch sight of him, shuffling awkwardly and gesturing as if I need to head out. As is typical, Bishop Flores either doesn't get it or intentionally ignores it, instead pulling his cart up parallel to mine and stopping to chat. "Just— grocery shopping."

He raises his eyebrows and looks between me and my cart. "I can see that."

"Right, of course." I shake my head and grip the handle of my cart a little too tightly. "I should probably get back to it, you know."

"We haven't seen you at church in a while. And Todd tells me that you've not been to Institute, either."

"Save the lecture," I snap, then immediately cringe. "No, I'm sorry, that's not— I just mean... I know, it's been a while."

To his credit, he doesn't flinch. "If you ever need someone…"

"You're only a phone call away, I know," I grumble, raising my shoulders to hide my neck even further in my hoodie. "Don't know that it'd help, but I know."

"I'm here for you. Anything you need."

"I need to go back to being alive!" I half-shout, then immediately sink back into myself, flushing under the gaze of other shoppers. Continuing in an angry whisper, I say, "I'm unique! No one knows what I'm going through!"

"Well," he says, and I can see where this is going before he speaks next, "Jesus—"

"Never had to forgive someone for literally *murdering him*—"

His expression is mostly concerned, but the flicker of amusement? I can't fault him for that. "Yeah, okay, I realised as I said it."

I don't look back as I push my cart down the aisle, curling my shoulders inwards. I don't have everything on the list, but I don't care. I pay for everything and leave as quickly as I can.

My phone buzzes again as I get back home.

j.c.caesar: *pictures are all good to go! :) any publication in mind or should i just pick for u?*

I click through the attached pictures. I don't even look like myself.

I'm smiling in the flower shop, but it doesn't meet my eyes. There's a hardness to my jaw on the sofa upstairs. My hair falls in to my eyes while I make a note in the stockroom.

In every photo, I'm surrounded by plants. That's the only thing that seems familiar.

I text back that she should just pick for me, and then, leaving the groceries still bagged in the kitchen, I go back to sleep.

68.

Charlie was right; the pictures being out there does satisfy a curiosity, and the photographers dissipate pretty quickly over the next few days. I'm able to go back to work without the boiling feeling in my stomach every time I look outside. I spend the next several weeks throwing myself into it. I barely think of anything else, not allowing myself to dwell on the dichotomy of Xander and Legion, or whatever.

New Years Eve comes and goes. I decline an invite to a dance with Ava and Zoram, telling them playfully that I don't want to third wheel, and then avoid texts from the other YSA in our ward offering me lifts. Caesar invites me to the penthouse because it has a phenomenal view of the fireworks, and I am tempted, but I tell him I have plans with my mom. Then, I go to my mom and make plans. We unfold the sofa bed and watch the fireworks on tv, eating pizza and popcorn and other foods starting with 'p' while in our pyjamas. I do text the superkids! chat at midnight, though. I don't want to be a complete dick.

Mom brings up Ace again, trying to sound casual, when she sees who I'm messaging. There's a stab of guilt at that. I'd meant to go visit her ages ago, but I still haven't spoken to Ace, even via text. She's been pretty quiet on the superkids! chat lately.

She does reply to my new years message with a string of celebratory emojis, and I make a quiet resolution to go see her within three days.

I go to the apartment she shared with her roommates, and the cute one answers the door. I used to have a fluttery sort of crush on him, before I died, but I haven't even spared it a thought since. He tells me that Ace moved out almost as soon as she got back to the city, which happened while I was away, and gives me directions to her new place.

He offers me a gentle smile and tells me that it's good to see me alive and well, and I can barely bring myself to say, "You, too." Thankfully, he doesn't seem offended, and just waves and closes the door.

Ace's new place isn't too far away, so I shove my hands into the pockets of my denim jacket— the one that used to be my dad's— and walk with my shoulders hunched.

"Is that Xander Pae? Legion?" I hear, and I have to resist the urge to turn around. The voice is young, probably only thirteen or fourteen.

"Maybe," says someone I assume is a friend or a sibling. "Go ask him."

I quicken my pace, and manage to lose anyone who might be following. I used to laugh when Abyss got stopped for pictures or autographs or anything else, because I knew I'd never have to deal with that. Shows what I know. Putting the cart before the horse, and all that.

Ace is in an apartment on the third floor. Apartment 5C. I knock on the door, and when she answers, she's wearing a bright red peacoat and matching lipstick. "Oh!" she says, blinking her wide eyes at me. "Xander! I was, uhm, I was just... heading out."

She used to say that she lies professionally. I'm not sure I'm buying it.

"You've been avoiding me," I accuse, and she drops her shoulders, sighing.

"No, I haven't," she says, and then cringes at how fake it sounds. When she turns to take her jacket off, she gestures for me to come in. "Do you want anything to drink? I'll be honest, I've mostly only got alcohol, but I think there's some orange juice in the fridge. Or soy milk, but, uhm. That's disgusting on it's own."

I don't think it's very good *not* on it's own, but I don't say so. I just shake my head. Her apartment is small, with an open plan living room and kitchen, and two doors on either side of the tv that presumably lead to a bedroom and a bathroom. The couch is obviously secondhand, but it's white with red stitching, incredibly Ace. There's a low table made of coffee colour wood, a lamp, a tv stand with a cheap flatscreen, tiny circular dining table and two mismatched chairs. She stands awkwardly in the middle of the room until I sit and slide my jacket off, and then she sinks onto the couch next to me.

"My mom keeps bringing you up," I tell her. "She says she misses you. Granted, I don't know when you and my mom got that close, but it's what she's said, so."

"Xander," Ace says, cutting me off. She has her hair cut short. Her beachy waves come to a stop just below her jaw. It suits her, makes her look older. "You died. Her whole family was dead. My whole family is dead. It was... I don't know. I guess we just understood

463

each other, y'know? And then, uhm. You came back, and that was hard for me."

"If you think that means my mom stopped caring about you, then you don't know her very well," I say, because I don't know what else to say. They were grieving, and able to share that grief. I'm grateful that someone was able to do that for my mom. I may not have been close to Ace before, but I feel a surge of affection for her now.

"No, hun," she says, like I'm incredibly dumb. "*You came back*. That's hard for me."

"Oh," I say, because maybe I'm incredibly dumb. I came *back*. Her family *didn't*. "I'm sorry."

"Only you would apologise for not being dead," she says, and she laughs. "Don't be stupid. *Of course* I'm glad that you're back. This is a me thing."

I smile lightly at her. "You should still go visit my mom at some point. She misses you. With Abyss out of the house now, too, I think she's… I think she got used to having a girl around."

Ace grins at that, resting her elbow on the back of the couch and her face on her hand. "I'll go over tomorrow. Hey, tell me. Are you okay?"

I go to shrug it off, but she fixes me with stern look. "I don't know," I admit. "It's all very… weird. I *died*. But I didn't. I don't remember it. Did it really happen to *me*? Or was that someone else? I've always felt like me and the duplicates are all one person, I've never had to

464

have this… identity crisis, or whatever, but I *died* and I didn't at the same time. And there's three months worth of stuff that I don't know anything about, and I feel like I missed a lifetime."

Ace blinks at me a few times. "Okay… I'll be honest, I don't know how to help with most of that."

I laugh, but it's not very humorous. "I don't think anyone does."

"It's a bit, um… philosophical for me," she shrugs apologetically. After only a beat, she sitting up straight and hitting my knee. "I can't help with the other stuff, but I can fill you in on what you missed. But, okay. Oh damn, has anyone told you about how *awful* Cee and Abs were? Like, honestly, it was *painful*."

"No one's told me in any detail, no."

We spend the next forty minutes chatting about Caesar and Abyss. Ace has some hilarious commentary on the whole situation. "I mean, I'd go to the diner with Caesar one day, and he'd tell me that he told her she was 'endlessly fascinating' and I'd die of laughter because he still hasn't put together that he loves her, right? Or if he has he still hasn't *told* her. And then the next day I'd be at the gym with Abs, you know? 'We were in bed,' she'd say, 'and he said he's endlessly fascinated by me. What is that supposed to mean? We sleep in the same bed, Caesar, can you at least tell me if you love me or not?'"

I'm cracking up at her disgusted, disbelieving expression, with her nose wrinkled and her mouth twisted up. She shakes her head back and forth slowly. "This is what I had to put up with, you know. And it only got worse once they did their whole 'mental connection' thing." She waves her hand next to her temple like a jellyfish.

"What?"

"Oh, don't worry about missing out on that," she says, shrugging. "They haven't told anyone. Cee only told me because I caught him doing this thing where he'd stop paying attention mid-sentence. I thought he was just getting spacey, but then I noticed Abyss doing the same thing, and then when they're in the same room, they'll go quiet at the same time and then get matching facial expressions. Caesar said something to me once about how much he loves being in her head, so I put two and two together and got seventeen, if you know what I mean. Called him on it, and he told me it's amazing."

"That's why they go all weird and quiet?"

"Man, *yes*," she says, rolling her eyes. "I mean, personally, I'd hate to have someone in my head twenty-four/seven, but I guess it works for them."

She fills me in on Caesar's birthday party, proudly telling me about the decorations she picked, which sound hideous to me. She tells me about her time undercover, because I haven't heard anything about that yet, and then she tells me that she's stopped or at least mostly stopped her hunt for that company. "It wasn't doing me any good," she says, smiling. "I'm back in high school! I'm going to get my diploma and try to live a normal life, you know? Not that I won't still help you guys out when you need it, though."

My chest constricts at that. I don't know if I'm still a superhero. On a whim, I ask, "What ever happened to that DNA drug?"

"It's still out there," she tells me darkly. "There's been a few more deaths linked to it. I can ask around, if you want. Put some, uh, feelers out, see what I can find."

"Sure," I agree. "Let me know what you hear."

When I leave, we're both smiling much more genuinely then we were when I arrived. Ace comes to the apartment the very next day, and I can tell my mom is thrilled.

69.

I pass January quietly. Ace texts me everything she hears about DNA, and I go back and forth on what to do with it all. I put on Legion's uniform a few more times, but I never make it past the fire escape, maybe the roof.

February brings Valentine's Day, which is busy season at a florists. We won't make any bouquets until day-of, but we're still kept occupied with purchasing stock and managing orders. I barely notice when Jamboree shows up.

She's hovering outside Pae's Flowers, stealing looks inside and trying to play casual. It's the suit that gives her away; emerald green, velvet. We're only an hour from closing, and it's quiet enough in the store that I can sigh, push the door open, and beckon her in.

"Can I show you something?" she says, all in a rush, after she shakes her head and refuses to come inside.

"Where?" I ask warily, but I step out of the shop anyway. Instinctually, I try to summon up a duplicate to take my place inside. I can practically feel my heart stop when nothing happens.

"A museum," she assures me. Then, with a smirk that looks much more familiar to me, adds, "It's in another universe, granted, but... It's only a museum."

I debate it for only a moment. After the debacle of our last interaction, I think I probably owe her one. "I'll have to tell my mom where I'm going. And I'm only agreeing to be gone for an hour. You can't— I can't—"

I don't finish my sentence. She seems to understand what I'm getting at anyway. She nods, and I go back inside to tell my mom.

"Do you know what you're doing?" she asks, voice low, looking out the window. Jamboree looks nervous, I think, rubbing her arms and bouncing on her feet.

I'm not worried about what Jamboree will do to me. I still don't really understand what she's hoping to get out of showing up at my house at all hours of the day and night, but she hasn't tried to hurt me even once. And, from the looks of the news, she hasn't tried to hurt anyone else, either. I'm more worried about what I might do, once we're out of sight, in a universe that's not my own.

I set my shoulders and try to smile. "I'm going to forgive her."

"Xander," she says, voice breaking. "Be *careful*."

Mom knows she can't stop me. I should probably feel bad about that, but instead I lean down to kiss her cheek, and, leaving my apron on the counter, go back outside to meet Jamboree. She nods to the alley, by the fire escape, and we wander down in an awkward silence. The portal opens with its usual fanfare, and she steps through first, leaving it open behind her. I guess she's giving me the chance to follow, or back out. I stand in front of the portal. The swirling, purple-blue tint to the edges is kind of hypnotic. Through it, I see glass cases and statuettes. It is, genuinely, a museum.

I step through the portal. What's the worst that can happen? I'm already four-fifths dead.

The museum has shiny glass floors with inky black wood underneath and the ceiling, easily twenty feet high, is made entirely of windows, letting the afternoon sun stream in, lighting the whole room. We're in a long room filled almost entirely of marble statues, with three or four glass cases near the front, where the portal is. Jamboree is ages way now, nearly at the other end, so I start walking in her direction. The dress shoes that I wear to work click satisfyingly against the clear floors.

Jamboree is standing in front of the statue that must be the focal point of the room. It's bigger than any of the other ones, even if it weren't on the circular, raised platform that it is. I let my eyes drag up, and I stop short at the sight.

It's clear who I'm looking at. Caesar sits on the ground, one leg bent to point straight up and the other stretched out in front of him. He's barefoot, wearing only a pair of cut-off shorts, the line of his flat stomach stretched out as he leans back onto his hands. Even made out of stone, his curls look soft to the touch. Somehow, he even has freckles scattered over his nose and bare shoulders. He's looking, his eyes crinkled in the corners with obvious joy, at Abyss. She's sitting up straighter, her legs tucked under her, her hands in the air like she's mid-thought. Her hair is woven into her signature braids, and instead of sunglasses her eyes are covered with a ribbon that ties behind her head and then drapes over her shoulders. Her head is pointed towards Caesar's, and she's smiling, just the barest upturn of her lips.

They look beautiful, ten feet tall and made of marble.

I come to a stop next to Jamboree, silent from equal parts awe and shame.

"This statue is thousands of years old," she says, low and tired sounding. "Here, they're worshipped as *gods*. They'll never worship me, you know?"

It's barely audible, but her voice goes up slightly at the end, turning it into a question. I look at my hands. I only have two, not ten. "Yeah, I think I do."

"I didn't— I couldn't explain it to her," she says, closing her eyes. "She said she wanted to help me, and she left. She said she wanted to help superhumans, but she left. You know?"

I feel like I almost understand. It's dancing right at the cusp of my mind. "You…" I start, but I trail off. "If it helps," I add after a second, squeezing my two hands into fists. "They'll never worship me, either."

Jamboree looks at me oddly, her brow furrowed. "What? Of course they do. Look," and she points, and I follow it to another statue, only a little smaller, to the left of the room.

It's like looking in a mirror; that's my hair, my eyes, my lean muscle.

There's five of me, of course. One of them is standing, shoulders squared, chin tilted upwards, hands curled into fists. The other four are positioned lower to the ground, kneeling or crouching or laying down. They're inlaid with gold, and it sparkles in the sunlight. In the glass floor, I can only see the one that's standing, looking defiantly across the room.

"There's got to be one of you," I say, swallowing thickly and turning away from the painful reminder of everything I'm missing.

She laughs. "There's really not. I've looked. That's my point."

Again, I think I could get it. "You…" I start again, uncurling my fists. "What? You felt like Abs abandoned you?"

"Didn't she?" she asks wryly, and crosses her arms in front of her. "She went searching for these universes, and she said she did it for *me*. And then she joins your team and… said she did it for superhumans. Or at least that's what Caesar said, and she agreed with him, and she didn't come find me. All these other universes… in so many others, she found me. Why not in *mine*?"

"She was scared," I tell her. "She missed you. She told me. Abyss… well, that's just it, isn't it? She's *Abyss*, now. Not Jenna-Louise. Not *Jenny*. She was always so scared of what you'd think of her. It's why she never went home."

"But *I'm* superhuman. I would've— she must know I would've understood."

"Scared people are stupid," I say, and allow myself to smile, just a little. I know it all too well, lately. "Even if they are actual, certified geniuses."

There's silence for a few moments longer, while we both stare at the statue of Caesar and Abyss. It's more beautiful the longer I stare at it. It's painfully accurate, down to the dimple on Caesar's cheek and the tiny scar on Abyss' nose.

"Maybe…" I pause. "I don't know if this is comforting, but maybe you don't exist in this universe, and that's why there's no statue."

"Nah," she says. "That's the kicker. I can only see universes where I exist."

I wonder if Abyss knows that. I wonder if Jamboree has ever admitted a limitation like that to anyone before.

"I'm sorry," I say. "For all of this. For the way I acted last time."

She shrugs, jerky. "It's fine. I deserved it."

My head snaps to face her. "No, it isn't. No, you didn't."

She purses her lips, and doesn't say anything.

"I can't make duplicates anymore," I say on a whim, since we're in a sharing mood. "They— I— this body is a duplicate, and duplicates never could make more. Only the original could. That's what I mean when I say that they won't worship me. I'm not— I'm not superhuman anymore."

Jamboree shrugs, and it's that same forced nonchalance from our three a.m. chat. "That sucks, man. Come on, we better get you home."

The portal she opens blocks the statue from our view. I go through it first, and she doesn't follow.

70.

"Are you okay, Xander?" Bishop Flores asks me, the next day, while Mom is busy chatting and I'm standing awkwardly a few feet away from Ava and Zoram's painful flirting. "We haven't seen you too much."

I think back to our conversation in the grocery store. "I've been coming to church more."

He nods, chewing on his lip. "But Todd says that you still haven't been to Institute. And I know for a fact that you skipped out on the New Years Eve dance, and the bowling activity that the YSA did. I've also heard you don't have Valentine's Day plans. It's unlike you."

"I…" I don't have a defence. I haven't been preparing for this particular conversation. "I've been working through some stuff."

He looks at me with kind, worried eyes. "You know, Xander, we're all here for you." He taps a painting on the wall. "He's here for you. He's pretty unique too."

I look at the picture. It's of Jesus, knocking on a door without a handle, waiting for someone to open it. I've seen it thousands of times. I think I understand it slightly more, now. I've been cutting myself off from everything, haven't I?

"How do you think He did it?" I ask, and Bishop Flores looks curiously at me. "How He— forgave the people who killed Him?"

He blinks at me, clearly caught off guard. "I think He knew them," he says, after a moment. "I think He loved them, for knowing them. Why do you ask?"

"Because I died," I say, swallowing. "And I'm not entirely sure how to forgive the person who caused it, however unintentional it was… But I'm starting to get to know her. I'd like to be able to look at her without— I just wanted to know how you thought He did it."

There's silence for a long, stretching moment. "If you ever need me, Xander," he says, smiling kindly at me and letting his hand rest on my shoulder. "You let me know, okay?"

71.

I don't have a date for Valentine's Day. I've had a date every year for the past five years, ever since I turned sixteen, even if it was something casual, so it feels a little weird to be seeing all the couples being affectionate. We have even more customers than usual, so I'm glad that we managed to sort out the photographer problem before now.

Charlie calls, to order something extravagant for Farah. I grin while I note it down, because Farah, meanwhile, is talking to Mom, placing an order of her own. Zoram gets a small bouquet for Ava, which she loves. Abyss was never a flower person, despite my many attempts to change her mind, so I'm not surprised that Caesar doesn't call. I send them a bouquet anyway, made up of chrysanthemum and iris, because they're my best friends.

I don't have anyone else to buy flowers for. I debate getting some for Jamboree, if only to continue my apology, but I wouldn't know where to send them.

I spend Valentine's Day with Mom. I make heart shaped pancakes and she actually sits in the same room as me while I play video games. Abyss and Caesar send me a picture of the two of them with their flowers, both smiling. I'm happy for them. I've never seen Abyss smile so much, or this brightly. However they came to be together, it's clearly done good things for her.

ace: *wanna go paint the town??*

me: *dont u have a bf???*

ace: *hes away and im bored… come on, itll give us a reason to get all fancy*

ace: *plus ur not doing anything tonight r u?? i can wing woman you a date*

me: *i dont want a date a*

ace: *fine, we can just dance*

me: *i dont really go to clubs*

ace: *got you covered. theres a jazz place near cees place, it's all proper dancing, not club dancing*

ace: *i know youll like it*

me: *…okay, fine*

ace: *:)!!!*

She's at my window quickly enough that I know she was already ready to go and possibly on her way before I agreed to go. She's chatting to Mom while I pull on a nice shirt in my bedroom.

"How's your boyfriend?" Mom asks, and Ace laughs.

"Fantastic, as always," she replies. "You know, it was actually his idea that I ask Xander to come out. He's not much of a dancer, and I think he knows that Xander needs a friend."

I probably do, but I don't love to hear it coming from someone who I've never met.

Ace is wearing a black velvet dress with a flared skirt over a red turtleneck and a pair of heels that look dangerous to walk in. She beams when she sees me, clapping her hands together and dragging me in for a picture. She captions it 'PALentines day' and sends it off to several people, only half of which I know.

"Come on, we need to get a cab," she says, and before I can speak, interjects with, "I know you'd drive, but we're doing an *experience* thing today."

We race down the fire escape, ignoring the way it creaks, while I laugh at Ace's enthusiasm and she laughs at my laughter. She whistles for a taxi, something I could never quite master, and reels off an address as soon as we've climbed in. We chat and gossip and laugh the whole way to club which, as promised, is an upscale jazz place. Through the window, I see girls in loose dresses twirling around the room, and guys in nicely fitted suits holding them in their arms.

She smiles at the bouncer, who doesn't even check her ID. He does check mine. "You're underage," I whisper, once we're out of ear shot.

"Shh!" she chastises me. "I've been here before. They know me, and they *don't* know that. So keep your voice down. Come on, let's dance."

She grabs my hands and takes me out to the dance floor, where we fumble through the steps. Ace is clearly out of her element with this kind of thing, and all I have is a few tricks I picked up at church dances, but we make do, and we have fun. We stay on the floor for several songs, all of which are fast paced and happy sounding, and don't leave much room for conversation. Her hair goes all mussed and frizzy, and I end up paying to have my coat stashed, and we carry on dancing.

When a slower song finally plays, she steps closer to me and wraps her arms around my neck. I rest my hands on her waist, naturally assuming we're switching positions for the dance. Instead, she tilts her head towards my ear and whispers, "There's someone here who's selling DNA."

I freeze, but only for a half-second, and given how bad we've been at dancing all night, we manage to play it off. "So this wasn't just to get me out of the house, then?"

"Course it was," she replies, and I can hear her smile even if I can't see it. "Get you out of the house, get you back in the game, same difference, right? Turn around."

I step in a slow circle, in time to the music, so that we're facing in opposite directions. "See that guy in the burgundy suit? The one with the hat, not the one with the ascot."

As we sway back and forth, I scan along the men opposite us, flicking right over the one with the ascot and landing on a shorter man with a fedora worn at an almost jaunty angle. "Yeah, I see him."

"His name is Bruno," Ace tells me, her voice so low I have to strain to hear it over the music. "I've played poker with him before, so I know how good of a liar he is. If it weren't for the numbers, I wouldn't be able to beat him."

"Keeps his cards close to his chest, does he?"

Ace sighs, and I can't hold back a grin. "Something like that," she says, shaking her head. "Anyway, he, uh, offered me some DNA the last time I saw him. Woulda been… about a week ago. Nine days? Whatever. When I asked where he got it, he told me he's 'seen how it's made'."

"He could've been lying," I point out. "You said he's a good liar."

"And I have numbers that tell me the chances of things, don't I?" she snarks. "I checked. Seems legit. I think it's worth looking into."

"So how are we going to do this?"

"Oh, no," she laughs, tilting her head back and stepping a quarter inch back so we can actually see each others faces. "That's not how this works. I'm *retired*, remember? I've given you a… chance. It's up to you what you do with it."

As if on cue, the song ends, and Ace steps further away. She spins around and wanders towards the bar, leaving me standing dumbly in the middle of the club. The man, Bruno, hasn't noticed me, and is, instead, laughing with some tall, beautiful woman. I don't know what to do right now.

Xander Pae doesn't do the superhero thing, and Legion isn't here anymore. My heart pounds against my ribcage. What was Ace thinking, bringing me here? This is her thing, not mine.

Everyone around me is dancing again as a faster paced song picks up. Bruno and the tall women don't join in, but slink down a hall that I hadn't even noticed until now. I glance around, but Ace is still at the bar, talking into her phone, presumably to her boyfriend. My heart speeds up again. I think it might explode soon if I don't do *something*.

The hallway is narrow and intimate, lit with dim orange light. I'm half worried I'm going to interrupt some sort of hookup, rather than learn anything useful, but I press on anyway, keeping an ear out for any unsavoury sounds. There's only faint voices, too far away to hear properly, and the fading sound of music from the main room.

At the end of the hallway, there's a red curtain that looks heavy. I don't push it aside for fear of startling Bruno and the woman, but when I brush against it as I get closer, it's velvety smooth. I press my back against the wall to peer through the gap. Beyond the curtain is a large room that seems circular. Bruno is sitting on a desk, facing towards me, and the woman is facing him, cut off from my view.

"There's too much *press*," the woman says. She's got a rich voice, raspy like a smokers. "You understand that, don't you?"

"Relax," Bruno replies, like it's the easiest thing in the world. "I think it's a good thing. People know about it, then. Come looking for it."

"They know that it gets people killed! They know about kids jumping off of buildings and walking into the sea!"

"That was before," he says, waving a hand through the air. For a moment, I think he looks at me, and I pull sharply away from the curtain. I can't see what's going on anymore, but I can still hear well enough.

"Before what?" the woman's voice demands, followed by the sound of a chair against wood floors and the repeated click-clack of high heels pacing back and forth. "Because I really don't know how you come back from something like this."

"Before we perfected it," Bruno replies easily, like it was already in his mouth and he was simply waiting for her to ask. "It works, now."

The woman's breath catches in unison with mine, and her next words mirror my thoughts exactly. "It *works*? It really gives people abilities?" Bruno must nod, or offer a smug smile, because the woman immediately breathes, "Wow. This is huge! How will we market it?"

"Testing it as a street drug was good and bad," Bruno muses. "We got to see the effects real-time, and gauge people's reactions, but it will make going forward tricky. Don't worry, though. I'll think of something and keep you posted."

There's silence behind the curtain for a few seconds, and then I hear liquid pouring and glass clinking.

My phone chooses this exact moment to vibrate. Which wouldn't be so bad, except that it's in my back pocket, which is pressed against the wall, and so the vibration bounces against that and amplifies the sound.

"Crap, crap, crap," I whisper-shout, fishing my phone out of my pocket, but the damage is done. Those high heels are getting louder as the woman heads towards me. I'm off like a shot, barely glancing at the name on the screen. *Caesar? It's Valentines Day, you moron, what are you texting me for?*

I hear the curtain opening behind me, so I put on another burst of speed, nearly knocking into people as I round the corner. "Sorry, sorry," I apologise in a rush, pushing through the crowd. Bruno is only steps behind me when I chance a glance over my shoulder. Ace is still at the bar, so I dive towards her, grabbing her by the wrist and dragging her out of her seat. "Time to go!"

"What—"

She shakes her wrist out of my grip but follows behind me anyway. I swear this club wasn't quite so busy a moment ago, and now it feels like we're packed in sardine-tight. Bruno is by the bar, just where Ace was, and in front of me is a huge group of people dancing, a few tables loaded with drinks, and a band. I make a split second decision and, with both feet, jump up onto a table, then pause to kick the drinks backwards, towards Bruno. The drinks pour out, splashing against his shirt, and the glass falls to the ground of shatters. Ace steps up on to the stage, spinning around the performers and blowing a kiss to the crowd, who seem drunk and oblivious enough to barely notice us weaving through them.

Bruno, sputtering and wiping alcohol off of his face, chases after us, joined by two other men (including, somewhat ironically, the one with the ascot). We duck under a few outstretched arms and fly through the door, into the relative quiet of the street.

Our breathing is heavy, laboured. Ace tugs me down a side street and we round the corner with just enough time for Bruno to see us. He shouts something that neither of us hear over our pounding footsteps and manic laughter.

It doesn't take long, from there, to lose him. Ace is fast and I know the city better than most people. Before long, we're coming to a stop with our hands on our knees by the edge of the main road. After we've caught our breath a little, Ace waves for a taxi, and we ride back to my house in pleasantly exhausted silence.

When we arrive, we pay the driver and sit down underneath the fire escape. We don't realise until too late that the ground is wet. I'm not worried about my dark jeans, but Ace's velvet dress will likely be ruined. She doesn't seem to care, stretching her bare legs out over the ground anyway.

"So when you told my mom that this outing was your boyfriends idea," I ask, keeping my voice light, "how true was that?"

Ace laughs, clearly caught off guard by the question, and then tips her head back against the wall. "Completely," she shrugs. "I think it was as much for me as it was for you, though. Turns out I'm not great at this whole 'retirement' thing. Like, I know that I have to, but. I don't really want to."

I feel my eyebrows knit together involuntarily. "What do you mean?"

She sighs and shifts her shoulders so she's facing me slightly more. "Okay, uh. The whole 'superhero' thing was dangerous for me. And not like, "being a superhero is dangerous!", like, personally, for me and my mental health, it was... bad." She pauses, shrugs. I give her time to gather her thoughts.

"For me, everything is either zero or a hundred, with no in-between." She lists them off slowly, "Relationships. Friends. School. Passions. Family. Everything, yeah? And playing the superhero game had me —" she raises a hand in the air— "way up to a hundred and ten, you know? I would throw myself into it, isolate myself from everything else. Even the people I cared about at a one hundred, because... I don't know. It's not like with you," she looks at me with wide, sad eyes. "You've always been trying to help people, and I always wanted to hurt them."

I mull this over for a moment, chewing on my inner cheek. "So you decided to get out?"

"Well, yeah," she shrugs, laughing again. "I, uhm. It's like I said, you know, it was self-destructive. It cut me off from people. I wasn't helping the people I wanted to help, and I wasn't helping myself either. It's not like with you," she repeats. "When you're Legion... that's what's right for you."

I suck my lower lip in between my teeth and chew on that, too. "Can I confess something?"

She nods for me to continue. I can't quite convince myself to tell her about my lack of abilities, but I tell her about my complicated feelings about secret identities and how Legion and Xander were always so separate. I tell her how terrified I am that they can't be, anymore. "Legion wasn't bad," I say, "at least, I don't think he was. But he was able to be violent or dangerous and it wouldn't change the way people looked at me, you know?"

"I do," she says, nudging my shoulder. "I'm gonna tell you a secret, now."

I wait, watching her take a deep breath.

"Sophia," she whispers, her eyes wide and her brow low, her mouth in a tiny, wavering smile. "That's my name. I mean, not anymore, not really, but. Ace was what I told people after I got into all this, and it stuck. It was Sophia, and it was Ace, and they marked different parts of me. Now that's just who I am, but I do know what you mean. I think... I think that, uh, distinction isn't nearly as important as you think. It wasn't for me, in the end."

"You're nineteen," I tease, because I'm going to need more time than this to process what she's just said to me. "Hopefully you're a long way from the end."

She laughs, and stands up, and offers a hand to help me to my feet. I take it gladly, and we both brush ourselves off as best we can. "I should be heading home," she says, still smiling. "But I had a good night."

"Me, too." I smile at her, hug her, and climb up the fire escape. I watch as she hails another cab, and then watch until the headlights blink out of sight.

The next day, I send her some yellow roses.

72.

It works now.

That's what Bruno said, wasn't it? *It works now*.

Did DNA really work? Did it give people abilities?

Could someone *choose* what ability it gave them?

No. No, no, nope.

I'm not going to even let myself entertain the thought.

I'd been distracted on Valentine's Day; too busy running and laughing to process everything I'd heard Bruno say. Ace hadn't asked about it, either. I guess she's serious about leaving the superhero thing behind her. But she took me to the club for dancing and told me to investigate Bruno, and I did, and I heard *it works now*.

No! Not going there. Not thinking that. Not touching that.

This was a bad idea. Why did I ask Ace to look into it? Did some part of me always wonder if maybe, just maybe, there was a slim chance that it could *help*? I don't do drugs. I mean, I don't even drink coffee. But did I think, just a little, that it could help me be Legion again?

If it could, would I justify it?

Would I reason *it's not really a drug, it's not* really *breaking the word of wisdom, if it's to help me get better*?

The thought alone scares me, because I honestly think that I would.

I put on Legion's uniform again. It's a perfect fit, or it should be. It's Ava's design with C-Corp money behind it, but it still feels uncomfortable, wrong. I roll my shoulders, straighten the jacket, but it makes no difference. Without my ability, it's ill-fitted.

Ace said that the distinction isn't nearly as important as I think it is, but I don't think she quite understands. Legion was something other than myself, something bigger. Something *more*. Abyss always said it felt like we were playing pretend, but I didn't understand what she meant until now. I can't pretend anymore. I can't pretend to be Legion anymore.

I change back into my pyjamas, and go to bed.

I wake up less than an hour later to Abyss' voice. Abyss' voice? It takes me a second to work out why that's odd enough to wake me up. She lives with Caesar, now. Because they're together. I haven't seen them much, recently.

Mom is talking to her, and they seem excited about something. My door is open, so I can perfectly hear their laughter. I'm still wound up, bitter and angry, so I don't leave my room to see what the fuss is about.

When I hear Abyss' footsteps padding down the hall, I roll over and pretend that I'm still asleep.

"Xander, guess what? Oh," she says, from behind me. I can't hear her moving at all, but I make my breathing slow and deep anyway.

A weight on the opposite side of my bed tells me that she's come to sit with me. "I was so glad that you were okay," she says, quietly. "Maybe we didn't do enough to show it. Come on, Xander. We missed you so much, all of us. And now we hardly see you. I don't know if you're angry with us or just self-isolating, but it's two o'clock in the afternoon and you're asleep, alone…"

She sighs, and I almost feel guilty. They missed me before and they miss me now, because I'm not letting them be around me. It's not their fault, none of it is.

Before I can decide if I should roll over and speak to her, ask what's so exciting, she's standing, leaving the room, and swinging the door shut behind her.

I roll over.

Jamboree is leaning against the wall, right where the door was blocking moments ago. She's not wearing a suit jacket, for once, but has her button down shirt rolled up to her elbows, her hands in pressed trouser pockets.

"How do you keep getting in here without my mom noticing?"

She actually looks confused. "I make portals, you know."

"They make a lot of noise."

"She had the TV on!"

It's ridiculous enough that I laugh. The sound almost startles me. "How long have you been there?"

"I was going to wake you up just before Abyss arrived."

"Why didn't you leave when you heard her come in?"

"They turned the TV off."

I laugh again. She actually cracks a smile in response. It suits her, I can't help but think. No one looks their best when they're angry, ranting and raving, with a snarl on their face, and that's mostly how I've seen Jamboree before. But like this, with the ghost of a smile forming on her lips, she's actually quite pretty.

"She was coming to give you good news," she says, after a second, nodding towards the closed bedroom door, indicating Abyss. "Maybe you should have heard her out."

"Maybe," I admit. "It's hard. To be happy, lately."

She nods like she understands. Maybe she does.

We're quiet for a stretch, and then I sit up, shift so my back is pressed up against my headboard, and motion that she could come and sit, if she wants. She does, but she sits close to the edge, stiffly, like it's made of glass. I'll take what I can get.

"I don't think," she starts, voice strained and awkward, "that they necessarily want you to be *happy*. They just want *you*. Want you around. Miss you."

"It's all different, now," I say, waving a hand through the air in front of us. "I mean, we're all *different*, now. Caesar and Abyss are, like, in love? I guess? Does that happen in three months? I mean, okay, I know it does. It just… it almost feels weird being around them now. Like, before, it was the three of us, and now it's *them* and *me*, and I wasn't around to see it change so I have no idea how to navigate it. How does this change our friendship?"

"Does it have to change it at all?" She asks, her brow furrowed.

I throw my hands up wordlessly.

"You're overthinking this, Xander," she says, matter-of-fact. "You were dead, and now you're not, and so they want to be close to you. You heard her, worrying that you were self-isolating or whatever. They want you around, simple as. Have you really only been socialising with your *mom*?"

"My mom is great!"

She shrugs agreeably. "I never said she wasn't. But it's not great that she's your only source of… social interaction."

"I've spent time with Ace," I defend weakly, "and Charlie Caesar."

She shoots me an unimpressed look. I wonder when she started caring about my social life. Actually, I wonder when her appearing out of no where stopped being intimidating and started being almost relaxing. The museum had been… nice. Our civil conversations have actually been enjoyable. She's already made me laugh twice today.

"And you," I tack on, after a beat. She looks away.

"I don't know why you haven't kicked me out yet," she says in something quieter than a whisper.

I try to joke, "Fighting you didn't go so well for me last time."

She laughs, just a little bit, and shakes her head. "Or anytime."

"Hey!" I say, full of mock offence. "I'll have you know I could kick your butt any day of the week."

"In video games, maybe," she scoffs.

That's an idea. "Jamboree—"

"Julia," she says, aiming for light and missing. There's an awkward silence, and she looks ready to bolt when I don't say anything. Are we becoming *friends*?

"Julia," I correct myself, after only a second. "Are you any good at Street Fighter?"

She thinks for a second. "I'm better at Portal."

73.

I need to stop hiding. Jamboree— Julia— is right, after all. I haven't been being very social. I've been self-isolating, cutting myself off from my friends and people who care about me. I've been going to church but I haven't been getting very much out of it. I've been hiding in my room, sleeping the day away, eating dinner with my mom, and playing video games until my eyes turn square. I need more than that; I've always been a social creature, and I've been depriving myself of that for no good reason.

I spend an afternoon with Ava, drinking smoothies and kicking around a nearby park. She spits on a few rocks and we watch them dissolve away into nothing. "It would be a very useful ability," she jokes, as she often does, "if I could spit farther than three inches."

"Still a cool ability," I say, trying not to be bitter.

She lifts a shoulder, picking clay out from underneath her fingernails. "Not as cool as yours is."

No, not as cool as mine was.

Zoram takes me to see a movie. We share extra large popcorn and watch as the lead, a technopath hacker, directs a rag-tag group through a bank heist. It's enjoyable, funny in the right places and dramatic in others.

Afterwards we go to Institute, and I don't sit in the back, so I can actually get something out of the lesson. Six of us stay to play basketball in the gym. Me, Zoram, and Ava on one team, with Emily Snow, Margot Zhou, and Todd Flores on the other. From ages eight to eighteen, this group had been pretty much inseparable at church events. It's nice to be with them all again.

"I hope you don't mind us asking, Xander," Emily says as we wrap up, and Todd stops dribbling to listen in. "It's just, none of us have seen you since— before. Ava said you were *Legion*, and you weren't around for us to ask about it."

I swallow, tug my sweatshirt sleeves down over my hands. "What do you want to know?"

"What's it like?" Margot asks, sounding almost breathless. "Being a superhero?"

I don't have the heart to tell her that I'm not, not really, not anymore. Instead I take a steadying breath and lean against the stage, and answer as though it's still true. "Incredible," I say, aiming for light and just about landing there. "I always feel like… like I'm *helping*. I've been doing it for years, you know."

"Legion was the first superhero I heard anything about," Todd nods. "Even before that Caesar kid revealed his ability. Even before Abyss. I don't know how none of us put it together, though. You hang out with them both. Once Ava said it, it was obvious enough."

"You just never seemed like the type," Emily shrugs. "You know, out there punching bad guys, tracking drugs, battling it out with supervillians."

"You think of me differently, now?" I ask, heart hammering. This is why I wanted them separate, why I wanted a secret identity.

Emily shrugs again. "A little. I thought Legion was the scariest of them. Now that I know he's *you*, it's just... different."

"You were scared of Legion?"

"Sure," Todd says. "The mask, the posture, the multiple bodies thing. It's probably why we *didn't* catch on, honestly. You're so... gentle. You talk to plants, you know? And you can talk to anyone about anything, you're always smiling. We thought you were innocent," he laughs, nudges Zoram. "Didn't we? We thought we had to protect him."

Zoram cracks a tiny, awkward smile. I think he can tell that I'm stressed out by all of this.

My jaw twitches. "So," I say, fighting to keep my voice level. "Xander was weak, and Legion was *scary*. What am I now that you know I'm both?"

"I don't know," Emily says, frowning. "I guess you're just *you*. You're both."

"I never wanted to be both," I say, feeling heat in my cheeks and neck when my voice cracks. "They were always meant to be separate. Xander could be kind, and gentle, and soft-spoken, and loved, and whatever else, and Legion could go and fight crime and get bloody and be angry. I wanted— I *needed* them to be separate, because then no one would look at me how you're all looking at me right now!"

My voice has steadily risen in volume. The group flinches, slightly, wide-eyed and shocked. Emily's lips part in confusion, her eyebrows knit together.

"I hated it, though," I admit, making a concentrated effort to keep my voice low. "I hated it, because people were scared of Legion. They liked him well enough, I guess. Thought he was doing *good*, but wouldn't want to run into him themselves. He was *intimidating*, even when he joked with the press. The mask, the *posture*. People pitied Xander," I spit, put on a falsetto, "'likes flowers, too nice for his own good'. Doesn't have powers, hangs out with superheroes and brings nothing to the table. Weak, helpless, someone to look after. I hated it," I reiterate, a little louder. "But I *needed* it. And then I *died* and *came back* and I didn't even have the choice anymore! It was gone!"

I swallow thickly. They're all still looking at me, seemingly at a loss for words. So much for 'socialising'. What does Jamboree know, anyway? "Maybe I would've let it go, eventually," I shrug, a jerky movement. "But I didn't even have the choice."

"Xander," Ava says, finally, resting her hand on my upper arm. "I'm so sorry, if I'd known—"

"I know," I tell her, softly. The anger bleeds out of me as quickly as it came. This whole situation is messy and convoluted and putting into words why the distinction is so important is nearly impossible. "It's

499

just another thing I missed. The art show, Caesar's birthday, the chance to make that choice myself. Not that it matters much anymore."

"What do you mean?" Margot says, her almond eyes wide. "Why doesn't it matter?"

"Legion is dead!" I say, and I laugh, a little watery. If I don't laugh, I think I might cry. "I'm dead! I'm at least four-fifths dead! I can't make duplicates anymore!"

They stare at me, and I keep laughing, until I suddenly stop, dropping my arms to my sides. It finally sinks in, standing in the church gym in a floral sweatshirt, surrounded by people I've known most of my life. "I'm not superhuman, anymore," I say, lowly. "How can I be Legion if I'm not superhuman anymore?"

There's silence for a long moment, then I shake myself. "I need to go," I say, and I feel bad for that, I do, for monologuing to them and then disappearing, but I need to go to Caesar and Abyss, to tell them everything, finally.

"Can you meet me?" I say down the phone, standing in the parking lot.

"Of course," Caesar says without missing a beat. "Where are you?"

74.

I remember when I first came out. Not as a superhuman, because I couldn't have hidden that from Mom if I'd tried, but as bisexual. I'd agonised over it for months leading up to telling anyone; wondering what it meant, to have such strong faith, but to like boys just as much as I liked girls. I wondered if that was *allowed*, if I was somehow wrong, if this meant that I would have to leave the church. It felt impossible, but ultimately I'd come to the conclusion that I could have both.

I was never any good at keeping secrets from Mom. And I didn't *want* to be keeping secrets, anyway. So I told her, one evening, shaking and worried, and she didn't understand it at first, but we stayed up late talking, and she hugged me and said that she loved me, and I nearly melted.

While I climb in the backseat of Caesar's car, I keep thinking about that particular crisis of identity. I feel like I'm almost having the same one all over again; can I be both Legion and Xander? Is that wrong? I was so determined to keep them separate for so long, terrified of what it might mean to be both of them at once, but maybe it's okay to have them both together.

"Can we go to your place?" I ask him, once Aaron starts driving. "I need to talk to you and Abs."

He nods, and goes quiet. I remember what Ace said about their mental connection, and bite back a smile. I'm so happy for them.

"Are you okay?" he asks me. "Just… tell me if you're okay."

"I'm… getting there," I say, in an effort to be honest.

We stay in companionable silence until we arrive at the penthouse. The elevator takes us straight to his living room. Abyss is waiting on the couch, in a faded university sweatshirt with her sunglasses balanced on top of her head. She's holding a mug of coffee between both her hands, with her feet tucked up beside her. She looks domestic and comfortable in a way that she never did when she was living with me and Mom.

She lowers her glasses before looking at me, which I can't help but be grateful for. I'm glad that she's comfortable with the Void, but I don't know if, personally, I'll ever be. If Ace is right about their mental connection, then I suppose Caesar is. I'm glad for that, too.

She cuts to the chase. "What did you need to talk to us about?"

Her voice is less monotone, now. I hadn't noticed. She seems far more at peace in her own skin. I realise, again, how much I missed while I was gone, and just how much I've missed them since. Maybe Julia *was* right. I really do need to socialise.

"I don't have my abilities anymore."

Like ripping off a bandaid.

Caesar's jaw drops, but Abyss nods like maybe she'd suspected. I wouldn't be surprised if she had. There's a long moment of stunned silence, and then Caesar's nodding, too. Definitely *connected*, then.

I feel lighter just for having said it, happier than I've been since I came back. I've known since I woke up in the hospital, or at least since Caesar and Abyss had arrived and explained it all, but I've been terrified to say it out loud. Now, everyone knows. "You can speak *out loud*, you know," I huff, playful, rolling my eyes.

When they both look at me blankly, I laugh and sit down on the couch, next to Abyss. "Ace told me all about your *mental connection*."

"Caesar couldn't help but brag to her about it," Abyss says, with a fond sigh. The fact that I can recognise it as *fond* says a lot; she seems much more vocal about her emotions.

Caesar, bashful, rubs at the back of his neck. "That doesn't matter right now. You... don't have abilities anymore?"

"No," I reply, surprising myself with how level my voice is. "I can't make duplicates, anymore. I'm not... superhuman anymore."

I fill them in on everything that I'd told Ace; about how difficult it was, to have both of them living in me. I tell them how I haven't felt like myself, because I don't really know who I am, and about how coming back from the dead was enough on its own, but then, to have the choice of how to proceed be already gone made it even harder. "So,"

503

I finish, shrugging. "It's… been hard. But I guess I have to learn to accept it. That I'm not… you know."

Caesar opens his mouth, but Abyss rests a hand on his knee and he closes it again. I wonder what she'd said, if anything, or if this mental connection just means that they understand each other without any effort. There's a glint of something on her finger, and when I realise what it is, I break into a huge smile.

"You're engaged!" I say, pointing between them.

Abyss beams, holding her hand out so that I can inspect the ring. It's gorgeous, of course, undoubtably incredibly expensive, but nothing extravagant. Abyss wouldn't want anything too flashy. It's tasteful, sparkly, on a gold band.

Caesar wraps an arm around her, also wearing a face splitting smile.

"Why didn't you tell me?" I accuse.

"We tried!" Caesar protests, laughing. "Abs went over to yours, but you were sleeping, so she didn't get a chance."

Julia did say that Abyss had good news, didn't she? I feel silly for pretending to be asleep, I feel silly for locking myself away from my friends. Okay, I'll admit it: Julia was right, I need to be socialising more. I may be four-fifths dead, but I should probably focus on the part of me that's *alive*, right?

"Congratulations!" I say, grinning. "I'm so happy for you guys, really. I haven't been the best at showing it, but I am."

"Don't worry about it," Abyss says, squeezing my hand gently before pulling away. "You've been going through a lot yourself. We were worried about you."

"I'm sorry," Caesar says, frowning at me. "About everything. You were dead, and then you weren't, and then we didn't tell you everything we should have... I don't blame you for pulling away."

"You should," I say, scoffing. "I was being a dick. Yeah, I had stuff to work through, but I shouldn't have taken it out on you guys. It's... been hard, to be around you, when I know that I can't be *Legion* anymore."

"Ace said she took you out," Caesar says, and it sounds like a question.

I nod. "She did. We went dancing, and there was some guy who supposedly knew something about DNA, so I listened in. Then he heard me, and chased me out of the club. Not exactly a shining moment."

Abyss drums her fingers against her mug. "You're still *you*, though, aren't you?"

"What do you mean?"

"I mean, *you*, Pae Sun-Young Alexander," she says, with a small smile, "are *you*. That hasn't changed. You may not have your abilities anymore, you may not be able to split yourself into two or three or five, but you're still, underneath it all, the exact same person."

"Well," I agree, shrugging, "yeah. The duplicates always were me, and that— holds true now that I'm... a duplicate."

It feels weird to say it out loud, so I say it slowly, with my mouth sticky like peanut butter.

"So you're the same as you've always been?" Abyss asks again, like she's confirming something.

"Yeah?"

She smiles at me, shakes her head fondly, and takes a drink of her coffee. She doesn't offer any explanation, which is typical. She'll explain herself if and when it becomes absolutely necessary, and not a moment before.

I decide to distract them with wedding talk, which makes Caesar nearly vibrate with excitement and Abyss shake her head. "No more than fifty, Cee, I mean it," she says, when he starts ticking off guests. "I was at your sister's wedding, and there were way too many people there."

"Important people!"

"Important people to *Charlie* or important people to the *business*?"

Caesar relents the point, and I laugh at the sight of them, bickering back and forth, clearly outrageously in love with one another. I hadn't seen it, before, but now it's plain as day: Abyss, cross-legged with her hands in the air while she talks and Caesar, leaning back into his shoulders, watching her.

They look exactly like the statue Julia showed me. I almost tell them so, but that's one thing that I haven't touched on yet. In everything that I've filled them in on, I've been careful to avoid the topic. I don't know if she's been visiting either of them in tandem with her visits to me, and if she hasn't, I doubt that Abyss would love the idea of me hanging out with her.

And we have been. Hanging out, that is. Julia's been around a few times throughout the course of the week. We've been playing video games (my request) or watching old movies (hers), avoiding anything as heavy as the day in the museum but cultivating a careful, cautious friendship regardless. I think she's a better person than she let on, really.

I can forgive her for my death, but I can't forgive her on Abyss' behalf. So I don't bring it up.

We spent the next few weeks alternating between my house and Caesar and Abyss'. Sometimes, Ace will join us at either location. More often than she used to, actually, because now she doesn't go off on her own adventures.

Caesar and Abyss work on wedding plans, still occasionally going quiet and swapping ideas mentally. Ace and I share looks across the table, laughing silently together. She works on her homework and moans about dress codes, and I pick at the food.

It's not the same as it was; Caesar and Abyss are still superheroes, they still go out and lend a hand wherever they can, but they don't talk about it with us.

Ace will show up with tiny scraps of information— not nearly as much as she used to have on hand, but she's still got her connections and I know she still gambles— and they'll take them into consideration, speaking only through their connection. I burn with jealousy at the thought of it, that they're out there doing all the things that I used to. I try my best not to let on. It's not their fault.

One day, in May, Ace pulls me aside, and asks with a low voice, "Have you done anything with what you heard from Bruno?"

Aside from having a mental breakdown about whether or not I'd take the drug if the opportunity arose? No. I shake my head. She looks disappointed.

"I think you should."

"I'm not... I'm not a superhero anymore, Ace."

She shrugs. "Maybe not. But if you don't do something, who will?"

"Caesar. Abyss. *You.*"

"I'm retired."

"Convenient," I roll my eyes. "It doesn't have to be me, you know."

She shrugs again, turning back to her studying. "Maybe not. But I still think it should be. You've got better chances of success than you think."

75.

"The fact that Ace said my odds are good doesn't change anything!
Sure, okay, the numbers haven't ever been wrong before, but that
doesn't mean that they can't be, right?"

Julia blinks at me. She's sitting on my bed, holding one of my pillows
on her lap, fiddling mindlessly with the case. Her jeans have paint
splatters on them from helping Mom and I paint the living room. We'd
decided to change it from light yellow into pastel blue, and Julia had
crashed the party with no warning and offered to help. It surprised
Mom, but I think she understands that Julia is trying, in her own, off-
kilter way, to make amends.

The bedroom door is wide open and we can hear Mom, from the
kitchen, calling, "Stop *yelling*, Xander!"

I huff and crash down onto the bed. I repeat, "It doesn't change
anything."

"Sure it doesn't," Julia's sarcasm makes me huff again. "Maybe she's
on to something. I mean, Caesar and Abyss *are* busy, not only with
their superhero stuff, but with the wedding. You *know* the press has
been on them in a whole new way since they announced it."

I bite back a laugh at that. Abyss' struggle with interviews and
paparazzi has gotten worse in the last few months. She's going to be
a part of the Caesar family, and that comes with its own set of
challenges. I can only find it funny because I know she'll find her feet
eventually. "Yeah, but still. They're superheroes, I'm not."

"Aren't you?" Julia jumps up and goes to the door, closing it just enough to pick up Legion's uniform, which is still hanging on the back of the door. "You still have this."

"And you still have all your suits, doesn't mean you're still a supervillian." Her face closes off. I sigh, throwing an arm over my eyes. "You know what I mean."

"Yeah," she says tightly. "I do. I did kill you, so I guess it's fair play."

"You didn't kill me," I say, almost on impulse. "You *were* a supervillian, but I know that you're… trying."

"You *were* a hero," she says, and sits back down on the bed. "And you're *not* trying."

She's not one to mince words. I tell her as much, laughing and taking my arm away from my eyeshot look up at her. Despite her bluntness, though, she does seem more relaxed these days, not as tightly-wound as she was the first time she visited. She even almost smiles at me, a lot of the time.

"Can I ask you something?" I question, a little while later, when we're back in the living room, flicking through movies. She pauses, pushing her inky black hair over her shoulder while she turns to look at me. "Is there a universe where I kept being Legion, even after this?"

She doesn't even have to think about it. She says, "Not yet."

That night, after Julia has stepped through a portal and disappeared into some other universe, and Mom has turned in for the night, I stay up late, thinking.

Once, Abyss and I spoke about alternate universes. She said that for every single tiny choice that I made, there was another universe where I'd made a different one. She also said that she thought all of those other universes existed already, near identical to ours, waiting.

If I put on Legion's uniform again, and go out as a superhero again, I may not be the first or only one to make that choice. There may be hundreds of universes where I do the same thing. Do they matter? Or does only this universe, this choice, make any sort of difference?

Not yet, Julia said. *Not yet.*

Was it encouragement? She's been trying to make up for everything that she did, but she's always been careful not to overstep her bounds. But Ace took me out to a club to show me everything about DNA, and Abyss smiled knowingly when I said that I was still *myself*. Caesar opened his mouth to protest when I said I wasn't a superhero anymore.

It's like everyone is telling me to go back out there.

Ace said that being a superhero was self-isolating for her, but that it 'wasn't like that with me'. Was it the same in reverse? Was *not* being a superhero self-isolating in my case? I've been killing myself with jealousy at Caesar and Abyss, cutting myself off from something that I'd always felt was so *right* for me.

Not yet.

I still feel wrong in my own skin while I pull on Legion's uniform. In the mirror, I stare at myself through the mask. Wearing it was a way to hide my identity, to separate myself from… myself. That is what it was, in the end, wasn't it? Trying to divide myself in two as easily as I could split myself in five. Legion and Xander, Xander and Legion. It was an effective divide, clearly, but was it a healthy one? Is it a healthy one? I think of myself as two different people, and pretend that one of them is dead.

Legion is not dead.

I *am* Legion.

I tear off the mask, and I climb out the fire escape.

76.

The night air is cool, even as we lead into spring. I'm grateful that my uniform (my uniform! *mine*, not some other strange, separate persons!) has so many layers. Undershirt, C-Corp protective gear, shirt, jacket. It has *Legion* stitched careful, angular, into the back, telling the world who I am. Who *I* am!

How could I have gone so long without doing this? It feels like the world slots itself back into place as I make my way through the city. I have to bite my cheeks to keep from smiling.

I consider going to Ace, just to ask if this is how she felt when she decided to retire, but I don't want to bother her. She has homework and studying and finals, a real life that keeps her healthy and secure, and I have *this*, my real life, that's been waiting for me for months and months and months.

My uniform fits like a glove. I can practically feel it singing.

The city is mostly quiet; there's a few cars, some scattered voices, but nothing that warrants my attention. I don't care. I'm just happy to be out again, wearing this uniform, doing this job. I love the flower shop, but I don't think I could ever be happy doing just that when I know what it's like to do all this.

The shouting startles me.

It's why I'm out here, though, so I react quickly enough, racing around corners until I come to a sliding halt outside an apartment building. There are several open windows, and a teetering, broken fire escape leads up past all of them. The shouting continues, getting louder, so I don't even think. I just jump up the first few rusted steps of the fire escape and half-throw myself towards the first open window. It's the wrong one; only the TV is blaring, and there's no shouting involved.

The next steps creek dangerously as I race up them. They're rusted through enough that I'm worried one will break and I'll crash down. They don't break, but my foot catches and slips anyway. I have to reach for the hand hold— also rusted and disgusting— and I manage to pull myself on to the relative safety of the step above. I don't slow down, but I try to step more carefully.

The second window I check is obviously the right one. I crouch, barely poking my head far enough over the windowsill to see. From my un-ideal vantage point, I can see a woman, wrinkled but not old, with wide, terrified eyes. She's crouching in a position not dissimilar to mine, trying to make herself small and hidden.

There's a man approaching her, screaming senselessly, his meaty hands curled into fists. While I watch, he slams one down against the counter, rattling some dirty dishes and making the woman jump, and wraps her arms even more tightly around herself. He reaches towards her, grabs her by the forearm and drags her to her feet, spitting obscenities into her face.

Okay, that's it.

I pull myself back to my feet and vault through the window, intentionally stumbling around to draw attention to myself.

The woman whimpers, bringing a hand up to cover her wobbling mouth.

The man growls. He all but throws her away from him, and I track her movement more than his, watching her slump against the back of the couch. If I had duplicates, I would send one to her, get her out of here. But I don't. I have to come up with a better plan.

Caesar used to hang out in my head when we were out, tell me things that would help me. He could strategise better than me, what with the whole 'being-able-to-read-our-enemies-minds' thing. But today it's just me, just *me*, four bodies short of a whole person.

Okay, I think, I pray, *I'm gonna need some help.*

"What are you doing in my house?" the man demands, pulling himself up to his full height in an effort to look intimidating. It's not that I'm not scared— I am, I'm petrified— but I know that men like him always want to be more powerful than they are. And I may be many things; alone, without abilities, singular, without a team. But I'm not weak.

"I heard *shouting*," I say pointedly.

"That's not an excuse to break in!" He takes another step towards me. "I can and will defend my family from the likes of you."

It's supposed to be a threat, but it's a poor one. I glance at the woman, who's still shaking on the ground. "You're doing a stand-up job," I drawl. It's a Legion comment, the sort of thing I would've avoided saying without the mask, but now there is no mask and Xander Pae is Legion and Legion is Xander Pae. "Really, I'm impressed by how *safe* your home is for your *family*."

He, as I expected, lunges towards me after that comment. I dart away, guiding him towards the kitchen and away from the woman. He follows after me, lumbering and angry. He's not really that much bigger than me, but he's got the body of a weightlifter, and he clearly thinks that makes him the best person in the room. I've been fighting for most of my life, with and without four extra people, and I know that strength like that is not the be all and end all.

I slide around the kitchen, using his own force against him as I keep myself moving. He swings at me, a few times, but only one of them connects. I stumble, just a little, just enough for him to think he's got the upper hand, and when he reaches out for me, I duck under his arms and go behind him, shoving him forward. Combined with his own momentum, it's enough to send him reeling, crashing his head against the faucet. He slides down, catches his jaw on the edge of the sink, and, finally, tips over and smashes his head against the tile. He's unconscious, I'm sure, but for peace of mind I check his pulse anyway.

With a heave, I roll him over to his side. In the subsequent quiet, I can make out the woman's shaking breathing.

There was no duplicate to go to her, so I go to her now.

"Did you—" she asks, and breaks off, like she can't quite believe what she's thinking. She shakes her head. "No, no, you didn't. You *wouldn't*."

"He's unconscious," I tell her, keeping my voice level and low. "We're going to call an ambulance, okay?"

"Do we have to?" Her voice is barely a whisper. I drop to my knees in front of her, careful not to move too suddenly or touch her unexpectedly. "I could kill him. I could kill him right now."

I don't say anything, instead watching as she takes deep, steadying breaths. "He took some drug. DNA, I think he called it. He said it would give him super strength, make it so that not even *you* could stop him."

DNA. There it is again. It keeps popping up, it keeps hurting people. *It works now.* If it works now, it's even more dangerous.

"But you *did*," she continues, shaking. "You did stop him."

"Of course," I say, then, "What's your name?"

"Mindy."

"This isn't the first time, is it, Mindy?"

She hesitates a moment, then shakes her head. "It's the first time with the drug. But... not the first time, no."

"Okay," I say, already running through every scrap of information I have on places and people that might be able to help her. I have a list saved somewhere on my phone of numbers to give people, and I'm sure that there will be something that's applicable. "Let's get out of here, okay? We'll leave the door unlocked and call an ambulance once we've got a few blocks away. Grab anything essential. Money, ID, anything you can think of. But be fast."

Frantic, she races around the house shoving bits and pieces into her bag, which she throws over her shoulder with a determined look. I guide her out the front door and down to the ground level, and then out across the street. We phone an ambulance after we've walked for five minutes. As soon as I hang up, I go into my notes and read off a few numbers for her to make note of. "I'll take you to the shelter," I say. "And I'll put you in touch with some people who may have space for you to stay, after. Okay?"

Instead of answering, she bursts in to tears and wraps her arms around my middle. "You were my *favourite*," she says, between wracking sobs. "I cried for days when you died. He didn't like that much, but when you came *back*, he liked that even less. He said he was unbeatable, after the drug. And you *beat* him. I think I owe you my life."

"You don't owe me anything," I tell her, overwhelmed and reeling, but I wrap myself protectively around her anyway. "Just… look after yourself, Mindy."

She nods, and I escort her as far as the shelter, as promised.

77.

I'm barely awake the next day before Ace is hugging me. Bleary-eyed, I hug back. Mom snaps a picture, which makes me roll my eyes fondly.

"What's this for?" I ask, when Ace finally pulls away, beaming.

She does an excited little bounce and pulls her phone out. It's already open to a webpage with the headline: *LEGION-DARY: Xander Pae Dons Uniform Once More!* I hate the headline, but I shrug it off and keep reading.

Xander Pae, 21, recently made headlines when, presumed dead, he was confirmed to be none other than our favourite superhero of the moment, masked-crusader Legion. He then graced our newspapers and blogs once more when he returned from a hospital just outside his hometown virtually unscathed. Jocelyn Charlotte Caesar provided us with some phenomenal (and mouth-watering!) shots of him at work and home, and he's since been spotted out clubbing with fellow superhero and occasional teammate Ace Jackson.

Just last night, he was spotted in the Legion uniform for the first time since his revival. Accompanying an unknown— but clearly distressed — woman through the midnight streets, he commanded the attention of novice photographer Jamie Brown, who provided us with this soon-to-be iconic shot.

I wonder how I didn't notice this being taken. Our backs are to the camera, but I'm looking over my shoulder, mouth set in a hard line. I have my arm around Mindy, stretching the fabric of my jacket so the lettering is clearly visible. All anyone would see of Mindy is her dark red hair, but my face is almost dead-on to the camera. There's no denying that it's me, if there was any doubt.

"We didn't go clubbing," is the first thing that I can think to say.

"We went to *a club*," she responds, rolling her eyes. "I'm just so excited, Xander! You went out again!"

"I did," I agree, and I can't quite keep the wonder out of my voice. "I helped someone."

"I know!" she says, beaming. "Who is she?"

I tell her, in brief terms, what happened. As it goes on, she gets an odd look in her eye. "Give her my number," she says. "If she needs somewhere to go, later, she can come to me."

"Will your boyfriend be okay with that?"

"Absolutely," she says, nodding firmly. "If she needs us, we'll help."

I promise that I will, and it seems to relax her, just a little bit. "I have to go to school," she says, sticking her tongue out in an expression of exaggerated disgust. "But I was up early, anyway, so I thought I'd come speak to you. I'm excited for you, Xander!"

"It's like you said," i say, as she climbs out of the window to the fire escape. "Being a superhero, for you, was self-isolating. It's not like that, with me. It was the opposite way 'round."

She nods, and beams again, and races off.

I back away from the window, and before I can go much further Mom hugs me, too. "The point of having a team is to go out as a team," she says, pinching my nose. "You should tell them."

"I'm sure they already know."

Sure enough, when I pick up my phone, the superkids! chat is filled with messages. I scroll through them for a little while, grinning at their excitement about Legion being back.

caesarean: *we can see that ur reading these!!!*

me: *legion is back bay-bee!!*

abs: *i knw u wldnt sty awy*

ace: *im in class but i have to say that abs? that was horrific to red*

abs: *read**

me: *course i wouldnt stay away. just had to figure that out first lol*

caesarean: *means ur gonna come with us tonight yeah???*

me: *wouldnt miss it*

It makes me feel half-giddy to even be discussing it.

I go through my work day beaming, chatting to customers, making up bouquets. Without the duplicates, I can't be here and out there, being a superhero. I have to be in one place at one time, which twists me up inside, makes me feel guilty. Bad guys don't stop during daylight hours. I'm used to being a team of one— of five— even within the team with Caesar and Abyss. Maybe we should look at recruiting, getting a bigger group together. The teams that they have in Europe have more than three people, and our city has a bigger population than some countries over there.

We used to be, sort of, a team of seven (eight when Ace joined it), so maybe we should try to get our numbers back up. I make a mental note to talk to Caesar about it.

When I arrive at the penthouse, Caesar and Abyss are already suited up. Abyss is wearing her cape, but doesn't have anything covering her eyes. I try to avoid eye contact, not really wanting to get sucked into the Void. Caesar must be used to it, now, spending his time in her head and all.

"Ready?" Abyss asks me, smiling.

All in a breath, I say, "As I'll ever be."

And we go, racing down the many, many stairs instead of taking the elevator to warm ourselves up. I let out a 'whoop' as I jump down the last six steps. Abyss laughs at me. Caesar claps me on the shoulder as he passes, and we go out into the world. It's dusk, not quite dark, but the sun is dipping low over the horizon, painting the sky orange and purple and pink. The street-lamps are on, when we get out onto the more main streets, and people are starting to turn on their lights, flickering one, two, three, sending warm, yellow-toned light through their windows.

We don't have a specific lead to chase today, so we split off, each going off in separate directions. I feel the press of Caesar's mind against my own as we round a corner, and I try to relax against it. It's an uncomfortable feeling, someone else being in your head, but it's a useful one, too. Especially in our line of work.

I wander up and down random streets. I pause to take a picture with a group of teens, then, laughing, suggest we take another, sillier one. They walk away hollering and pushing at each other, and I walk away with a smile on my face. I check in at the women's shelter— Mindy gives me another hug, when she sees me— and then get distracted playing with a dog. Caesar protests at that, when he decides I've been doing it for too long, so I straighten up, a little disappointed, and walk until I find a street lined with clubs and bars.

Nice and easy, I think. Ease myself back into the job. Yesterday was intense, and important, and good, but today I should start small. Remind myself that there's only one of me, now. Get used to it. There's always something, in areas like this. There's always someone to help.

I wind my way around the streets, occasionally pausing to refuse a drink someone's trying to buy me, or to give a high five to someone who gets excited to see me. I break a few fights, standing in between the men and pushing them either side. I help a stumbling group of girls to their taxi, slipping a tip to the driver with a smile and a wink.

It's good, it feels good, to be back out here.

I turn a corner, and walk directly in to a drug deal.

They don't seem to notice me, so I side step into the shadow, pressing my shoulder against the faux brick and peering at them from a three-foot distance.

"You got it?" a feminine voice says, and I watch as she adjusts her skirt.

"Would I be here if I didn't?" a guy replies. "Yeah, I've got it. You got cash?"

She fumbles for her wallet. "The *right* stuff, right? The one that'll make me fly?"

"Yeah, yeah," he says urgently. "Hurry up, come on."

The stuff that'll make her fly. DNA? Or does she mean that metaphorically? I step just slightly closer. She hands him some cash, and he responds by pulling out a plastic bag. I can't see it from here, can't tell if it's DNA or something else, couldn't tell the difference, but it's got three little pills inside.

My heart pounds. *It works now.*

The girl doesn't waste any time. She pops one of the pills into her mouth eagerly, and dry swallows.

"It'll take about twenty minutes to kick in. Then you'll be soaring all over the place."

"Best *high* I've ever had," she says, giggling.

The guy shakes his head. "Whatever. Just don't use it all at once. It'll wear off in twelve hours, so don't go jumping off of any buildings too close to the end time. We don't want you ending up like that Brad Peters guy."

"Brett," I say, stepping out of the shadow and approaching them. I have one hand in my trouser pocket, the other raking through my hair. I swagger, which isn't a word I like to use, usually, but it fits in this instance. "Brett Peters. The guy is dead, man, the least you could do is get his name right."

The guy freezes, and the girl, still giggling, stumbles a few steps away. I can hear her saying 'wheee' to herself, clearly preparing to fly.

"You were dead too," he says, voice low and gravelly, as though I haven't just heard him talking in his uneven, higher pitch. He's definitely putting this on, trying to seem intimidating. "How'd you come back?"

"I was in a coma," I reply stiffly. "Not dead."

Kind of dead. But he doesn't need to know that.

"Coma, right," the guy says, pounding a fist into the palm of his other hand. "Wanna know what being dead really feels like?"

"Oh, come on, dude," I say, leaning into my shoulders in an exaggerated half-circle in time to my rolling eyes. "We both know that's not going to end well for you."

"Isn't it?" he asks, and cracks his knuckles.

As it turns out, he's absolutely right. I don't know if he's actually superhuman, or if he's doped up on DNA, but either way, he knocks the breath out of me with a single, well-placed swing. I'm fast, light on my feet, so I try to dart away, but he's faster, and follows me, shoves me to the ground. He seems to move almost faster than I can blink, blurring across my vision.

There aren't enough of me. I can't help but think it; if I had four others with me, I'd be able to stop him from running off. There is, however, some grim satisfaction at the fact that he does run— even with his abilities, he's scared that I'd beat him. Good.

The girl is staring at the wall, still giggling.

"What's the catch?" I ask her.

She blinks owlishly at me. "What do you mean?"

"With DNA, what's the catch? There's got to be some side effect, you know?"

She shakes her head. "You're crazy, Legion," she says, dragging out 'crazy' for far too long. "It's a, a, a miracle!"

Then she kicks up off the ground and jumps upwards, waving her hands through the air. She doesn't seem okay, and I want to help her find somewhere to sit down, have a glass of water, but she's not having it. As soon as I make a move towards her, she takes off in another direction.

In a few minutes, she'll be able to fly.

It works now.

No, no. Not doing that again.

Xander?

Ah, Caesar. I'd almost forgotten about his presence in my mind. Maybe going off on my own was a bad idea. I'm not used to this. I need backup.

Xander?!

No, no, not right now. Just in general. There needs to be more than one person, wherever I am, like there used to be. Also, I need to sort this DNA thing out.

I square my shoulders, leave the alley, and continue on.

78.

I can't expect Caesar and Abyss to be with me the whole time that we're out. It's impractical. Splitting up means that we can cover more ground. Unless there's something specific that we're going after, there's no point in all of us sticking together. Ace is retired. To varying degrees of success depending on the day, but it's clearly important to her, so I wouldn't ask her to give it up for me. I think about asking some of her old roommates, but they have their own team, so I don't think that's fair, either. Ava has no interest in being a superhero. She's made that clear since we were sixteen, so there's no point in asking her. I debate sticking up 'help wanted' posters before the obvious occurs to me.

Julia uses the fire escape now, like everyone else does. I imagine that she still uses portals to get to the bottom of the steps, but at least she knocks on the window now, instead of appearing at any and all hours of the day.

When I open it, instead of inviting her in, I step out side. "Hey," I say, with a signature grin. They've started coming more easily again. "Let's go out."

"What?" She looks genuinely baffled.

"It's a nice day." It's June, so the early summer heat is starting to roll in, and the sun is staying out longer and longer, stretching the days out. It's my favourite time of year. "Let's go to the park."

She continues to look at me oddly the whole way, but I don't pay it any mind. I'm wearing my dad's old denim jacket, with my hands stuffed into the pockets. It's not cold, but it may be cooling down by the time we decide to come home, so I like to be prepared. She's wearing cut-off shorts with a blazer, put together yet casual.

I haven't seen her in a full suit for weeks, maybe months. I haven't heard anyone say anything about Jamboree for even longer. When we finally arrive at the park, I guide us past picnic tables and fire pits to a slightly more secluded area just off the beaten path. The trees hide the sky, filtering sunlight through the leaves, and we end up just far enough away from anyone else to dull the sounds. There's some birds chirping, a warm breeze. I spread my jacket out and lay down, resting my head on one side of it, and gesture for Julia to join me.

"You're acting weird," she says as she sprawls out next to me.

I shrug, pull out my phone, connect some earbuds, and offer her one. She takes it, shifts until she's comfortable, and then closes her eyes. I play something soothing and slow. We lay there for the length of the song before she sits up.

"Seriously, Xander, what's going on?"

I sit up, too, stretching my arms towards the sky. "I wanted to do something nice for you."

Again, she wears that look of genuine bafflement. "Why?"

"Because you're my friend?" I say, knitting my eyebrows together. When she doesn't say anything for a long moment, I add, "Aren't you?"

"I don't…" She coughs awkwardly a few times before continuing. "I don't know why you'd want to be friends with me."

I shrug. "You didn't really give me much choice," I tell her, lightly. "Showing up all hours of the day. It was either fight you or friend you, and we both know I kinda sucked at the first one."

"Those are your two options?" She says, and I can tell that she's laughing at me from the way the corners of her mouth turn up by half-a-millimetre. "Fight or friend?"

"Yep," I agree, grinning. "There's not really an in-between for me."

"So you decided to be my friend because you sucked at fighting me?"

"Well, there's more to it than that."

"Is there?"

"'Course," I say, and I lean back against my palms. "You're clever, you're good at video games. You helped my mom paint our living room and you throw pillows at me when you think I'm being sort of dumb. *You* told me that I was still Legion."

"Loads of people told you that," she says, looking away from me.

"But you were the only one who knew I didn't have my abilities anymore." I pause, to let that sink in. "You never judged me for it."

"Of course I didn't!" She bursts out, suddenly loud with a cracking voice. "How could I judge you for it when it's *my fault!*"

I blink at her. She sighs and tips her head forwards, turning her long dark hair into a curtain that hides her face. "I *knew*," she says, after a moment. "What would happen. Or, even if I didn't know, I could make an educated guess. I'd seen that fight play out in however many different universes, and in so many of them, you fell and you died. In most of them, you came back, but not all. In most of them, if you came back, you'd be... different. I knew the *risk*—" she rips up a handful of grass and throws it, unsuccessfully, towards the nearest tree— "and I did it anyway. I always knew the risk and did it anyway."

I've forgiven Julia for her involvement. I know that there's no use blaming her for it. It was an accident, and it was no one's fault. People do things despite knowing the risks all the time. I hate that she's tearing herself up over it.

"It wasn't—" I start, but she glares at me, so I choose a different track. "Well, I've forgiven you, anyway," I say, shrugging. "People do stupid things all the time, and at the end of that day, that's all you did. A stupid thing."

"A big stupid thing," she says sourly. "A *massive* stupid thing."

"Maybe," I say, nudging her with my elbow. "But still just a stupid thing."

She turns to look at me dead-on, lips parted in surprise. "You really mean that, don't you? You really don't blame me at all?"

"Really," I agree with a nod. "I think you're a better person than you give yourself credit for. So you had a bad year. So what? You're clearly trying to get better now."

She smiles at me, genuinely smiles, even if it's a little shaky. "Yeah, I am. Wish I could do more, though."

It becomes incredibly clear what I should be doing. My chest feels lighter just for thinking it. I say, after a half-second to make the decision, "You could always help me?"

"With what?" She asks, but I think she's being purposely dumb. I shoot her a look and she deflates, just a little. "Okay, yeah, I know what you mean. Do you really think that's a good idea?"

"Why not?" I ask. She shoots me a deadpan look. "Really, why not? We could go together and do all the things that I do as Legion, but like, as a duo. I could show you the ropes of being a superhero! It'd be fun!"

"I'm not agreeing," she says, holding up a finger. "Not exactly. But... damn you and your overwhelming positivity. I'lll give it a try, okay? No promises."

I punch the air and shout "Yes!"

She laughs, actually laughs. I think it's the first time I've ever heard it. "You know," she says, after a beat, returning to her seat next to me, "people will think it's weird if you start hanging around with... Jamboree."

"We'll just rebrand you," I say, shrugging. She looks at me like I'm crazy, which maybe I am. "We'll call you Jubilee instead, or something."

"JuJu Jubilee," she says, shaking her head and scrunching her nose. "Plus, it's too similar. Maybe... Fanfare? Same sort of idea, but sounds completely different. I dunno." She smiles at me for a half-second. "What about you, though? Are you gonna rebrand too, what with the whole—" she holds up five fingers, then lowers four of them — "thing?"

I think about it for a second. "No... Legion was— is— about more than my powers, you know. Legion is... just me. It took me a while, but I know that now. Xander and Legion, Legion and Xander. I tried so hard to keep them separate, but they really aren't. I'm both of those things at once."

She nods and elbows me in the side. "Legion and Fanfare. You don't think it sounds silly?"

"Of course it does." I grin at her, wide and toothy. "That's half the fun."

79.

Bishop Flores sits across the desk from me. His hands are folded together with the fingers interlocked, and he's wearing a small, soft smile. "You wanted to speak to me, Xander?"

"Yeah," I say, and shift in my seat. "Remember a little while ago, when we talked about forgiveness?"

"I do," he says, and his face falls. He looks genuinely crushed. "Todd told me about what you said the other week. I thought you meant 'died' and 'killed' metaphorically, but you didn't, did you?"

"No, not really." I pause, trying to gather my thoughts. "I really *did* die."

"I had my suspicions. There was a body, after all."

"Yeah... But, uhm. I think I know how He did it, now. How He forgave them." Bishop Flores doesn't say anything, so I go on. "It's like you said, isn't it? He knew them and He loved them."

"You've been spending time with... Jamboree." He doesn't phrase it like a question, but I can hear the wariness in his voice, regardless. He hopes that I'm going to deny it.

"Julia," I say, instead. "Julia Lago, that's her name. And yes, I have been spending time with her. She helped my mom and I paint the living room walls."

"Does that seem safe, Xander?"

"Bishop, I... I needed to forgive her. For me. I was holding on to anger and depression and bargaining. I *needed* to forgive her, so I could let that go. So I did," I shrug, like it was that simple. And maybe it was, really. "And, as a happy side effect, I learned a lot about her. Got to forgive her for *her*, as well."

"It's admirable," Bishop Flores admits, "but..."

"Seventy times seven, right?" I shrug. "So unless she kills me four-hundred and eighty-six more times, I have to forgive her."

"It's the fact that she's, technically, already killed you more than once that's concerning to me," he says, with a pinched expression on his face. "Well, the fact that she's killed you at all, really."

"I forgave her, Bishop," I say in quiet voice. "I know not everyone can. But... I'm the only one who died because of her actions. I can give her another chance."

He lets out a long, heavy sigh. "If you die again, your mother will be distraught."

"I know," I nod a few times. "But I'm not planning on dying again for a long, long time. Actually, I'm thinking of going on a mission."

I didn't specifically mean to say it, but once it comes out I'm unsurprised to find that it's true. Bishop Flores blinks at me, clearly startled by the change in subject. "You are?" he asks, and furrows his brow.

"I mean," I say, looking anywhere but his face as I gather my thoughts, "the only reason that I didn't go when I was eighteen was because of my abilities, right? Because I felt like I was supposed to be doing *this* instead."

"I remember giving you that blessing," he says, nodding thoughtfully.

"Exactly. And now, I don't have those abilities. Maybe... it's time to serve in a different way."

Bishop Flores nods again. "We can start looking at getting your papers in, then."

I beam at him.

I'm still Legion. That's who and what I am, and there's no changing that. But I'm also Xander Pae. If I have to be Legion in a different way now, so why not be Xander in a different way too? This feels like a step in the right direction— like I'm doing something right again. It's the same way I felt when Ava first made me my mask, all those years ago, fourteen and still half-joking, or the way I felt the other week, the other month, taking it off and climbing out of the fire escape anyway.

80.

The first night that I go out with Julia, I don't tell anyone else. It's a trial run, just to get to grips with things. She shows up at my house, hovering outside on the fire escape, wearing athletic clothing. It's CrashTech, not C-Corp, but I suppose that's probably to be expected, given her history. She looks uncomfortable, tugging at her sleeves.

"Hey," I say, sliding through the window in my uniform. "Tried to dress for the occasion?"

"I've seen what Legion does," she replies, her lips pursed like she's sucking on a lemon. "I doubt my usual clothes would cut it."

"We'll get you a Fanfare uniform soon," I promise, and although she doesn't look appeased, exactly, her sour expression does drop a little. "Come on, let's go."

I set off, trusting that Julia will follow behind me.

She does, of course. She's changed a lot over these last months. The fact that she'd agreed to be here at all is proof enough of that, and that's she's shadowing me like this just solidifies it in my mind. I don't know if I'm quite at trusting her with the idea that's been rolling around in my mind since I met with Bishop, but I have time to decide. We'll start with tonight, and see where it goes.

She trails behind me, but never too far. We head away from my neighbourhood and into different areas of the city, walking shoulder to shoulder.

"What are we looking for?" she asks, after several minutes in silence.

"You've heard of DNA?" I ask, "The drug, not... y'know."

She rolls her eyes hugely. "Of course. It's been everywhere lately. Remember like a year ago? People were accusing *me* of being involved in it."

"Not really your MO, is it?"

She shakes her head primly. I laugh.

"Did you know that it works?"

She comes to a full stop, looking at me with wide eyes. They look almost black in the low lighting, and for a second I think they'll suck me in like Abyss' eyes do. "What?" She shakes her head. "It actually *works*, here?"

"It doesn't, in other universes?"

She shakes her head. "None that I've seen, anyway."

"I guess that's what makes this universe different."

"There's lots of things that make this universe different," she murmurs, then shakes her head. "Anyway, it works? What do you mean it works?"

"I heard a few different people talking about it. This guy Bruno seems to be in charge, and then he's got some lady backing him. Plus, I watched a deal going down the other day." I quickly explain to her what I've seen and heard, and her eyes seem to get wider and wider.

"Wow," she says, sounding awed. Then she narrows her eyes at me. "Xander, why do you want to find this?"

I blink at her, trying to feign innocence, but it clearly doesn't work. She crosses her arms over her chest. "Okay," I relent, dropping my shoulders and collapsing slightly forwards. "I've *thought* about it. Of course I have. But I'm not... I'm not going to take it. It's a drug, at the end of the day, and I bet you anything that there's a catch."

"Of course there is," Julia says, and rolls her eyes again. But she seems satisfied with my answer.

My heart is still racing as we continue on. The truth is, I'm still not entirely sure that I wouldn't take a dose if it could give me my abilities back, but I don't *want* to. Not actively, at least. Still, it is another reason to make sure that I don't go after this alone.

We wander around a little, keeping ears and eyes out. After a while, Julia sighs and asks, "Did you have a lead that brought you to this side of the city, or...?"

I shake my head. "Brett Peters lived around here."

"Brett Peters?"

"The first death associated with DNA," I reply. "Before it worked, I think. He jumped off a building thinking he could fly."

"He was a guinea pig," Julia says slowly. "While they were still trying to work out the kinks."

"Yeah," I nod. "That's what I think, too. I figure, if they found buyers around here before it even worked, won't they find buyers now that it does?"

"Will they? If someone died from it?"

"People die from all sorts of drugs, it doesn't stop people from taking them."

She hums noncommittally. "I don't know, Xander. Right in this area? His friends would know what happened to him, right? And I'm sure his family wouldn't want the drug kicking around, if they knew what happened to him."

"Well," I admit, "it was reported as a suicide. Chances are that his family *doesn't* know."

"If it was reported as a suicide, how do you know DNA was involved?"

"Ace. She's heard rumours and the numbers back them. She's our intelligence. Or was, I guess. She's retired."

Julia looks like she can't decide if she wants to hit me or not. "So you barely even have a *hunch* about this area? You just shoot blind, don't you?"

I flush and look down. "Caesar's the strategist."

"And he doesn't know that I'm here, does he?"

"To be fair," I say, after shaking my head, "he doesn't know that I'm here either."

"Most powerful telepath in the world," she sighs, "and he barely knows how to use it. No wonder you wanted me on board. You guys are hardly reaching your potential."

"Neither are you," I point out. She rolls her eyes at me.

We don't find anything related to DNA. Julia's right; I barely have a hunch, just a name and a stab in the dark. We do, however, find a tall building with a wide, flat roof on our way back towards city centre. Julia points it out, and then opens a portal beneath our feet. I see the briefest flash of some other universe, and then there's another portal, and we're on the roof.

"Neat trick."

Julia playfully flips her hair over her shoulder. "It's much more fun to get around that way."

"I bet. Why are we on this roof?"

She doesn't make eye contact when she answers. "I just thought… we could use the portals. Get you used to them. I bet that.. 'neat trick' could come in handy for your career."

"Your career too, now," I point out, breaking into a face-splitting grin.

She rolls her eyes again, but I catch her smiling. "Let's just try it out, okay?"

I nod, and we get to work.

81.

The TV is playing the eleven o'clock news, and, next to it, Abyss is standing with her arms crossed. I probably should've seen this coming, but I didn't even think of it. I didn't think anyone would be paying much attention to me anymore; it had felt like the novelty had worn off. Apparently, going out with Julia drew extra attention my way.

On screen, the news anchor reads, "In other news, Xander Pae, otherwise known as Legion, was spotted last night with the known supervillian Jamboree. Initially, it was assumed to be some sort of fight, but… see for yourself. We go now to footage of the event."

The video is shaky, and at a low angle, but there's no denying that it's me and Julia. We're on the roof, and she's throwing portals around, bouncing me from location to location with relative ease. As it goes on— and it must either be multiple videos or edited into chunks, because it skips a lot of time— I start to race towards the portals, and appear out of them ready for a fight. And we do fight, just not ruthlessly like we might have a year ago. We spar playfully, visibly laughing even in the poor quality of the video.

She drops a portal beneath my feet and one opens above her, and I drop down prepared for it, with a bend in my knees and my hands out for balance. I kick out almost immediately, swiping at her legs, and she jumps back, laughing. I know that she said, at this point, "I think we've got it!" but the video doesn't have audio beyond some whistling wind.

"The most damning bit of evidence," the newscaster says in voiceover, although I don't exactly know what he's trying to find evidence of, "comes in this final video. Take a look."

On screen, I take off at a run, grabbing Julia's hand as I go, and we race towards the edge of the building. Julia said, "Why are we jumping?" and I'd answered, "Presentation!" but, again, the video doesn't pick it up. It just shows us, hand in hand, jumping off the building, and disappearing into a hovering portal.

We'd only gone down to the bottom of the building and caught a bus home, but the video doesn't show that. It's played again, slowed down and zoomed in to show our hands.

I stand up, clapping my hands together. "I'm going to get some orange juice. Does anyone want anything?"

Abyss, still standing by the TV, and Caesar, sitting in the armchair next to her, stare at me and don't answer. I shrug, and go to the kitchen to grab a juice box.

When I get back, they've only moved to look at each other. I sigh, and flop down onto the sofa bed, which I'd unfolded for the express purpose of curling up under a duvet this morning. I'd been playing video games until Abyss and Caesar crawled through the window and changed the source without a word.

I'm still tired from last night, and I'm not due at work in the flower shop until late afternoon, so I'd thought I'd take it easy. Apparently, instead, I'm going to be fighting with my best friends. I've had enough of that to last a lifetime.

No one speaks, so I say, "I was thinking about getting more people on the team," forcing my voice to sound casual, then I take a slurp from my juice box.

"And you chose *Jamboree*?" Abyss demands, her arms crossed in front of her chest and her shoulders tilted towards me. Caesar, next to her, also looks dubious.

I shrug, forcing this movement, like my voice, to be casual. "We're thinking of changing her name. It's bad press, you know?"

"Change it to what?" Caesar asks, his voice torn between curious and annoyed.

Abyss sighs. "I hardly think that's the most important issue, here—"

"Not sure yet. It's up to her in the end," I cut her off, earning myself a glare. "Maybe Jubilee. Maybe Fanfare."

"Really, Cee? 'Fanfare sounds cool'?"

She must be responding to something in his head, because he hasn't spoken. I decide not to engage, and focus on finishing my juice box, instead.

After a moment, something seems to click in their minds simultaneously— typical, these days— and Abyss rounds on me with renewed anger. Mom and I were always pretty good at reading her, but it's a lot more obvious now. More physical. Easier to spot without knowing her. I am glad for it— it's good that she's more at ease with herself— but I wish her anger wasn't directed at *me*.

"'*We're* thinking'?" she says, and she doesn't have to remove her sunglasses for me to know that she's narrowing her eyes. "Exactly how long have you and Jamboree been talking?"

I have to think, and make a show of counting backwards on my fingers. "Well, the first time I saw her was the day that I found out about the two of you."

I think it's sensible to leave out the fact that I'd run off that day, as well, but of course Abyss brings it up again. "Is that where you disappeared off to?"

"No," I say with a bit of a scowl. "This was after. She showed up the night— it doesn't matter. The point is, that was the first time. Then I saw her again the day I did the photoshoot, and after that it was three days before Valentines day. I guess that's when we became friends," I muse. I haven't thought about it too much in retrospect. "She took me to a museum."

"A museum?" Abyss deadpans.

"In another universe."

Caesar perks up at that. "What was it like?"

I think about it. "Weirdly intimidating. There was this massive statue of *you*, which was very off-putting."

I decide that they're going to need a more in-depth explanation of this all, so I take them through it, starting with the first time she appeared in my house and ending with the events of last night. They both seem more convinced as time goes on, especially as I explain everything she said about my pseudo-death. "She feels terrible about it," I tell them. "You'll hear how she sounds when it's brought up."

Abyss sighs. She'd finally sat down as I was telling them everything, and seems to be a least a little bit more open to the idea now. "You trust her, Xander?"

"Yeah," I reply. "I know it sounds crazy, after everything, but... I do. I think she was hurt, and isolated and alone and just trying to figure out who she was."

"She felt like I abandoned her. Like I didn't trust her," Abyss says, and Caesar comes to sit next to her, wrapping an arm around her shoulders. There's two many of us on the bed now, but I don't mind it. "I should've realised. It's why she kept showing me our old apartment, and the universes we used to watch. I should've helped her."

She looks back at me, lips just barely parted. "You helped her, I guess?"

"I tried. She helped me too."

Caesar nods. "Well, I'm convinced to give her a shot at least. We should see her, though?"

Abyss and I nod in unison. I say, "I'll call her."

They blink at me, and I guess that despite talking about it for the last forty-five minutes, it's still a weird adjustment. I can't really blame them. Really, I should've told them from the start, but I was worried that they'd try to put a stop to it. If they had, maybe Julia and I would never have become friends. It's a weird thought to entertain, but I'm sure that there's a universe where it's true.

I step out of the room to throw away my now-empty juice box and make a quick call. "Heads up," I say, once she's agreed to come. "Cee and Abs are here. I think they want to feel you out."

"So," she says, and she doesn't sound angry, just resigned. "When you asked me to help *you*, you really meant that you want me to join your team, right?"

"Maybe?"

She just sighs, but a second later a portal opens up and she steps into my kitchen. She's wearing one of her suits again. I don't know if it'll do her any favours, but I don't mention it. Her jaw is visibly clenched. She doesn't need anything else to put her on edge.

"It's gonna be okay," I promise in a whisper. "They know that you've helped me, okay? They're just worried."

"Can't blame them," she says tightly.

We walk back to the living room.

I prepare myself for the worst.

82.

Abyss and Caesar are still sitting close together. Abyss has brought her feet up on to the sofa-bed, and is sitting cross-legged. Caesar has a hand resting on her thigh, leaning back against the headrest. He's trying to look nonchalant, but failing. His head is tipped at a forty-five degree angle, his brow low.

"Jamboree," he says stiffly.

"Fanfare, actually," she corrects, and she's clearly aiming for light. I think she misses. "Recent change."

"Last time I saw you," Caesar says, and his faux-light tone is much more convincing. "You were throwing me into another universe and threatening me. And Abyss."

"Yeah, well," she shrugs jerkily. "Last time I saw *you*, you told me that Xander was dead, and you were wrong, too."

It's the 'too' that does it. It's not an apology, not really, and I somehow doubt that anyone is going to apologise. Julia hasn't ever said she's sorry for my death, not in so many words, but I know she is. I just have to hope that Caesar and Abyss know that this means that she is. She's admitting she was wrong, after all. Even if it was phrased disdainfully.

Maybe I don't have to prepare for the worst after all.

"You came to my family's house," Abyss says, in her crystal-clear monotone. She hasn't used it around me for some time now, not since I came back and she was more open, easier to read. I'd forgotten how intimidating it is, to be met with something so blank.

Julia drops her gaze to the floor, and I can see her jaw tighten. I don't know where Abyss is going with this.

Abyss stands up, goes to stand in front of Julia, and rests her hands on her arms in a not-quite hug. Julia looks up, scanning over Abyss' face, although I'm not sure what she hopes to find. Even if she wasn't wearing her sunglasses, her eyes are hardly easy to read these days. She doesn't seem to find anything, anyway, and looks back down.

"I'm sorry," Abyss says, catching me off guard. I hadn't anticipated any apology from any side. "That I made you feel abandoned. You're my best friend. Do you know how often I thought about messaging you? It was never about not trusting you. It was about not knowing who I was. And this— the superkids, the superhero thing... I did it because of *you*. Because I knew how much it would've meant to you, to see it."

Julia's eyes are wide as she looks up at Abyss again.

Caesar stands up as well, to stand next to his fiancé, and stares, long and hard at Julia. She meets his eyes, but her expression is carefully blank. After a moment, he nods.

"So, Fanfare, then?"

She half smiles at him, and he returns it, and that's that. She's in.

83.

Ava takes even more convincing than Caesar and Abyss. I had a feeling that she would. After all, Abyss at least has fond memories of Julia, and Caesar is in her head. He could be in Julia's too, I suppose, and from the long, hard look he gave her the other day, I think he might have been. Ace has neither of these advantages and only knows Julia as Jamboree, the one who killed me. I want to point out that Julia didn't actually kill me, and even if she had, it wasn't intentional, but she's standing right next to me, and always goes funny when I talk about that, no matter how positively.

Ava looks her up and down, making no effort to hide her distaste. "You want me to design for her?" she asks, looking back at me. I've known her since we were fourteen, and I know just how to get her on my side.

I smile, and lift a shoulder into a half-shrug I've been told is adorable. "Come on, it'll be fun! Maybe not quite as fun as Legion and Acid Spit, but..."

She scowls, and I'm sure she knows exactly what I'm trying to do, but she doesn't protest any further. "Legion and Fanfare, then." She adds, with a pointed look at Julia, "I guess you want to, uh, distance yourself from the reputation you earned?"

"Ava!" I say sharply. "Leave it!"

Julia finally speaks, pushing her shoulders up off the wall she's been leaning against. "No," she says, walking until she's directly in front of Ava. "Let her speak."

Ava raises her chin to look down on Julia. There's maybe two inches between them, but Ava makes it count. "I don't need your permission to talk."

"Maybe not," Julia allows, "But you have it anyway. Tell me what you think."

"I think you need to stay away from Xander." She crosses her arms over her chest. "I think that you're dangerous and manipulative and a murderer, and playing superheroes isn't going to change that."

Julia gets a hard, stony look in her eye. "I'm not playing."

I look between the two girls, nerves shot. I have to bounce on the balls of my feet to stop from interfering. Ava asks, "Aren't you?"

"Nope," Julia says, popping the 'p'. I recognise this immediately for what it is. She's posturing, like she always did when she was acting as Jamboree. The way she'd call Abyss 'pet', or mock Caesar in Spanish, or say 'Just checking that this universe is the same as all the others.' I also recognise that Ava will not take it well. I almost want to cover my eyes. "I've never been playing, not once. I've always taken this seriously. Maybe I'm dangerous or manipulative or a murderer. I guess I wasn't playing then, huh, and now's no different. This isn't a game. Has it ever been a game to Xander?" She pauses for a half-second. "Acid Spit?"

For a moment, I think that Ava's actually going to do it; that she's going to spit in Julia's face.

It's more than a sign of disrespect coming from her, and Julia's clearly angling for it, in some intense game of chicken that I'm not going to pretend I don't understand. Instead, the tension seems to drain out of Ava, and I watch her shoulders settling down and back. "No, I guess you're right. It never has been a game for him, has it? Even when we were kids. And he's smart enough that he wouldn't get you on board if he didn't trust you."

Julia seems to falter at that and looks towards me with an expression that I can't quite read. Her eyes are wide and her mouth is in a tight line.

To rescue her, I sweep over, wrap an arm around Ava's shoulder, and grin. "Are you done talking about me like I'm not here?" I ask, trying to sound playful. "I do trust her, for the record. And Cee and Abs gave their stamp of approval, too! Does this mean that you're going to style her?"

Ava hesitates for a second longer. "Yes. But *I* still don't trust her."

She throws another wary look at Julia, who seems unbothered now. I can't tell if she's putting it on or not, but she just shrugs and lets Ava guide her out of the room to take measurements.

It hits me that none of my friends particularly trust Julia. I guess why would they? But I've gotten to know her, over these months, and I know that I can rely on her to have my back. And take my place, once I go on my mission.

That's been bouncing around my head, too, ever since my talk with Bishop. I have to leave the city with someone else to look after it. Caesar and Abyss would, and they'd do it happily, but I know that, with the wedding and the company and the science that Abyss is inevitably going to want to pursue again, they won't have time. And we reintroduced superheroes to the world. Or at least had a hand in it. It's important to me that they stick around.

So, I'm going to work with Julia until she really *is* a superhero inside and out, and then, when I go, I'll leave the city in her capable hands.

Julia's uniform is finished within a couple of weeks, which Ava says is 'thanks to C-Corp resources' when she delivers it to me at church. "I should be on their payroll by now," she mock grumbles.

"Aren't you?" I'm genuinely surprised.

She shakes her head. "I've been hired freelance. Which is great! They pay me generously, but... I don't know. I spoke to Abyss about it ages ago. I finish my degree this year, and then I have to try to find work. It's stressful."

"C-Corp would hire you, if you applied."

"I'm sure Caesar would," she says, which is what I meant, really, "but... I don't know. I don't want to accept handouts."

"It's not a handout, Ava," I say, nudging her. "You're really good."

She playfully flips her hair over her shoulder. "I try, I try."

"I'm serious. Even if you don't want to apply there, you should get someone you worked with to write you a letter of recommendation or something, to put with your resumé."

"That's not a bad idea, you know."

"All of my ideas are good!"

She looks dubiously at the package in my hand, then shakes her head. "I sure hope you're right, Xander."

I call Julia as soon as we get home, and she comes over to try on her uniform. The base is a black top and trousers, not-dissimilar to Abyss', a pair of sturdy black boots, and some gloves which leave her fingers and knuckles exposed. The star of the show, though, is the bright purple blazer that seems to sparkle in the light as she moves around, creating an illusion that's quite like the edges of her portals.

I clap at the sight, and she takes a sweeping bow.

"The jacket makes me feel like a magician," she says, but she sounds thrilled about it. "I guess people *did* call me an illusionist when I was a kid, so it's fitting. But that's not even the best bit!"

"What's the best bit?" I ask, because I'm obviously supposed to and her excitement is catching.

She spins around.

On the back of the blazer, in a contrasting bright white, is the word *fanfare*.

"We match!"

I laugh. I can't help it. She's so excited by the prospect of it, and I find that incredibly endearing. I know that is is Ava's stamp of approval, the same way that Abyss' small apology was hers, and Caesar's hard stare and eventual nod was his. I think Ava has worked out, at least a little, what I'm trying to do. This is her way of saying she accepts it, and supports me. She may not trust Julia, but she trusts me.

"We'll go out tomorrow, okay? Maybe during the day, so that people can get used to the sight of you."

We spend most of the following week going out and about in the city, helping where we can. We practice with her portals until I'm as comfortable diving in and out of them as I was making a duplicate— or as close as I'll get to anything like that.

I'm completely caught off guard when Ace texts me. I haven't heard from her since two weeks ago, when everyone found out about my friendship with Julia. I haven't put that together until now.

ace: *we need to talk*

me: *about what??*

ace: *about jamboree*

ace: *fanfare*

ace: *julia. whatever. we need to talk about her*

me: *why??*

ace: *please, xander*

84.

Ace is playing with the handle of a teacup when I arrive in the cafe she'd suggested we meet at. It smells like peppermint— not lavender — when I sit down opposite of her with my mug of hot chocolate, extra whip cream and marshmallows. I almost hadn't come; I'm certain that this is going to be another argument about Julia, and I'm not sure I want to go through that another time. But she'd said 'please'.

Ever since I've been back, she's been dressing more boldly, decked out in reds and whites and blacks— playing card colours, that's her scheme— with trendy accents and bright makeup. Caesar said it was like she was 'performing herself', but I think it's more that she's finally found her footing. 'Retiring', whether entirely accurate or not, has been good for her, and it's shown in the way she cut her hair.

Today, she's wearing black jeans, boots, and a ringer tee with white trim. There's also a little ghost over the heart. I'm pretty sure it's an old shirt of *mine*, actually, but I don't mention it. If she's got it, it probably means that she helped Mom go through my things while I was dead, so I'm grateful she was there to help. Still, the relatively solid black is unlike her.

She looks up at me and half-smiles. "Hey."

"Hey," I reply, "what was so important?"

"I just—" she shakes her head. "I need to make sure you're okay."

"Of course I'm okay," I say. "Why wouldn't I be?"

Ace shakes her head, sending her hair bouncing around her face. She seems to debate speaking for a long time, chewing on her bottom lip and casting her eyes around to look anywhere but at me. I let her think.

After a moment, she brings her tea to her mouth and takes a long drink. When I first realised she was a tea drinker, rather than the coffee person I would've pegged her for, I was surprised. Even more so when I discovered it was herbal tea. She's swapped lavender for peppermint, and that's almost as surprising. It seems odd to change her preference after so long.

"You remember when I faked my death?" she finally says.

"How could I forget?"

She nods, once, twice, three times. "Right. Do you know why?"

"You said you got too close to a lead," I say, tipping my head to one side, wondering where this is going. "Put yourself at risk."

"That's... half true."

I wait for her to elaborate.

"That— company, that I was going after? I, um, met one of their employees. One of my roommates was missing, you know, and I thought he was there to, like, brag or something. Hold it over me. He didn't. He, uh… bought me tea. Lavender, my favourite. Don't know how he knew that, but…" she shrugs. "I didn't ask. He said he would help me get my roommate back. And I… I trusted him, even though he never really did anything to deserve it."

"You think it's the same with me and Julia?"

She shrugs, looking helplessly around the room, unable to meet my eyes. "I don't know! But I told him things, and let him in, and *loved* him, and he… he wasn't a good person, Xander. At the end of the day, he was still a bad guy. Still the enemy, but I let him get close and —"

She cuts herself off and shakes her head aggressively. Her eyes squeeze shut and, on the table, her hands ball in to fists.

I reach across to rest a hand over her wrist, and she snaps back into herself. She looks back at me, her eyes wide. "I can't drink lavender tea anymore," she admits. "It's ruined for me. I don't… I don't want you to have anything ruined for you."

"It's… Ace, I'm sorry," I say, squeezing her arm.

She takes my hand in hers and looks intently at me. "I look at you and Jamboree-" I decide not to correct her- "and I can't help but think… You trust her so much. You jump into her portals without even looking! And you got her a uniform and defended her to *Abyss* and I worry that… you're trusting her for no reason. Like I did."

"She's given me lots of reasons to trust her," I assure her. "And, just so we're clear— this isn't the boyfriend I've been hearing about?"

She shakes her head. "No, no. He's great."

We fall quiet, Ace sipping her tea and me slipping my hot chocolate. After a few moments, she says, "Xander... just promise me you'll be careful? It's easy to... get sucked in to something, you know? And all these reasons that she's given you... who knows how true they are?"

"I know," I say softly. I don't want to undermine her feelings— even with only a few sentences, I feel like I've learned a lot about her. I remember her saying, immediately and firmly, that I should give Mindy her number. I'm looking at it in a slightly different light, now. "I know that they're true, but... I promise I'll be careful. And if I'm ever unsure, I'll come straight to you."

There's a brief period of dead silence, and then Ace nods once, firmly. "I'll hold you to that."

On impulse, I go around to the other side of the table and wrap her in a hug. She hugs me back, tightly, hands splayed across my shoulders. When we pull away few seconds later, and I return to my seat, she lets out a long breath through pursed lips.

"Thanks for... looking out for me," I smile at her, gratified when she returns it. "I like that I have you on my side."

"Yeah, well," she scoffs. "Someone's got to, if you're gonna be dumb."

"I'm not being dumb!"

She laughs, previous tension dissipating. "I just had to make sure. Your mom would kill me if I let you die again."

"I have no plans on it," I promise, holding up three fingers. "Scouts honour."

"Were you a *scout*?"

"We did it through church— they've stopped it, now, but yeah, I was one. Earned all sorts of badges, made racing cars out of water bottles and things."

"You know," Ace says, grinning, "that actually explains a lot about you. Like, as a person. Just, you know. You're such a good person. Want to help everyone, yeah? And you were a *scout*, it just makes a lot of sense."

I roll my eyes fondly. "I'm thinking of going away—"

She narrows her eyes. "Why?"

"—On a mission," I finish, raising my eyebrows. She holds her hands up in apology. I probably could've worded that better, given *her* reasons for 'going away', that we literally just talked about. "I think… I didn't go before, because I was busy being Legion and that felt right."

"You're still busy being Legion," she points out. Literally points, directly at my chest.

"Well, yeah, sure," I reply, "I'm Legion, I'll always *be* Legion, we've already worked through this particular identity crisis."

"Do you have many identity crisises? Crisies? What's the plural of crisis?"

"Who knows? But yes, I've had a fair few. Especially over the last year. Anyway, point is, I'm still Legion, but I want to do *this*, too. It feels right. You know, the whole time I've been working through this, I've been thinking, 'how can I move on from this?', 'how can I be Legion if I'm not superhuman?', 'how can I forgive Julia, or Caesar, or Abyss, or Ava, or Zoram?' And yes, I did blame all of them for at least some amount of time."

"Didn't blame me though," she says, raising her teacup and tipping it towards me like someone might do with a glass of champagne.

I poke my tongue out at her, but continue as if she hadn't spoken. "For me, the answer was my faith. Took me a while to get there, but… I got frustrated, speaking to the bishop, saying how Jesus said to forgive everyone, but *he'd* never had to forgive people for literally killing him…"

Ace raises her eyebrows. "My mama was Catholic, and I'm pretty sure that's not right."

"I realised as soon as I said it," I say, flushing pink. I can feel the heat of it on the tips of my ears. "And that made it easier to forgive. I want to share that with people. I know that not everyone needs it or wants it, but I think that it can help people, and I want to share it. Plus, it's not all about that stuff. It's also about, just, serving. Doing good."

"You can do that *here*," she says.

I shake my head. I don't really expect my non-member friends to understand. "It's just... different."

"You can be someone different if you go somewhere else," she says, and I blink.

Maybe she does get it.

"It feels..." I trail off, but she doesn't push, just lets me get my thoughts together. I used to try to keep Legion and Xander so separate, so individual of each other. But we're not two different people. I'm one person. "Like it's a natural fusion of Xander and Legion. Doing good, talking to people. And... I need to figure out how to be both of them— me— at once, you know? Maybe I need some space to do that."

"Makes sense," she says, nodding thoughtfully. "You need to figure out how... to be *you*, but you, uhm, need to do it by *being* you?"

"Exactly!"

She smiles. "When I was undercover, I learned a lot about myself. And I think it shows— Caesar keeps telling me that I 'seem good', like, every time I see him. Maybe a mission will do the same for you."

"I hope so."

"How long is it for?"

"Two years."

Ace chokes on her drink. "You think your mom will be cool with it? I mean, after everything that's gone down over the last two years, you think she's gonna be alright with you disappearing for another two?"

"She *was* worried about it at first," I admit. "But… they have just changed the rules so that I can call home every week, and it's something that we used to talk about a lot. She supported me being Legion, and that was a lot more dangerous."

"Well, good luck," she says, shaking her head. "But what about the city? I'm retired-" I resist the urge to snort- "and we both know Cee and Abs are gonna be too busy with their wedding— they've set a date now, did they tell you?— and even if my friends are kicking around, they take on a drastically different crowd than you did. Do."

"That's where Julia comes in."

"Ooooooh," Ace says, and a tiny smile appears on her face. "*That's* what the name change is all about. Does she know this is the plan? Is she on board?"

"Not yet," I laugh. "But I think she's coming around."

After a long, long pause, Ace smirks. The expression spreads over her face slowly, almost purposefully. "You still wanna take down DNA?"

I nod.

"I know where Bruno is going to be on Tuesday. Will you be ready in time?"

85.

We're on the roof again.

Without a secret identity, there's no reason for me to go anywhere else. Plus, I'm only on my lunch break. It's much easier to race up the stairs for a forty-five minute break than it is to find somewhere fancy to practice at weird times. Julia meets me on the fire escape, and we practice with her portals and I teach her everything I know about being a superhero.

"Why the sudden *rush*?" she asks me, panting. She was always able to hold her own against five of me, but we've been pushing each other harder and harder throughout our time on the same team. Her hair is slicked to the sweat on her forehead; normally pin-straight, it's almost curled from the wetness.

For my part, I'm covered in bruises up the entire lengths of my arms. Julia's a *grabber*, and she's got an iron grip. Between that, and falling out of portal after portal while I attempt to understand it all and land properly, I'm aching and sore almost all the time.

Since Wednesday, when I saw Ace, I've been pushing the two of us harder and harder. It's Saturday now, and on Tuesday, Bruno's going to be attempting to get funding for DNA. Publicly. With a press conference. I don't understand how he managed to swing it, but I know we have to stop it. Caesar is chasing after his contacts in the Caesar Corporation's business partners, finding out the opinions of those likely to fund it. So far, no one seems quite sure what to make of it. Abyss is holed up in the lab Caesar got her, testing and retesting the samples that Ace got her, all those months ago. Over a year, really. How time flies.

"You know why," I tell Julia and she scowls, but nods.

When she comes at me again, I'm unprepared, and she knocks me flat onto my back. I groan, but jump back up after less than two seconds, and chase her to the other side of the roof. I manage to grab her arm. She shakes me off easily.

Instinctually, I try to call a duplicate.

My face must drop, because Julia stops short, and rests a hand on my shoulder.

"Can't shake the habit," I say, shaking my head. "It's been *months* of this! I should know better."

"You're used to the advantage," she says, her voice low and steady. She squeezes her hand to massage my shoulder, looking at me sideways. "It's... normal."

"Do we have a frame of reference, suddenly?" I snark. Then I sigh, leaning into her touch. "I just... I can't help but wonder, sometimes, if maybe DNA isn't the worst thing in the world."

"Xander..."

I shake my head again. "I'm not— I mean, I don't think..."

"Are you sure you want to be doing this?" she asks gently. "Caesar and Abyss are working on it. I'm working on it. You could... sit this one out and it'd be okay."

It's relieving to hear; Julia calling her 'Abyss' without a trace of irony, putting the three of them on the same side and the same team. I know that when I leave, they'll be able to hold on to this delicate balance they've struck. Julia, doing good however badly. Caesar, leading the pack. Abyss, designing everything they'd need. Even Ace, keeping a wary eye on everything from a half-step away. *That's* the team.

But I'm *Legion*, and I've lost the very thing that DNA claims to be able to give. "If I took a dose," I say, slowly. "It wouldn't... make me any more than I already am. It'd probably make me *worse*."

"Yeah," Julia agrees. "I think you're right."

"It wouldn't make me Legion any more than I already am, right?"

"Course not. You're Legion, you don't need abilities for that."

"I'm glad you stopped blaming yourself for that," I tell her, and she winces.

She doesn't look me in the eyes. "I know it drives you crazy... but it's the same way that you can't stop reaching for the duplicates. I *can't stop* blaming myself for taking them away from you. For hurting Abyss. For scaring Caesar. I'm a monumental fu-"

"What have I said about swearing in my mother's house?"

"Technically, we're not *in* her house." I shoot her a look and she sighs. "Fine, I'm a *screw-up*, but... I'm trying to make it right."

"That means you aren't a screw-up," I tell her.

Before she can respond, my phone buzzes three times in rapid succession.

cee said to **superkids!**: *its gonna be v hard for bruno to get funding*

abs said to **superkids!**: *brng ff & gt t pnths*

ace said to **superkids!**: *WAS THAT SUPPOSED TO BE 'PENTHOUSE' IM LIVID*

"Come on," I say to Julia, flashing the texts in her direction.

After a beat, she says, "She wants you to bring me?"

"That's what she said, isn't it? Come on, we'll say goodbye to Mom on the way out."

"Won't she be mad that you're skipping work? This was supposed to be lunch-hour training, after all."

I shake my head. "You know my mom. She'll be fine. Now come on!"

Mom does, of course, get it, and Julia and I are debating calling a cab when Caesar's driver pulls up. I think he may have an ability; he always arrives just in time, never hits a red light, and never gets lost. "Mr Caesar sent me," he says, "For yourself and Miss Julia."

"Perfect! Thank you, Aaron."

He nods, and Julia and I climb into the backseat. The drive, as any in this car, goes by quickly. We pull up to the building and ride the elevator straight to the top. This, I realise, will be Julia's first time in the penthouse. She's worrying her bottom lip between her teeth. I nudge her with my shoulder. "You good?"

She shrugs. "Didn't think they'd invite me here. Even if… I've been trying, this still feels kinda like enemy territory."

I don't know what to say to that. I feel like that a lot with Julia. Instead of answering, I just bump my shoulder against hers again and smile encouragingly. It's all I have time for, anyway, because as soon as I've finished the motion, the elevator doors open, and we're in the penthouse.

Abyss greets us immediately by saying, "Bruno is a liar."

86.

"What?"

"DNA doesn't work!" Caesar says, from his spot on the couch. He's sprawled out, slouched down enough that his head is resting on the top of the cushion, his arms wide across the back of the couch. His laptop is open and balanced on his knees. "Anyone who's said that best be hanging from a telephone wire."

I pinch my eyebrows together. "Are you okay?"

"I'm very tired," he admits, then, in a sing-song, says, "Liar, liar, pants on fire…"

I don't even know how to answer that, so I turn my attention back to Abyss. She's shaking her head at Caesar. "We haven't really slept for the past three days," she admits, "and Cee is suffering from sleep deprivation, I think. His side of the connection is all funny. The point is, DNA doesn't work."

Julia runs a hand through her hair, raking her fingernails from the top of her forehead to the top of her scalp. "How do we know that?"

"Jessica Smalls," Caesar says, twirling a finger through the air. "We're on video chat right now."

I go over to sit next to Caesar. Jessica Smalls is wearing a hospital gown, and her hair is hanging limp around her face. There are dark bruises around her otherwise very pretty green eyes, giving her a sunken, haunted look. She waves when she sees me come on screen.

"I know you!" I say, recognition dawning when I see her smile. "You wanted to fly!"

She nods. "Didn't work out for me."

The story that Jessica tells me goes like this:

The first dose was fine; fun, even. She didn't fly, but she felt like she was. Apparently, even if it can't actually give you abilities, it does a very good job of tricking you into thinking it does. "I kept seeing all these buildings and things below me, like I really was up in the air. And I *believed* that if I climbed up somewhere and jumped, I'd be just fine."

Her second dose was not as much fun. "The come down is a nightmare. I stopped seeing things, but the… belief didn't go away."

"Brett Peters," I whisper. "Jumped off a building thinking he could fly."

"I was scared," she says, "and I decided I wouldn't take anymore. But… even only two days later, I was begging for it. Whatever they have in there might not do what they say, but it's *good*, I guess. Keeps you wanting more. I took another pill. It was even worse that time. Luckily, this superhero kid turned the glass I fell onto into something like… soft? Almost bouncy, like a trampoline. I guess he was a friend of yours, cause the first day I was I here, someone gave me Caesar's contact information."

I recognise the ability; one of Ace's old roommates. "Are you okay?" I ask, and she nods.

"Well, not yet," she admits. "But the doctors are looking after me, and they think I'll make a full recovery. Only had some fractures, some bruising. I haven't really slept. Withdrawal is hell. They're going to put me in rehab after this, as well. Get me clean. Probably for the best… but I don't even want to think about what my dad's gonna say."

"Good luck," I tell her, and she thanks me.

Abyss chimes in. "Jessica told me where her dorm is, so I snagged a few of her leftover pills to run tests on. Plus, since we had her consent, the doctors have been helpful."

"I can't believe people thought I was involved in this," Julia says, and when I glance up over the monitor, her lip is twisted in disgust. "People spend years telling superhumans exactly what they can and cannot be, treat us like trends…"

Jessica looks uncomfortable, but she nods her agreement. "It's true. Superhumans became cool again, so people wanted to be them. Everyone wants to be a superhero, you know?"

"There are better ways than this," I sigh, rubbing at my forehead. "You don't *need* abilities for it."

"Not everyone can see that," Jessica says, shrugging and looking at something offscreen. "I mean, do you know any superheroes who aren't superhuman?"

"What do we do," I ask a few minutes later, after Jessica has hung up, "now that we know this? Bruno will try to sell it as a way to be a superhero, and *we've* made being a superhero cool."

"We tell the truth," Abyss says, like it really is that simple.

Caesar nods his agreement. "I mean, everyone knows that Abyss is a genius. We've got the research to back it and Jessica said she'd speak, if we need her to."

I glance around the room and shake my head. "People will believe what they want to believe, guys. And it's like she said—" I gesture to the black screen— "people want to be superheroes."

"It's not right," Julia sighs. "But it's true. I don't know that it'll be as simple as just... sharing the facts."

"Well then what do you recommend?" Abyss snarks.

Julia just shrugs.

"We'll figure it out," I say, looking at Caesar, "right? We always do."

Caesar rolls his head to the side and blinks slowly at me. "Yeah," he says after a beat. He sits up straighter, rubs at his eyes, and shakes himself. "Yeah, 'course we will. First thing— you."

He points to Julia, who's still standing by the windows, and she recoils slightly. "What did I do?!"

"How does this go in other universes?" he asks, "Is there anything we can learn from that?"

She closes her eyes for a second. Abyss leans forwards, her tongue poking out from her lips just a little. Caesar glances over at me, like he expects my reaction to mean anything. Julia hasn't properly shown me any alternate universes since the museum; any time I've spent in them has been almost unbearably quick in the turnaround, using the portals more as transportation than anything else. I'm as intrigued as the others.

Julia raises one hand until her fingers are in line with her temple. Three portals appear behind her almost simultaneously, blocking the mid-day sun and casting the room into shadow. The sound of it is almost deafening, and as it finally fades, she opens her eyes. "What do you want to see first? Ones where you win?"

She pauses meaningfully, looking between us. "Or ones where you lose?"

87.

We pick lose. End on a high note, right?

We realise quickly that watching ourselves crash and burn over and over is incredibly demoralising.

"Remember," Julia says, standing in front of the most recent portal, through which we've just watched Caesar have his arm broken, "Every universe is different. Don't get hung up on the details. And, to be fair, in most of these universes, you don't have me on your side. That'll make a difference."

"Can you just show us some where we win?" Caesar asks, and he sounds exhausted again. Abyss' lip is twisted with concern, her hand resting on his arm. Maybe this was a bad idea; he and Abyss really should be getting some sleep. We still have time to come up with a plan, and if he's so overtired, we won't have much success anyway.

I say as much, and Caesar shakes his head, blinks multiple times, and does all he can to look more energised. "We've got to come up with *something* first."

Julia's eyes close again, her fingers moving in a slow circle through the air, like she's flicking through papers. I assume she's cycling through universes in her mind, trying to find the right ones to show us. "I could just stick Bruno in another universe," she says, and shrugs with her eyes still closed. "That would solve the problem, wouldn't it?"

"Is it that hard to find a universe where we did a good job?" Abyss asks.

In the same moment, I say, "We're not sticking some other universe with our problems!"

Julia shrugs again, looking unbothered, but I'd bet my left arm that she's still filing the idea away for later use. "You always do a good job," she says, addressing Abyss. "It just doesn't always work out for you. Honestly, though," and she finally opens her eyes to look at each of us in turn, "you win more times than you lose, and there's not all that much to be learned from watching those."

"You could show us anyway," Caesar says, and she sighs.

"Look in to my head, *guapo*," she suggests to him, "comb through them all with me, come up with a plan. *Lead*, et cetera."

Caesar goes quiet for several minutes, then looks sidelong at Abyss, who nods. They're all sharing some great secret, and it doesn't take a telepathic leader, or a million universes, or an actual, certified genius to figure out what.

It makes me sick.

Caesar calls Ace, who answers in her typical, peppy fashion. "If we go against Bruno," he asks, "exactly as we are now, what are the chances that we win?"

"Fifty-nine percent," she replies, then pauses, humming. "You really need to sleep, man. And let Xander do the talking on Tuesday, okay?"

"Do our odds go up then?"

"Yeah," she says, but doesn't say by how much. "You're more likely to win than to lose."

"That's *literally* what I just said," Julia moans.

"I don't like that I'm agreeing with her," Ace says pointedly, but I think she's teasing. "I dunno what it's like in other universes, obviously, but in *this* one, you're gonna be okay. Just get some sleep, and Tuesday will be fine."

"In the other universes, where we win," I say, speaking for the first time and staring directly at Julia, "I still have my ability, don't I?"

Julia stares back for three full seconds before she breaks eye contact to nod.

"Are there any where we win, but I *don't* have them?"

She looks back at me, eyes flitting up and down like she's nervous and says, "Not yet."

88.

Not yet.

Not yet.

It works now.

It doesn't work now; Jessica had said it and Abyss had proven it. It *doesn't work.* I have to keep repeating it to myself, over and over, *it doesn't work.*

When I'd asked if there were any universes where I'd lost my abilities and kept being Legion, Julia had said, 'not yet' and it had felt like encouragement. This time around, it feels more like a warning. I wonder aloud who I *am* in other universes, and Julia, next to me, shakes her head.

"You don't want to know."

"That's the worst thing you could've said!"

She winces. "I know. Just… they aren't *you.* You're different. Take it from someone who knows, Xander, it's not always nice to see who you might've been."

"What do you mean?"

She chews on the inside of her cheek for a moment. "I've seen all these different universe and tried to work out their turning points. There are all these tiny little differences that can be nearly impossible to see. But I've... I've seen who I am when I'm not friends with you, and I don't like it."

I open my mouth to speak, although I've not entirely sure what I'm going to say. I'm almost relieved when she cuts me off.

"Equally, though, I've seen universes where we *are* friends, and I don't like them very much either." She shrugs her shoulders up to her ears. "As interesting and informative and whatever else as they can be, it's... it's not really *us*, in those universes. All those tiny changes make big differences, you know?"

"I guess." I still wonder, though, about those different places with those different people, with versions of myself who still have all five of their bodies. Those universes where I never died, or came back as not-Legion, or the ones where I never came back at all. I shiver, and I can't even blame it on the chill. It's summer, now, and even early evening is accompanied with sunshine.

Julia nudges me. "You're the best version of you out there. Promise."

She grins when she says it. I know that's not how it works. Even if she can see all those other universes, it's not like there's really a sliding scale, top to bottom, best to worst. I appreciate it anyway.

"I'm sure you're the best of you, too."

She rolls her eyes. She doesn't believe me. I intend to keep saying it until she does.

We've come to a stop outside the flower shop. She opens a portal with a wave of her hand, and smiles at me one last time before disappearing through it. I still don't know where she lives, if anywhere. Maybe she could stay with Mom while I'm on my mission. I know she's missed having a girl around.

Speaking of my Mom, she's sitting on the sofa bed when I get upstairs. It's unfolded, which is far more rare these days, and she's got a blanket draped across her legs. "Xander," she greets me warmly when I walk in, and I take a seat next to her, allowing her to wrap an arm around me. "I love you."

"I love you too, Mom."

"It just hit me today that you'll be leaving," she says, and brushes her fingers soothingly through my hair like she did when I was a kid. She sounds choked up when she speaks again, "I'm so proud of you."

"I haven't even got my call yet," I say, shifting to a slightly more comfortable position.

"I don't just mean that." She takes my chin in her fingers and forces me to look at her. "It's everything. You've always been so determined to do the right thing. For you or others. Being Legion, making friends, standing up for yourself, serving a mission. Coming back, after everything…"

We both freeze for a second, still stumbling over the whole 'I was dead' situation, but Mom breezes past it and continues by saying, "You've adapted to everything so well. You're my hero."

"Mom!"

"It's true! I can't believe I raised you."

"*I* can," I tell her, and I hug her tightly enough that she protests. "You're *my* hero. You're the best mom in the whole world."

She makes a tutting sound.

"It's true!" I mimic, and we both burst in to laughter.

"Your call will be here any day now," she says, after a brief moment. "Anywhere you'd like to go?"

"I haven't thought about it," I admit. "People at church keep asking me and I honestly don't know. I just want to... *go—*"

"*—and do the things the Lord commands.*" Despite not growing up with them, Mom learned primary songs when she first joined the church, still getting to grips with the language, and she sings them, sometimes, while she wanders around the house. I'll miss it when I'm gone. It's starting to hit *me* that I'll be leaving.

"When my call arrives, I want to open it straight away," I tell her. "If I'm out, call me, and then Ava and Zoram, and Ace, and I'll get Abyss and Caesar and Julia to come with me. We can open it together. But

I'm not going to, like, set a date. Just tell me when it gets here and I'll open it as soon as possible."

She promises she will. Then she asks me, "Are you ready for Tuesday?"

I can only say, "Not yet."

89.

I'm still not ready when Tuesday does roll around, in all honesty. I don't tell Mom this.

Instead, I pull on my uniform and meet Julia, wearing hers, where she's hovering on the fire escape. Bruno's press conference is being held in the city centre. The repairs have only just been completed, and as we approach, I can see Julia's eyes flicking over the buildings. I nudge her with my shoulder.

"Best version of you," I say, and she rolls her eyes.

She smiles, too, though, so I count it as a win.

We meet Caesar and Abyss outside a café. Both of them are wearing their uniforms, and Caesar has his arm wrapped around her shoulders. She doesn't wear her engagement ring when we go out like this, saying she doesn't want to risk losing it, and for a while the tabloids went wild over it. I don't know why they bothered; one glance at the two of them and I feel nauseous with how in love they are.

"Okay," Caesar says, as soon as we've come to a stop. "Here's the plan..."

We stick out in out uniforms, highly stylised and famous, so we don't attempt to hide our approach. There really wouldn't be much point. Instead, we go a bit over the top.

Julia's portals create a loud enough *fanfare* to drown out Bruno's voice, and from them, Caesar, Abyss, and I walk out into the crowd from three different angles. We draw as much attention to ourselves as possible. Caesar and Abyss draw their own, smaller crowds on either side, and for me, in the middle, the crowd parts. It may be the set in my jaw or the line of my shoulders, but for all the faux whispering and pointing fingers, no one tries to approach me for an autograph like they do to my friends. They provide me with a straight shot to the temporary stage and the podium that Bruno is standing behind.

Charlie Caesar, wearing her press pass around her neck, is the only exception. At the very front of the crowd and the base of the stage, she's turned around to face me and lifted her camera to her eyes. The flash goes off, far enough away that it doesn't blind me even as I stare right at it. When she lowers her hands, she's beaming at me.

Eliza Caesar is with her, standing a few steps away, which surprises me. She shoots me a thumbs up as I catch her eye, and mimes shouting. I get the message— she'll project my voice for me.

"Hey, Bruno."

Ace did say that I should do most of the talking.

Bruno is trying and failing to get the crowd re-interested in whatever it was he was saying before we showed up. People are murmuring about us, about the portals, about Jamboree ("*no, stupid, it's Fanfare now—*"). People are looking at *me*, not Bruno, wondering why I'm here and what I have to say.

What do I have to say?

"Legion," Bruno finally says, giving up his efforts and acknowledging me as I continue to walk towards the stage. "Xander Pae. Which is it, these days?"

"Either works," I tell him, but I'm not looking at him. The crowd split down the middle for me, looking curious and nervous and wondering. I beam at them, wave to them, watch them watch me.

Bruno doesn't like that no one is paying attention to him. "Where's the rest of you?"

"Caesar's that way," I say, and point, "And Abyss is over there somewhere."

"That's not what I meant. We haven't see very many of you since you came back."

Oh.

This is why Ace said to let me do most of the talking.

If we win solely with our abilities, it wouldn't stop people wanting DNA. People want to be superheroes, and I need to show them that they can be, regardless of superhuman status. I need to make DNA *un*cool, the same way we live and die to make superhumans cool. I need to make it unattractive, unappealing, unsatisfying.

I need to do it by refusing it.

Are there any universes where I—

Not yet.

This is my universe. My choice.

I swallow.

"There aren't very many of me around since I came back," I say, slowly. Another wave of murmuring passes through the crowd. "I'm… singular, now."

As I expected, Bruno latches on to this.

I glance to either side. I see Abyss has made her way through the crowd and is coming to stand near me. Mom said that she calls me her brother, sometimes, but today I look at her and for the first time I think *my sister*. Caesar falls in to place on my other side, my best and oldest friend. Julia opens another portal behind me, and I don't have to look to know that she's standing behind me. I am surrounded on all sides.

I am not alone.

I close my eyes for a half second to take that in. I am singular. I will always feel like one piece of a whole, chasing after aspects of my identity that I don't know how to categorise anymore. I don't know if

I'm superhuman or not, if I'm fully alive or not, if I am Xander or Legion or not. But I am not alone.

"We could fix that," Bruno says, and now that I'm closer I can see his eyes shining excitedly. I wish, for a split second, that he could. But it is only a split second. "We could give you your abilities back."

I think of my friends— the ones here and the ones who are not. The rest of the Caesars, Ace, Ava, Zoram. I think of Mom, stroking my hair as a baby and an adult, telling me that she's proud of me.

I am not alone.

I believe in a perfected body. Does that extend to my *bodies*, plural? When I die properly, and see my dad again, will I be all of me? I think I will. Even if DNA works, which I know, *I know*, it doesn't— anything it could offer me would be a cheap imitation of what I was, am, and will be.

I take a deep breath.

"I'm good," I say, beaming up at Bruno. I hear Julia exhale heavily. Over my shoulder, I smile at her, too. "See, the thing is, even if it worked— which it doesn't, by the way," I tell the crowd, "ask Abyss, she's got all the science to prove it— it's not going to make me any better than I already am. It wouldn't make me a better person or son or friend or... florist or superhero. My abilities have no impact on any of that. With or without them, I'm Xander."

I stop speaking for a half second to jump up onto the low stage, and stand, with my shoulders square and my jaw set, in front of him. I narrow my eyes and look down my nose. My voice is clear and sharp when I tell him and everyone watching, "I'm Legion."

Naturally, in response, he takes a swing at me.

90.

Things get pretty ruthless after that.

The punch doesn't even have a chance to connect, of course. I move out of the way before he's finished swinging. But that doesn't stop the crowd from gasping, breaking in to shouts and screams. Julia is on the stage before anyone else, bouncing between portals, her hands balled in to fists and her mouth twisted into an unattractive snarl. Caesar manages to hold her back, up on stage a few heartbeats after her, but he doesn't have enough hands to stop Abyss from executing one very well placed kick.

Bruno doubles over, bringing his face to Abyss' eye level.

I can barely hear Abyss cursing him out. "—you," she spits, and her voice is far louder now she's finished swearing. Well done, Eliza, keeping this PG. "For trying to pass this off as anything other than a dangerous scam."

"I'm a scientist!" Bruno protests, which is probably the worst thing he could've said to Abyss. "I'm trying to figure out what makes it all tick!"

"Genetics, dumbass!" Caesar shouts, finally letting go of Julia.

She takes the opportunity to go over to Bruno and slap him across the face. He stumbles and drops to the ground. This is not the same man who chased after me and Ace. This man is *scared*. "You're not *clever*," she tells him, her voice dripping with disdain. "You're not *smart*. You haven't done anything groundbreaking. You're a liar."

"It doesn't work," I say, and my friends move out of the way with some hesitation. Before, I may have been offended that they thought I couldn't defend myself. Now, I know it's all stemming from love. I don't have to do it all by myself. I have two hands instead of ten, but I am not alone.

"It doesn't," I say again, "and my abilities didn't make me a superhero any more than your drug could if it did."

I crouch down across from him, shrugging in faux apology.

He glares at me. "How did you survive?"

I know he means physically. He's asking how there was a body and a funeral and a recovery that I never explained. I don't answer that question. Instead, I look over my shoulder at my team. I called us the superkids! as a joke, but I think that we *were*. I think we've all done a lot of growing up.

"My friends helped me," I tell him. "Wouldn't be here without them."

91.

I don't keep up with the court case that follows, but sometimes either Abyss or Ace will text the group chat news about it. DNA is being looked at a lot more closely, by scientists not on Bruno's payroll. They use Abyss' research as a starting point, and they confirm and reconfirm her findings. The deaths linked to DNA, like Brett Peters, are reexamined. Jessica Smalls testifies. Mindy writes a blog post about how the drug affected her ex-husband.

Popular opinion decides the outcome indirectly. Even if a judge lets Bruno off, no one is going to support his drug any more. That's what matters, in the end.

What else matters: I didn't take it. I miss the rest of me like a limb, and I'm sure that I will continue to for the rest of my life. But I didn't take it when I believed that it worked, and I didn't take it when Bruno offered it. I didn't even want to.

Julia and I sit on the fire escape two days afterwards, after dragging duvets and quilts out to make it more comfortable, and eat Chinese takeout from paper boxes. The city is quiet, but if that changes I know that she'll jet off to fix it. She's one of us now.

I tell her as much and she doesn't even roll her eyes.

"Best version of you," I tell her.

She says the same back to me. Mom, sitting on the sofa inside, a few feet away, says, "Is that how it works?"

"Nah," I say, turning around to grin at her with the tip of my tongue poking between my teeth. Mom just sighs, smiling fondly.

"Does this mean I'm a— what do you call each other? Superkids?"

I pull out my phone.

you added **juju jubilee** to **superkids!**

caesar: *welcome*

juju jubilee: *it rly is ofcal... a sprkd... id lik to thnk th acdmy...*

ace: *omg*

me: *there's two of them........*

abs: *whr do u thnk i gt it frm*

I look at Julia and laugh, and it's catching. Mom doesn't even bother asking what we find so amusing.

My mission call comes less than a week after that. Mom and I are working, and we can't close the shop on such short notice. I don't want to wait, though, so I text all of my friends to come to the shop as soon as possible. Within an hour, we're all crowded in amongst the flowers.

I rip open the letter despite the customers and shout, "Busan Korea Mission!"

Mom practically squeals and immediately starts listing all the places I have to go once I'm there, forgetting, for a split second, that this isn't a holiday. I am excited to learn that I have extended family in the area, and wonder if I'll meet any of them. Zoram moans that I won't even have to learn a language, or even a dialect if that's where my parents come from. Ava makes me promise to take a million pictures, which of course I will.

Caesar asks, "when do you leave?"

I return my gaze to the letter. "October twenty-third."

"That's ages away," Ace says, furrowing her brow. "I thought you said Zoram left, like, four weeks after his letter came."

"It is a while," Mom agrees, but Caesar and Abyss both look slightly disappointed.

"Our wedding isn't until the fifth of November." Abyss' careful monotone is back.

I don't want to miss it, of course. They're my best friends and I love them and I want to celebrate with them. But I can't postpone this. "We'll celebrate beforehand," I promise, and they nod solemnly, looking sidelong at each other but staying silent. I don't even try to guess what they're think-talking about.

I spend the next three months preparing myself, trying to divide my time between everyone I love. Two years suddenly feels like a long time, but also no time at all. It was two years ago that Caesar first asked me to lunch to discuss superhumans, and it will be two years until we go for lunch again. It's surreal, but exciting, and I don't want to miss out on anything, and my friends are more than willing to spend extra time with me.

Ace takes me out dancing again, and this time we just dance, spinning around the floor and laughing every time we get a step wrong. Abyss and Caesar spend just as many nights in my apartment as I spend in their penthouse. Julia gets me to go out with her in uniform nearly every night, but slowly I start to say no, and she goes out on her own, or with Abyss and/or Caesar. I look at my friends, at this weird little team, and I know that the city is in good hands.

When Abyss comes to the flower shop in early October, the only odd thing is her white off-the-shoulder top. We're not far from closing, so she waits around until we lock up, and then invites me and Mom for a meal. Mom smiles like she knows a secret.

We walk through the city for a while, until Abyss takes an abrupt turn, and Ace is suddenly in front of us. "You know," she drawls, when she sees Abyss, "it's unusual for the bride to be late to her own wedding."

"Bride? Wedding?"

Abyss smiles at me. "We wanted you here more than anything. I never wanted a big wedding anyway, and Caesar agreed that this would be fun. It's just friends and family. We'll still have the one in November for the press and the like, but this is the real one."

"Which is why you need to put this on," Ace says, and Abyss indulgently takes the small box she holds out.

"Something borrowed," she explains to me, and clasps a necklace around her neck.

"Caesar's tie is the something blue," Ace natters, guiding us into the courthouse. "And he's wearing his granddad's watch for something old. Abyss' *something new* isn't anything you need to concern yourself with."

Abyss sighs, but I can tell it's fond.

Friends and family includes me, my mom, Caesar's immediate family, and a nice looking family that must be Abyss'. There's also Ace, obviously, who's very clearly been involved in planning all of this, and is, I imagine, the only reason that Abyss is wearing white for it at all. Julia's around too, standing half-awkwardly in a corner, in a lilac dress. When I smile at her, she returns it, but makes no move to join any conversation.

"Will you sign as our witness?" Abyss asks me. "Caesar wanted you as best man, but we aren't really doing that, for obvious reasons. And your mom did the flowers, because we wanted to surprise you with this. Cee knew that you wanted to be here, and... it wouldn't be the same if you weren't a part of it."

I nod, speechless. Abyss beams— actually *beams*. "You're family, Xander, you know that. Come on, come meet my parents. And my brother!" She practically drags me over to them, and my initial reaction seems to be correct: they're very nice. Her brother, Jordan, is also an astrophysicist, and they chat a mile a minute about things I don't even want to pretend to understand. Her parents both shake my hand, and we make quiet conversation about the weather and the wedding.

The wedding is simple.

We all sit on fold-out chairs and face Caesar and Abyss, who have their hands joined. Abyss' hair is loose, with her sunglasses pushed up into it, so her eyes are on display for her husband (her husband!). Caesar is beaming, beaming, beaming, like he can't quite believe that he gets to be here, in this place, in this moment.

They've written their own vows, which turn out to be nothing more than each of them saying, "My mind is ours." I suppose they don't need much more. It is *literal*, for them, after all.

When I go up to sign the paper as their witness, I can hear several half-stifled sobs. My eyes might be shining a little bit, too. Weddings!

For the reception, we go out for a nice meal in a restaurant with a private room, where we subtly toast the happy couple. They sit at the head with face splitting smiles, leaning in to each other and playing with each other's fingers and hair.

Julia does appear properly for this. She seems shocked to have been invited, and keeps fiddling with the sleeves of her dress. She's sitting next to me, next to Caesar, and I nudge her shoulder with mine any time I catch sight of the action.

Ace, who is next to Abyss, across from me, stands abruptly, a glass of expensive champagne in her hand.

"I wanna make a toast," she says, and Caesar gestures for her to go ahead. "To Cee and Abs, who're so oblivious they didn't work out they loved each other until after they'd shared a bed for, like, a month."

Caesar's siblings laugh and whistle, but Caesar is smiling too wide to blush. Abyss just flips Ace off.

"Genuinely, though," Ace continues, after a moment to pull a face at them, "I'm so happy for you guys. These last two years have been insane for all of us. There's been so, so much good, but a lot of bad. And a lot of weird."

She points at me as she says this, and I laugh without thinking about it. It feels good to laugh about it. "That's fair," I say, shrugging, "that's definitely fair."

"And you two—" she points back to Caesar and Abyss— "have been so incredible to each other throughout all of it. I'm glad you found each other. I'm glad you found... happiness in each other."

She's talking to Cee and Abs, but it gets me choked up anyway. It's been a crazy couple of years, and it's going to continue to be crazy for a lot more. Such is the nature of life, I guess. Especially with the lives that we've chosen for ourselves. We're friends and family and superheroes, and we're all still figuring out our place. We've grown up a lot. I bet we have to grow up a lot more.

"To the happy couple! Hopefully they'll be a lot more good to come."

Caesar stands as soon as Ace is sitting down again. "Lots of good," he says, looking fondly at Abyss. "But probably bad, too. And given our lives, probably a lot more weird. But we've got each other…"

Abyss takes his hand and squeezes, smiling up at him.

He continues, "And we've got all of you. Thanks for being our friends and our family. Thanks for being people we can rely on. And a special thanks to Ace, Xander, and Julia, for being the best coworkers in the world."

We all protest that title, because we're obviously supposed to, but Caesar just laughs and holds up a hand. "To the superkids!"

It's ridiculous and perfect and we're all so, so happy. Everyone on the table raises their glasses and we echo it back.

"To the superkids!"

THE END

ACKNOWLEDGEMENTS

This book (and, in fact, the superkids in general) would not be what it is without the incredible group of people that met them first. So, first of all, a huge thank you to those who I roleplayed with; Malakh, Michael, Jordan, and many, many others. Your collaboration helped me to learn these characters, and develop my own writing skills. Thank you.

But I can't talk about roleplaying the superkids without mentioning Fate, who not only roleplayed them with me, but encouraged me to take the step to write this book, provided feedback and support during the writing process, and was, of course, the first person to read it. Your enthusiasm for the superkids (and others!) has kept me going over the last year. Thank you!

Next, thank you to Emma and Maddie, also beta readers. Your feedback was essential during the editing process. Emma (@emmatopdesign on instagram) also designed and illustrated the cover— and isn't it beautiful?

Thank you to Steve, my college creative writing teacher, who all but forced me to try my hand at first person, despite my insecurities towards the form. If not for that, this book would have been told in a very different (and much less effective!) way.

Thank you to my Mum and Dad, who support my many creative endeavours and never tell me that it will be impossible— only that it will be hard.

And finally to you, dear reader. Thank you.

Printed in Poland
by Amazon Fulfillment
Poland Sp. z o.o., Wrocław

54835233R00357